Saturn

BEN BOVA

Saturn

Hodder & Stoughton

A CIP catalogue record for this title
is available from the British Library

ISBN 0 340 76766 9

Typeset in Plantin by Hewer Text Ltd, Edinburgh
Printed and bound in Great Britain by
Mackays of Chatham Ltd, Chatham, Kent

Hodder and Stoughton
A division of Hodder Headline
338 Euston Road
London NW1 3BH

Once more to dearest Barbara, and to Dr. Jerry Pournelle, a colleague and friend who originated the term 'shepherd satellites' but never received the credit for it that he deserves.

ACKNOWLEDGEMENTS

My thanks to all the friends and colleagues who provided information and ideas for this novel, especially Jeff Mitchell, Ernest Hogan, and, from Columbia University's Biosphere 2, Gilbert LaRoque and John S. Engen.

There are some questions in Astronomy to which we are attracted . . . on account of their peculiarity . . . [rather] than from any direct advantage which their solution would afford to mankind . . . I am not aware that any practical use has been made of Saturn's Rings . . . But when we contemplate the Rings from a purely scientific point of view, they become the most remarkable bodies in the heavens . . . When we have actually seen that great arch swing over the equator of the planet without any visible connection, we cannot bring our minds to rest.

James Clerk Maxwell

As the new century begins . . . we may be ready to settle down before we wreck the planet. It is time to sort out Earth and calculate what it will take to provide a satisfying and sustainable life for everyone into the indefinite future . . . For every person in the world to reach present U.S. levels of consumption would require [the resources of] four more planet Earths.

Edward O. Wilson

BOOK I

For the same reason I have resolved not to put anything around Saturn except what I have already observed and revealed – that is, two small stars which touch it, one to the east and one to the west, in which no alteration has ever yet been seen to take place and in which none is to be expected in the future, barring some very strange event remote from every other motion known to or even imagined by us. But as to the supposition . . . that Saturn is sometimes oblong and sometimes accompanied by two stars on its flanks, Your Excellency may rest assured that this results either from the imperfection of the telescope or the eye of the observer . . . I, who have observed it a thousand times at different periods with an excellent instrument, can assure you that no change whatever is to be seen in it. And reason, based upon our experiences of all other stellar motions, renders us certain that none will ever be seen, for if these stars had any motions similar to those of other stars, they would long since have been separated from or conjoined with the body of Saturn, even if that movement were a thousand times slower than that of any other star which goes wandering through the heavens.

Galileo Galilei
Letters on Sunspots
4 May 1612

Selene: Astro Corporation Headquarters

Pancho Lane frowned at her sister. 'His name isn't even Malcolm Eberly. He changed it.'

Susan smiled knowingly. 'Oh, what diff's that make?'

'He was born Max Erlenmeyer, in Omaha, Nebraska,' Pancho said sternly. 'He was arrested in Linz, Austria, for fraud in 'eighty-four, tried to flee the country and—'

'I don't *care* about that! It's ancient! He's changed. He's not the same man he was then.'

'You're not going.'

'Yes I am,' Susan insisted, the beginnings of a frown of her own creasing her brow. 'I'm going and you can't stop me!'

'I'm your legal guardian, Susie.'

'Poosh! What's that got to do with spit? I'm almost fifty years old, f'real.'

Susan Lane did not look much more than twenty. She had died when she'd been a teenager, killed by a lethal injection that Pancho herself had shot into her emaciated arm. Once clinically dead Susan had been frozen in liquid nitrogen to await the day when medical science could cure the carcinoma that was raging through her young body. Pancho had brought her cryonic sarcophagus to the Moon when she began working as an astronaut for Astro Manufacturing Corporation. Eventually Pancho became a member of Astro's board of directors, and finally its chairman. Still Susan waited, entombed in her bath of liquid nitrogen, waiting until Pancho was certain that she could be reborn to a new life.

It took more than twenty years. And once Susan was revived and cured of the cancer that had been killing her, her mind was almost a total blank. Pancho had expected that; cryonics reborns

3

usually lost most of the neural connections in the cerebral cortex. Even Saito Yamagata, the powerful founder of Yamagata Corporation, had come out of his cryonic sleep with a mind as blank as a newborn baby's.

So Pancho fed and bathed and toilet trained her sister, an infant in a teenager's body. Taught her to walk, to speak again. And brought the best neurophysiologists to Selene to treat her sister's brain with injections of memory enzymes and RNA. She even considered nanotherapy but decided against it; nanotechnology was allowed in Selene, but only under stringent controls, and the experts admitted that they didn't think nanomachines could help Susan to recover her lost memories. Those years were difficult, but gradually a young adult emerged, a woman who looked like the Susie that Pancho remembered, but whose personality, whose attitudes, whose *mind* were disturbingly different. Susan remembered nothing of her earlier life, but thanks to the neuroboosters she had received her memory now was almost eidetic: if she saw or heard something once, she never forgot it. She could recall details with a precision that made Pancho's head swim.

Now the sisters sat glaring at each other: Pancho on the plush burgundy pseudoleather couch in the corner of her sumptuous office, Susan sitting tensely on the edge of the low slingchair on the other side of the curving lunar glass coffee table, her elbows on her knees.

They looked enough alike to be immediately recognized as sisters. Both were tall and rangy, long lean legs and arms, slim athletic bodies. Pancho's skin was little darker than a well-tanned Caucasian's, Susan's a shade richer. Pancho kept her hair trimmed down to a skullcap of tightly-curled fuzz that was flecked with spots of fashionable gray. Susan had taken treatments to make her dark brown hair long and luxurious; she wore it in the latest pageboy fashion, spilling down to her shoulders. Her clothing was pop mod, too: a floor-length faux silk gown with weights in its hem to keep the skirt hanging right in the low lunar gravity. Pancho was in a no-nonsense business suit of powder gray: a tailored cardigan jacket and flared slacks over her comfortable lunar softboots. She wore sensible accents of jewelry at her earlobes and wrists. Susan was unadorned, except for the decal across her forehead: a miniature of Saturn, the ringed planet.

Susan broke the lengthening silence. 'Panch, you can't stop me. I'm going.'

'But . . . all the way out to Saturn? With a flock of political exiles?'

'They're not exiles!'

'C'm on, Soose, half the governments back Earthside are cleaning out their detention camps.'

Susan's back stiffened. 'Those fundamentalist regimes you're always complaining about are encouraging their non-believers and dissidents to sign on for the Saturn expedition. Encouraging, not deporting.'

'They're getting rid of their troublemakers,' Pancho said.

'Not troublemakers! Freethinkers. Idealists. Men and women who're ticked with the way things are on Earth and willing to warp off, zip out and start new lives.'

'Misfits and malcontents,' Pancho muttered. 'Square pegs in round holes.'

'The habitat will be populated by the best and brightest people of Earth,' Susan retorted.

'Yeah, you wish.'

'I *know*. And I'm going to be one of them.'

'Cripes almighty, Soose, Saturn's ten times farther from the Sun than we are.'

'What of it?' Susan said, with that irritating smile again. 'You were the first to go as far as the Belt, weren't you?'

'Yeah, but—'

'You went out to the Jupiter station, di'n't you?'

Pancho could do nothing but nod.

'So I'm going out to Saturn. I won't be alone. There'll be ten thousand of us, f'real! That is, if Malcolm can weed out the real troublemakers and sign up good workers. I'm helping him do the interviews.'

'Make sure that's all you're helping him with,' Pancho groused.

Susan's smile turned slightly wicked. 'He's been a perfect gentleman, dammit.'

'Blister my butt on a goddam Harley,' Pancho grumbled. And she thought, damned near thirty years I've been working my way up the corporation but ten minutes with Susie and she's got me talkin' West Texas again.

'It's a great thing, Panch,' said Susan, earnest now. 'It's a mission, really. We're going out on a five-year mission to study the Saturn system. Scientists, engineers, farmers, a whole self-sustaining community!'

Pancho saw that her sister was genuinely excited. Like a kid on her way to a thrill park. Damn! She said to herself. Susie's got the body of an adult but the mind of a teenager. There'll be nothing but grief for her out there, without me to protect her.

'Say it clicks, Panch,' Susan asked softly, through lowered lashes. 'Tell me you're not ticked at me.'

'I'm not sore,' Pancho said truthfully. 'I'm worried, though. You'll be all alone out there.'

'With ten thousand others!'

'Without your big sister.'

Susan said nothing for a heartbeat, then she reached across the coffee table and grasped Pancho's hand. 'But Panch, don't you see? That's why I'm doing it! That's why I've got to do it! I've got to go out on my own. I can't live like some little kid with you doing everything for me! I've got to be free!'

Sagging back into the softly yielding sofa, Pancho murmured, 'Yeah, I suppose you do. I guess I knew it all along. It's just that . . . I worry about you, Susie.'

'I'll be fine, Panch. You'll see!'

'I sure hope so.'

Elated, Susan hopped to her feet and headed for the door.

'You'll see,' she repeated. 'It's gonna be great! Cosmic!'

Pancho sighed and got to her feet.

'Oh, by the way,' Susan called over her shoulder as she opened the office door, 'I'm changing my name. I'm not gonna be called Susan anymore. From now on, my name is Holly.'

And she ducked through the door before Pancho could say a word more.

'Holly,' Pancho muttered to the closed door. Where in the ever-lovin' blue-eyed world did she get *that* from? she wondered. Why's she want to change her name?

Shaking her head, Pancho told the phone to connect with her security chief. When his handsome, square-jawed face took shape in the air above her desk, she said:

'Wendell, I need somebody to ride that goddamned habitat out to Saturn and keep tabs on my sister, without her knowin' it.'

'Right away,' the security chief answered. He looked away for a moment, then said, 'Um, about tonight, I—'

'Never mind about tonight,' Pancho snapped. 'You just get somebody onto that habitat. Somebody good! Get on it right now.'

'Yes, ma'am!' said Pancho's security chief.

Lunar Orbit: Habitat *Goddard*

Malcolm Eberly tried to hide the panic that was still frothing like a storm-tossed sea inside him. Along with the fifteen other department leaders, he stood perfectly still at the main entrance to the habitat.

The ride up from Earth had been an agony for him. From the instant the Clippership had gone into Earth orbit and the feeling of gravity had dwindled to zero, Eberly had fought a death struggle against the terror of weightlessness. Strapped into his well-cushioned seat, he had exerted every effort of his willpower to fight back the horrible urge to vomit. I will not give in to this, he told himself through gritted teeth. Pale and soaked with cold sweat, he resolved that he would not make a fool of himself in front of the others.

Getting out of his seat once the Clippership had made rendezvous with the transfer rocket was sheer torture. Eberly kept his head rigidly unmoving, his fists clenched, his eyes squeezed down to slits. To the cheerful commands of the flight attendants, he followed the bobbing gray coveralls of the woman ahead of him and made his way along the aisle hand over hand from one seat back to the next until he glided through the hatch into the transfer vehicle, still in zero gravity, gagging as his insides floated up into his throat.

No one else seemed to be as ill as him. The rest of them – fifteen other men and women, all department leaders as he was – were chatting and laughing, even experimenting with allowing themselves to float up off the Velcro carpeting of the passenger compartment. The sight of it made Eberly's stomach turn inside out.

Still he held back the bile that was burning his throat. I will *not* give in to this, he told himself over and over. I will prevail. A man can accomplish anything he sets his mind to if he has the strength and the will.

Strapped down again in a seat inside the transfer rocket, he stared rigidly ahead as the ship lit off its engines to start its flight to lunar orbit. The thrust was gentle, but at least it provided some feeling of weight. Only for a few seconds, though. The rocket engines cut off and he felt again as if he were falling, endlessly falling. Everyone else was chattering away. Several of them boasting about how many times they had been in space.

Of course! Eberly realized. They've all done this before. They've experienced this wretchedness before and now it doesn't bother them. They're all from wealthy families, rich, spoiled children who've never had a care in their lives. I'm the only one here who's never been off the Earth before, the only one who's had to fight and claw for a living, the only one who's known hunger and sickness and fear.

I've got to make good here. I've got to! Otherwise they'll send me back. I'll die in a filthy prison cell.

Through sheer mental exertion Eberly endured the hours of weightlessness. When the woman in the seat next to him tried to engage him in conversation he replied tersely to her inane remarks, desperately fighting to keep her from seeing how sick he was. He forced a smile, hoping that she would not notice the cold sweat beading his upper lip. He could feel it soaking the cheap, thin shirt he wore. After a while she stopped her chattering and turned her attention to the display screen built into the seat backs.

Eberly concentrated on the images, too. The screen showed the habitat, an ungainly cylinder hanging in the emptiness of space like a length of sewer pipe left behind by a vanished construction crew. As they approached it, though, the habitat grew bigger and bigger. Eberly could see that it was rotating slowly; he knew that the spin created a feeling of gravity inside the cylinder. Numbers ran through his mind: the habitat was twenty kilometers in length, four kilometers across. It rotated every forty-five seconds, which produced a centrifugal force equivalent to normal Earth gravity.

In his growing excitement he almost forgot the unease of his stomach. Now he could see the long windows running the length of the gigantic cylinder. And the Moon came into view, shining brightly. But seen this close, the Moon was ugly, scarred and pitted with countless craters. One of the biggest of them, Eberly knew, housed the city-state of Selene.

Swiftly the habitat grew to blot out everything else. For a moment Eberly feared they would crash into it, even though his rational mind told him that the ship's pilots had their flight under precise control. He could see the solar mirrors hugging the cylinder's curving sides. And bulbs and knobs dotting the habitat's skin, like bumps on a cucumber. Some of them were observation blisters, he knew. Others were docking ports, thruster pods, air-locks.

'This is your captain speaking,' said a woman's voice from the speakers set above each display screen. 'We have gone into a rendezvous orbit around the habitat. In three minutes we will be docking. You'll feel a bump or two: nothing to be alarmed about.'

The thump jarred all the passengers. Eberly gripped his seat arms tightly and waited for more. But nothing else happened. Except—

His innards had settled down! He no longer felt sick. Gravity had returned and he felt normal again. No, better than normal. He turned to the woman sitting beside him and studied her face briefly. It was a round, almost chubby face with large dark almond eyes and curly black hair. Her skin was smooth, young, but swarthy. Eberly judged she was of Mediterranean descent, Greek or Spanish or perhaps Italian. He smiled broadly at her.

'Here we've been sitting next to each other for more than six hours and I haven't even told you my name. I'm Malcolm Eberly.'

She smiled back. 'Yes, I can see.' Tapping the name badge pinned to her blouse, she said, 'I'm Andrea Maronella. I'm with the agrotech team.'

A farmer, Eberly thought. A stupid, grubbing farmer. But he smiled still wider and replied, 'I'm in charge of the human resources department.'

'How nice.'

Before he could say more, the flight attendant asked them all to get up and head for the hatch. Eberly unstrapped and got to his feet, happy to feel solid weight again, eager to get his first glimpse of the habitat. The inner terror he had fought against dwindled almost to nothing. I won! He exulted to himself. I faced the terror and I beat it.

He politely allowed Maronella to slide out into the aisle ahead of him and then followed her to the hatch. The sixteen men and women filed through the hatch, into an austere metal-walled chamber. An older man stood by the inner hatch, tall and heavyset; his thick head of hair was iron gray and he had a bushy gray moustache. His face looked rugged, weatherbeaten, the corners of his eyes creased by long years of squinting in the open sun. He wore a comfortable suede pullover and rumpled tan jeans. Two younger men stood slightly behind him, clad in coveralls, obviously underlings of some sort.

'Welcome to habitat *Goddard*,' he said, with a warm smile. 'I'm Professor James Wilmot. Most of you have already met me, and for those of you who haven't, I look forward to meeting you and discussing our future. But for now, let's take a look at the world we'll be inhabiting for at least the next five years.'

With that, one of the young men behind him tapped the keyboard on the wall beside the hatch, and the massive steel door swung slowly inward. Eberly felt a puff of warm air touch his face, like the light touch of his mother's faintly remembered caress.

The group of sixteen department leaders started through the hatch. This is it, Eberly thought, feeling a new dread rising inside his guts. There's no turning back now. This is the new world they want me to live in. This huge cylinder, this machine. I'm being exiled. All the way out to Saturn, that's where they're sending me. As far away as they can. I'll never see Earth again.

He was almost the last one in line; he heard the others oohing and aahing by the time he got to the open hatch and stepped through. Then he saw why.

Stretching out in all directions around him was a green landscape, shining in warm sunlight. Gently rolling grassy hills, clumps of trees, little meandering streams spread out into the hazy distance. The group was standing on the gentle slope of a knoll, with a clear view of the habitat's broad interior. Bushes thick with vivid red hibiscus flowers and pale lavender oleanders lined both sides of a curving path that led down to a group of low buildings, white and gleaming in the sunlight that streamed in through the long windows.

A Mediterranean village, Eberly thought, set like steps on the flank of a grassy hill, overlooking a shimmering blue lake. This is some travel brochure vision of what a perfect Mediterranean countryside would look like. Far in the distance he made out what looked like farmlands, square little fields that appeared to be recently plowed, and more clusters of whitewashed buildings. There was no horizon. Instead, the land simply curved up and up, hills and grass and trees and more little villages with their paved roads and sparkling streams, up and up on both sides until he was craning his neck looking straight overhead at still more of the carefully, lovingly landscaped greenery.

'It's breathtaking,' Maronella whispered.

'Awesome,' said one of the others.

A virgin world, Eberly thought, untouched by war or famine or hatred. Untouched by human emotions of any kind. Waiting to be shaped, controlled. Maybe it won't be so bad here after all.

'This must have cost a bloody fortune,' a young man said, in a strong, matter-of-fact voice. 'How could the consortium afford it?'

Professor Wilmot smiled and touched his moustache with a fingertip. 'We got it in a bankruptcy sale, actually. The previous owners went broke trying to turn this into a retirement center.'

'Who retires nowadays?'

'That's why they went bankrupt,' Wilmot replied.

'Still . . . the cost . . .'

'The International Consortium of Universities is not without resources,' said Wilmot. 'And we have many alumni who can be very generous when properly approached.'

'You mean when you twist their arms hard enough,' a woman joked. The others laughed; even Wilmot smiled good-naturedly.

'Well,' the professor said. 'This is it. This will be your home for the next five years, and even longer for many of you.'

'When do the others start coming up?'

'As the personnel board approves applicants and they pass their final physical and psychological tests they will come aboard. We have about two-thirds of the available positions already filled, and more people are signing up at quite a brisk pace.'

The others asked more questions and Wilmot patiently answered them. Eberly filtered their nattering out of his conscious attention. He peered intently at the vast expanse of the habitat, savoring this moment of discovery, his arrival into a new world. Ten thousand people, that's all they're going to permit to join us. But this habitat could hold a hundred thousand easily. A million, even!

He thought of the squalor of his childhood days: eight, ten, twelve people to a room. And then the merciless discipline of the monastery schools. And prison.

Ten thousand people, he mused. They will live in luxury here. They will live like kings!

He smiled. No, he told himself. There will be only one king here. One master. This will be *my* kingdom, and everyone in it will bend to my will.

Vienna: Schönbrunn Prison

More than a full year before he had ever heard of habitat *Goddard*, Malcolm Eberly had been abruptly released from prison after serving less than half his term for fraud and embezzlement.

The rambling old Schönbrunn Palace had been turned into a prison in the aftermath of the Refugee Riots that had shattered much of Vienna and its surroundings. When Eberly first learned that he would serve his sentence in the Schönbrunn he had been hopeful: at least it wasn't one of the grim state prisons where habitual criminals were held. He quickly learned that he was wrong: a prison is a prison is a prison, filled with thugs and perverts. Pain and humiliation were constant dangers, fear his constant companion.

The morning had started like any other: Eberly was roused from sleep by the blast of the dawn whistle. He swung down from his top bunk and waited quietly while his three cell mates used the sink and toilet. He had become accustomed to the stench of the cell and quite early in his incarceration had learned that complaints led only to beatings, either by the guards or by his cell mates.

There was a hierarchy among the convicts. Those connected with organized crime were at the top of the prestige chain. Murderers, even those poor wretches who killed in passion, were accorded more respect than thieves or kidnappers. Mere swindlers, which was Eberly's rap, were far down the chain, doomed to perform services for their superiors whether they wanted to or not.

Fortunately, Eberly had maneuvered himself into a cell where the top con was a former garage mechanic from the Italian province of Calabria who had been declared guilty of banditry, terrorism, bank robbings and murders. Although barely literate, the Calabrian was a born organizer: he ran his section of the prison like a medieval fiefdom, settling disputes and enforcing a rough kind of justice so thoroughly that the guards allowed him to keep the peace among the prisoners in his own stern manner. When Eberly discovered that he needed a man who could operate a computer to keep him in touch with his family in their mountain-top village and the remnants of his band, still hiding in the hills, Eberly became his secretary. After that, no one was allowed to molest him.

It was the mind-numbing routine of each long, dull day that made Eberly sick to his soul. Once he came under the Calabrian's protection, he got along well enough physically, but the drab sameness of the cell, the food, the stink, the stupid talk of the other convicts day after day, week after week, threatened to drive him mad. He tried to keep his mind engaged by daily visits to the prison library, where he could use the tightly monitored computer to make at least a virtual connection to the world outside. Most of the entertainment sites were censored or cut off altogether, but the prison authorities allowed – even encouraged – using the educational sites. Desperately, Eberly enrolled in one course after another, usually finishing them far sooner than expected and rushing into the next.

At first he took whatever courses came to hand: Renaissance painting, transactional psychology, municipal water recycling systematics, the poetry of Goethe. It didn't matter what the subject matter was, he needed to keep his mind occupied, needed to be out of this prison for a few hours each day, even if it was merely through the computer.

Gradually, though, he found himself drawn to studies of history and politics. In time, he applied for a degree program at the Virtual University of Edinburgh.

It was a great surprise when, one ordinary morning, the guard captain pulled him out of line as he and his cell mates shuffled to the cafeteria for their lukewarm breakfasts.

The captain, stubble-jawed and humorless, tapped Eberly on the shoulder with his wand and said, 'Follow me.'

Eberly was so astonished that he blurted at, 'Why me? What's wrong?'

The captain held his wand under Eberly's nose and fingered the voltage control. 'No talking in line! Now follow me.'

The other convicts marched by in silence, their heads facing straight ahead but their eyes shifting toward Eberly and the captain before looking away again. Eberly remembered what the wand felt like at full charge and let his chin sink to his chest as he dutifully followed the captain away from the cafeteria.

The captain led him to a small, stuffy room up in the executive area where the warden and other prison administrators had their offices. The room had one window, tightly closed and so grimy that the morning sunlight hardly brightened it. An oblong table nearly filled the room, its veneer chipped and dull. Two men in expensive-looking business suits were seated at it, their chairs almost scraping the bare gray walls.

'Sit,' said the captain, pointing with his wand to the chair at the foot of the table. Wondering what this was all about, and whether he would miss his breakfast, Eberly slowly sat down. The captain stepped out into the hallway and softly closed the door.

'You are Malcolm Eberly?' said the man at the head of the table. He was rotund, fleshy-faced, his cheeks pink and his eyes set deep in his face. Eberly thought of a pig.

'Yes, I am,' Eberly replied. Then he added, 'Sir.'

'Born Max Erlenmeyer, if our information is correct,' said the man at the pig's right. He was prosperous-looking in an elegant dark blue suit and smooth, silver-gray hair. He had the look of a yachtsman about him. Eberly could picture him in a double-breasted blazer and a jaunty nautical cap.

'I had my name legally changed when—'

'That's a lie,' said the yachtsman, as lightly as he might ask for a glass of water. An Englishman, from his accent, Eberly decided tentatively. That could be useful, perhaps.

'But, sir—'

'It doesn't matter,' said the pig. 'If you wish to be called Eberly, that is what we will call you. Fair enough?'

Eberly nodded, completely baffled by them.

'How would you like to be released from prison?' the pig asked.

Eberly could feel his eyes go wide. But he quickly controlled his reactions and asked, 'What would I have to do to be released?'

'Nothing much,' said the yachtsman. 'Merely fly out to the planet Saturn.'

Gradually they revealed themselves. The fat one was from the Atlanta headquarters of the New Morality, the multinational fundamentalist organization that had raised Eberly to manhood back in America.

'We were very disappointed when you ran away from our monastery in Nebraska and took up a life of crime,' he said, genuine sadness on his puffy face.

'Not a life of crime,' Eberly protested. 'I made one mistake only, and now I'm suffering the consequences.'

The yachtsman smiled knowingly. 'Your mistake was getting caught. We are here to offer you another chance.'

He was a Catholic, he claimed, working with the European Holy Disciples on various social programs. 'Of which, you are one.'

'Me?' Eberly asked, still puzzled. 'I don't understand.'

'It's really very simple,' said the pig, clasping his fat hands prayerfully on the table top. 'The International Consortium of Universities is organizing an expedition to the planet Saturn.'

'Ten thousand people in a self-contained habitat,' added the yachtsman.

'Ten thousand so-called intellectuals,' the pig said, clear distaste in his expression. 'Serving a cadre of scientists who wish to study the planet Saturn.'

The yachtsman glanced sharply at his associate, then went on, 'Many governments are allowing certain individuals to leave Earth. Glad to be rid of them, actually.'

'The scientists are fairly prestigious men and women. They actually *want* to go to Saturn.'

'And they are all secularists, of course,' the yachtsman added.

'Of course,' said Eberly.

'We know that many people want to escape from the lives they are leading,' the pig resumed. 'They are unwilling to submit to the very necessary discipline that we of the New Morality impose.'

'The same thing applies in Britain and Europe,' said the yachtsman. 'The Holy Disciples cleaned up the cities, brought morality and order to the people, helped feed the starving and find jobs for the people who were wiped out by the greenhouse floods.'

The pig was nodding.

'But still, there are plenty of people who claim we're stifling their individual freedoms. Their individual freedoms! It was all that liberty and license that led to the near-collapse of civilization.'

'But the floods,' Eberly interjected. 'The greenhouse warming and the droughts and all the other the environmental disasters.'

'Visitations by an angry God,' said the pig firmly. 'Warnings that we must return to His ways.'

'Which we have done, by and large,' the yachtsman took up. 'Even in the bloody Middle East the Sword of Islam has worked miracles.'

'But now, with this mission to Saturn—'

'Run by godless secularists.'

'There will be ten thousand people trying to escape from the righteous path.'

'We cannot allow that to happen.'

'For their own good.'

'Of course.'

'Of course,' Eberly agreed meekly. Then he added, 'But I don't see what this has to do with me.'

'We want you to join them.'

'And go all the way out to the planet Saturn?' Eberly squeaked.

'Exactly,' the yachtsman replied.

'You will be our representative aboard their habitat. We can place you in charge of their human resources department.'

'So that you'll have some hand in selecting who's allowed to go.'

The pig added, 'Under our supervision, of course.'

'In charge of human resources? You can do that?'

'We have our ways,' said the yachtsman, grinning.

'Your real task will be to set up a God-fearing government

aboard that habitat,' the pig said. 'We mustn't allow the secularists to control the lives of those ten thousand souls!'

'We mustn't let that habitat turn into a cesspool of sin,' the yachtsman insisted.

'A limited, closed environment like that will need a firm, well-controlled government. Otherwise they will destroy themselves, just as the people of so many cities did here on Earth.'

'You're too young to remember the food riots.'

'I remember the fighting in St. Louis,' Eberly said, shuddering inwardly. 'I remember the hunger. My sister dying from the wasting disease during the biowar.'

'We don't want that happening to those poor souls heading out for Saturn,' said the pig, his hands still folded.

'Whether they realize it or not,' the yachtsman said, 'they are going to *need* the kind of discipline and order that only we can provide them.'

'And we are counting on you to lead them in the direction of righteousness.'

'But I'm only one man,' said Eberly.

'You'll have help. We will plant a small but dedicated cadre of like-minded people on the habitat.'

'And you want me to be their leader?'

'Yes. You have the skills, we've seen that in your dossier. With God's help, you will shape the government of those ten thousand souls properly.'

'Will you do it?' the yachtsman asked, earnestly. 'Will you accept this responsibility?'

It took all of Eberly's self-control to keep from laughing in their faces. Go to Saturn or remain in jail, he thought. Be the leader and form a government or live another nine years in that stinking cell.

'Yes,' he said, with quiet determination. 'With God's help, I accept the responsibility.'

The two men smiled at one another, while Eberly thought that by the time the habitat reached Saturn he and everyone in it would be far away from the strictures of these religious fanatics.

Then the pig said, 'Of course, if you fail to accomplish our goals, we'll see to it that you return here and serve out the remainder of your sentence.'

'We might even add a few more charges,' said the yachtsman, almost genially. 'There's a lot in your dossier to choose from, you know.'

Departure Minus 45 Days

James Coleraine Wilmot was the son of a peer of the realm, a baron who had left his native Ulster in the wake of the Irish Reunification despite his family's five hundred-odd years of residence there.

To his credit, he felt no bitterness about the family leaving its ancestral home. They had never been wealthy; for nearly a dozen generations they had struggled to maintain a shabbily dignified lifestyle by raising sheep. Wilmot had no interest whatsoever in animal husbandry. His passion was the study of the human animal. James Coleraine Wilmot was an anthropologist.

He was also a very able administrator, and as adroit as they came in the quietly fierce internecine warfare of academe. He felt that being named to head this strange collection of people in their mission out to distant Saturn would be the acme of his career, a real, carefully controlled research program, an actual experiment in a field that had never been able to conduct experiments before.

A closed, carefully limited community in a self-sufficient ecology and a self-contained economy. Every feature of their physical existence under control. Individuals from Europe, the Americas, Asia and Africa. Freethinkers, mostly, people who chafed under the restrictions of their own societies. And the scientists, of course. The avowed purpose of this mission was the scientific study of the planet Saturn and its giant moon, Titan.

Wilmot knew better. He knew the true purpose of this flight to Saturn, and the reason its real backers wanted their financial support kept secret.

The Chinese had refused to join the experiment, as usual; they kept to themselves, isolationists to their core. But otherwise most racial and religious groups were represented. What kind of a society would these people create for themselves? An actual experiment in anthropology! Wilmot glowed inwardly at the thought of it, even though the purpose behind this experiment, the underlying reason for this venture to Saturn, troubled him deeply. Yet he put aside such worries, content to revel in the prospects lying before him.

His office was a reflection of the man. It was as close to a duplicate of his office at Cambridge as he could make it. He had brought up his big clean-lined Danish-styled desk and its graceful chair that molded itself to his spine, together with the bookcases and the little round conference table with its four minimalist chairs. All in white beech, clean and efficient, yet warm and comfortable. Even the carpet that almost covered the entire floor had been taken from his Earthside office. After all, Wilmot reasoned, I'm going to be living and working here for five years or more. I might as well have my creature comforts around me.

The only new thing in the office was the guest chair, another Danish piece, but of shining chrome tubular supports and pliant butterscotch-brown leather cushions.

Manuel Gaeta sat in it, looking much more relaxed than Wilmot himself felt. The third man in the room was Edouard Urbain, chief scientist of the habitat, a small, slim, dark-bearded man, his thinning hair slicked straight back from his receding hairline; he was seated in one of those spare, springy-looking chairs from the conference table in the corner. Wilmot did not particularly like Urbain; he thought the man an excitable Frenchman, despite the fact that Urbain had been born and raised in Quebec.

'I can see that you're physically and mentally fit,' Wilmot was saying to Gaeta, gesturing toward the wallscreen that displayed the man's test scores. 'More than fit; you are an unusual specimen, actually.'

Gaeta grinned lazily. 'It goes with the job.'

His voice was soft, almost musical. He was on the small side, but solidly built, burly. Lots of hard muscle beneath his softly-pleated open-necked white shirt. His face was hardly handsome: his nose had obviously been broken, perhaps more than once; his heavy jaw

22

made him look somewhat like a bulldog. But his deepset dark eyes seemed friendly enough, and his grin was disarming.

'I must tell you, Mr. Gaeta, that—'

'Manuel,' the younger man interrupted. 'Please feel free call me Manuel.'

Wilmot felt slightly perplexed at that. He preferred to keep at least a slight distance from this man. And he noted that although Gaeta seemed quite able to speak American English, he pronounced his own name with a decided Spanish inflection. Wilmot glanced at Urbain, who did nothing except raise one eyebrow.

'Yes, sorry,' Wilmot said. Then, 'But I must tell you, Mr . . . um, Man-well, that no matter what your backers believe, it will be impossible for you to go to the surface of Titan.'

Gaeta's smile did not fade one millimeter. 'Astro Corporation has put up five hundred million international dollars for me to do the stunt. Your university consortium signed off on the deal.'

Urbain broke his silence almost explosively. 'No! It is impossible! No one is allowed to the surface of Titan. It would be a violation of every principle we are guided by.'

'There must have been a misunderstanding,' Wilmot said more smoothly. 'No one has been to Titan's surface, and—'

'Pardon me,' said Gaeta, 'but that's just the point. If somebody else had already been to Titan there'd be no reason for me to do the stunt.'

'Stunt,' Wilmot echoed disapprovingly.

'I have the equipment,' Gaeta went on. 'It's all been tested. My crew comes aboard tomorrow. All I need from you is some workshop space where they can set up my gear and check out the equipment. We're all set with everything else.'

Urbain shook his head vehemently. 'Teleoperated probes only will be sent to the surface of Titan. No humans!'

'With all respect, sir,' Gaeta said, his voice still soft and friendly, 'you're thinking like a scientist.'

'Yes, of course. How else?'

'See, I'm in show biz, not science. I get paid to do risky stunts, like surfing the clouds of Jupiter and skiing down Mt. Olympus on Mars.'

'Stunts,' Wilmot muttered again.

'Yeah, stunts. People pay a lotta money to participate in my stunts. That's what the VR gear is for.'

'Virtual reality thrills. Vicarious experiences.'

'Cheap thrills, right. It brings in the big bucks. My investors'll make their half-bill back the first ten seconds I'm on the VR nets.'

'You risk your life so that other people can get their adventure plugged into a virtual reality set,' Urbain said, almost accusingly.

If anything, Gaeta's smile widened. 'The trick is to handle the risks. Do the research, buy or build the equipment you need. They call me a daredevil, but I'm not a fool.'

'And you want to be the first man to reach the surface of Titan,' Wilmot said.

'Shouldn't be that tough. You're going out there anyway, so we hitch a ride with you. Titan's got an atmosphere and a decent gravity. Radiation levels are nowhere near as bad as Jupiter.'

'And contamination?' demanded Urbain.

Gaeta's brows hiked up. 'Contamination?'

'There is *life* on Titan. It is only microscopic, I grant you: single-celled bacterial types. But it is living and we must protect it from contamination. That is our first duty.'

The stuntman relaxed again. 'Oh, sure. I'll be in an armored spacesuit. You can scrub it down and bathe me in ultraviolet light when I get back. Kill any bugs that might be on the suit's exterior.'

Urbain shook his head even more violently. 'No, no, no. You don't understand. We are not worried about the microbes contaminating you. Our worry is that *you* might contaminate *them*.'

'Huh?'

'It is a unique ecology, there on Titan,' Urbain said, his blue eyes burning with intensity, his beard bristling. 'We cannot take any chances on your contaminating them.'

'But they're just bugs!'

Urbain's jaw sagged open. He looked like a Believer who had just heard blasphemy uttered.

'Unique organisms,' corrected Wilmot sternly. 'They must not be disturbed.'

'But they've landed probes on Titan,' Gaeta protested, 'lots of 'em!'

'Each one was as thoroughly disinfected as science can achieve,' Urbain said. 'They were subjected to levels of gamma radiation that almost destroyed their electronic circuits. Some of them *were* actually disabled during the contamination procedures.'

Gaeta shrugged. 'Okay, you can decontaminate my suit the same way.'

'With you inside it?' Wilmot asked quietly.

'Inside? Why?'

Urbain replied, 'Because when you get into your suit you will be leaving a veritable jungle of microbial flora and fauna on every part of its exterior that you touch: human sweat, body oils, who knows what else? One fingerprint, one *breath* could leave enough terrestrial microbes to utterly devastate Titan's entire ecology.'

'I'd have to stay in the suit while you fry it with gamma rays?' Wilmot nodded.

Urbain said flatly, 'That is the only way we will allow you to go to Titan's surface.'

Departure Minus 38 Days

He's really handsome when he smiles, Susan noted silently. But he's always so serious!

Malcolm Eberly was peering intently at the three-dimensional display floating in mid-air above his desk top. To Susan he looked like a clean-cut California surfer type, but only from the neck up. His blond hair was chopped short, in the latest style. He had good cheekbones and a strong, firm jaw. Chiseled nose and startling blue eyes, the color of an Alpine sky. A killer smile, too, but he smiled all too rarely.

She had bent over backwards to please him: dressed in the plain tunics and slacks that he preferred, let her hair go natural and cut those stubborn curls short, taken off the decal she had worn on her forehead and now wore no adornments at all except for the tiny asteroidal diamond studs in her ears. He hadn't noticed any of it.

'We've got to be more selective in our screening processes,' he said, without looking up from the display. His voice was low, richly vibrant; he spoke American English, but with an overlay of a glass-smooth cultured British accent.

'Look.' Eberly thumbed his remote controller and the display rotated above the desktop so that Susan could see the three-dimensional chart. The office was small and austere: nothing in it but Eberly's gray metal desk and the stiff little plastic chair Susan was sitting in. No decorations on the walls. Eberly's desk top was antiseptically bare.

She leaned forward in the uncomfortable squeaking chair to inspect the series of jagged colored lines climbing steadily across the chart floating before her eyes. Just as she had remembered it from last night, before she'd gone home for the evening.

'In the two weeks since you've started working in the human resources office,' Eberly said, 'successful recruitments have climbed almost thirty percent. You've accomplished more work than the rest of the staff combined, it seems.'

That's because I want to please you, she said to herself. She didn't have the nerve to say it aloud; didn't have the nerve to do anything more but smile at him.

Unsmilingly, he continued, 'But too many of the new recruits are convicted political dissidents, troublemakers. If they caused unrest on Earth, they'll probably cause unrest here.'

Her smile crumpled. She asked, 'But isn't that the purpose of this mission? The reason we're going to Saturn? To give people a new chance? A new life?'

'Within reason, Holly. Within reason. We don't want chronic protesters here, out-and-out rebels. The next thing you know, we'll be inviting terrorists to the habitat.'

'Have I done that bad a job?'

She waited for him to reassure her, to tell her she was doing her job properly. Instead, Eberly got to his feet and came around the desk.

'Come on, let's go outside for a bit of a stroll.'

She shot to her feet. She was just a tad taller than him. From the shoulders down Eberly was slight, skinny really. Thin arms, narrow chest, even the beginnings of a pot belly, she thought. He needs exercise, she told herself. He works too hard in the office. I've got to get him outside more, get him to the fitness center, build him up.

Yet she followed him in silence down the hallway that led past the habitat's other administrative offices and out the door at its end.

Bright sunshine was streaming through the long windows. Colorful butterflies flitted among the hyacinths, multi-hued tulips and blood-red poppies that bloomed along the path. They walked in silence along the path that ran past the cluster of low white buildings and down the shoulder of the hillside on which the village was built. The tan-bricked path wound around the lake at the bottom of the ridge and out into a pleasant meadow. A bicyclist passed them, coasting down the gentle slope. Leafy young trees spread dappled shade along the path. Susan heard insects humming in the bushes and birds chirping. A complete ecology, painstakingly established and maintained. Looking at the grassy field and the clumps of taller trees standing farther along the gently curving path, she found it hard to believe that they were inside a huge, man-made cylinder that was hanging in empty space a few hundred kilometers above the surface of the Moon. Until she glanced up and saw that the land curved completely around, overhead.

'Holly?'

She snapped her attention back to Eberly. 'I . . . I'm sorry,' she stuttered, embarrassed. 'I guess I wasn't listening.'

He nodded, as if accepting her apology. 'Yes, I forget how beautiful this is. You're absolutely right, none of us should take all this for granted.'

'What were you saying?' she asked.

'It wasn't important.' He raised his arm and swept it around dramatically. '*This* is the important thing, Holly. This world that you will create for yourselves.'

My name is Holly now, she reminded herself. You can remember everything that happens to you, remember your new name, for jeep's sake.

Still, she asked, 'Why'd you want me to change my name?'

Eberly tilted his head to one side, thinking before he answered. 'I've suggested to every new recruit that they change their names. You are entering a new world, starting new lives. A new name is appropriate, don't you agree?'

'Oh, right! F'sure.'

'Yet,' he sighed, 'very few actually follow my suggestion. They cling to the past.'

'It's like baptism, isn't it?' Holly said.

He looked at her and she saw something like respect in his

piercing blue eyes. 'Baptism, yes. Born again. Beginning a new life.'

'This'll be my third life,' she told him.

Eberly nodded.

'I don't remember my first life,' Holly said. 'Far's I can remember, my life started seven years ago.'

'No,' Eberly said firmly. 'Your life began two weeks ago, when you arrived here.'

'F'sure. Right.'

'That's why you changed your name, isn't it?'

'Right,' she repeated, thinking, he's so bugging *serious* about everything! I wish I could make him smile.

Eberly stopped walking and slowly turned a full circle, taking in the world that stretched all around them and climbed up over their heads to completely encircle them.

'I was born in deep poverty,' he said, his voice low, almost a whisper. 'I was born prematurely, very sick; they didn't think I would live. My father ran away when I was still a baby and my mother took up with a migrant laborer, a Mexican. He wanted me to die. If it weren't for the New Morality I would have died before I was six months old. They took me into their hospital, they put me through their schools. They saved me, body and soul.'

'I'm glad,' Holly said.

'The New Morality saved America,' Eberly explained. 'When the greenhouse warming flooded all the coastal areas and the food riots started, it was the New Morality that brought order and decency back into our lives.'

'I don't remember the States at all,' she said. 'Just Selene. Nothing before that.'

He chuckled. 'You certainly seem to have no trouble remembering anything that's happened to you since. I've never seen anyone with such a steel trap of a mind.'

With a careless shrug, Holly replied, 'That's just the RNA treatments they gave me.'

'Oh, yes, of course.' He started walking again, slowly. 'Well, Holly, here we are. Both of us. And ten thousand others.'

'Nine thousand, nine hundred and ninety-eight,' she corrected, with an impish grin.

He dipped his chin slightly in acknowledgement of her arithmetic, totally serious, oblivious to her attempt at humor.

'You have the opportunity to create a new world here,' Eberly said. 'Clean and whole and new. You are the most fortunate people of the ages.'

'You too,' she said.

He made a little gesture with one hand. 'I'm only one man. There are ten thousand of you – minus one, I admit. *You* are the ones who will create this new world. It's yours to fashion as you see fit. I'm completely satisfied merely to be here, among you, and to help you in any way that I can.'

Holly stared at him, feeling enormous admiration welling up within her.

'But Malcolm, you've got to help us to build this new world. We're going to need your vision, your . . .' she fumbled for a word, then . . . 'your dedication.'

'Of course, I'll do what I can,' he said. And for the first time, he smiled.

Holly felt thrilled.

'But you must do your best, too,' he added. 'I expect the same dedication and hard work from you that I myself am exerting. Nothing less, Holly.'

She nodded silently.

'You must devote yourself totally to the work we are doing,' Eberly said. 'Totally.'

'I will,' Holly answered. 'I already have, f'real.'

'Every aspect of your life must be dedicated to our work,' he insisted. 'There will be no time for frivolities. Nor for romantic entanglements.'

'I don't have any romantic entanglements, Malcolm,' she said, in a small voice. Silently she added, wish I did. With you.

'Neither do I,' he said. 'The task before us is too important to allow personal considerations to get in the way.'

Holly said, 'I understand, Malcolm. I truly do.'

'Good. I'm glad.'

And Eberly thought, Carrot and stick, that's the way to control her. Carrot and stick.

Departure Minus Two Hours

Eberly chose to stand with his back to the oblong window of the observation blister. Beyond its thick quartz the stars were swinging by slowly as the mammoth habitat revolved lazily along its axis. The Moon would slide into view, so close that one could see the smoothed launching pads of Armstrong Spaceport, blackened by decades of rocket blasts, and the twin humps of Selene's two buried public plazas, as well as the vast pit where workers were constructing a third. Some claimed they could even see individual tractors and the cable cars speeding along their overhead lines to outlying settlements such as Hell Crater and the Farside Observatory.

Eberly never looked out if he could help it. The sight of the Moon, the stars, the universe constantly swinging past his eyes made him sick to his stomach. He kept his back to it. Besides, his work, his future, his destiny was *inside* the habitat, not out there.

Standing before him, facing the window with apparently no ill effect, stood a short heavyset woman wearing a gaudy arm's-length tunic of many shades of red and orange over shapeless beige slacks. Sparkling rings adorned most of her fingers and more jewelry decorated her wrists, earlobes, and double-chins. Ruth Morgenthau was one of the small cadre of people the Holy Disciples had planted in the habitat. She had not been coerced into this one-way mission to Saturn, Eberly knew; she had volunteered.

Beside her was a lean, short, sour-faced man wearing a shabby pseudoleather jacket of jet black.

'Malcolm,' said Morgenthau, gesturing with a chubby hand,

'may I introduce Dr. Sammi Vyborg.' She turned slightly. 'Dr. Vyborg, Malcolm Eberly.'

'I am very pleased to meet you, sir,' said Vyborg, in a reedy, nasal voice. His face was little more than a skull with skin stretched over it. Prominent teeth. Narrow slits of eyes.

Eberly accepted his extended hand briefly. 'Doctor of what?' he asked.

'Education. From the University of Wittenberg.'

The ghost of a smile touched Eberly's lips. 'Hamlet's university.'

Vyborg grinned toothily. 'Yes, if you can believe Shakespeare. There is no mention of the Dane in the university's records. I looked.'

Morgenthau asked, 'The records go back that far?'

'They are very sketchy, of course.'

'I'm not interested in the past,' Eberly said. 'It's the future that I am working for.'

Vyborg nodded. 'So I understand.'

Eberly glanced sharply at Morgenthau, who said hastily, 'I have explained to Dr. Vyborg that our task is to take charge of the habitat's management, once we get underway.'

'Which will be in two hours,' Vyborg added.

Eberly focused his gaze on the little man, asking, 'I have seen to it that you are highly placed in the communications department. Can you run the entire department, if and when I ask you to?'

'There are two very prominent persons above me in the department,' Vyborg replied. 'Neither of whom are Believers.'

'I know the organization chart!' Eberly snapped. 'I drafted it myself. I had no choice but to accept those two secularists above you, but *you* are the one I have chosen to run the department. Can you do it?'

'Of course.' Vyborg answered without hesitation. 'But what will become of my superiors?'

'You can't ship them home, once we get started,' Morgenthau pointed out, a smile dimpling her cheeks.

'I will take care of them,' Eberly said firmly, 'when the proper moment comes. For now, I want to know that I can rely on you.'

'You can,' said Vyborg.

'Completely and utterly. I want total loyalty.'

'You will have it,' Vyborg said firmly. Then he smiled again and added, 'If you can make me head of communications.'

'I will.'

Morgenthau smiled, satisfied that these two men could work together and further the cause that she had given her life to serve.

Holly was getting frantic. She had searched everywhere for Malcolm, from his austere little office to the other cubbyholes in the human resources section, then down the corridors in the other sections of the administration building. No sign of him anywhere.

He'll miss the breakout! she kept telling herself. She had it all planned out. She would take Malcolm to the lakeside site down at the edge of the village. Professor Wilmot and his managers had arranged more than a dozen spots around the habitat where people could gather and watch the breakout ceremonies on big vid screens that had been set up out in the open. The lakeside was the best spot, Holly thought, the prettiest and closest to their offices.

But Malcolm was nowhere to be found. Where could he be? What's he doing? He'll miss everything! People were streaming along the paths toward the assembly areas where the big screens had been set up, couples and larger groups, chatting, smiling, nodding hello to her. Holly ignored them all, searching for Eberly.

And then she saw him, striding along the path from the woods with that overweight Morgenthau woman beside him. Holly frowned. He's spending a lot of time with her, she thought. But a smile broke across her face as she watched them: Morgenthau was puffing hard, trying to keep up with Malcolm's longer strides. Serves her right, Holly thought, as she started down the path to intercept them and bring Malcolm over to the shore of the lake. She wanted him standing beside her as the habitat started its long flight to Saturn. Nobody else, she told herself. He's got to stand with me.

Sitting up in bed, Pancho Lane stared unhappily at the hologram image of *Goddard* hanging in space. It seemed as if one half of her bedroom had disappeared, to be replaced by the darkness of space with a miniature habitat floating in the middle of the scene, revolving slowly. The Moon edged into view, pockmarked and glowing brightly. Pancho could see the laser beacon that marked the top of Mt. Yeager, just above Selene, not all that far from her own bedroom.

She's really doing it, Pancho grumbled to herself. Sis is really going off on that danged tin can, getting as far away from me as she can get. I saved her life, I broke my butt paying her medical expenses and the cryonics and all that, I nursed her and taught her and wiped her shitty ass, and now she goes traipsing off into the wild black yonder. That's gratitude. That's a sister's love.

Yet she couldn't work up real anger. She knew that Susie needed to break away, needed to start her own life. Independently. Every kid's got to go out on her own, sooner or later. Hell, I did myself when Susie was just a preteen.

Not Susie, she remembered. She calls herself Holly now. Got to remember that when I call her. Holly.

Well, if things don't work out for her I'll send a torch ship out to bring her home. All she's got to do is ask. I'll fly out to her myself, by damn.

The holographic view of *Goddard* winked out, replaced by a life-sized image of Professor Wilmot. To Pancho, watching from her bed, it seemed as if the man's head and shoulders hovered in midair across her bedroom.

'Today we embark on an unprecedented voyage of discovery and exploration,' Wilmot began, in a slow, sonorous voice.

'Blah, blah, blah,' Pancho muttered. She muted the sound with a voice command and then ordered her phone to get her security chief. I just hope Wendell got somebody really good to keep an eye on Sis. If he hasn't I'll toss him out on his butt, no matter how good he is in bed.

'Vyborg makes a good addition to our cadre,' Morgenthau said as she walked beside Eberly, heading back to the lakeside village.

Eberly brushed at a brilliant monarch butterfly that fluttered too close to his face. 'He's ambitious, that's clear enough.'

'There's nothing wrong with ambition,' said Morgenthau.

'As long as he can follow orders.'

'He will, I'm sure.'

Inwardly, Eberly had his doubts. But I've got to work with the material at hand, he told himself. Morgenthau has practically no ambition, no drive for self-aggrandizement. That makes her a perfect underling. Vyborg is something else. I'll have to watch him closely. And my back, as well.

To Morgenthau he said, 'Information is the key to power. With Vyborg in communications we'll have access to all the surveillance cameras in the habitat.'

'And he could help us to tap into the phones, as well,' Morgenthau added.

'I want more than that. I want every apartment bugged with surveillance cameras. Secretly, of course.'

'Every apartment? That's . . . it's a tremendous task.'

'Find a way to do it,' Eberly snapped.

Holly tried not to run, she didn't want to appear *that* anxious, but the closer she got to Eberly and Morgenthau, the faster she trotted. As she approached, she wondered why Malcolm had chosen to be with Morgenthau. She's not much to look at. Holly giggled to herself. Really, she's *too much* to look at. And all decked out like she's going to some wild-ass party. She'd be pretty if she dropped twenty-thirty kilos.

Eberly looked up and recognized her.

'Malcolm!' Holly called, slowing to a walk. 'Come on! The ceremonies've started already. You're gonna miss it all!'

'Then I'll miss it,' Eberly said severely. 'I have work to do. I can't waste my time on ceremonies.'

He walked right past her, with the Morgenthau woman slogging along beside him. Holly stood there with her mouth hanging open, fighting desperately to keep from crying.

Breakout

Hardly anyone aboard *Goddard* knew about the 'bridge.' Actually, the massive habitat's navigation and control center was in a compact pod mounted on the outside skin of the huge cylinder like a blister on a slowly rotating log.

Captain Nicholson's title was an honorific. She had skippered spacecraft out to the Asteroid Belt and had once even commanded a trio of ships on a resupply mission for the scientific bases on Mars.

Of the four-person crew that ran the navigation and control center, Nicholson, her first mate and her navigator intended to return to Earth as soon as they had established *Goddard* in orbit at Saturn. Only the systems engineer, Ilya Timoshenko, had signed on for the mission's full duration. In fact, Timoshenko never expected to see Earth again.

Samantha Nicholson did not look like a veteran spacecraft commander. She was a petite woman who had allowed her hair to go silvery white. The descendant of a long line of shipping magnates, she was the first of her family to heed the call of space, rather than the sea. Her father disowned her for her stubborn, independent choice, her mother cried bitterly the first time she left Earth. Nicholson consoled her mother and told her father she neither needed nor wanted the family fortune. She never returned to Earth, but made Selene her home instead.

Timoshenko admired the captain. Nicholson was capable, intelligent, even-handed whenever a dispute arose, and when necessary she could peel four layers of skin off a man with language that would have made her mother faint.

'X minus thirty seconds,' said the computer's synthesized voice.

Timoshenko eyed his console. Every single icon was in the green.

'Ignite the thrusters on my mark,' said Captain Nicholson.

'Roger,' the first mate replied.

Normally Timoshenko would have sneered at her insistence on human control. The four of them knew perfectly well that the computers actually ran the propulsion system. This lumbering oversized sewer pipe would be pushed out of lunar orbit at precisely the right instant even if none of them were on the bridge. But the captain kept the old traditions, and even Timoshenko – normally as dour and scornful as a haughty, patronizing academic – respected the old lady for it.

The computer said, 'Ignition in five seconds, four . . . three . . . two . . .'

'Fire thrusters,' the captain said.

Timoshenko grinned as his console showed the computer command and the human action taking place at the same instant.

The thrusters fired. *Goddard* broke out of lunar orbit and began its long flight path to the planet Saturn.

Even with Duncan Drive fusion engines, an object as massive as the *Goddard* habitat does not flit through the solar system the way passenger carriers or even automated ore haulers do.

Part of the problem is sheer mass. At more than a hundred thousand tons, the habitat is equal to a whole fleet of interplanetary ships. To push the habitat to an acceleration of even one-tenth *g* would require enormous thrust and therefore a bankrupting amount of fusion fuel.

Yet the major problem is the spin-induced gravity inside the habitat. A major acceleration from rocket thrust would turn the world inside the cylinder topsy-turvy. Instead of feeling a gentle Earthlike pull 'downward' the inhabitants would also sense an acceleration pushing them in the direction of the rocket thrust. Life within the habitat would become difficult, even weird. It would feel to the inhabitants as if they were constantly struggling uphill, or traipsing downhill, even when walking on normal-looking flat ground.

So *Goddard* accelerated away from the Moon at a leisurely pace, a minute fraction of a *g*. The force went unnoticed by the ten thousand inhabitants, although it was closely monitored by the habitat's small crew of propulsion engineers.

It would take fourteen months to reach the vicinity of Jupiter, giant of the solar system. There *Goddard* would replenish its fusion fuels, isotopes of hydrogen and helium delved from Jupiter's deep, turbulent atmosphere by automated skimmers operated from the space station in orbit around the enormous planet. Jupiter's massive gravity would also impart a slight extra boost to the habitat as it swung past.

Eleven months after the Jupiter encounter, *Goddard* would slip into orbit around ringed Saturn. By then, more than two years after departing the Earth/Moon vicinity, anthropologist James Wilmot expected the subjects of his experiment would be ready to form the political systems and personal bonds of a new society. He wondered what form that society would take.

Malcolm Eberly already knew.

Departure Plus Three Days

The great advantage of having a scientist in charge of the habitat, thought Malcolm Eberly, is that scientists are so trustingly naive. They depend on honesty in their work, which leads them to behave honestly even outside their sphere of expertise. In turn, this makes them believe that those they associate with are honest, as well.

Eberly laughed aloud as he reviewed his plans for the day. It's time to start things in motion. Now that we're on our way, it's time to start these people looking to me as their natural leader.

And who better to begin with than Holly, he thought. My newborn. She had been sulky, pouting, since he had been so curt with her at the breakout ceremony. He saw that his morning's messages included one from her; she had called him twice yesterday, as well. Ah well, he told himself, Time to make her smile again.

He told the phone to locate her. The holographic image that appeared above his desktop showed that she was in her office, working.

As soon as she recognized Eberly's face her expression lit up with hope, expectation.

'Holly, if you have a moment, could you come to my office, please?' he asked pleasantly.

She said, 'I'll be there FTL!'

FTL? Eberly wondered as her image winked out. What could— Ah! Faster Than Light. One of her little bits of slang.

He heard her tap on his door, light and timid.

Let her wait, he said to himself. Just long enough to make her worry a bit. He sensed her fidgeting uncertainly outside his door.

When at last she tapped again he called, 'Enter.'

Holly wasn't pouting as she stepped into Eberly's office. Instead, she looked apprehensive, almost afraid.

Eberly got to his feet and gestured to the chair in front of his desk. 'Sit down, Holly. Please.'

She perched on the chair like a little bird ready to take flight at the slightest danger. Eberly sat down and said nothing for a few moments, studying her. Holly was wearing a forest green tunic over form-fitting tights of a slightly lighter green. No rings or other jewelry except for the studs in her earlobes. Diamonds, he saw. Since the asteroid belt had been opened to mining, gemstones were becoming commonplace. At least she's taken off that silly decal on her forehead, Eberly noted. She's rather attractive, really, he thought. Some men find dark skin exotic. Not much of a figure, but she's got good long legs. Should I find someone to get her involved with romantically? No, he concluded. I want her attention focused on me, for now.

He made a slow smile for her. 'I hurt you, didn't I?'

Holly's eyes went wide with surprise.

'I didn't mean to. Sometimes I become so wrapped up in my work that I forget the people around me have feelings.' With a sigh, he continued, 'I'm truly sorry. It was thoughtless of me.'

Her expression bloomed like a flower in the sunshine. 'I shouldn't be such a pup, Malcolm. I just couldn't help it. I wanted to be beside you at the ceremony and—'

'And I let you down.'

'No!' she said immediately. 'It was my own dimdumb fault. I should've known better. I'm sorry. I didn't mean to cause you any trouble.'

Eberly leaned back in his comfortable chair and gave her his patient fatherly smile. How easily she's maneuvered, he thought. She's apologizing to me.

'I mean,' Holy was prattling on, 'I know you've got lots to do and all the responsibilities for the whole habitat's human resources and all that and I shouldn't have expected you to take time out and stand around watching the ridic' ceremonies with me like some schoolkid at commencement or something . . .'

Her voice wound down like a toy running out of battery power.

Eberly replaced his smile with a concerned expression. 'Very well, Holly. It's over and done with. Forgotten.'

She nodded happily.

'I have an assignment for you, if you can find the time to work on it.'

'I'll make the time!'

'Wonderful.' He smiled again, the pleased, grateful smile.

'What's the assignment?'

He called up the habitat's ground plan and projected it against the bare wall. Holly saw the villages, the parks and farmlands and orchards, the offices and workshops and factory complexes, all neatly laid out and connected by paths for pedestrians and electric motorbikes.

'This is our home now,' Eberly said. 'We're going to be living here for at least five years. Some of us – many of us – will spend the rest of their lives here.'

Holly agreed with a nod.

'Yet we have no names for anything. Nothing but the engineers' designations. We can't go on calling our home towns "village A" and "village B" and so forth.'

'I click,' Holly murmured.

'The orchards should have names of their own. The hills and the woods – everything. Who wants to go shopping in "retail complex three?"'

'Yeah, but how will we pick names for everything?'

'I won't,' Eberly said. 'And you won't, either. This is a task that must be done by the residents of the habitat. The people themselves must choose the names they want.'

'But how—'

'A contest,' he answered before she could complete her question. 'Or rather, a series of contests. The residents of each village will have a contest to name that village. The workers in a factory will have a contest to name their factory. It will engage everyone's attention and keep them busy for months.'

'Cosmic,' Holly breathed.

42

'I need someone to work out the rules and organize each individual contest. Will you do this for me?'

'Absotively!'

Eberly allowed himself to chuckle at her enthusiasm. He went on, 'Later, you'll have to form committees to judge the names entered and count the votes.'

'Wow!' Holly was almost trembling with anticipation, he could see.

'Good. I want you to make this your top priority. But tell no one about this until we're ready to announce it to the general populace. I don't want knowledge of this leaking out prematurely.'

'I'll keep it to myself,' Holly promised.

'Fine.' Eberly leaned back in his chair, satisfied. Then he cocked an eye at her and said, 'I notice that you called me several times. What is it you wanted to talk to me about?'

Holly blinked as if suddenly shaken awake from a dream. 'See you? Oh, yeah. It's prob'ly nothing much. Just some details, not a big deal, really, I guess.'

Leaning slightly forward, Eberly thought that her persistent calls were merely a thinly disguised attempt to get to see him. He rested his arms on his desk. 'What is it, then?'

With a concerned knitting of her brows, Holly said, 'Well . . . I was running routine checks on the dossiers of the last batch of personnel to come aboard and I found some discrepancies in a few of them.'

'Discrepancies?'

She nodded vigorously. 'References that don't check out. Or incomplete forms.'

'Anything serious? he asked.

'Ruth Morgenthau, for example. She's only got one position filled in on the prior-experience section of her application.'

'Really?'

'It's a wiz of a good one,' Holly admitted, 'chief of administrative services for the Amsterdam office of the Holy Disciples.'

Eberly smiled faintly. 'That *is* rather impressive, don't you think?'

'Uh-huh, but it's only one and the form calls for at least three.'

'I wouldn't worry about it.'

She nodded. 'Kay, no prob. But there's one guy, he claims references from several universities but I can't find any mention of him in any of their records.'

'False references?' Eberly felt a pang of alarm. 'Who is this person?'

Holly pulled a palmcomp from her tunic pocket and pointed it at the wall opposite the one showing the habitat's layout. She glanced at Eberly, silently asking permission. He nodded curtly.

A human resources dossier appeared on the wall. Eberly felt himself frowning as he saw the name and photo at its top: Sammi Vyborg.

Scrolling down to the references section of the dossier, Holly highlighted the names of five university professors.

'Far's I can dig, he never attended any of those schools,' she said.

Eberly leaned back in his chair and steepled his fingers, hiding his intense displeasure, thinking furiously. 'Have you contacted any of those professors?'

'Not yet. I wanted you to see this before I go any deeper.'

'Good. Thank you for bringing this to my attention.'

'I can query each of the profs. But what do we do with Vyborg if they don't back him?'

Eberly spread his hands. 'Obviously we can't let the man remain in the post he's been assigned to. *If* he has falsified his references.'

'We can ship him back Earthside when we refuel at Jupiter, I guess,' Holly mused. 'But what do we do with him till then? Put him to work in the farms or something?'

'Or something,' Eberly temporized.

'Kay. I'll query the—'

'No,' he said sharply. 'I will contact these professors. Each one of them. Myself.'

'But you've got so much to do.'

'It's my responsibility, Holly. Besides, they're much more likely to respond quickly to a query from the chief of human resources than from one of the chief's assistants.'

Her face fell briefly, but she quickly brightened. 'Yeah, guess so.'

'Besides, you're going to be very busy arranging the contests.' She grinned at that.

'I'll take care of it myself.' Eberly repeated.

'Doesn't seem fair,' she murmured. 'I'm sorry I brought it to you. I should have done it without bothering you.'

'No, Holly. This is something that should have been brought to my attention. You did the right thing.'

'Kay,' she said, getting slowly to her feet. 'If you say so. Still . . .'

'Thank you for bringing this to me,' Eberly said. 'You've done a fine job.'

She beamed. 'Thanks!'

'I'm sure it's just a mistake or a misunderstanding somewhere along the line. I know Vyborg personally. He's a good man.'

'Oh! I didn't know . . .'

'All the more reason to check this out thoroughly,' Eberly said sternly. 'There can be no personal favoritism here.'

'No, of course not.'

'Thank you, Holly,' he said again.

She went to the door, slowly, as if reluctant to leave his presence. He smiled at her and she finally left his office, sliding the door shut quietly.

Eberly stared at the dossier still on his wallscreen, the false references still highlighted.

Idiot! he fumed. There was no need for Vyborg to pad his dossier. He let his ego override his judgment.

Still, Eberly said to himself, a mistake like this gives me a little leverage over him. Something to make him more dependent on me. All to the good.

Now to correct his folder. And Eberly began dictating to his computer the glowing references from each of the university professors that would be placed in Vyborg's dossier.

Departure Plus 28 Days

'Come on,' groused Manuel Gaeta, 'there's gotta be a way. There's *always* a way, Fritz.'

Friederich Johann von Helmholtz got up from his knees and drew himself to his full height. Despite his imposing name, he was a short, slim, almost delicately built man. And the best technician in the solar system, as far as Gaeta was concerned. At the moment, however, there was precious little goodwill flowing between them.

Fritz's buzz-cut head barely rose to Gaeta's shoulders. Standing beside the muscular stuntman, the technician looked almost like a skinny child. Both of them were dwarfed by the massive cermet-clad suit standing empty in the middle of the equipment bay.

'Of course there is a way,' Fritz said, in precisely clipped English. 'You get into the suit. We seal it up. Then we go through the sterilization procedure that Professor Wilmot and Dr. Urbain insist upon, including the gamma-ray bath. And then you die.'

Gaeta huffed mightily.

Fritz stood beside the empty suit, his arms folded implacably across his slim chest.

'Jesoo, Fritz,' Gaeta muttered, 'those Astro Corp suits paid half a bill for me to be the first man to set foot on Titan. You know what they'll do to me if I don't do it? If I don't even *try* 'cause some tight-ass scientists are worried about the bugs down there?'

'I would imagine they will want their half billion returned,' Fritz said calmly.

'And we've already spent a big chunk of it.'

Fritz shrugged.

'They'll take it outta my hide,' Gaeta said, frowning with worry. 'Plus, nobody'll ever back me for another stunt. I'll be finished.'

'Or perhaps dead.' Fritz said it without the faintest flicker of a smile.

'You're a big help, *amigo*.'

'I am a technician. I am not your financial advisor or your bodyguard.'

'You're *un fregado*, a cold-blooded machine, that's what you are.'

'Insulting me will not solve your problem.'

'So what? You're not solving my problem. Nobody's solving my problem!'

Fritz pursed his lips momentarily, a sign that he was thinking. 'Perhaps . . . no, that probably would not work.'

'Perhaps what?' Gaeta demanded.

Reaching up to pat the bulky suit on its armored upper arm, Fritz mused, 'The problem is to insert you into the suit after it has been sterilized without contaminating it.'

'Yeah. Right.'

'Perhaps we could wrap you in a sterile envelope of some sort. A plastic shroud that has been decontaminated.'

'You think?'

Cocking his head to one side, Fritz added, 'The problem then becomes to get you sealed into the shroud without contaminating it.'

'Same problem as getting into the *maldito* suit in the first place.' Gaeta broke into a string of Spanish expletives.

'But if we did it outside the habitat, in space,' Fritz said slowly, as if piecing his ideas together as he spoke, 'then perhaps between the ambient ultraviolet flux out there and the hard vacuum the contamination requirements could be satisfied.'

Gaeta's dark brows shot up. 'You think?'

Fritz shrugged again. 'Let me run some numbers through the computer. Then I will talk with Urbain's planetary protection team.'

Gaeta broke into a grin and thumped Fritz on the shoulder hard enough to make the smaller man totter. 'I knew you could do it, *amigo*! I knew it all along.'

Departure Plus 142 Days

Eberly had sat for more than two hours, utterly bored, as each of the habitat's sixteen department heads gave their long, dull weekly reports. Wilmot insisted on these weekly meetings; Eberly thought them pointless and foolish. Nothing more than Wilmot's way of making himself feel important, he told himself.

There was no need to spend two or three hours in this stuffy conference room. Each department chairman could send in his or her report to Wilmot electronically. But no, the old man has to sit up at the head of the table and pretend that he's actually doing something.

For a community of ten thousand alleged troublemakers, the habitat was sailing on its way to Saturn smoothly enough. Most of the population were relatively young and energetic. Eberly, with Holly's unstinting help, had weeded out the real troublemakers among those who applied for a berth. Those whom he accepted had run foul of the strictures of the highly organized societies back on Earth one way or another: they were unhappy with their employment placement, displeased when the local government refused to allow them to move from one city to another, unwilling to accept a genetic screening board's verdict on a childbearing application. A few had even tried political action to change their governments, to no avail. So here they were, in habitat *Goddard*, in a man-made world that had plenty of room for growth. They turned their backs on Earth, willing to trek out to Saturn in their ridiculous quest for personal freedom.

The trick is, Eberly thought as the chief of maintenance droned on about trivial problems, to give them the illusion of personal freedom without allowing them to be free. To make them look to

48

me for their freedom and their hopes for the future. To get them to accept me as their indispensable leader.

It's time to begin that process, he decided as the maintenance chief finally sat down. Now.

Yet he had to wait for the security director's report. Leo Kananga was an imposing figure: a tall, deeply black Rwandan who insisted on being addressed as 'Colonel,' his rank in the Rwandan police force before he volunteered for the Saturn mission. His head shaved bald, he dressed all in black, which accentuated his height. Despite his impressive appearance, he had nothing new to report, no great problems. A few scrapes here and there in the cafeteria, usually young men making testosterone displays for young women. An out-and-out brawl at a pick-up football game in one of the parks.

'Sports hooligans,' Kananga grumbled. 'We get fights after vids of major sporting events from Earth, too.'

'Maybe we should stop showing them,' suggested one of the women.

The security chief gave her a pitying smile. 'Try that and you'll have a major disturbance on your hands.'

Great God, Eberly thought, they're going to argue the point for the next half hour. Sure enough, others around the table joined the discussion. Wilmot sat in silence at the head of the table, watching, listening, occasionally fingering his moustache.

Which of these dolts will be loyal to me? Eberly asked himself as they wrangled on. Which will I have to replace? His eyes immediately focused on Berkowitz, the overweight chairman of the communications department. I've promised his job to Vyborg, Eberly thought. Besides, Berkowitz would never be loyal to me; I couldn't trust a Jew who's spent all his life in the news media.

At last the teapot-tempest over sports hooligans ended. Without a resolution, of course. That type of discussion never produces results, Eberly thought, only hot air. Still, I should remember sports hooligans. They might become useful, at the proper moment.

49

Wilmot stroked his moustache again, then said, 'That completes the departmental reports. Have we any old business to take up?'

No one stirred, except that several people seemed to eye the door that led out of the conference room.

'Any new business? If not—'

'I have a piece of new business, sir,' said Eberly, raising his hand.

All eyes turned toward him.

'Go ahead,' Wilmot said, looking slightly surprised.

'I think we should consider the matter of standardizing our clothing.'

'Standardizing?'

'You mean you want everyone to wear uniforms?'

Eberly smiled patiently for them. 'No, not uniforms. Of course not. But I've noticed that great differences in clothing styles cause a certain amount of . . . well, friction. We're all supposed to be equals here, yet some of the people flaunt very expensive clothing. And jewelry.'

'That's a personal decision,' said Andrea Maronella. She was wearing an auburn blouse and dark green skirt, Eberly noticed, set off with several bracelets, earrings, and a pearl necklace.

'It does cause some friction,' Eberly repeated. 'Those sports enthusiasts, for example. They wear the colors of the teams they favor, don't they?'

Colonel Kananga nodded.

Berkowitz, of all people, piped up. 'Y'know, some people show up at the office dressed like they were going to work on Wall Street or Savile Row, while the technicians come in looking like they've been dragged on a rope from lower Bulgaria or someplace.'

Everyone laughed.

'But isn't that their right?' Maronella countered. 'To dress as they choose? As long as it doesn't interfere with their work.'

'But it does interfere with their work,' Eberly pounced, 'when it causes jealousy and rancor.'

'Those hooligans wear their team colors just to annoy the buffs who root for other teams,' Kananga said.

'I think that if we offered guidelines about dress codes,' Eberly said, calm and reasonable, 'it would help considerably. Not mandatory codes, but guidelines for what is appropriate and expected.'

'We could offer counseling,' said the chief of medical services, a psychologist.

'And advice about style.'

They wrangled over the issue for more than half an hour. Finally Wilmot put it to a vote, and the board decided to generate voluntary guidelines for appropriate dress during working hours. Eberly graciously accepted their decision.

The first step, he told himself.

Memorandum

To: All personnel
From: M. Eberly,
Director, Human Resources Dept.
Subject: Dress codes

In an effort to reduce tensions arising from differences in apparel, the following dress codes are suggested. These codes are not mandatory, but voluntary adherence will help eliminate frictions arising from apparent differences in clothing style, expense, accessories, etc.

1. All personnel are required to wear their identity badges at all times. These badges include name, job position, a recent photograph plus electronically-stored background data from the individual's dossier on file in the Human Resources Department. In an emergency, such data is vital to medical and/or rescue teams.

2. Suggested dress codes are as follows:
   a. Office workers should wear a solid-color tunic and slacks, with personal adornment (such as jewelry, tattoos, hair styling, etc.) kept to a minimum.
   b. Laboratory workers should dress as in (a), above, except that they should wear protective smocks, eye shields, etc., as required by their tasks.
   c. Factory workers . . .

Selene: Astro Corporation Headquarters

Pancho paced across her office as she spoke, feeling frustrated because there was no feedback from the person she was addressing. Communications beyond the Earth/Moon vicinity were almost always one-way affairs. Even though messages flitted through space at the speed of light, the distances to Mars, the Belt, and beyond were simply too great for real-time, face-to-face chat.

So Pancho rattled on, hoping that Kris Cardenas would reply as quickly as possible.

'I know it's a lot to ask, Dr. Cardenas,' she was saying. 'You've spent a lot of years there at Ceres and made a life for yourself. But this migration out to Saturn is a chance to build something brand new for yourself. They'll be happy to have your expertise, you can count on that. There's probably a million ways your knowledge of nanotechnology will help them.'

By force of habit Pancho glanced up at the image floating in the middle of her office. Instead of Kris Cardenas' face, it showed only her own neatly typed words.

'I'll personally pay all your expenses and add a big bonus,' Pancho went on. 'I'll pay for a major expansion of your habitat out there at Ceres. She's my little sister, Kris, and she needs somebody to watch over her. I can't do it; I'm hoping that you can. Will you do this for me? Just for a year or so, just long enough so Sis gets squared away and can stand on her own feet without doing anything foolish. Will you help me on this, Kris? I really think it'll be to your advantage and I'd appreciate it enormously.'

Pancho realized she was practically begging. Almost whining. So what? she asked herself. This is Susie I'm talking about.

But she took a breath and said more evenly, 'Please get back to me as soon as you can on this, Kris. It's important to me.'

In her cozy quarters aboard the habitat *Chrysallis*, in orbit around the asteroid Ceres, Kris Cardenas intently watched Pancho's earnest face as the Astro Corporation board chairman paced back and forth across her plushly furnished office. Cardenas noted the tension in every line of Pancho's lanky body, every gesture, every word she spoke.

I don't owe her a thing, Cardenas told herself. Why should I uproot myself and trundle out to Saturn on that weird expedition?

Yet, despite herself, she felt intrigued. Maybe it's time for a change in my life. Maybe I've done enough penance.

Despite her calendar years, Dr. Kristin Cardenas looked no more than thirtyish, a pert, sandy blond woman with a swimmer's shoulders and strong, athletic body, and bright cornflower-blue eyes. That was because her body teemed with nanomachines, virus-sized devices that acted as a deliberate, directed immune system that destroyed invading organisms, took apart plaque forming in her blood vessels atom by atom, and rebuilt tissue damaged by trauma or aging.

Cardenas had won a Nobel prize for her research in nanotechnology, before the fundamentalist governments of Earth succeeded in banning all forms of nanotech on the planet. She had carried on her work at Selene for years, helping the lunar nation to win its short, virtually bloodless war against the former world government. But because she had taken nanomachines into her own body she was not allowed to return to Earth, even for a brief visit. She had lost her husband and children because they dared not come to Selene and risk being exiled from Earth with her. Cardenas bitterly resented the short-sighted attitudes of the 'flat-landers' who had cost her her children and grandchildren, a bitterness that led her to homicide. She allowed her knowledge of nanotechnology to be used to sabotage a spacecraft, which caused the death of industrialist Dan Randolph.

The government of Selene locked her out of her own nanotech

lab. She fled to the mining station on Ceres, in the Asteroid Belt, where she remained for many years, serving as a medical doctor and eventually as a member of Ceres' governing board. Penance. She helped to build the miners' community at Ceres, and she had refused to do any nanotech work since fleeing from Selene.

Am I being foolish? she now asked herself. Should I apply for a slot on the Saturn expedition? Would they take me if I did apply?

Staring at Pancho's engrossed image frozen on her wallscreen, Cardenas decided to try. It's time to begin a new life in a new world, she thought. Time for a new start.

When she received Cardenas' request, Holly raced from her desk to find Eberly. He was in the office complex's cafeteria, sitting with Morgenthau and a lean, skeletally-thin man whose complexion was darker than her own, the nearly purple black of the true African. They were deep in an intense discussion, their heads leaning forward like conspirators.

Holly scurried up to their table and stood at Eberly's elbow. None of them paid any attention to her. They continued to talk in hushed, confidential tones, too low for Holly to hear their words over the clatter and conversations that clanged off the bare walls of the busy cafeteria.

She waited several moments, fidgeting impatiently, then broke into their tête-à-tête with, 'Excuse me! Malcolm, I hate to interrupt but—'

Eberly looked up sharply at her, displeasure clear in his piercing eyes.

'I'm sorry, Malcolm, but it's important.'

He took a breath, then said, 'What is important enough to intrude in my discussion?'

'Dr. Cardenas wants to join us!'

'Cardenas?' asked Morgenthau.

'Kristin Cardenas,' Holly said, grinning enthusiastically. 'The nanotech expert. She won the Nobel Prize! And she wants to come with us!'

Eberly seemed less than pleased. 'Do we need an expert in nanotechnology?'

'That's a dangerous area,' said the black man, his voice a surprisingly high tenor. His scalp was shaved bald, although there was a fringe of a beard outlining his jawline.

'It's outlawed on Earth,' Morgenthau agreed, adding a muttered, 'Unholy.'

Holly was surprised at their obtuseness. 'Nanotech could be really helpful to us. We could use nanomachines to do most of the habitat's maintenance work. And health-wise, nanomachines could—'

Eberly stopped her with an upraised finger. 'Nanomachines are outlawed on Earth because they could run wild and devour everything in their path.'

'Turn everything into gray goo,' Morgenthau muttered.

'Only if somebody programs 'em to do that,' Holly countered. 'Those flatlanders back Earthside are scared of terrorists or nutcases going wild with nanomachines.'

Morgenthau glared at her but said nothing.

'Shouldn't we be concerned about that, as well?' Eberly asked mildly.

'We've screened everybody aboard,' Holly said. 'We don't have any violent types here. No fanatics.'

'How can we be sure of that?' Morgenthau was obviously unconvinced.

Looking at Eberly, the black man said slowly, 'Properly used, nanomachines could be of great help to us.'

Eberly stared back at him for a long moment. 'You believe so?'

'I do.'

'Would Dr. Cardenas agree to work under our terms, I wonder?' Eberly mused.

'We could ask her and find out,' Holly prompted. 'She's on Ceres now. We could pick her up when we go through the Belt. I checked the flight plan; we'll be within a day's flight of Ceres. She could buzz out to us on a torch ship, no prob. I could get my sister to set up a flight for her, betcha.'

56

Eberly stroked his chin. 'Even though we have a full complement now, I suppose we could make room for one person of Dr. Cardenas' caliber.'

'If Wilmot approves of it,' said Morgenthau.

'Wilmot.' Eberly almost sneered. 'I'm in charge of human resources decisions, not Wilmot.'

'But something like this—'

'I'll take care of it,' he insisted. Turning to Holly, he said, 'Inform Dr. Cardenas that I would like to discuss this with her personally.'

'Cosmic!' Holly blurted.

She was about to turn and head back to the human resources office when Eberly grasped her wrist.

'You haven't met Colonel Kananga, have you?'

The black man got to his feet like a jointed scaffolding unfolding. He was almost two meters tall, a full head taller than Holly.

'Our director of security, Colonel Leo Kananga, from Rwanda,' said Eberly. 'Holly Lane, from Selene.'

Kananga extended his hand. Holly took it in hers. His long fingers felt cold and dry. His grip was strong, almost painful.

Kananga smiled at her, but there was no warmth in it. Just the opposite. Holly felt an icy shudder run down her spine. It was like looking at a skull, a death's head.

Departure Plus 145 Days

As she climbed the stairs to the roof of the administration building, Holly wondered why Eberly had summoned her to the rooftop. She stepped through the metal door and looked for him. No one else was there. She walked to within two steps of the roof's edge and turned full circle. She was alone.

He's always so prompt, she thought. Why isn't he here?

Then she realized that she was more than a minute early, and she relaxed somewhat. He'll be here, she told herself, right on the tick.

Gazing out from the three-storey-high roof, Holly could see the other buildings of the village, low and gleaming white in the sunlight. The long slash of the solar window overhead was too bright to look at for more than a momentary glimpse. Even so, the afterimage of its glare burned in her eyes.

Everything is going well, Holly thought. The habitat is functioning smoothly, everybody doing their jobs as they should. Some trouble with one of the solar mirrors a few days ago, but the maintenance crew went out in spacesuits and fixed it. Now it was swiveling properly again, keeping sunlight streaming through the long windows while the habitat rotated along its axis.

We need sunshine, Holly thought. No matter where we go, no matter how far from Earth we travel, human beings need sunshine. It's more than simple biology, more than the need for green plants at the foundation of the food chain. Sunlight makes us happy, drives away depression. Must be awful back Earthside when they have clouds and storms and they don't see the Sun for days and days. No wonder the flatlanders are a little crazy.

She glanced at her wrist again. He'll be here, she told herself.

He's always on time. Why's he want to see me up here, though? Just the two of us. She felt a nervous thrill race through her. Just the two of us. Maybe he feels about me the way I feel about him. Maybe just a little, but—

'There you are.'

She whirled and focused her attention on Eberly, who was walking slowly across the rooftop's slightly rubbery surface toward her. He really is handsome, she saw. So full of energy. But he ought to dress better, Holly thought, scrutinizing the baggy gray slacks and darker shapeless tunic that hung a size or so too big from his shoulders.

'I wanted to have a word with you outside the office,' he said as he stopped an arm's length from her.

'Sure, Malcolm.' She had to make a conscious effort to keep her hands from fidgeting.

'There are too many listening ears down there,' he went on, 'and what I have to say is for you only.'

'What is it?' she asked, trembling.

He looked over his shoulder, as if expecting to find someone hiding behind him.

Turning back to Holly, he said, 'I see from your reports that you are ready to launch the naming contests.'

Business, Holly realized, crestfallen. He wants to talk about business.

'You are ready, aren't you?' he asked, oblivious to her letdown.

'Right,' she said, thinking, Nothing but business. I don't really mean a thing to him.

'You've set up the rules for each contest?'

Holly nodded. 'It was pretty easy, f'real. And I think that using a lottery to pick the committees for judging each individual contest is the best way to go.'

'I agree,' Eberly said. 'You've done a fine job.'

'Thanks, Malcolm,' she said glumly.

'I'll have to get Wilmot's approval, and then we can launch the contests. I should be able to make the announcement within a few days.'

'Fine.'

His face grew serious. 'But there is something else, Holly.'

'What is it?'

He drew in a breath. 'I don't want you to think of this as a reprimand—'

'Reprimand?' A pang of alarm raced through her. 'What did I do?'

He touched her shoulder with one extended finger. 'Don't be frightened. This is not a reprimand.'

'But . . . what?'

'You and I have been working together for several months now, and in general your work has been excellent.'

She could see there was bad news coming. She tried not to cringe or let her fear show in her expression.

'However, there is one thing.'

'What is it, Malcolm? Tell me and I'll fix it.'

The corners of his lips curled upward slightly. 'Holly, I don't mind you addressing me by my given name when we're alone,' he said softly, 'but when we are with other people, that is altogether too familiar. You should call me Dr. Eberly.'

'Oh.' Holly knew from Eberly's dossier that his doctorate was honorary, awarded by a minor Web-based college that sold courses on languages and public speaking.

'When I introduced you to Colonel Kananga a few days ago,' he went on, 'it was altogether improper for you to address me by my first name.'

'I'm sorry,' she said in a small voice. 'I didn't realize . . .'

He patted her shoulder in a fatherly manner. 'I know. I understand. It really isn't all that important, except that for persons such as Kananga and Morgenthau and such, respect is very essential.'

'I didn't mean to be disrespectful, Mal – I mean, Dr. Eberly.'

'You can continue to call me Malcolm when we're alone. But when there is a third person present, it would be better if you observed the formalities.'

'Sure,' Holly said. 'No prob.'

'Good. Now, we'd both better be getting back to work.'

60

He turned and started for the door that led back inside the building. Holly scampered after him.

'About Dr. Cardenas,' she said.

'Yes?' Without turning or slowing his pace.

'She's agreed to work under our guidelines. She'll be joining us at our closest approach to Ceres. It's all set.'

'Good,' Eberly said, unsmiling. 'Now we need to draw up the guidelines that will regulate her work.'

'We'll need Professor Wilmot's approval for that, won't we?'

He grimaced. 'Yes, we will. Unless . . .'

Holly waited for him to finish the thought. Instead, Eberly yanked open the door and started down the metal stairs toward his office.

Two days later, Eberly sat behind his bare desk studying the face of Hal Jaansen, head of the habitat's engineering department.

Ruth Morgenthau sat beside Jaansen, looking worried. She wore one of her colorful tunics and enough jewelry, Eberly thought, to tilt the entire habitat in her direction. She's paying absolutely no attention to the dress codes, he said to himself. She's flaunting her independence, making me look like a fool. But he kept the distaste off his face as he watched Jaansen.

The man doesn't look like an engineer, Eberly thought. Jaansen was one of those pale blond Norsemen; even his eyelashes were so light that they were practically invisible. He had a clean, pink, well-scrubbed look, and instead of the engineer's coveralls that Eberly had expected, Jaansen wore a crisply starched old-fashioned shirt with an open collar and neatly creased chocolate brown trousers. The only clue to his profession that Eberly could see was the square black palm-sized digital information processor that rested on his thigh, balanced there precariously. Jaansen touched it every now and then with the fingers of his left hand, as though to reassure himself that it was still there.

'Nanotechnology is a two-edged sword,' he was saying, somewhat pompously, Eberly thought. 'It can be used for a tremendous variety of purposes, but it also poses grave dangers.'

61

'The gray goo problem,' Morgenthau murmured.

Jaansen nodded. His face was square-cut, stolid. Eberly decided that the man had very little imagination; he was a walking bundle of facts and information, but beyond his technical expertise he had no interests, no knowledge, no ambitions. Good! Eberly said to himself.

'Gray goo is one thing,' Jaansen replied. 'Nanobugs have also been deliberately programmed to destroy proteins. Take them apart, molecule by molecule.'

'So I've been told,' said Eberly.

'We're made of proteins. Nanobugs can be designed to be killers. That's a real danger in a closed ecology like this habitat. They could wipe out everybody in less than a day.'

Morgenthau gasped a disbelieving, 'No! Less than a day?'

Jaansen shrugged his slim shoulders. 'They can reproduce themselves out of the materials around them in milliseconds and multiply faster than plague microbes. That's why they're usually programmed to be de-functioned by near UV.'

'De-functioned?' asked Eberly.

'Near UV?' Morgenthau inquired.

'De-functioned, deactivated, broken up, killed, stopped. Near ultraviolet light is softer – er, not so energetic – as ultraviolet light of shorter wavelength. So you can use near UV to stop nanobugs without causing damage to people.' He broke into a toothy grin as he added, 'Except maybe they get a suntan.'

Eberly steepled his fingers. 'So nanomachines can be controlled.'

'If you're *verrry* careful,' Jaansen replied.

'But the risks are frightening,' Morgenthau said.

Jaansen shrugged again. 'Perhaps. But take the EVA we had to do on the solar mirrors a few days ago. Nanomachines could have been inserted into the mirror motors and repaired them without anyone needing to go outside.'

'Then they could be very useful,' said Eberly.

'They'd be extremely helpful in all the maintenance tasks, yes, certainly,' Jaansen replied. 'They would make my job much easier.'

Before either of the other two could speak, he added, 'If they're kept under strict control. That's the hard part: keeping them under control.'

'Can they be controlled well enough to do only do what they're programmed to do, without running wild?' Morgenthau asked.

'Yes, certainly. But you've got to be *verrry* careful with the programming. It's like those old fairy tales about getting three wishes, and the wishes always backfire on you.'

'We'll have Dr. Kristin Cardenas to be in charge of the nano-technology group,' Eberly said.

Jaansen's ash-blond brows rose a respectful few centimeters. 'Cardenas? She's here?'

'She will be, in a few months.'

'That's good. That's extremely good.'

'Then it's settled,' Eberly said. 'You will work with Cardenas to draw up guidelines for using nanomachines.'

Jaansen nodded enthusiastically. 'I'll be glad to.'

'I don't like it,' Morgenthau said, grim-faced. 'It's too dangerous.'

'Not if we can keep them under control,' said Eberly.

Jaansen got to his feet. 'As I said, it's a two-edged sword. Cardenas is the top expert, though. We'll be lucky to have her.'

'I don't like it,' said Morgenthau, once the engineer had left. 'Nanomachines are dangerous . . . evil.'

'They're tools,' Eberly countered. 'Tools that could be useful to us.'

'But—'

'No buts!' Eberly snapped. 'I've made my decision. Dr. Cardenas will be welcome, as long as she works under our guidelines.'

Looking doubtful, almost fearful, Morgenthau said, 'I'll have to discuss this with my superiors in Amsterdam.'

Eberly glared at her. 'The Holy Disciples asked *me* to direct things here. I won't be second-guessed by a board of elders sitting back on Earth.'

'Those elders asked me to assist you,' said Morgenthau. 'And to make certain you didn't stray off the path of righteousness.'

Eberly leaned back in his desk chair. So that's it. She's the link back to Amsterdam. She's here to control me.

Keeping his voice calm, he said to Morgenthau, 'Well, I've made my decision. Dr. Cardenas will be joining us in three months, and there's nothing that Amsterdam or Atlanta or anyone else can do about it.'

She looked far less than pleased. 'You still have to convince Wilmot to let you introduce nanotechnology into the habitat.'

Eberly stared at her for a silent moment. Then, 'Yes, so I do.'

Confidential Report

To: M. Eberly
From: R. Morgenthau
Subject: Surveillance of living quarters

I discussed the problem of installing surveillance cameras in every living space in the habitat with H. Jaansen, of Engineering. He informed me that microcameras, no larger than a pinhead, have been developed for the probes that the planetary scientists plan to send to Titan. Such cameras are also used by the medical department for examining patients' innards. They can be manufactured in large numbers with existing facilities.

Jaansen suggests having the medical department initiate a program of spraying each apartment in the habitat with a broad-based disinfectant or aerosol antibiotic, under the guise of preventing the outbreak of airborne diseases. The cameras would be installed in each apartment during the spraying procedure.

This program will require the cooperation of several lower-level personnel from the medical, maintenance, engineering, and security departments. It will also require a significant amount of time to complete.

If you can recruit satisfactory personnel for this program, I suggest we begin the 'spraying' effort as soon as feasible.

In addition, Vyborg has successfully tapped into the communications net and is now routinely recording phone conversations and the video programming that individuals watch in their homes. The amount of information is enormous, as you may well imagine. Vyborg will need guidelines from you as to who should be monitored on a regular basis. He will also need personnel and/or automated equipment to accomplish said monitoring.

Departure Plus 268 Days

'And this is where we grow most of our fruit,' Holly was saying as she and Kris Cardenas strolled leisurely through the orchard's long straight rows of trees: oranges on their left, limes on their right. Grapefruit and lemons were behind them; they were approaching apples, pears, and peaches. The trees were lined up as precisely as marching cadets.

Cardenas had arrived aboard the habitat the day before. Now she seemed lost in wonder. 'I haven't seen a tree in so many years . . .' She turned and laughed, head upturned. 'Not one tree since I left Selene and here you've got a whole orchard full of them! It's like California, almost!'

Holly asked, 'There aren't any trees on Ceres?'

'Not a one,' replied Cardenas, a bright smile on her youthful face. 'Nothing but hydroponics tanks.'

'We have hydroponics farms, too,' Holly said, 'as a backup in case any troubles come up with the crops.'

'And bees!' Cardenas exclaimed. 'Aren't those bees?'

'Uh-huh. We need them for pollinating the trees. They make their hives in those white boxes over there.' Holly pointed toward a set of square white skeps sitting among the trees. Laughing, she added, 'Would you believe, one of my hardest problems was finding a couple of bee-keepers.'

Cardenas looked at her with those brilliant blue eyes of hers. 'You know, you really don't realize how much you miss open spaces and trees and . . . well, even *grass*, for god's sake. Not until you see something like this again.'

They walked on through the orchard, heading for the farms out beyond the trees. Eberly had given Holly the task of showing Dr.

Cardenas around the habitat. He called it orientation; Holly called it fun.

As they walked through the neatly aligned rows of trees, they heard a thin, quavering voice off to their left. Singing.

'Who's that?' Cardenas wondered.

Holly ducked through the low branches of a young peach tree and cut toward the edge of the orchard, Cardenas close behind her.

The orchard ended in an earthen embankment that led down to the irrigation canal. Water flowed smoothly through the sloping concrete walls of the canal. Up ahead of them they saw a solitary man lugging a double armful of sticks and leafy bushes, singing in a high, scratchy voice. Spanish, Holly thought. It sounds like a Spanish folk song.

'Hello,' Cardenas called to the man.

He dropped his burden and squinted through the late afternoon sunlight at them. Holly saw he was elderly. No, he looked *old*. Lean body half bent with age, skinny arms, wispy white hair that floated about his head like a halo, scraggly dead white beard. She had never seen a truly old person before. He wore a droopy shirt that had once been white, sleeves rolled up above his elbows, and shapeless, baggy blue jeans.

'*Hola!*' he called back to them.

The two women approached him. 'We heard you singing,' Holly said.

'It was very lovely,' Cardenas added.

'Thank you,' said the man. 'I am Diego Alejandro Ignacio Romero. My friends call me Don Diego, because of my age. I am not truly a nobleman.'

The women introduced themselves. Then Holly asked, 'You must work for the maintenance department, right?'

Don Diego smiled, revealing perfect teeth. 'My occupation is in the communications department. On Earth, I taught history. Or tried to.'

'What are you doing here, then?'

'The Church was not happy with my studies of the Counter-Reformation and the Inquisition.'

68

'No, I mean, working out here by the canal.'

'Oh, this? This is my hobby. I am attempting to create a little wilderness.'

He gestured along the canal, and Holly saw that there were bushes and small trees set up haphazardly along the sloping packed-earth banks. Someone had moved a few good-sized rocks here and there, as well.

'Wilderness?'

'Yes,' said Don Diego. 'This habitat is too neat, too ordered. People need something more natural than rows of trees planted precisely two point five meters apart.'

Cardenas laughed. 'A nature trail.'

'Si. Yes, a nature trail. Built by hand, I'm afraid, because nature is a stranger to this place.'

'Why did you sign up for this mission?' Cardenas asked.

Don Diego pulled a checkered handkerchief from his shirt pocket and mopped his brow. 'To help build a new world, of course. And perhaps to teach anyone who expressed an interest in history, if I am allowed.'

'You'd like to teach?'

'I was professor of Latin American History at the University of Mexico until I was forcibly retired.'

Without thinking, Holly asked, 'How old are you?'

He eyed her for a moment, then smiled. 'You don't see many as aged as I, do you?'

Holly shook her head.

'I have ninety-seven years. Ninety-eight, in four months.'

Cardenas said, 'You could take rejuvenation treatments—'

'No,' he replied amiably. 'Not for me. I want to grow old gracefully, but I am unwilling to postpone death indefinitely.'

'You *want* to die?' Holly blurted.

'Not necessarily. I maintain my health. I have taken injections to grow my third set of teeth. Also injections to rebuild the cartilage in my joints.'

With a smile, Cardenas said, 'You're getting your rejuvenation treatment one shot at a time, instead of all at once.'

He thought about that for a moment. Then, 'Perhaps. It would not be the first time I have played the fool on myself.'

Holly asked, 'Does the maintenance department know what you're doing here?'

For the first time, Don Diego looked apprehensive. 'Eh . . . not yet,' he said slowly.

Before Holly could say anything more, he added, 'I have not interfered with the flow of water in the canal. If anything, I believe I have made this area more beautiful, more natural and serene.'

Cardenas looked at the tangle of bushes and rocks, then up over the embankment's edge at the straight rows of fruit trees. Finally she looked back into the old man's red-rimmed eyes.

'I agree,' she said. 'You've created some beauty here.'

'You will not report this to the maintenance department?' Don Diego asked.

Cardenas glanced at Holly.

'I will tell them myself, of course,' he said, 'when I have finished this stretch of the canal.'

Holly grinned at him. 'No, we won't tell anybody.'

Cardenas agreed with a nod.

'May we come and help you, now and then?' Holly asked.

'Of course! I am always glad for the company of lovely women.'

Less than three kilometers away from them, Malcolm Eberly and Professor Wilmot were following a lab-coated technical manager through one of the small, highly automated factories that produced the habitat's manufactured goods. This one was turning out the pharmaceutical pills and drugs that the habitat's population needed to maintain their health, and the meat-based proteins they required for a balanced diet. The two men were inspecting the rows of processors that produced the medications and engineered food: shoulder-tall stainless steel vats that gleamed in the overhead lights. The factory was practically silent; the only sound other than their own voices was the background hum of electrical power.

'. . . can't allow infectious diseases to get a start here,' the factory manager was saying as he led the two men down the row of processors. 'In a closed ecology like this, even the sniffles could be dangerous.'

Eberly turned to Wilmot, beside him. 'That's one of the reasons why I approved Dr. Cardenas' application to join us. With her knowledge of nanotechnology—'

'You should have consulted me first,' Wilmot said sharply. He stopped in the middle of the aisle and fixed Eberly with a severe gaze.

Eberly stopped too, and glanced at the factory manager, who pretended not to hear as he kept on walking slowly along the row of humming vats.

'But, Professor,' Eberly said placatingly, 'I sent you a memorandum. When you didn't reply, I naturally assumed you approved of our taking Dr. Cardenas aboard.'

'You should have come to me in person to discuss it,' Wilmot said. 'That's what I expected.'

'You placed me in charge of human resources matters. I assumed you would be elated to have Dr. Cardenas with us.'

'You assume too much.'

The factory manager, a bland-looking technician in a long pale blue lab coat, cleared his throat and said, 'Um, the rest of the processors are pretty much just like these here. We can program them to produce any of the medications required out of the raw materials coming in from the chem labs.'

'Thank you,' said Wilmot, dismissing the man with a wave of his beefy hand.

The manager scurried away, leaving Eberly alone with the professor. As far as Eberly could tell, the manager was the only human on the factory's staff.

He looked up at Wilmot. The professor was much taller than Eberly, big-boned. He looked decidedly displeased.

'You don't approve of allowing Dr. Cardenas to join us?' Eberly asked in what he hoped was a properly obsequious whine.

Wilmot opened his mouth, shut it again, and fingered his moustache momentarily before replying, 'I'm not certain that I would have approved her application, no.'

'But she is here,' Eberly said. 'She arrived from Ceres yesterday morning.'

'I know. You exceeded your authority by inviting her, Dr. Eberly.'

'But I didn't invite her! She *asked* for permission to join us.'

'Even so, you should have brought the matter to me. Immediately. I am the one in charge here, and I have to justify every decision I make to the university consortium board back on Earth.'

'I know, but—'

'You know, but you bypassed the rules of procedure,' Wilmot hissed. 'You acted on your own authority.'

'I thought you would be pleased,' Eberly bleated.

'This habitat must run on established procedures,' Wilmot said, his voice as low as Eberly's but much stronger. 'We cannot have anarchy here! There is a set of regulations that was drawn up by the best minds the consortium could tap. We will follow those regulations until we arrive at Saturn and the people select the form of government they desire. Is that clear?'

'Yes, sir. Perfectly clear.'

Wilmot drew in a deep breath. Then, somewhat more softly, he went on, 'Once we've achieved orbit around Saturn the people can draw up a constitution for themselves and elect officers and all that. Form their own government. But while we are in transit we will follow the regulations set down by the consortium. No one will deviate from those regulations. No one!'

'I thought you would be happy to have Dr. Cardenas.'

Wilmot fiddled with his moustache again. 'Nanotechnology,' he muttered. 'Serious stuff, that.'

Eberly realized that the professor was not angry. He was worried, perhaps frightened. A weight lifted from Eberly's shoulders; he had to consciously keep himself from smiling.

'Ah, yes,' he said, in a hushed tone. 'Nanotechnology. In a closed environment such as ours . . .' He let the thought peter out in mid-sentence.

Wilmot resumed walking along the nearly silent processors. 'I realize that nanomachines can be of enormous help to us. And I know that Dr. Cardenas is the leading expert in the field. Still . . .'

Thinking quickly, Eberly suggested, 'If you don't want her here, I can order her back to Ceres.'

Wilmot looked shocked. 'Throw her out? We can't do that! We've already accepted her. You did, rather, but you did it in the name of our community and we can't go back on our word.'

'No, I suppose not,' Eberly agreed meekly.

Wilmot paced on, determined to get to the end of the row of processors, even though each one looked alike and there was no longer anyone with them to explain anything.

Matching the professor's long-legged strides as best as he could, Eberly said, 'I suppose we could order her not to engage in any nanotechnology work. She served as a medical caregiver in Ceres, I understand.'

The professor glared down at Eberly. 'We can't do that! She's a bloody Nobel laureate, for the lord's sake! We can't have her dispensing pills.'

'But nanotechnology has its dangers—'

'And its advantages. We'll have to supervise her work very closely. I want foolproof safeguards around her laboratory. Absolutely foolproof!'

'Yes, of course,' Eberly replied, thinking, The only fool here is you, Professor. You're the one who's frightened of nanotechnology, yet you will allow it here in the habitat because you're too unbelievably *polite* to send Cardenas back to Ceres.

It was all he could do to keep from laughing in the professor's face.

Instead, he shifted the subject. 'Sir, have you had a chance to study the proposal for naming the various parts of the habitat?'

'This silly contest thing?' Wilmot snapped.

'A series of contests, yes. The psychologists believe it will be beneficial to the general mental health—'

'The psychologists actually endorse the idea?'

Realizing that Wilmot had no more than skimmed the proposal, at best, Eberly went on, 'The political scientists we consulted with back on Earth believe such contests can help to strengthen group solidarity.'

'Hmph,' muttered Wilmot. 'I daresay.'

'All the proposal needs is your approval, sir,' Eberly urged subtly. 'Then you can announce it to the general population.'

'No, no,' said the professor. 'You make the announcement. It's your idea, after all.'

'Me?' Eberly asked as innocently as he could.

'Yes, of course. I can't be bothered with it. You announce the contests. Damned silly business, if you ask me, but if all those consultants endorse it, I won't stand in your way.'

Eberly could barely contain his elation. He wanted to leap into the air and give an exultant whoop. Instead he meekly paced along the row of processors beside Professor Wilmot, thinking to himself, He chastised me about Cardenas, so he felt he had to placate me about the contests. How wonderfully predictable he is.

'I haven't walked this much in years,' Kris Cardenas said, puffing slightly. 'I feel kind of lightheaded.'

Holly smiled. 'It's the gravity. We've climbed closer to the midline; the *g* force gets lighter.'

They had left Don Diego at the irrigation canal and walked through the plowed farmlands, then climbed the grassy hills down at the endcap of the habitat. Cardenas sat on the grass, her back propped against a young elm tree. One of the habitat's ecologists had made a personal crusade of trying to save the elm from the extinction it faced on Earth.

Cardenas huffed out a breath. 'Whew! I'm glad I spent all those hours in the centrifuge at Ceres. Mini-gee can be seductive.'

'You're in good shape,' Holly said, sitting beside her.

'So are you.'

The habitat stretched out before them, a green inside-out world, like a huge tunnel that had been landscaped and dotted with tiny toy villages here and there.

'What did you think of that crazy old man?' Holly asked.

Cardenas looked out at the landscaped perfection of the habitat:

everything in its place, everything neat and tidy and somehow almost inhuman. It reminded her of store window displays from her childhood.

'I think we could use a few more crazies like him,' she said.

'Maybe so,' Holly half-agreed.

They sat in silence for a few moments, each absorbed in her own thoughts.

'I read your bio,' Holly said at last. 'I expected you to look a lot older than you do.'

Cardenas didn't flinch, exactly, but she gave Holly a quick sidelong glance. 'If you've read my bio then you know why I look younger than my years. And why I was living at Ceres.'

Ignoring the tension in her voice, Holly asked, 'How old do you think I am?'

Within ten minutes they were fast friends: two women whose bodies were far younger than their ages.

Infirmary

The man lay wheezing on the gurney, his eyes swollen nearly shut.

The young doctor looked perplexed. 'What's the matter with him?'

'I don't know!' said the woman who had brought him in. She was close to hysteria. 'We were walking out in the park and all of a suddenly he collapsed!'

Leaning over the patient, the doctor asked, 'Do you know what happened to you?'

The man tried to speak, coughed painfully, then shook his head negatively.

Glancing up at the monitors that lined the wall of the emergency cubicle, the doctor saw that it couldn't be a heart attack or a stroke. He felt a surge of panic: not even the diagnostic computer could figure out what was wrong! The male nurse standing on the other side of the gurney looked just as puzzled and scared as he felt.

The head nurse pushed past the woman and into the cubicle. 'Take his shirt off,' she said.

The doctor was too confused and upset to argue about who gave orders to whom. Besides, if the gossip around the infirmary was anywhere near the truth, this tough Afro-American had put in plenty of years with the peacekeeping troops. She had a reputation that scared him.

With the male nurse helping, they pulled the man's shirt off. The patient's chest and arms were lumpy with red welts. His skin felt hot.

'Hives?' the doctor asked.

The nurse turned to the woman, staring wide-eyed at them, hands clenched before her face.

'Walkin' in the park?' she asked.

The woman nodded.

'Anaphylactic shock,' the nurse said flatly. 'Epinephrine.'

The doctor gaped at her. 'How could he—'

'Epinephrine! Now! He was stung by a fuckin' bee!'

The doctor barked to the male nurse, 'Epinephrine! Now!'

The head nurse pulled a magnifying lens out of its slot on the cubicle wall and extended its folding arm across the patient's body. The doctor accepted the hint and took the lens in one hand. Within seconds he found the barb of the bee's stinger imbedded in the patient's left forearm, just above the wrist. With tweezers he gently pulled the stinger out, rather deftly, he thought.

When he looked up the head nurse had gone and the patient was already breathing more easily.

'I never saw a bee sting before,' he admitted to the woman, who also looked much better now. 'I interned in Chicago, downtown.'

The woman nodded and even managed to smile. 'He must be allergic.'

'Must be,' the doctor agreed.

The male nurse unclipped the patient's ID badge from the shirt they had dropped to the floor and slid into the computer terminal. The man's name, occupation, and complete medical history came up on the display. No mention of allergies, although he did have a history of bronchial asthma. The doctor noted that the patient had grown up in Cairo and had been a lawyer before running into trouble with the Sword of Islam and accepting permanent exile instead of a fifty-year prison term for political agitation. Aboard the habitat he worked in the accounting office.

'A lawyer?' the male nurse grumbled after the patient had recovered enough to walk home with his girlfriend. 'Shoulda let him croak.'

Departure Plus 269 Days

The next morning when Holly arrived at her cubbyhole office, there was a message on her desktop screen from Eberly. Without even sitting at her desk, she went straight to his office.

The door was open; he was already at his desk, deep in discussion with a young Asian couple. She hesitated. Eberly glanced up at her and nodded briefly, so she stayed in the doorway and listened.

'We understand the regulations and the reasoning behind them,' the young man was saying, in Californian English. Holly saw that he was tense, sitting stiffly on the front five centimeters of the chair.

'It's my fault,' said the woman, leaning forward and gripping the edge of Eberly's desk with both hands. 'The protection I used was not sufficient.'

Eberly leaned back in his chair and steepled his fingers. 'The rules are quite specific,' he said gently. 'Your only choice is an abortion.'

The man's face crumpled. 'But . . . it's only this one case. Can't an exception be made?'

'If an exception is made for you,' Eberly said, 'others will expect the same consideration, won't they?'

'Yes. I see.'

Eberly spread his hands in a gesture of helplessness. 'We live in a limited ecology. We're not allowed to expand our population. Not until we arrive at Saturn and prove that we can sustain larger numbers will anyone be allowed to have children.'

'I must have an abortion, then?' the woman asked, her voice shaking.

'Or we could put you off when we refuel at Jupiter and you could return to Earth.'

The young man shook his head slowly. 'We can't afford the transport fare. Everything we had was invested in this habitat.'

Eberly asked, 'Do you have religious inhibitions against abortion?'

'No,' the man answered, so quickly that it made Holly wonder.

'Is there no other way?' the woman asked, almost begged.

Eberly steepled his fingers again and tapped them against his chin. The young couple strained forward unconsciously, waiting for a word of hope.

'Perhaps . . .'

'Yes?' they said in unison.

'Perhaps the fertilized zygote could be removed and frozen – kept in storage until it's decided that we can expand our population.'

Frozen! Holly shuddered at the idea. Yet it had saved her life. No, she thought. It had allowed her to begin a new life after her old one ended in death.

'Then the zygote can be re-implanted in your womb,' Eberly was saying. 'You'll have a perfectly normal baby; you'll simply have to wait a year or two.'

He smiled brightly at them. They looked at each other, then back to him.

'This can be done?' the young man asked.

'It would require special permission,' said Eberly, 'but I can take care of that for you.'

'Would you?'

He hesitated just a fraction of a second, then smiled again and answered, 'Yes. Of course. I'll handle it for you.'

They were unendingly grateful. It took a full ten minutes of handshaking and bowing before Eberly could usher them out of his office. They did not even notice Holly standing by the doorway as they left, still bowing their thanks.

'That was wonderful of you, Malcolm,' Holly said as she went to the chair that the woman had been sitting in.

'Population control,' he muttered as he stepped behind his desk and sat down. 'I made certain that the human resources department got that responsibility. The ecologists wanted it, but I wrangled it away from them.'

Holly nodded.

Pointing to the still-open doorway with a grin, Eberly said, 'There's a couple who will be loyal to me forever. Or until their child becomes a teenager.'

Holly did not see any humor in that. 'You wanted to see me?' she said.

'Yes,' he said as he snapped his fingers, the signal for his computer to boot up.

Holly waited in silence as the image formed above Eberly's desk. It was a list of some sort. It was facing him, so to her the hologram was turned backwards. She sat and waited while he studied the list. The office seemed small and bare and, somehow, cold.

At last he looked up from the image and gazed directly at her. Holly felt those laser blue eyes penetrate to her soul.

'There are going to be some changes in this office,' he said, without preamble, without asking how she was or noticing that she was wearing a plain sky blue tunic over her slacks, with no adornments other than her name badge, just as the dress code guidelines called for.

'Changes?'

'Yes,' Eberly said. 'I won't be able to continue directing the day-to-day operations of this office. I will be busy organizing the government of the habitat.'

'Government? But I thought—'

'Holly,' he said, leaning forward slightly in his desk chair, toward her. She leaned toward him slightly, too. 'Holly, we have ten thousand men and women here. They must have a voice in choosing the kind of government they want. And their leaders.'

Holly said, 'You mean the government we'll create once we get to Saturn.'

Eberly shook his head. 'I don't believe we should wait until we arrive in Saturn orbit. The people should decide on the government they want now. Why wait?'

'But I thought that as long as we're in transit out to Saturn we have to—'

'We must follow the protocols set down by the consortium,' Eberly finished for her.

'Yes,' Holly said.

'Why?' he demanded. 'Why should we allow ourselves to be governed by rules written by a group of university graybeards who remained behind on Earth? What right do they have to force us to obey their rules?'

Holly thought a moment. 'That's what we agreed to, though.'

'It's time to end that agreement. What difference does it make if we do it now or wait until we arrive at Saturn?'

She thought his question cut both ways. Why rush into this now?

'We should *not* allow arrogant old men to tell us what we can and cannot do,' Eberly said, with some heat. His face was reddening, Holly saw.

'Maybe not,' she agreed, half-heartedly.

'Of course not,' he said. 'The people must decide for themselves.'

'I guess.'

'These contests you're setting up to pick names for the villages and everything else, they are a part of my plan,' he confided.

That surprised her. 'Your plan?'

'Yes. By themselves, the contests are little more than trivia, entertainment for the masses. But they serve a larger purpose.'

'I click,' Holly said. 'Getting the people to vote in the contests will be like a sort of training exercise, right? It'll prepare the people to vote for their government when the time comes.'

Eberly gave her the full radiance of his best smile. 'You are extremely bright, Holly. Extremely bright.'

She could feel her cheeks grow warm.

'While you are running the contests,' he said, growing serious once again, 'I must devote all my efforts to drawing up a constitution for the people.'

'So, if you're going to be busy setting up this new constitution and everything, who's going to run the office here?'

'You will.'

Holly gulped. 'Me?'

He smiled at her surprise. 'Of course you. Who else?'

'But I can't be in charge,' she squeaked. 'I'm just an assistant, a house mouse—'

Eberly's smile widened. 'Holly, haven't you been *my* assistant? What better qualifications for the task can there be?'

She wanted to turn handsprings. 'But . . . d'you think the prof will okay me being named director?'

The smile vanished. 'Wilmot,' he muttered. 'No, he would definitely not approve of someone as junior as you being named director. Him and his rigid regulations.'

Holly watched his face, waiting for a ray of hope.

'I want you to head this office, Holly,' he said. 'You can do the work, I know you can.'

'I'd do my warping best.'

'Of course you will. But since I can't officially name you director, I must place someone else in the acting director's position. A figurehead. To placate Wilmot.'

'Figurehead? Who?'

'Ruth Morgenthau will fill the role nicely. She's working in the administrative services office at present. I can transfer her here and Wilmot won't blink an eye.'

Morgenthau, Holly thought. So that's why he's been spending so much time with her.

'She's rather lazy, you know,' he said, grinning naughtily. 'And rather vain. We'll let her sit at this desk and stay out of your way. You will run the department.'

'She would do that?'

Nodding, he replied, 'She'd leap at the chance. More prestige, less work. She'll love it.'

'I click.' Holly tried to grin back at him, but it was forced.

He reached across the desk and lifted her chin so he could stare into her eyes. 'It all depends on you, Holly. Will you take on this responsibility? Will you do this for me?'

Holly felt a rush of emotions surge through her: gratitude,

loyalty, a longing to please Malcolm Eberly, a yearning to have him love her.

'Yes,' she said breathlessly. 'I'll do anything for you, Malcolm.'

He smiled dazzlingly. And thought, this ought to make Morgenthau happy: the trappings of authority, a whole department to lord it over. It should keep her busy enough to stay out of my way.

What's In A Name?

To: All residents
From: M. Eberly,
Director Human Resources Dept.
Subject: Naming Contests

You, the people of this habitat, will decide the names to be given to the five villages, the various work complexes, and the natural areas (farms, orchards, woodlands, lakes, etc.) by participating in contests to select such names.

Residents of each village will select the name for the village in which they reside. Workers in each factory, processing plant, farm, aquaculture complex, etc., will select the names for such centers. If desired, individual buildings may be given specific names.

Each contest will consist of three phases. In the first phase, all citizens will decide on the categories from which names will be eventually chosen. For example, residents will decide whether they wish to name the villages after national heroes, or cities on Earth, or great artists or scientists, etc.

In the second phase, specific names from each chosen category will be nominated and discussed. The list of names for each specific site will be shortened to five, using a secret ballot.

In the third and final phase, permanent names will be chosen from the short lists of five nominees, again by secret ballot.

The human resources department will manage the various contests. The human resources department may appoint one or more panels of citizens to serve as judges, researchers, or in other capacities, as needed.

A public meeting will be convened at 22:00 hours Thursday in the cafeteria to discuss this activity. All residents are urged to attend.

Memorandum

To: All habitat personnel
From. R. Morgenthau,
Acting Director, Human Resources Dept
Subject: Medical prophylaxis

As a proactive measure to prevent the outbreak of airborne infectious diseases, every individual's living quarters will be treated with a disinfectant antibiotic spray over the course of the next four weeks.

Each individual will be notified when her or his building is to be treated. Such treatment will be done during normal working hours; it is neither necessary nor desirable for individuals to remain in their quarters during the spraying procedure.

The First Rally

Although there were two full-service restaurants in the habitat, virtually everyone ate in the big, noisy cafeteria almost every day. The restaurants were small, intimate, run by harried entrepreneurs who obtained their foods directly from the people who ran the farms and the fish tanks. Just as the nutritionists of Selene had learned, aquaculture produced more protein per unit of input energy than barnyard meat animals could. Before leaving the Earth/Moon region, several farmers had suggested bringing rabbits or chickens aboard for their meat. Wilmot had sternly rejected the idea, citing horror stories from Australia of runaway rabbit overpopulation and the diseases that cooped-up birds caused.

So the habitat's residents got their protein from fish, frogs, soy derivatives, and the processed products of the food factory, popularly known as 'McGlop'. When they did not make their own meals in their quarters, they usually ate in the cafeteria.

The cafeteria was the biggest enclosed space in the habitat, and between meals it often served as a makeshift theater or auditorium. It was after the habitat had cleared the asteroid belt and started on the leg of its flight that would take it to Jupiter, that Eberly called a public meeting there.

The meeting was set for 22:00 hours, and there were still a few people finishing their dinners when Eberly's team – including Holly – began to move all the tables and chairs to one side of the spacious room to clear the floor for the incoming audience.

Eberly stood frowning impatiently at the far end of the room, next to the little stage on which he planned to make his speech. He could see the cafeteria staff and its robots, across the way, cleaning their steam tables and display cases, rattling piles of dishes and glassware. He did not see a large crowd assembling.

Ruth Morgenthau scanned the thinly scattered audience. 'All the people from my department are here,' she claimed.

'Not many others, though,' said Sammi Vyborg.

Colonel Kananga smiled thinly. 'This is all being vidded. I'll have the names and dossiers of everyone here.'

'It's the names of those who are *not* here that I want,' Eberly growled.

'A simple matter of subtraction,' said Kananga. And he smiled as if amused by some inside joke.

Once the last of the diners had gotten up and their tables were shoved out of the way, Morgenthau heavily climbed the three steps of the speaker's platform and spread her arms for silence. The muted buzz of the crowd's many separate conversations slowly stopped and everyone turned toward her expectantly.

Holly had been positioned by the main door, which opened out into the village's central green. Her duty, Eberly had told her, was to encourage anyone outside to come in, and to discourage anyone inside from leaving. He had given her two rather large, muscular young men from the security department to help her in the latter task. She felt disappointed that so few people had turned out for Eberly's speech. There was no other public entertainment on the agenda for this evening, she had made certain of that before scheduling his appearance. With ten thousand people in the habitat, she had expected more than a couple of hundred to show up.

At least Dr. Cardenas had come in, giving Holly a cheerful hello as she strode through the open door. But where's everybody else? Holly wondered.

Still, Morgenthau smiled jovially at the audience as if everyone this side of Calcutta had crowded the cafeteria floor. She thanked the people for coming and promised them an evening 'of the greatest importance since we started this long journey into a bright and glorious future.'

Holly watched the faces of the onlookers. They appeared more curious than anything else; hardly fired with enthusiasm for a glorious future.

Then Eberly climbed up onto the stage and stepped to the podium. He nodded curtly to Morgenthau who, still smiling, stepped to the back of the stage.

Why doesn't she get off the stage? Holly wondered. She's distracting people's attention from Malcolm.

For several long moments Eberly simply stood at the podium, gripping its sides, staring out at the audience in cold silence. The crowd begin to stir uneasily. Holly heard muttering.

At last Eberly began to speak. 'Each of you has received an announcement of the series of contests to be held for the purpose of naming the villages and other features, both natural and architectural, of this habitat.'

'I didn't get an announcement,' came a man's low grumble from the audience. Kananga glared and pointed; two husky young black-clad men converged on the man.

Eberly smiled at the heckler, though. 'The announcement is in your mail. Simply check your computer; it's there, I promise you.'

The man looked startled by the two security officers now standing on each side of him in their black coveralls.

Eberly resumed, 'This is your habitat. It is your right to choose the names you want for its natural and man-made features. Besides, these contests will be fun! You will enjoy them, I promise you.'

People glanced at each other and murmured. A few turned around and started walking toward the door.

'I'm not finished,' Eberly said.

The crowd paid scant attention. It began to break up. A woman raised her voice loudly enough for everyone to hear, 'I don't know about you, but I've got work to do tomorrow morning.' More people began drifting toward the door.

'Listen to me!' Eberly demanded, his voice suddenly deeper, stronger, more demanding. 'You are the most important people in this habitat. Don't turn your backs on your own future!'

Their muttering stopped. They turned back toward Eberly, every eye focused on him.

89

'The others,' Eberly said, in a voice more powerful than Holly had ever heard before, 'those who are too lazy, or too timid, or too poorly informed to be here, will envy you in time. For you are the ones who are wise enough, strong enough, brave enough to begin to seize the future in your own hands. You understand that this is *your* habitat, *your* community, and it must be controlled by no one except yourselves.'

'Right!' someone shouted.

Holly was staring at Eberly, dimly aware that everyone in the crowd was doing the same now, listening, hearing that richly vibrant voice and the mesmerizing message it carried.

She jumped nearly out of her skin when someone tapped her on the shoulder.

'Hey, I didn't mean to spook you.'

Holly saw a smiling solidly built youngish man with a rugged bulldog face. Dark eyes and darker hair.

'What's going on?' he asked in a stage whisper.

Holly gestured toward the stage and whispered back, 'Dr. Eberly is giving a speech.'

'Eberly? Who's he?'

She shook her head and touched a finger to her lips, then pantomimed for him to come into the cafeteria and listen. Still smiling, the man stepped past her, then stood at the rear of the crowd and crossed his beefy arms over his chest.

Eberly was saying, 'Why should you be governed by rules made hundreds of millions of kilometers away, written by old men who know nothing of the conditions you face? What do they know of the problems you encounter every day? What do they care? It's time for you to create your own government and choose your own leaders.'

Someone began clapping. The rest of the crowd took it up, applauding and even cheering out loud. Holly clapped along with the others, although she noticed that the newcomer kept his arms folded.

Soon Eberly had them roaring their approval with almost every sentence he spoke. The crowd became a single, unified creature:

an animal with many heads and hands and bodies, but only one mind, and that mind was focused entirely on Eberly's message.

'It's up to you to build this new world,' he told them. 'You will be the leaders of tomorrow.'

They applauded and stamped and whistled. Holly thought they would storm the platform and carry Eberly off on their shoulders.

The newcomer turned to her and shouted through the noisy accolade, 'He knows how to turn 'em on, doesn't he?'

'He's wonderful!' Holly yelled back, hammering her hands together as loudly as she could.

Eberly smiled brilliantly and thanked the audience several times and finally stepped down from the platform, to be immediately surrounded by admiring people. The rest of the crowd began to break up and drift outside.

The newcomer asked Holly, 'Am I too late to get something to eat?'

'The cafeteria's closed until tomorrow morning,' Holly said. Gesturing toward the food dispensers, she added, 'You can get something from the machines.'

He wrinkled his pug nose. 'Stale sandwiches and sodas that make you belch.'

Holly giggled. 'Well, there are the restaurants. They stay open till midnight, I'm pretty sure.'

'Yeah,' he said, 'I guess that's it.'

The last of the crowd was leaving, little knots of two or three, talking about Eberly's speech.

Kris Cardenas stopped beside Holly. 'I'm going over to the Bistro for some dessert. Would you like to join me?'

The newcomer said, 'Why don't the two of you join me?'

Holly glanced at Cardenas. She knew the man's face, but she couldn't recall his name or occupation.

Sensing her puzzlement, he said, 'My name is Manuel Gaeta. I'm not part of your regular population here, I'm—'

'You're the stuntman,' Holly blurted, remembering now.

Gaeta smiled, almost shyly. 'My publicity people say I'm an adventure specialist.'

'You're the one who wants to go down to the surface of Titan.'

He nodded. 'If Professor Wilmot lets me do it.'

'Why on Earth would anyone want to go to the surface of Titan?' Cardenas asked.

Gaeta grinned at her. 'Because it's there. And nobody's done it before.'

With that, he took each of the women by the arm and started off for the Bistro, halfway across the village.

Professor Wilmot's Quarters

James Coleraine Wilmot followed a comfortable routine almost every night. A lifelong bachelor, he usually had an early dinner with friends or colleagues, then retired to his quarters for an hour or two of watching history and a glass of whisky, neat.

He had known that Eberly intended to make a speech of some sort that evening, but had not let the knowledge interfere with his nightly custom. Eberly ran the human resources department well enough, Wilmot thought, which meant that no one brought complaints about the department to Wilmot's attention. He exceeded his authority by allowing that nanotechnology woman to join the community without Wilmot's approval, but that could be handled easily enough. If the man wants to make a speech, what of it?

He felt a bit rankled, therefore, when his phone chimed in the middle of one of his favorite vids, *Secrets of the Star Chamber*. He checked the phone's screen and saw that it was a minor assistant calling. With an irritated huff, Wilmot blanked the holographic image and opened the phone channel.

Bernard Isaac's face appeared in mid-air: round, apple-cheeked, tightly curled hair. He seemed flushed with excitement, or perhaps worry.

'Did you hear his speech?' Isaacs asked urgently.

'Whose speech? Do you mean Eberly and his silly contests?'

'It's more than contests. He wants to tear up the protocols and write a new constitution, form a new government!'

Wilmot nodded, wondering what the problem was. 'When we reach Saturn, yes, I know. That's in our plan of—'

'No!' Isaacs interrupted. 'Now! He's telling them they should do it now.'

'Telling who?'

'Anyone who will listen!'

'Can't be done,' Wilmot said, completely calm. 'Everyone signed the agreement to stick by our protocols until we establish the habitat safely in Saturn orbit.'

'But he wants to do it now!' Isaacs repeated, his voice rising half an octave.

Wilmot raised a hand. 'That's not possible and he knows it.'

'But—'

'I'll have a talk with him. See what he's after. Possibly you misunderstood his intention.'

Isaac's round jaw set stubbornly. 'I'll send you a vid of his speech. You can see for yourself what he's up to.'

'Do that,' Wilmot said. 'Thank you very much for informing me.'

He clicked the phone connection off, noting that the red RECORDING light immediately lit up. Isaacs was sending Eberly's speech. Wilmot's brows knitted slightly. Isaacs isn't the excitable type; at least he hasn't been until now. I wonder what's got the wind up in him?

Wilmot resolved to review Eberly's speech. But not until he finished the vid on Henry VIII's means of extracting confessions from his subjects.

Two hours later, after watching Eberly's speech several times and helping himself to another healthy-sized whisky, Wilmot sat back in his favorite easy chair with an odd little smile playing across his lips.

So it's finally begun, he said to himself. The experiment begins to get interesting. At first I was afraid they would all be anarchists, troublemakers, but so far they've behaved rather well, damned little sign of rebelliousness or mischief. Probably they're all getting themselves accustomed to their new world, adapting to life in the habitat. Most of them have never had it so good, I suppose. But this man Eberly wants to rouse them a bit. Very good.

Fascinating. Eberly puts out this silly damned dress code, and no one complains. They either ignore it, or they decorate their clothes with scarves and sashes. These people aren't going to be led around by their noses, that's clear enough.

But Eberly wants to control them, apparently. I wonder what ticked him off? Most likely it was that little dressing-down I gave him about the Cardenas woman. Instead of submitting to authority or sulking, he takes political action. Fascinating. Now the question is, what will the general population do? He only got a handful of people to listen to him, but by the start of the workday tomorrow the entire habitat will know of his speech. How will they react?

More importantly, he thought, how should I react? Move to thwart him? Cooperate with him?

Wilmot shook his head. Neither, he decided. I must not insert my own prejudices into this experiment. It won't be easy to stay out of it, though. I can't simply disappear; I have a role to play. But I mustn't let it interfere with their behaviors.

Of course, he thought, none of them knows the *real* purpose of this mission. No one even guesses that it exists. And I must keep it that way. If anyone got the slightest hint of it, that would skew the experiment terribly. I'll have to be very careful in phrasing my report back to Atlanta. It wouldn't do to have some snoop in the communications department find out what's really going on here.

He got up from his chair, surprised at how stiff he felt, and headed for his bedroom. I'll play it strictly by the book, he decided. The agreed-upon protocols will be followed at all times. That should offer enough resistance to Eberly to force his next move. I wonder what it will be?

Eberly finally got rid of his admirers and made his way to his own quarters, flanked only by Morgenthau, Vyborg and Kananga.

Once inside his spartan apartment, he said excitedly, 'They loved me! Did you see the way they reacted to me? I had them in the palm of my hand!'

'It was brilliant,' said Vyborg quickly.

Morgenthau was less enthusiastic. 'It was a good beginning, but only a beginning.'

'What do you mean?' Eberly asked, disappointment showing clearly on his face.

Morgenthau sat heavily on the room's only couch. 'It wasn't much of a crowd. Fewer than three hundred.'

Vyborg immediately agreed. 'Less than three percent of the total population.'

'But they were *with* me,' Eberly said. 'I could feel it.'

Looking up at him, Morgenthau said, 'Three percent might not be all that bad.'

'What about the other ninety-seven percent?' Kananga asked.

She shrugged. 'It's as Malcolm said in his speech. They're too lazy, too indifferent to care. If we can capture and hold an active minority, we can lead the majority around by its collective nose.'

'What will Wilmot's reaction be?' Vyborg asked.

'We'll know soon enough,' said Eberly.

A crafty expression came over Morgenthau's fleshy face. 'Suppose he simply ignores us?'

'That's impossible,' Vyborg snapped. 'We've made a direct challenge to his authority.'

'But suppose he feels so secure in his authority that he simply ignores us?' Morgenthau insisted.

Eberly said, 'Then we will raise the stakes until it's impossible for him to ignore me.' He smacked his fist into the open palm of his other hand.

Kananga said nothing, but a wisp of a smile curled his lips slightly.

Holly, Cardenas and Manuel Gaeta were the last customers in the Bistro. The human hostess had gone home, leaving only the simple-minded robots to stand impassively by the kitchen door, waiting for the people to leave so they could clean the last remaining table and the floor around it.

96

'. . . your basic problem is contamination?' Cardenas was asking the stuntman.

Gaeta glanced at the dessert tray the hostess had left on their table: nothing but crumbs. They had finished the coffee long ago.

'Contamination, right,' Gaeta said, suppressing a yawn. 'Wilmot and the geek boys are scared I'll hurt the bugs down there on the surface.'

'That's an important consideration,' Holly said.

'Yeah, right.'

Cardenas said, 'I can solve your problem, I'm pretty sure.'

Gaeta's eyes widened. 'How?'

'I could program nanomachines to break down any residues of perspiration or whatever organic materials you leave on the outside of your suit. They'll clean it up for you, break down the organics into carbon dioxide and water vapor. No sweat.'

'Literally!' Holly accented the pun.

Gaeta did not smile. 'These nanomachines . . . they the type that're called gobblers?'

'Some people call them that, yes,' Cardenas replied, stiffly.

'They can kill you, can't they?'

Holly swiveled her attention from Gaeta's swarthy, wary face to Cardenas, who was suddenly tight-lipped.

For a long moment Cardenas did not reply. At last she said, 'Gobblers can be programmed to attack proteins, yes. Or *any* carbon-chain organics.'

'That's pretty risky, then, isn't it?' he asked.

Holly saw that Cardenas was struggling to keep her voice calm. 'Once you're sealed inside the suit, the nanobugs can be sprayed over its outer surface. We can calculate how long it would take them to destroy any organics on the suit. Double or triple that time, then we douse the whole assembly in soft UV. That will deactivate the nanobugs.'

'Deactivate?' Gaeta asked. 'You mean, like, kill them?'

'They're machines, Manny,' she said. 'They're not alive. You can't kill them.'

'But would they come back later and start chewing on organics again?'

'No, we'll wash them all off. And once they're deactivated, they don't revive. It's like breaking a motor or a child's toy. The pieces don't come back together again spontaneously.'

Gaeta nodded. But Holly thought he didn't look convinced.

The Morning After

'What did you think of his speech last night?'

Ilya Timoshenko looked up his console in *Goddard*'s navigation and control pod. There was very little actual work for them to do; the habitat was sailing through the solar system on a course that Isaac Newton could have calculated to a fine accuracy. The fusion engines were purring along smoothly, miniature man-made suns converting hydrogen ions into helium and driving the habitat along on the energy released. Bored as usual with the utterly routine nature of his duty shift, Timoshenko had been daydreaming about the possibilities of designing a fusion engine that converted helium into carbon and oxygen. After all, that's what the stars do when they run low on hydrogen; they burn the helium they've accumulated. The carbon and oxygen from helium fusion would be valuable resources in themselves, he realized.

But Farabi, the pipsqueak navigator, wants to get me involved in politics, Timoshenko thought sourly.

'What speech?' he muttered. The two men were alone on the bridge. Captain Nicholson had decided that there should be two of them in the control center at all times, despite the fact that the computer actually ran everything. We humans are redundant here, Timoshenko often told himself. Yet the captain insisted, and her three underlings obeyed.

'Eberly's speech,' Farabi said. 'Last night in the cafeteria. I thought I saw you there.'

'Not me,' said Timoshenko. 'You must have seen somebody else and thought it was me.'

'It was you. I saw you.'

Timoshenko glared at the man. Farabi claimed that he was an

99

Arab, from one of those desert lands that had once supplied the world with oil. He was small and wiry, his skin nut-brown, his nose decidedly hooked. Timoshenko thought he was more likely a Jew from the ruins of Israel hiding from the real Arabs. Timoshenko himself was as Russian as could be, only slightly taller than Farabi, but thick-bodied, muscular, with a heavy thatch of unruly auburn hair.

It was politics that had gotten him exiled to this newfangled Siberia. His career in engineering, his coming marriage, his family ties that went all the way back to Heroes of the Soviet Union – all wiped out because he couldn't keep his mouth shut once he started drinking. So they set him up with this woman who accused him of rape and now he was on his way to Saturn, courtesy of the government and those pissant psalm-singers who ran the government.

'I wasn't there,' he insisted, even though it was a lie. 'I have no interest in politics.'

Farabi gave him a disbelieving look. 'Have it your own way, then,' he said softly.

Timoshenko focused his attention on the glowing icons spread across the top of his console. Why can't people behave as predictably as machines? he asked himself. Why can't people just do their jobs and leave me alone?

'I just thought,' said Farabi, sitting at the next console, 'that Eberly raised some good points. We should get involved in the management of the habitat. After all, it's our home, isn't it?'

Wiping sweat from his forehead, Timeshenko bit back the reply that sprang to his lips. He wanted to say, this isn't a home, it's a prison. No matter how comfortable it is, it's a prison and I'm going to be locked inside it for the rest of my life, while you'll be free to go back to Earth after we reach Saturn.

Instead, he said only, 'I have no interest in politics.'

'Maybe you should become interested.'

'Politicians.' He spat the word. 'They're all alike. They want to be the boss and make you jump to their tune. I want nothing to do with them.'

★   ★   ★

Nadia Wunderly was one of the few people in the habitat who had followed Eberly's suggestion and changed her name. Her parents, staid New Hampshire dairy farmers, had christened her Jane, but she had always thought the name was too ordinary to suit the adventure in her soul. All through her school years she had been plagued with the 'Plain Jane' tag; she hated it, even though she had to admit when she looked into a mirror that she was indeed rather plain. Her figure tended toward the rotund unless she exercised mercilessly and dieted like a penitent monk; her face was also round, although she thought her big gray eyes were attractive. Owl eyes, she thought, remembering that the goddess Athena was owl-eyed, too.

Wunderly was always trying new hairdos; nothing seemed to help her straight mouse-brown hair. When she came aboard the habitat as part of the science team, she immediately dyed her hair brick red, gave herself the goal of loosing ten kilos by the time they reached Saturn, and changed her name to the smoky, exotic-sounding Nadia.

As she watched the morning news vid replay of Eberly's speech, she wondered what the man was driving at. We have a government, don't we? she asked herself while spooning up her breakfast cereal and soymilk. And we all know why we're going to Saturn: to study the planet and its moons and life forms and most of all its rings. Those glorious, beautiful rings. This is a science mission. Doesn't Eberly understand that?

She dressed in the approved tunic and slacks and took one of the electrobikes standing in the racks at the entrance of her apartment building. Running late, she realized, so she let the bike's quiet little electric motor speed her along the winding path to the science offices up at the top of the hill. I'll pedal home, she told herself, all the way. That'll recharge the battery and burn off some calories.

Nadia said hello to everyone she passed as she hurried through the corridors to her workspace, which was nothing more than a cubicle barely large enough to house a desk, chair, and some filing shelves. She saw Dr. Urbain hurrying by; he passed too quickly for her to catch his eye. Later, she thought. After I've finished the proposal and it's ready to show to him.

She started working on the proposal. Urbain demanded a fully documented plan of research from each scientist on the staff. All the others were avid to study Titan and the organisms living there. They were competing with one another like grad students trying to finagle a fellowship. Which was fine, as far as Nadia was concerned. She was interested in those blessed rings. And she had them all to herself. The rest of the staff were all slobbering over Titan, leaving the rings to her alone.

I can't miss, Nadia thought. I'm the only one. I've got them all to myself.

She pulled up the latest telescopic views of the rings and soon became completely engrossed in watching their mysterious, tantalizing dynamics. How can they weave those strands? she asked herself. What makes those spokes appear and disappear like that?

Above all, why does Saturn have such a glorious set of rings, in the first place? They can't be very old, their particles will fall into the planet in a matter of a few million years. How come they're sitting out there for us to see? How come we're so lucky? How come Jupiter and the other gas giants have teeny little dark rings that you can hardly see, while Saturn has this gorgeous set hanging around it? What makes Saturn so special?

Hours went by as she watched the rings in their convoluted, hypnotic ballet. She forgot about the other scientists' competing for Urbain's favor. She forgot about the proposal she needed to finish. She forgot about Eberly and his speech and everything in her endless fascination with Saturn's glowing, beckoning rings.

Oswaldo Yañez could think of nothing except Eberly's speech. He buttonholed other doctors in the infirmary, he stopped nurses on their rounds to ask their opinions, he chattered about the speech with each of the patients he saw that morning.

As he tapped the chest of a construction mechanic who came in complaining of a strained back, Yañez spoke glowingly of Eberly's ideas.

'The man is absolutely right,' he insisted. 'He's a genius. It takes real genius to cut through all the details and get to the heart of the situation.'

His patient, wincing slightly as he sat up on the edge of the examination table, replied, 'Just gimme a shot, doc, and let me get back to work.'

All through the morning Yañez prattled on in his animated, rapid, Spanish-accented English to anyone and everyone who came within earshot of him. He was a round little man with a round, cheerful leprechaun's face that was very animated, especially when he was as excited about a subject as he was about Eberly's speech.

Yañez was not a political exile, nor a rebel, nor a convicted criminal. He was an idealist. He had run foul of the medical orthodoxy of Buenos Aires because he believed that their ban against therapeutic cloning was based on outmoded religious beliefs rather than the clear evidence of medical gain to be had by regenerating tissues damaged by disease or trauma. The medical board had given him his choice: he could go on the Saturn mission or he could remain in Buenos Aires and be stripped of his license to practice medicine. Yañez made up his mind immediately: a new, clean world was preferable to the slow death of the spirit that would inevitably destroy him if he remained. He asked only that his wife be allowed to accompany him. She was quite surprised when he broke the news to her.

Now he was exhilarated by Eberly's bold words. 'We *should* take charge of this habitat,' he repeated all day long. 'We should form our own government and build this new world the way it should be built. And Eberly is clearly the man to lead us.'

Departure Plus 284 Days

Professor Wilmot leaned back in his desk chair, enjoying the familiar comfort of the padded leather upholstery. The holowindow to his left showed a three-dimensional view of the rocky coast where the River Bann emptied into the cold and restless North Channel. It was like looking through a window in the old family estate. Strange, he thought, the only time I miss the old country is when I look at scenes like this. Distance lends enchantment, I suppose.

The phone buzzed and announced, 'Dr. Eberly to see you, sir.'

Wilmot sighed heavily and blanked the view of his ancestral homeland. Back to the business at hand, he told himself as he ordered the office computer to open the door from the ante-room.

Malcolm Eberly stepped in, with one of his young assistants, a leggy, tawny-skinned young woman wearing a hip-length tunic of pale green that showed her slim legs to good advantage. No decorations of any kind, except her name badge. She's being an obedient little underling for him. Wilmot almost smiled. If you think you can distract me with her, my boy, you have another think coming.

Wilmot smiled genially and said, 'Come in! Sit down. It was good of you to come on such a short notice.'

Eberly was in a sky-blue tunic and blue-gray slacks. The shoulders looked padded to Wilmot's critical eye.

'When the chief administrator calls,' Eberly said good-naturedly, 'it's best to come at once.'

Nodding graciously, Wilmot said, 'It's good to see you again, Miss Lane.'

She looked surprised for a moment, then smiled, pleased that the chief administrator remembered her name, forgetting that it was spelled out on the tag above her left breast.

'I saw the speech you made last night,' Wilmot said to Eberly. 'Very impressive.'

Eberly clasped his hands together as if praying. 'I'm pleased that you think so.'

'You realize, of course, that we will not be able to make any changes in our governing regulations until we establish ourselves in Saturn orbit.'

With a slight shake of his head, Eberly said, 'I see no reason to delay.'

'Obviously,' said Wilmot. 'But the regulations are in force and we all agreed to follow them.' Before Eberly could reply, Wilmot asked, 'Tell me, why are you in such a rush to change things? Are there problems that I'm not aware of?'

Eberly pursed his lips and tapped his prayerful fingertips against them. Stalling for time to think, Wilmot reckoned.

At last, Eberly answered, 'The regulations are too stifling. They allow the people no flexibility. They were written by administrators and academics—'

'Like myself,' Wilmot interjected, with a good-natured smile.

'I was going to say, administrators and academics who remained back on Earth; political theoreticians who've never been off the Earth. Nor ever plan to be.'

Wilmot edged forward in his chair and glanced at the young woman. 'Miss Lane, do you feel that our existing protocols are stifling you?'

Her eyes went wide, startled, then she looked at Eberly.

'Miss Lane?' Wilmot repeated. 'Are we stifling you?'

'I've never been on Earth,' Holly replied slowly, hesitantly. 'At least, I don't remember my life there. As far as I can recall, I've spent my whole life in Selene. And now here in the habitat, of course. Living in Selene was . . .' she struggled briefly for a word, 'well, easier, in some ways. I mean, if you ran into a problem you could always go to one of the governing boards and appeal. Like, for your monthly water allotment, or to increase the size of your quarters.'

'And we have no such boards of appeals here,' Wilmot said softly.

'No, we don't,' Holly replied. 'Everything's set in cement. There are the rules and nothing else. End of story.'

Wilmot brushed his fingertips against his moustache thoughtfully.

'The real problem,' Eberly burst out, 'is that these regulations were written by people who live in a world that must be tightly controlled. They all share the same basic, underlying view that society must be hierarchical and controlled from the top.'

Wilmot felt pleased that the discussion was moving into his field of interest. 'Aren't all societies controlled from the top? Even the so-called democracies are ruled by a small elite group; the only difference is that a democracy can shift its elite without bloodshed and give the general populace the illusion that they have made a telling change.'

'There are too many controls,' Eberly repeated. 'Back on Earth, with a global population climbing well past ten billions despite the greenhouse warming and all the other ecological disasters, tight control is very necessary. But this is not Earth.'

Wilmot pretended surprise. 'Don't you believe that we must regulate our population size? Don't you understand the need to mete out our resources according to our ability to replenish them? We live in a very limited environment, you know.'

Obviously struggling to contain his impatience, Eberly said, 'This habitat could feed and house ten times the existing population. Why must we behave as if we are on the brink of famine?'

'Because we will be on the brink of famine if we don't control population size,' Wilmot replied mildly.

Eberly shook his head vigorously. 'You assume that we are a closed ecology, that we have nothing available to us except what we produce for ourselves.'

'Isn't that the truth?' Wilmot shot back.

'No! We can trade for resources with the asteroid miners, with the bases on Mars and in Jupiter orbit, with Selene, even.'

'Trade what?' Wilmot asked. 'What do we have to trade with?'

Eberly smiled as if he were turning over his trump card. 'We will have the most precious resource of them all: water.'

Wilmot felt his eyebrows go up. 'Water?'

'Saturn is surrounded by massive rings, which are composed of pieces of ice. Water ice. We can become the providers of water for the entire solar system once we reach Saturn.'

'Water,' Wilmot repeated, in a near whisper.

'Water,' Eberly said again. 'And fusion fuels, too. Once we are in Saturn orbit, it will be cheaper for us to scoop fusion fuels from the planet's atmosphere than it is to scoop them from Jupiter.'

'But we'll be twice as far from Earth—'

'I've had experts do the analysis,' Eberly said, almost smugly. 'You can check the numbers yourself. Once we are in Saturn orbit we can drive the Jupiter operation out of business!'

'Extraordinary,' Wilmot murmured, looking up at the ceiling panels, thinking furiously. 'Even if that is a workable proposition,' he said, 'it will have to wait until we are at Saturn, won't it?'

'Yes, of course.'

'Then there is no point in trying to alter our system of governance until then, is there?'

Eberly placed his hands on his thighs and said very reasonably, 'The people should be ready to launch into action as soon as we reach Saturn. Why should they delay? They should be free to select the form of government they want, the form that will work best for them, *now*, while we are in transit, so that the new government can be in place when we get to our destination.'

With you at its head, Wilmot added silently. That's what you're after, isn't it? This is nothing more than a power game. Fascinating.

Aloud, he said to Eberly, 'Perhaps there is some merit in your idea.'

Holly blurted, 'You think so?'

Wilmot smiled at her and said, 'Why don't we agree on this: You can start the process of writing a new constitution. Canvass the population and determine what kind of a government they want for themselves. Begin the process immediately.'

'We'll have to poll the people, draw up various types of constitutions, nominate candidates—'

'Yes, yes,' Wilmot said. 'Do all that while you're carrying out your little contests about naming things. But there will be no change in our governing regulations until we are firmly established in orbit about Saturn. Is that clear? You can spend the time left in transit to form your new government, but it will not be installed in office until we are at our destination.'

Eberly thought a moment, eyes cast downward, then looked squarely at Wilmot and said, 'Yes, I can agree to that.'

'Good,' said Wilmot, getting to his feet and extending his hand across the desk. 'We are agreed, then.'

Eberly and Holly stood up and shook Wilmot's hand in turn. As they left his office, Wilmot sank back into his chair, thinking that he should write up this encounter and have it ready to send back to Atlanta as quickly as possible.

Data Bank

It is the most beautiful sight in the solar system: Saturn and its glowing, glorious rings.

They arch above the planet's equator like a bridge of light, circling the ponderous flattened sphere of the planet, hovering above its middle as if in splendid defiance of gravity.

The second largest planet of our solar system, Saturn is slightly smaller than Jupiter, but orbits twice as far from the Sun as Jupiter. Like Jupiter, Saturn is a gas giant world, composed almost entirely of the lightest elements, hydrogen and helium. If you could build a swimming pool nearly ten times the size of Earth, Saturn would float in it: the planet's density is slightly less than water's.

Approaching Saturn, the planet's pale yellow and tan clouds churn across a disc that is noticeably flattened by its frenetic spin rate. Saturn's day is a scant ten hours and thirty-nine minutes. Yet to the ancients, Saturn was the farthest planet they could see, and the slowest in making its way around the sky. At ten times the Earth's distance from the Sun, it takes 29.46 Earth years for Saturn to circle the Sun once.

The ring system is what makes Saturn so beautiful, so intriguing. Jupiter and the farther worlds of Uranus and Neptune have narrow, faint rings circling them. Saturn has broad bands of *rings*, shining brilliantly, suspended about the planet's middle, hanging in emptiness like a magnificent set of halos.

When Galileo first turned his primitive telescope to Saturn he thought he saw a triple planet: his small lenses could not make out the rings; to him they looked like strange ears sprouting on either side of the planet. He wrote to the German astronomer Johannes Kepler a letter in code, so that it could be read only by its intended recipient. 'I have observed the highest planet to be triple-bodied,' Galileo wrote in an anagram. Kepler misunderstood, and thought that Galileo meant he had discovered two moons of Mars.

As telescopes improved, astronomers discovered those impossible rings. To this day, Saturn is one of the first objects that amateur astronomers turn to. The sight of the ringed planet never fails to inspire admiring, delighted sighs.

Saturn's beautiful rings are composed of particles of ice and ice-covered dust. While most of the particles are no larger than dust motes, some are as big as houses. The rings are about 400,000 kilometers across, yet not much thicker than a hundred meters. They have been described as 'proportionally as thick as a sheet of tissue paper spread over a football field.'

The rings' total mass amounts to that of an icy satellite no more than 100 kilometers in diameter. They are either the remains of one or more moons that got too close to the planet and were broken up by gravitational tidal forces, or left-over material from the time of the planet's formation which never coalesced into a single body because they were too close to Saturn to do so.

The rings are *dynamic*. Hundreds of millions of particles circling the mammoth planet, constantly colliding, bouncing off one another, breaking into smaller fragments, banging and jouncing like an insane speedway full of lunatic drivers.

The dynamics of the rings are fascinating. There are gaps between the major rings, spaces of emptiness caused by the gravitational pulls of Saturn's several dozen moons. The rings are accompanied by tiny 'sheep-dog' satellites, minuscule moons that circle just outside or just inside each ring and apparently keep them in place with their tiny gravitational influence. The rings are self-sustaining: as particles are sucked down into the planet, new particles are chipped off the 'shepherd' moons by constant collisions with the hurtling, jostling particles; abraded off these tiny moonlets as they grind their way around the planet, constantly bombarded by the blizzard of tiny icy particles through which they orbit.

The main rings are actually composed of hundreds of thinner 'ringlets' that appear to be braided together. Spacecraft time-lapse photos also show mysterious spokes weaving through the largest of the rings, patterns of light and dark that remain unexplained and fascinating. Perhaps Saturn's extensive magnetosphere electrically charges the dust particles in the ring and levitates them, which may give rise to the spokes.

The planet itself presented an enigma to the inquisitive scientists from Earth. Like the more massive Jupiter, Saturn is heated from within, its core of molten rock seething from the pressure of the giant world squeezing down upon it. But Saturn is smaller than Jupiter, farther from the Sun, and therefore colder. Where Jupiter harbors a flourishing biosphere of aerial organisms in its thick hydrogen atmosphere, and an even more complex ecology of sea-going creatures in its deep planet-wide ocean, Saturn seems bereft of life, except for the cold-adapted microbes that dwell in its upper cloud deck.

'Saturn is a dead end, as far as multicellular life is concerned,' pronounced a disappointed astrobiologist after the earliest probes scanned the vast ocean that swirls beneath the ringed world's perpetual clouds, 'just over the edge of habitability for anything more complex than single-celled organisms.'

Wistfully, he added, 'Just a little warmer and we would have had a duplicate of Jupiter.'

Among the billions of ice particles that make up the rings, some prebiological chemical activity has been detected by robotic probes, but no evidence for living organisms has been found, as yet.

Saturn's giant moon, Titan, is an altogether different matter, however. A rich ecology of hydrocarbon-based microbes exists there, placing Titan off-limits for any development or industrial exploitation. No one but scientists is allowed near Titan, and even they have refrained from sending to its surface anything except completely sterilized robot probes.

The scientific community and the International Astronautical Authority are agreed that humans must not endanger Titan's ecology with the threat of contamination.

But others do not agree.

Intradepartmental Memorandum

To: All Human Resources Department personnel
From: R. Morgenthau, Acting Director
Subject: Prayer meetings

Several staff members have asked for a clarification of departmental policy concerning prayer meetings. Although habitat regulations do not specifically call for such meetings during normal working hours, neither do said regulations forbid them.

Therefore it will be the policy of the human resources department to allow HR staff to conduct prayer meetings during working hours, providing such meetings are cleared beforehand with the Acting Director, and further providing that such meetings are no longer than thirty (30) minutes in duration.

Staff members are encouraged to attend prayer meetings. The human resources department will, furthermore, encourage all other departments to follow a similar policy. Those who oppose prayer meetings are obviously attempting to impose their secularist opinions on the general population of this habitat.

Time, Tides And Titan

Edouard Urbain imagined himself standing on the shore of Titan's hydrocarbon sea.

Larger than the planet Mercury, Titan is a cold and dark world, some ten times farther from the Sun than Earth is. Only pale and weak sunlight filtered through the clouds and smog of Titan's thick, murky atmosphere.

Urbain pictured himself standing on an outcropping of ice, staring through his spacesuit helmet's visor at the black, oily sea surging across the rough, jumbled ice field below. In the distance a sooty 'snow storm' was approaching, a wall of black hydrocarbon flakes blotting out the horizon as it came closer.

Then the bleak, frozen landscape suddenly grew brighter. He looked up, and the breath caught in his throat. The clouds had broken for a moment and he could see Saturn riding high above, magnificently beautiful, ten times larger than a full Moon on Earth, its rings a slim knife edge slicing across the middle of the gaudily striped body of the planet. There was no lovelier sight in the entire solar system, he thought.

But the tide was coming in. Pulled by the immense gravitational power of Saturn, the hydrocarbon sea was a frothing tidal wave swiftly advancing across the broken landscape of ice, a slimy crawling monster swallowing everything in its path, submerging spires and boulder-sized chunks of ice, covering the frozen ground in hissing, bubbling black oil, flooding the world from horizon to horizon. Soon it would drown even the prominence Urbain was standing on, slithering halfway across Titan before reversing its course.

Someday I will stand by that sea, Urbain told himself, equipped to sample it and search for living organisms in the black, oily liquid. Someday.

He sighed and looked around his cramped little office, returning to reality. No one will go to the surface of Titan, not for many years to come, he knew.

Then his eyes fell on the three-dimensional schematic of the landing vehicle that hovered above his desk. It looked bulky and cumbersome, but to Urbain it was the epitome of pragmatic elegance. *You* will go down to Titan's surface, my beauty, Urbain said silently to the drawing.

Designing the lander had been little more than child's play, he realized. It was being built by his engineers and technicians, under his meticulous direction. That much was actually rather simple.

The big accomplishment was carrying it to Saturn, establishing this habitat in orbit around the ringed planet, where Urbain and his scientists could control the lander in real time.

Time had defeated earlier attempts to explore Titan remotely. It took more than an hour to send a signal from Earth to Saturn, even when the two planets were at their closest. Remotely controlled probes failed, no matter how sophisticated they were, because of that time lag. For decades scientists on Earth had gnashed their teeth in frustration as one probe after another trundled blithely into a crevasse or was blanketed in oily black snow, simply because it took hours for their human controllers to get the proper commands to them.

No longer, Urbain told himself. Now we will control the lander from mere light-seconds away. If necessary, we can establish a command post in orbit around Titan itself and cut the reaction time to less than a second.

But no human will set foot on Titan, he knew. Not for many years. The thought saddened him, in his heart of hearts. He wanted to plant his own boots on that cold, dark, black-ice surface. Deep in the place where he kept his most secret desires, Edouard Urbain wanted to be the first man to reach the surface of Titan.

Departure Plus 317 Days

'Jezoo, it's like a movie set down here.'

Holly was leading Manuel Gaeta along the utilities tunnel that ran beneath the village. Overhead lights flicked on automatically as they walked along the tunnel, then went dark again once they had passed. The walls were lined with electrical conduits, plumbing pipes, valves, control panels, phone screens spaced every hundred meters. More pipes ran overhead, color-coded blue for potable water, yellow for sewage heading to the recyclers, red for hot water going to the waste heat radiators outside the habitat. The tunnel hummed with the constant throb of pumps and electrical equipment. Holly could feel the metal deck plates vibrating through the soles of her softboots.

'What's a movie set?' she asked.

'Where they shoot vids,' Gaeta replied, eying all the ductwork around them as they moved along the tunnel. 'You know, if they need to do a scene in ancient Rome they build a set to look like ancient Rome.'

'Oh. Sure. I click. But how does this look like a movie set?'

He grinned at her. 'Like the back side of a set. They're all fake, just a façade, usually made out of plastic. You go behind, it's all propped up with girders and scaffolds.'

'And this reminds you of that?' she asked, puzzled.

'Kinda,' he replied. 'I mean, a couple dozen meters over our heads is the village—'

'No, we're past the village now,' Holly corrected. 'We're underneath the park, heading for the farms.'

'Whatever. Up top it all looks so real, but down here you realize it's all fakery.'

115

'It is not!' she said, with some heat. 'It's as real as real can be. You eat the food we grow on the farms, don't you? You sleep in an apartment in the village. How real can it get?'

Gaeta held up both hands in a mock surrender. 'Hey, whoa. Don't take it so personal. I just meant, this whole habitat is an artificial construction. It looks like a real village and real farms and all that, but when you're down here you realize it's all inside a big machine.'

'Well, f'sure,' Holly said. 'Everybody knows that.'

They walked in silence for a while, the overhead lights turning on for them and off again once they passed. Like magic, Holly thought. Then she remembered that she should have been in the office, working. But this is fun, she told herself, exploring the tunnels. Why work all the time? A person ought to have a little fun now and then.

The tunnel branched up ahead, and one wall opened up to reveal another tunnel that crossed theirs at a lower level.

'This way,' Holly said, swinging a leg over the guard rail.

'Down there?' Gaeta asked.

'Sure.' She flipped over the metal railing, grasped its bottom rung and hung there for an instant, then dropped to the metal flooring of the lower tunnel, four meters below.

'Come on,' Holly called up to Gaeta. 'It's a shortcut to the farms.'

He leaned over the rail, looking dubious. Then slowly, methodically, he clambered over the rail and let himself drop down beside her, landing lightly on the balls of his feet.

'For a stunt guy,' she chided, 'you're warping cautious.'

'That's how a stunt guy stays in one piece,' he replied, grinning. 'There are old stuntmen and bold stuntmen, but there are no old, bold stuntmen.'

Holly laughed, understanding.

'How far to the farms?' Gaeta asked.

'Not far now.'

'How far?'

She wrinkled her brow for a moment, then answered, 'Less than three kilometers.'

'You certain of that?'

'I've got all the tunnels memorized,' Holly told him.

'All of them? Every one? Every kilometer?'

'Every centimeter.'

He laughed. 'All up in your head, huh?' he teased, tapping his own temple.

Holly pulled her handheld from her tunic pocket and pressed the locater key with her thumb. The screen showed a schematic of the tunnels that threaded beneath the habitat's landscaping, with a blinking red cursor identifying their location.

Gaeta peered at the little screen over her shoulder. She could fell his warm breath on the back of her neck, sense his body heat.

'I'll be damned,' he said, slightly awestruck. 'You were right on the button.'

'I told you, didn't I? I've memorized the whole layout of the habitat. Every centimeter of it.'

Gaeta placed his hand on his heart and made a little bow. '*Perdone mi, senorita.* I apologize for doubting you.'

'*Da nada,*' said Holly, which just about exhausted her knowledge of Spanish. She promised herself she would learn more.

Their adventure had started just before lunch, when Gaeta had popped into Holly's office asking about authorization for an excursion outside the habitat.

'Gotta test the suit,' he explained. 'We've made half a dozen modifications to it and we need to test it in hard vacuum.'

Looking up at him from her desk chair, Holly noticed that his eyes were the darkest brown she had ever seen.

'You need to see the safety department about that,' she said. 'This is human resources.'

Gaeta made a small shrug. 'Yeah, I know, but I thought maybe you could help me with it. I don't know any of the people in the safety department, and at least you and I have met before.'

She thought that sounded something like a lie. Or maybe an excuse to see me? Holly wondered. With hardly a moment's thought, she phoned the safety office and made an appointment for Gaeta to talk with them.

Then he asked her to lunch and they began chatting about his plans for getting down to the surface of Titan and living in the habitat and before she knew it Holly was telling him her life story, or as much of it she remembered.

'Let's take the afternoon off,' he suddenly suggested.

Holly sipped at her coffee, thinking that there was too much work waiting at her desk even though Manny was kind of handsome in a beat-up way and when he smiled like that those dark, dark eyes lit up like candles on a birthday cake.

'And do what?' she asked.

He spread his hands and grinned at her. 'Nothing. Just loaf. Take it easy for a few hours.'

'I have a better idea,' Holly said, putting her coffee cup down with a tiny clink.

'What?' he asked.

'Let's go exploring,' said Holly.

So she led him to one of the access hatches built into the back of the administration building and down the metal ladder into the utilities tunnel.

'Like going down to the Morlocks,' he muttered as they clambered down the ladder.

'Oarlocks?' Holly asked, puzzled.

Gaeta just laughed.

As they walked along the tunnel, talking, looking, discovering, Holly realized that here she was all alone with this guy and nobody knew where she was. What'll I do if he starts to come on to me? she wondered. And another part of her mind asked, what'll you do if he doesn't come on to you?

He's a stallion, all right, Holly thought as they prowled along the tunnel. Not much taller than she, but strong, muscular. She had never had the chance to do any sexual experimenting while under her sister's watchful eye, although according to what Pancho had told her she'd had her share of toy boys – and even serious lovers – when she'd been in school, before she'd died.

Could I make Malcolm jealous? she wondered. He hasn't paid

any attention to me at all. Maybe if he finds out I'm seeing this stud, he'll take some notice. Maybe—

'How well do you know Dr. Cardenas?' Gaeta asked as they paused at a fork in the tunnel.

Holly hesitated a moment, picturing the tunnel layout in her mind. 'That way,' she pointed, 'leads out to the farms. This way goes to the factories.'

He scratched his chin. 'We gonna walk all the way back to the village?'

'Sure. It's only three-four klicks.'

'There's no transportation?'

Holly laughed. 'Don't tell me you're tired!'

'Naw, not really. I was just thinking it's getting close to dinner time and I ought to take a shower, you know, and get into some fresh clothes.'

Holly felt her pulse speed up. *Is he trying to get me to his apartment?*

'I got a dinner date with Dr. Cardenas,' he explained, 'and I oughtta look decent for her.'

Holly's face fell. 'With Dr. Cardenas?'

He must have seen her disappointment. She realized that a blind man could have seen it.

'It's the only time we got to talk about how she can make the nanobugs to decontaminate my suit,' he explained. 'She's so damn' busy setting up her lab the only chance I get to talk with her is at dinner.'

'Oh.'

'It's strictly business.'

'Yeah. I click.'

Gaeta gave her a sheepish little-boy look. 'You wanna come, too? Bring a friend, we can make it two couples.'

With a start, Holly realized she didn't have a friend she could call for a dinner date. She had plenty of acquaintances, but most of them were from the office. Ever since coming into the habitat she had spent all her time, all her thoughts, on Eberly. Until this day when Gaeta had popped into her office.

And now this.

'No,' she said firmly. 'Thanks anyway. I have a lot of work to catch up on.'

He nodded glumly. 'I've taken you away from your work, huh?'

'That's all right,' Holly said. 'It was a fun afternoon.'

She started back down the tunnel in the direction they had come from. Gaeta quickly caught up with her.

'Maybe you could have dinner with me tomorrow?' he suggested.

Holly brightened. 'Tomorrow? Sure, why not.'

'Great,' he said, smiling at her.

When Gaeta got back to his apartment he stripped, showered, and decided the depilatory was still working well enough so that he didn't need to shave yet. As he pulled on his clothes, one eye on the digital clock by his bed, he commanded the phone to send a message to Wendell Sloane, in Selene.

'Mr. Sloane,' he said, slightly uncomfortable at being so formal. 'Progress report on Ms. Lane. Nothing much new to report. She's still working in the human resources department. Doesn't appear to have any personal attachments; no boyfriends, not much of a social life at all. I had lunch with her this afternoon. She's really a fine young lady: very bright, very sharp. She seems happy in her work here in the habitat. Tell her sister she's got nothing to worry about as far as she's concerned. But I'll keep on looking out for her, just like you want. Just wanna let you know there's no problems here.'

That oughtta keep the suits back in Selene satisfied for a while. Without their backing, this whole Titan stunt would go down the tubes. Astro Corporation was the major funding source for Manuel Gaeta and his team.

Sammi Vyborg sat rigidly at his desk, looking past the open door of his cubbyhole office at the larger office across the corridor. It belonged to his immediate superior, Diego Romero.

Vyborg glanced at the numerals of the digital clock flashing away in the corner of his desk. Every day it's the same routine, Vyborg grumbled to himself. He spends the morning pretending to work, takes his lunch, then goes out for the afternoon. I sit here buried in duties and chores and he spends every afternoon out of the office. The number two man in the department, and he only puts in half a day, at best.

Don't get mad, Vyborg reminded himself. Get even. It's time to set this lazy old incompetent against the director. With a bit of luck, I can bring them both down.

Romero stepped out into the corridor and slid his office door shut. Turning, he noticed Vyborg watching him.

'*Buenos tardes*,' he said, with a smile and a slight bow.

Vyborg smiled back at him, sourly.

As soon as Romero was gone, Vyborg got up from his desk and walked down the corridor to the office of the communications department's director, Zeke Berkowitz. He rapped once on the half-open door, making it rattle against its track.

'Come on in,' Berkowitz called. As Vyborg slid the door all the way open and stepped into the office, Berkowitz smiled and said, 'Ah, Sammi. What can I do for you?'

Amiable was the word for Berkowitz. The man had spent a long and successful career in the video news business, first as a local reporter, then as a network anchorman, and finally as a global executive. He had never made an enemy, although in the cut-throat world of news broadcasting many people had tried to chop him down, stab him in the back, or even forcibly retire him. He survived it all with a smile and a homily about Christian charity, liberally sprinkled with self-deprecating Jewish humor.

When he reached mandatory retirement age, the still-youthful Berkowitz moved into academia, happily teaching a new generation of would-be journalists and public relations flacks the realities of the communications business. It was at an international conference that he had met James Wilmot, the famous anthropologist; the two men became instant friends, even though they lived and taught on opposite sides of the Atlantic Ocean. Years later, when Wilmot invited Berkowitz to be head of the communications department on the Saturn-bound space habitat, Berkowitz – recently a widower after fifty years of loving marriage – had accepted the opportunity to get as far away from his memories as he could.

Now he sat back in his desk chair, handsome and suntanned, slightly chubby, a series of holograms on the wall behind him showing him at tennis tournaments and on golf courses. He smiled warmly at the dour, pinch-faced Vyborg.

'What's the matter, Sammi?' Berkowitz asked jovially. 'You look as if you swallowed something ugly.'

Taking the chair in front of Berkowitz's desk, Vyborg began, 'I don't enjoy bringing this to your attention—'

'But you're going to do it anyway. Must be important.'

'I think it is.'

'Okay. Out with it.'

'It's Romero.'

'Old Don Diego? What's he done that bothers you?'

Vyborg hesitated just long enough to show Berkowitz that what he was doing was distasteful to him. 'It's very difficult for me to say this, since he's my direct superior, but . . . well, he's simply not pulling his own weight.'

'He isn't.'

'No, he isn't. He spends only half a day in the office and then he's gone. How can he do his work?'

'That's why we've got you, Sammi.'

Startled, Vyborg blurted, 'What?'

Berkowitz put on his most amiable grin and, clasping his hands prayerfully on the desktop, said, 'Diego Romero is a wonderful old coot, a great teacher with a very distinguished career behind him.'

'Behind him,' Vyborg echoed.

'He's in this department more or less because Wilmot wanted him aboard this habitat and had to find a place for him somewhere. So he's working with us.'

'But he's *not* working,' Vyborg snapped. 'He's hardly ever at his desk.'

'That's okay, Sammi. I haven't given him much to do. I rely on you to get the work done. Leave Don Diego alone, he's going to be very valuable to this habitat – as a teacher.'

'A teacher?' Vyborg gasped. 'They got rid of him in Mexico because he was teaching unauthorized garbage. Do you want him teaching his blasphemies here?'

Berkowitz's smile diminished by less than a millimeter. 'Freedom of thought is not blasphemous, Sammi. He's a great teacher.'

Vyborg muttered, 'Yes, and he's teaching the rest of the office staff how to get by without working.'

'If you find anybody goofing off in this department, you tell me about it. Pronto. Don Diego's a special case. Leave him alone.'

Admitting defeat, Vyborg nodded and rose from his chair. 'I understand. I'm sorry to have bothered you.'

'No bother at all,' Berkowitz said grandly. 'My office door is always open to you, Sammi.'

Vyborg looked around the director's office. It was much more spacious than his own. It even had a window that looked out onto the park and the shimmering lake beyond. Without another word he turned and walked out, thinking, I'll have to get rid of them both, somehow.

By the time he got back to his own office, Vyborg had brightened considerably. Berkowitz wanted to allow Don Diego to teach heretical ideas, he realized. That makes Berkowitz just as guilty as the old man himself. Perhaps I can get them both in one swoop.

But as he sat at his desk again his mood darkened once more. That means I'll have to wait until we're established at Saturn. Much too long. I can't wait all those months, more than a year, actually. I want to get rid of them *now*.

Departure Plus 318 Days

When Holly got to her office the next morning there was a message on her screen: SEE ME IMMEDIATELY. MORGENTHAU.

It still bothered Holly to see Ruth Morgenthau sitting at Eberly's desk. Even though nearly two months had passed since Eberly had left the office, Holly always expected to see Malcolm there. Instead, when she opened the director's office door, Morgenthau was behind the desk, her fleshy face dark and ominous.

Even before Holly could sit down, Morgenthau demanded, 'Where were you yesterday afternoon?'

Holly stiffened. 'I took the afternoon off. I caught up on my work from my quarters, after dinner.'

Morgenthau asked, 'Were you ill?'

Holly thought that a simple lie could end this conversation. Instead, she replied, 'No. I – I just needed some time away from the office, that's all.'

'Do you think you're working too hard?'

'I enjoy my work.'

Morgenthau drummed her chubby fingers on the desk top. Despite the dress code they had agreed to, the woman's fingers were heavy with jeweled rings, and her tunic ablaze with colors. Holly noticed that the desk was littered with papers. Malcolm always kept it immaculately clear.

'Sit down, please, Holly,' Morgenthau said.

Holly took one of the chairs in front of the desk, feeling resentment simmering inside her. I'm entitled to take an afternoon off if I want to, she said to herself. I'm running this warping office. I'm doing all the work. I can go off and have a little fun if I want to. But she said nothing and meekly sat down.

Morgenthau stared at her for a long moment, then said, 'You know, and I know, that you are really running this office. I'm just a figurehead covering for Malcolm while you do all the real work.'

Holly almost blurted out her agreement, but she managed to keep silent.

'I don't mind that arrangement,' Morgenthau continued. 'In fact, I find it quite satisfactory.'

Holly nodded warily, expecting worse to come.

'But,' Morgenthau resumed, 'you don't have to rub my face in it. You must show at least some outward respect for my position.'

'I do!'

'Yesterday you did not. It is not proper for you to take the afternoon off without informing me. Actually, you should ask my permission, but I don't want to be a stickler. Still, how does it look when someone like Professor Wilmot asks me a question and I tell him that my assistant will look up the information and my assistant isn't at her desk? Isn't even in the office? And I don't know where she is?'

'You could have called me. I always carry my comm.'

'You should keep me informed of your whereabouts at all times. I shouldn't have to search for you.'

Holly's temper was rising. 'You don't like me very much, do you?'

For an instant Morgenthau looked surprised, almost startled. Then she admitted, 'You are not a Believer. And, worse, you're a reborn. I find that . . .' she struggled for a word, '. . . distasteful. Almost sinful.'

'It wasn't my decision. My sister did it when I was too sick to know what was happening to me.'

'Still. You tried to avoid God's judgment on you. You tried to cheat death.'

'Wouldn't you?'

'No! When God calls me, I'll be happy to go.'

The sooner the better, Holly snarled silently.

'But my religious beliefs are not the subject of this conversation. I want you to keep me informed of your whereabouts at all times.'

Holding back her anger, Holly replied, 'I understand.'

Breaking into a smile that looked forced to Holly, Morgenthau added, 'During office hours, of course. What you do when the office is closed is on your own conscience, of course.'

'Of course.'

'Unless it involves Dr. Eberly.'

So that's it! Holly realized. She's cranked up because she can see that I'm interested in Malcolm. Maybe she knows more than I do. Maybe she can see that Malcolm's interested in me!

'Dr. Eberly is much too busy for personal involvements of any kind, Holly. You should stop trying to distract him.'

She's trying to protect him. She's standing between Malcolm and me.

Holly got to her feet. 'I should have told you I was taking the afternoon off,' she said coldly. 'It won't happen again.'

'Good!' Morgenthau smacked her hands together loudly enough to startle Holly. 'Now that *that's* out of the way – I'll be out of the office all day. You'll be in charge.'

Surprised at her sudden change in tone, Holly asked, 'Where will you be?'

Morgenthau laughed lightly and waggled a finger in the air. 'No, no, it's not necessary for me to tell you where I'm going. I'm the department chief, remember. I can come and go as I wish.'

'Oh, right. F'sure.'

'For your information, however,' Morgenthau said as she pushed herself up out of the desk chair, 'I will be with Malcolm all day. We are going over several drafts of possible constitutions.'

Eberly sipped herbal tea while Vyborg and Jaansen argued with quiet passion. Kananga was obviously bored with the argument, while Morgenthau watched it in silence as she nibbled on pastries.

Kananga's a man of action, Eberly thought. He doesn't think very deeply, which is good. He makes a useful tool. Morgenthau, though, she's different. She just sits there watching everything, silent as a sphinx. What's going on inside her head? How much of this is she reporting back to Amsterdam? Everything, I suppose.

'If you allow the people all these personal freedoms,' Vyborg was saying, almost hissing, actually, 'the result will be chaos. Anarchy.'

'Most of the inhabitants have come to this habitat to escape repressive regimes. If their individual liberties are not guaranteed, they'll reject the constitution altogether.' Jaansen leaned back on the sofa, smiling as if he had won the argument.

'Individual liberties,' Vyborg spat. 'That's the kind of license that nearly caused the collapse of civilization. If it weren't for the New Morality—'

'And the Holy Disciples,' Morgenthau interjected, then, glancing at Kananga, she added, 'And the Sword of Islam.'

Jaansen frowned at her and Vyborg, both. 'No matter what you think, these people will not accept a constitution that doesn't guarantee their historical freedoms. They're here because they got fed up with the restrictions back on Earth.'

Vyborg thought otherwise. He continued to argue.

Sitting at the end of the coffee table, Eberly thought that Vyborg, in the room's best armchair, with his skinny legs tucked under him, looked rather like a coiled snake: lean, small, dark, his eyes glittering menacingly. Jaansen was just the opposite: cool, pale, but as immovable as a glacier. And he kept that damned palm-comp in his hand, fiddling with it like some voodoo charm.

Kananga butted in. 'In a closed ecology like this, we can't tolerate fools and troublemakers. Pop them out an airlock without a suit!'

Morgenthau laughed. 'My dear colonel, how can we resort to airlock justice if each citizen is guaranteed due process of the law for any offence they might commit?'

'Exactly my point!' Vyborg exclaimed, staring straight at Jaansen. 'We have no room here for the legal niceties.'

Pursing her lips for a moment, Morgenthau said, 'There is another possibility.'

'What?'

'I've heard that some scientists on Earth are experimenting with electronic probes they put inside peoples' skulls. They attach the probes to the brain—'

'Bioelectronics,' Jaansen said.

'Yes,' agreed Morgenthau. 'With these probes attached to various brain centers they can control a person's behavior. Prevent violent criminal behavior, for example.'

Vyborg scowled. 'What of it?'

'Perhaps we can use such probes to control behavior here,' said Morgenthau.

'Insert neural probes to control peoples' behavior?' Jaansen shuddered.

'It could work,' said Morgenthau.

'They would have to agree to the operation,' Vyborg pointed out.

Kananga countered, 'Not if they were found guilty of criminal behavior.'

'It might be a way to control the people,' Morgenthau said.

Shaking his head, Jaansen said, 'The population would never agree to it. These people aren't stupid, you know. They wouldn't give the government that kind of power over them.'

'We wouldn't have to tell them,' Kananga said. 'Just do it.'

That started an argument that grew steadily more fervent. Eberly watched and listened, sipping his tea, while they squabbled louder and louder.

At last he asked them, 'May I make a point?' He spoke softly, but all eyes immediately turned to him.

'Even in the so-called democracies back on Earth, the desperate conditions caused by the greenhouse crash have led to very authoritarian governments. Even in the United States, the New Morality rules most of the large urban centers with an iron fist.'

'Which is why most of these people joined this habitat,' Jaansen pointed out. 'To find more freedom for themselves.'

'The illusion of freedom,' muttered Kananga.

'Secularists,' grumbled Morgenthau. 'Troublemaking unbelievers. Agnostics and outright atheists.'

Jaansen shifted the palmcomp from one hand to another as he said, 'I don't disagree with you, really. I'm a Believer, too. I understand the need for firm control of the people. But those secularists aren't fools. Many of them are scientists. Even more are engineers and technicians. All I'm saying is that if you try to get them to agree to a constitution that does not include the kind of individual liberties they expect, they'll reject the constitution.'

'Not if *we* count the votes,' Morgenthau said with a heavy wink.

'Be serious,' Jaansen countered.

'It's been done,' she said, snickering.

Eberly let out a long sigh. Again, they all turned to him.

'None of you understand history,' he said. 'If you did, you would see that this problem has been faced before, and resolved properly.'

'Resolved?' Vyborg snapped. 'How?'

Smiling with superior knowledge, Eberly said, 'More than a hundred years ago Russia was part of the conglomeration called the Union of Soviet Socialist Republics.'

'I know that,' Vyborg said sourly.

'Soviet Russia had a constitution, the most liberal constitution on Earth. It guaranteed freedom and brotherhood to everyone. Yet their government was among the most repressive of them all.'

Jaansen seemed intrigued. 'How did they manage that?'

'It was simple,' Eberly replied. 'In the midst of all those high-flown constitutional phrases about liberty and equality and the brotherhood of man there was one tiny little clause that said, in effect, that all the rest of the constitution could be suspended temporarily in case of an emergency.'

'An emergency,' repeated Kananga.

'Temporarily,' said Vyborg.

Eberly nodded. 'It worked quite well. The Soviet Union was in a permanent state of siege, and the government ruled by terror and deceit. It worked for nearly three-quarters of a century, until the Soviet government collapsed under pressures from the western nations, especially the old United States.'

'We would have no outside pressures to contend with,' Vyborg said.

Eberly spread his hands. 'So we give the people the sweetest, kindest, most liberal constitution they have ever seen. But we make certain that we have that emergency clause in it.'

Morgenthau laughed heartily. 'Then, once the constitution is in effect, all we have to do is find an emergency.'

'Or make one,' Vyborg added.

Even Jaansen smiled. 'And then, if anyone objects—'

'We stick a neural probe into his brain,' Morgenthau said, 'and turn him into a model citizen.'

'A model zombie,' Jaansen muttered.

'Or better yet,' said Kananga, grinning, 'out the airlock with them.'

Jupiter Encounter Minus Three Days

Eberly asked Jaansen to sweep his apartment for bugs at least once a week.

'Are you really worried that Wilmot is spying on you?' the tall, pale Norseman asked as he walked across the bedroom, electronic detector in his hand.

Eberly, shorter, darker, replied, 'It's what I would do if I were in his place.'

'Are you bugging his office?' Jaansen asked, with a smile.

'Of course.'

'Well, in three days we fly past Jupiter,' said Jaansen. 'It's a milestone.'

Eberly agreed with a curt nod. 'I'm more interested in what happens inside the habitat than outside.'

Jaansen, ever the engineer, pointed out, 'We'll be taking on fresh fuel. Without it we won't be able to get to Saturn.'

'I have other things on my mind. More important things.'

'Such as?'

'The coming elections.'

Jaansen clicked off the detector and announced, 'You're all clean. No cameras, no microphones, no electrical power drain anywhere, down to the microvolt. Nothing that shouldn't be here.'

'Good.' Eberly walked him back into the sitting room and gestured him to the sofa.

Sitting himself in the easy chair, Eberly said, 'Sooner or later, we must get the people to vote on a new constitution and new leaders.'

Jaansen nodded, tucked the detector into one pocket and pulled out his inevitable handheld computer from another.

'I've been thinking about the elections,' Eberly said.

'They're a long way off.'

'Less than a year now. We must prepare for them.'

Jaansen nodded, fiddling with his palmcomp.

'The scientists will vote for one of their own, probably Urbain.'

Another nod from Jaansen.

'They form a sizable bloc of votes.'

'Not a majority, though.'

'Not of themselves,' said Eberly. 'But suppose the engineers and technicians vote with them.'

Recognition dawned on Jaansen's face. 'That could be a majority. A solid majority.'

'Therefore we must somehow split the engineers and technicians away from the scientists,' Eberly said.

'How can we do that?'

Eberly smiled. 'Let me explain what I have in mind.'

Edouard Urbain tried to control the trembling he felt inside him as he stared out the observation port. The giant planet Jupiter, no more than a bright star only a few days ago, was now a discernible disk even to the naked eye, obviously flattened at its poles, streaked with muted colors from bands of clouds racing across the face of that enormous world. Four tiny stars flanked the disk: the moons that Galileo discovered with his first telescope.

Tucked into a close orbit just above those multi-hued clouds, Urbain knew, was the research station *Thomas Gold*. I could have been there, he told himself for the thousandth time. I could have been leading the teams studying the life forms on Europa and Jupiter itself. Instead I am here in this glorified ark, stuck in along with renegades and madmen like this Gaeta fellow.

He knew it was his imagination, but Jupiter seemed to be getting larger as he watched. No, we are not that near to it yet, Urbain said to himself. Three days from now, that is when the spectacle will occur.

Habitat *Goddard*'s complement of scientists and their equipment was far smaller than Urbain had asked for. The university consortium was unwilling to send their best people on a multi-year voyage out to Saturn. Let them sit on their thumbs while the habitat lumbers its way out to that distant planet? No, never. Urbain recalled the face of the consortium's chief scientist with perfect, painful clarity:

'We can't tie up our best people for several years like that, Edouard. You take a skeleton team out to Saturn. Once you're established in orbit about the planet, we can shoot our top researchers out to you on a torch ship, get them there in a month or two.'

The implied insult still burned in Urbain's heart. I am not one of their top people. A lifetime of work on Mars and the Moon, three years in orbit around that hellhole of Venus, a life dedicated to planetary science, and all they think me capable of is playing nursemaid to a skeleton crew of also-rans.

It rankled. It cut. His wife had refused to come with him; instead, she had sued for a divorce. She had warned him, over the years, that he was foolish to ignore the political aspects of his career.

'Make friends,' Jeanne-Marie had told him, over and again. 'Play up to those who can do you good.'

He could never do it. Never play that game. He had done good work, solid work, perhaps not the level that wins Nobel prizes, but important contributions nevertheless. And now this. The end of the road. Exiled to Saturn. I'll be retirement age by the time I can work my way out of this habitat.

I should have paid more attention to Jeanne-Marie. I should have heeded her advice. I should have paid more attention to the New Morality counselors. They pull the strings behind the scenes. Mediocre Believers get promotions while honest researchers like me are left behind.

A wasted life, he thought.

Yet, as he looked out at Jupiter glowing like a beacon in the dark depths of infinite space, the old excitement simmered within him. There's a whole universe out there to explore! Worlds upon worlds! I won't be able to study Jupiter or its moons, but I'll be at Saturn before any of the others. I'll be directing the first real-time probes of Titan's surface.

He thought of the tracked rover vehicle that his staff was building. It will roam across the surface of Titan and obtain more data about that world in a few weeks than all the scientists back on Earth have been able to amass in their lifetimes. Before the bright youngsters get there on their torch ships I'll already be getting data from Titan. And from the cloud deck of Saturn. And the ice rings.

Perhaps my life won't be a waste, after all, thought Edouard Urbain. Perhaps this time I'll hit the jackpot. Perhaps there is a Nobel prize waiting for me in the future, after all.

Perhaps, he even thought, Jeanne-Marie will return to me.

In the workshop where he and his team labored, Manny Gaeta was walking Kris Cardenas around his EVA suit. Von Helmholtz and his four technicians stood at the benches that ran along two walls of the chamber, watching their boss and the nanotech expert as they slowly paced around the heavy, bulky suit, like shoppers inspecting a new outfit built for Frankenstein's monster.

She had arrived at the lab carrying a small briefcase, which she had left on the floor by the door as soon as Gaeta came over to greet her. The technicians stayed well clear of it.

Now she and Gaeta stared up at the suit, looming head and shoulders above them, gleaming in the light from the ceiling lamps.

'It's big,' Cardenas murmured. With its helmet and jointed arms, it reminded her of a medieval suit of armor.

'It's gotta be big,' Gaeta said as they paced slowly around it. 'Lots of gear inside.'

'You've got room in there for a cafeteria,' she joked.

With a rueful grin, Gaeta answered, 'Nope. Just enough room inside for me to squeeze in. The rest is packed with sensors, cameras, VR transmitters, servomotors to move the arms and legs, radiation armor, life support systems—'

'Systems? Plural?'

'You bet. Redundant systems are the only way to go. One craps out, you can live on the other.'

Cardenas peered at the gleaming armor's bright finish. 'Is this cermet?'

'Partly,' said Gaeta. 'Lots of organometallics in it, too. And semiconductor surfaces, protected by borosilicates and buckyfilament shields.'

'How do you put it on?'

He walked her around to the suit's back. 'You climb in through the hatch.'

Cardenas broke into a laugh. 'Like the trapdoor in old-fashioned long johns!'

Gaeta tilted his head to one side. 'I never thought of it like that, but yeah, you're right. Kinda like that.'

Sobering up somewhat, Cardenas said, 'Could you show me how you get into it?'

'Sure. You want to go in? It's okay, I can help you.'

Cardenas shook her head. 'No. You get into it.' Nodding toward the briefcase she had left by the door, 'Then I can take samples of whatever residues you leave on the outside.'

'Samples?'

'If you want nanomachines specifically tailored to clean up your residues, I have to know exactly what they are, down to the molecular level.'

Gaeta nodded his understanding. 'Okay.' He called to von Helmholtz, 'Yo, Fritz, I gotta get inside.'

Von Helmholtz and the four techs started for the suit. The chief technician hesitated, though, and asked, 'Dr. Cardenas, will you need your case?'

'Yes, I will, thank you.'

He brought the briefcase to Cardenas while two of the technicians began unsealing the suit's hatch and the other two booted up the monitoring consoles standing along the far side of the lab.

'You plan to go outside when we pass Jupiter?' Cardenas asked Gaeta as von Helmholtz handed her the briefcase.

'Yep. We'll have a couple million VR viewers sharing the experience as we zip past Jupiter. Should be fun.'

'Flying past Jupiter as seen from outside. I'd like to experience that myself,' Cardenas said.

The technicians swung open the hatch in the back of the suit and

Gaeta stepped to it. Over his shoulder he told Cardenas, 'Sure, why not? Fritz can fix you up with a VR rig, can't you Fritz?'

'It would be an honor,' said von Helmholtz. Cardenas couldn't decide if he meant it or he was being snotty.

She watched as Gaeta hiked one leg up over the rim of the hatch, grabbed the sides with either hand, and then pulled his other leg in. His head disappeared into the darkness inside.

She heard a thud, then a string of muffled Spanish curses.

'It's pretty tight in there,' one of the technicians said, grinning at her.

Gaeta called, 'Okay, I'm set.' The techs closed the hatch and sealed it shut.

Walking around to the front of the suit, Cardenas had to crane her neck to see Gaeta's face through the heavily tinted visor of the helmet.

The right arm of the suit stirred into motion with a buzz and whirr of servomotors.

'Hello, Kris,' boomed Gaeta's voice, amplified powerfully, as he waved at her. 'Wanna dance?'

But she was already on one knee, opening the briefcase that carried her analysis tools, all business.

Jupiter Encounter Minus Two Days

The cafeteria was bustling and noisy with the clatter of silverware and a hundred buzzing conversations. Ilya Timoshenko ignored the lines of people waiting at the various counters, preferring to punch out his lunch selections from the automated dispensers. He had filled his tray with a McGlop sandwich and a bowl of steaming soup; now he stood before the drinks dispenser.

'Decisions, decisions.'

Timoshenko turned his head to see that it was Jaansen, one of the top engineers, standing next to him, tall and lean and pale as the winter sun.

Without a word, Timoshenko slid his plastic cup beneath the cola nozzle and leaned on the button. Then he walked away, looking for a table where he could be alone. As he unloaded his tray, though, Jaansen walked up to the table, carrying a salad and a glass of milk.

'Do you mind if I sit here?' Jaansen asked, already putting his sparse lunch on the table. 'I need to talk with you.'

Timoshenko said, 'About what?' Jaansen was one of the bosses, several rungs up the ladder above him.

'Politics,' said Jaansen as he pulled out his chair and sat down.

Suddenly Timoshenko had no appetite. He sat facing the pale Norseman. 'I have no interest in politics.'

'You did once. You were quite an activist.'

'And look where it's got me.'

Jaansen waved a hand vaguely. 'This isn't so bad, is it? If you have to be exiled, this is better than most places.'

Despite himself, Timoshenko asked, 'Were you exiled?'

'No, I chose to come here. For me, this is an opportunity to be in charge of a major engineering operation.'

'To be a boss, you mean.'

'You could be a boss, too,' Jaansen said. 'The biggest boss of all.'

Timoshenko scowled at him.

'I mean it, Ilya. You could run for the office of chief administrator, once the new constitution is put into effect.'

'You're joking.'

'I'm serious. You could run, and you could win. All the engineers and technicians would vote for you. That's a major bloc of votes.'

'Why would they vote for me?'

'Because you're one of us. Everybody knows you and respects you.'

Timoshenko grunted derisively. 'I have very few friends. Hardly anybody knows me, and those who do don't like me very much. I can't say that I blame them, either.'

Jaansen would not be put off. Pulling his palmcomp from his tunic pocket he began tapping out numbers as he spoke.

'Politics boils down to arithmetic,' he said, pecking away. 'You are much more respected by your fellow workers than you think. They'll vote for you in preference to Urbain, and—'

'Urbain? He'll be running for office?'

'Of course. He's head of the science department, isn't he? The scientists think they own this habitat. They think we're all here to serve them. Of course he'll run. And he'll win, unless you can rally the engineers and technicians.'

Timoshenko shook his head. 'I have no interest in politics,' he repeated. But he stayed and listened and looked at the numbers Jaansen was pecking out on his palmcomp.

Half an hour later, on the other side of the crowded, noisy cafeteria, Edouard Urbain was trying to finish his lunch and get back to his office. The cold potato soup was a poor imitation of vichyssoise. He hadn't had a decent meal since leaving Montreal. *Wilmot has no interest in cuisine, of course. Once I become chief administrator I will see to it that the cooks learn how to cook.*

There were a thousand things to do, construction of the roving vehicle was running into difficulties and the Jupiter encounter was almost upon them and this man Eberly wanted to draft a constitution for the habitat and make himself the chief administrator. Impossible! Urbain told himself as he sipped the unappetizing soup. This is a scientific mission, the entire purpose of this habitat is science. A scientist must head the government.

'Are you as excited as I am?'

Urbain jumped as if someone had poked him. Looking up, he saw the chief engineer, the Norseman Jaansen, smiling gently at him. Reluctantly, Urbain gestured him to the empty chair on the other side of his table.

'Excited?' he asked as Jaansen took the proffered chair.

'About the Jupiter fly-past.'

'Ah. Yes. I suppose I am,' Urbain muttered as he spooned up the last of the mediocre soup. Then he noticed that Jaansen was empty-handed. 'Aren't you having lunch?'

'I've already eaten,' said the engineer. 'I was on my way out when I saw you sitting alone.'

Urbain preferred to eat alone. But he said nothing and reached for his cup of tea. They served wine, of a sort, in the restaurants. The cafeteria did not.

Jaansen said, 'I can't think of anything but the fly-past. And the refueling procedure. I've checked everything associated with the procedure a dozen times, but still I can't help worrying that I've forgotten something.'

'That is why we create checklists,' Urbain said tartly.

Jaansen smiled. 'Yes, I know. But still . . .'

Urbain finished his tea. 'If you'll pardon me,' he said, starting to push his chair back from the table.

Jaansen touched his sleeve. 'Do you have a minute? There's something I'd like to discuss something with you.'

'I must get back at my lab.'

Jaansen nodded, his ice blue, pale-lashed eyes looking disappointed. 'I understand.'

Nettled, irritated at the pang of guilt he felt, Urbain conceded, 'A minute, you say?'

'Maybe two.'

'What is it?' Urbain asked. He leaned over to pull his tray from beneath the chair and began placing his dishes on it.

'I need your help. Your guidance.'

'About what?'

The engineer glanced around almost furtively before replying, 'You know that the chief of Human Resources is forming a committee to draft a new constitution for us.'

'Yes, so I have heard.'

'And once the constitution is put into effect, we will vote on a government.'

Urbain nodded as he asked himself, What is he driving at?

'I presume that you will head that government,' Jaansen said.

'Ah. Yes. I suppose I will.'

Looking quite earnest, Jaansen asked, 'Are you prepared to make such a sacrifice? It will be a heavy responsibility.'

Urbain began to reply, hesitated, then formed the words in his mind before answering, 'I have thought about this quite seriously. It is a serious responsibility, you are entirely correct there. But since this is a scientific endeavor, it must have a scientist at its head. As chief scientist, I really have no choice in the matter. I must accept the responsibility.'

'Assuming the people elect you,' said Jaansen.

'Of course they will elect me? Who else could they vote for?'

Jupiter Encounter Minus One Day

'And where will you be when we fly past Jupiter?' asked Don Diego.

Holly looked up from the raspberry bush she was planting along the embankment. 'In my office,' she said with a smile. 'I've got to get my work done sometime.'

The old man wiped his sweaty forehead with the back of a gloved hand. 'You don't consider what we are doing as work?'

'This is fun. I mean, it's physical labor, y'know. But it's fun. Besides, when I say "work" I mean the job I was hired to do.'

'You seem to spend part of each day here with me,' Don Diego said as he tugged at a stubborn coil of steel cable, half buried in the ground.

'I like being out here.' Holly realized that she enjoyed being outdoors, away from her office. She enjoyed working and talking with this older man, this serious yet light-hearted man who listened so well and had so much to teach her.

'Careful,' Holly warned as he strained to pull the stubborn cable out of the ground. 'That might be connected to something important.'

He shook his head. 'No, it is just some of the junk that the construction crews left behind. Instead of cleaning up the area as they were paid to do, they threw most of their leftovers down the embankment, figuring that no one would notice it.'

Holly went over to help him. Together they pulled the coiled length of cable free. Sure enough, it was connected to nothing. Just leftover trash from the habitat's construction.

'Maybe we ought to organize cleaning crews to go through all the culverts and embankments,' Holly thought aloud. 'We could prob'ly scavenge some useful materials.'

'I worry more about the effects on our health. Steel rusts, and the rust seeps into our drinking water supplies.'

'Everything's purified when the water's recycled,' Holly said.

He nodded warily. 'Still, I worry.'

Holly returned to the raspberry bush, tamped down the fresh-turned earth around it, then straightened up slowly, hands on the small of her back.

'That's enough for me,' she said, looking up at the long solar window. It was half in shade. 'Dinner time.'

'Will you allow me to make dinner for you at my hacienda?' Don Diego asked, pulling off his stained, soiled gloves.

Holly smiled. His hacienda was a one-bedroom apartment, she knew, just about the same size and layout as her own.

'Why don't I cook tonight?' she suggested.

He looked embarrassed for a moment, then said, 'You are a wonderful person in many ways, Holly, but I think I'm a better cook than you.'

'Will you teach me how to make chili?' she asked eagerly.

'Out of soymeat and pinto beans,' he replied. 'Of course. I will even show you how to prepare the beans so they do not cause gas.'

'Ain't I *ever* gonna get dinner?' Manny Gaeta complained. 'The cafeteria's probably closed by now.'

'Then it doesn't matter, does it,' retorted Fritz von Helmholtz.

Inside the armored suit, Gaeta was standing a good half-meter off the deck plates. He looked down at von Helmholtz through the heavily tinted visor of the helmet.

'*Cabrón*,' Gaeta muttered. Fritz can be a real pain in the ass sometimes, he thought.

Von Helmholtz looked up from his handheld and frowned at him. 'We have to do the vacuum test first.'

'It's damned hot in here. I'm sweating.'

'Turn up the cooling,' von Helmholtz said, unfazed.

'I don't wanna run down the batteries.'

'We can recharge them overnight.'

Gaeta knew he could stop the test by simply powering down the suit and popping the hatch. He'd been in the clunker for hours now, going through every procedure that they would need to record the Jupiter fly-by. Gaeta felt tired and sweaty and uncomfortable.

But Fritz was right, he knew. Check everything now. Make certain everything is working. Don't want any surprises when you're outside.

'Vacuum test, right,' he muttered, scanning the Christmas tree of monitoring lights set into the collar of the helmet. Everything in the green, except for two amber lights: a low battery and an air fan that was running slower than design nominal. Maybe that's why it's so damn' hot in here, he thought.

Fritz was over by the big monitoring console, studying the diagnostics screen. 'That fan will have to be replaced,' he said into the pin mike at his lips.

One of the technicians nodded glumly. 'There goes my dinner date,' he grumbled.

Straightening up and turning toward Gaeta, Fritz curled a beckoning finger. 'Come, my little sylph. To airlock number fourteen.'

Gaeta began to walk. The suit felt stiff, despite the servomotors that were slaved to his arms and legs. 'I feel like the Tin Woodman in here,' he told Fritz. 'Oil can! Oil can!'

Fritz did not smile one millimeter. 'The bearings are self-lubricating. As you exercise the suit, the joints will smooth out.'

'Yeah. Sure.'

Gaeta followed Fritz toward the wide double doors of the lab. One of the other techs opened them. Gaeta was surprised to see Holly Lane standing in the hallway outside. Her eyes went wide when she saw the suit clunking toward her.

He moved one arm slowly and flexed the fingers in a robotic wave. 'Hi, Holly,' he called.

'Manny? Is that you in there?'

'It's me.'

She hefted a small plastic bag. 'I brought you some chili. Homemade.'

Von Helmholtz said, 'We have no time for a meal at present. We are very busy.'

'Come on along, Holly,' Gaeta called. We're goin' down to airlock fourteen.' He resumed his plodding walk out into the hallway.

'You're going outside now?' Holly asked, scampering out of his way.

'Naw. The safety guys nixed my EVA. They got a whole crew out there to take on the fuel tanks comin' up from Jupiter. I'll just stay in the 'lock while they open it to the outside, keep out of their way. We'll vid the Jupiter pass tomorrow; that's when we'll be closest.'

'Can I watch?'

'Sure,' Gaeta said, enjoying the nervous tic in Fritz's right cheek. 'Come on along.'

Tanker *Graham*

'Hey, Tavalera, look sharp now, we're starting the rendezvous maneuver.'

Raoul Tavalera grumbled an obscenity under his breath. I know we're starting the frigging rendezvous maneuver, he answered the skipper silently. Why the fuck else are we out here?

The *Graham* was little more than a pair of powerful fusion engines and a habitation pod that housed its crew of two: the hard-assed skipper and Tavalera, who was counting the days until his obligatory Public Service duty was finished and he could return to his native New Jersey. Once he got back, he planned to kiss the ground and never, ever leave the surface of planet Earth again.

Cramped little *Graham* towed three enormous spheres full of the hydrogen and helium isotopes that fed fusion engines. They would soon be attached to the approaching habitat; once that task was finished, *Graham* and her two-person crew could return to the relative safety and dubious luxury of station *Gold,* in orbit around massive Jupiter.

The skipper was buckled into her command chair, her ugly, pasty face almost completely hidden beneath her sensor helmet. All Tavalera could see of her was her mean, lantern jaw and the cruddy coveralls that she'd been wearing ever since they had left the space station, four days ago.

When Tavalera had first come out to Jupiter he had been excited by the prospects of skimming the Jovian clouds. He pictured a daredevil operation, diving into the upper fringes of Jupiter's swirling clouds, scooping those isotopes out of the planet's incredibly deep atmosphere. Risky and exciting. And vitally necessary. Jovian fusion fuels fed civilization's electrical power generators and nuclear rockets all across the solar system, from Earth out to the asteroid belt and beyond.

Back then, Tavalera had envisioned an exhilarating life of thrilling missions into Jupiter's clouds and swarms of adoring chicks begging for his attention. The reality was boringly different. The screaming dives into the maelstrom of clouds were done by robot spacecraft, teleoperated from the safety of station *Gold*. Tavalera's only flight missions were routine ferrying jobs, transferring fuel tanks to ships from the Earth/Moon region or the Belt. And the women aboard the space station chose their men by rank, which meant that Tavalera – a mere grubby engineer doing his Public Service tour of duty – was quite low on the totem pole. Besides, he growled inwardly, most of the women were ugly, and the few pretty ones were likely to be dykes.

He began to count the missions, count the days and hours and minutes until he could be released and go home. This mission had been particularly dull, four frigging days towing three enormous fuel containers, plodding out to a rendezvous point to meet the approaching habitat, on its way to Saturn. Tavalera's own coveralls stunk with four days' accumulated crud. The skipper had tweaked him about it, asked him why he couldn't take a shower with his clothes on. Bitch! he thought.

Now all he had to do was sit tight and watch the control panel displays while the skipper maneuvered those three huge tanks to the approaching habitat. It had been a difficult mission; they'd used up most of *Graham*'s own fuel climbing up over Jupiter's north pole to get clear of the fifty-million-electron-volt synchrotron radiation that hugged the planet's equator. Then they had to maneuver farther from Jupiter than any of his earlier missions had been, a full twenty diameters upsun, outside the bowshock of the planet's enormous magnetosphere and its own fearsome radiation. Downsun the magnetosphere's tail stretched all the way out to Saturn's orbit.

The main display screen showed the habitat in a false-color infrared image. Tavalera looked up at the observation window and saw it dimly outlined in sunlight that glinted off its long, tubular body. To him it looked like a section of sewer pipe floating silently through empty space.

'Releasing tank number one,' said the skipper, mechanically.

Tavalera saw that the release light winked on, green. Cranking up the magnification on his screen, he watched a small army of technicians in spacesuits and one-man transfer flitters hovering at the far end of the habitat, waiting to grapple the spherical tank and attach it to the flying sewer pipe.

Tank one went smoothly, as did tank two.

Then the skipper said, 'Oh, oh.'

Tavalera's heart clutched in his chest. Trouble.

'Got a hangup on tank three,' she said calmly. 'You'll have to go outside and clear it.'

Tavalera had been dreading that possibility. He didn't mind flying through the dead vacuum of space inside a ship, even a gnat-sized one like *Graham*. But being out there in nothing more than a flimsy spacesuit – that was scary.

The skipper raised the sensor helmet off her face. 'Well, brightboy, didn't you hear me?' she snapped. 'Get into your suit! We've got to clear that hangup before that bugger of a habitat sails out of our range.'

We, Tavalera muttered to himself. She said 'we' have to clear the snag. But she means me. She's staying in here.

Reluctantly he unstrapped and pushed himself off his chair, floating to the rear of the module where the spacesuits were stored. It took only twenty minutes or so to get into the suit and connect all the lines, but from the way the skipper swore at him it seemed like hours. She came back to check him out, and did it so swiftly that Tavalera knew she couldn't have done it right. Then she shoved him toward the airlock.

'Get going, chump.'

Gaeta felt hungry, tired, sweaty and generally dismal as he waited for the technicians to open the airlock's inner hatch. Looking down on them from inside the armored suit, he wondered what was taking the *idiotas tarugas* so long to simply tap the right numbers on the airlock's wall-mounted keyboard.

147

Fritz pressed one hand to his earplug and muttered something into the pin mike at his lips.

'What's the holdup?' Gaeta demanded.

'Safety director,' said Fritz. 'They have a team of people EVA and they want to make certain they're nowhere near this airlock when we open it.'

'*Maldito*. I'm not going outside, I'm just going to stand in the open airlock. Haven't you told them that?'

'They know—' Fritz tilted his head and pressed at the earplug again. 'Say again?' He listened, nodded, then looked up at Gaeta. 'Five more minutes. Then we can cycle the airlock.'

'Five minutes,' Gaeta grumbled.

Holly stepped in front of him, looking almost like a little elf as she peered up toward the visor of his helmet.

'Is there any way I can get some of this chili to you?' she asked with a smile. 'You must be starved in there.'

He grinned back at her, wondering how much of his face she could see through the heavily-tinted visor. Silently he thanked her for her unwitting beneficence to him. Gaeta had tried for more than a year to hitch a ride on the Saturn-bound habitat. Then Wendell had called from the Astro corporate headquarters and in less than two weeks everything had been arranged. All he had to do was keep an eye on this skinny kid, which was no hardship at all. In fact, as Gaeta looked down on Holly, he realized that she wasn't skinny; she was slim, trim, and altogether pretty damned attractive. *Una guapa chiquita.*

'I'm starving, all right,' he said to Holly, 'but there's no way to open this tin can without ruining the test we want to make.'

She nodded, a little glumly.

Fritz abruptly waved her away from Gaeta as he said to the technicians, 'Open the inner hatch.'

'I thought you said five minutes,' Gaeta snapped, surprised.

As one of the techs tapped out the hatch's code, Fritz said tightly, 'Five minutes until we can open the outer hatch. We can get ready for that now. I haven't had any supper, either.'

Gaeta laughed as the heavy hatch popped slightly ajar. Two of the techs swung it all the way open. Massive though it was, his suit could only fit through the outsized airlock hatches designed to receive cargo. The suit was not built to bend at the waist or to flex in any way except at the arms and legs. Inside it, Gaeta felt as if he were driving an army tank.

He caught a glimpse of Holly standing to one side, watching intently, as he thumped across the coaming of the hatch and planted both his booted feet inside the airlock.

'Closing the inner hatch,' came Fritz's brittle voice in the ear-phones built into his helmet.

'Copy you're closing inner hatch,' Gaeta said.

They were all behind him now, outside his field of view. He could see the airlock's control panel on the bulkhead to his left, red and green displays. The light dimmed as the inner hatch closed and one of the red telltales flicked through amber to green. Gaeta was sealed alone inside the blank-walled chamber, like an oversized robot in a metal womb. He felt a need to urinate, but that always happened when he was nervous. It would go away. It better, he thought; we didn't bother to connect the relief tube.

'Pumping down,' said Fritz.

'Pump away,' he replied.

He couldn't hear the pumps that sucked the air out of the chamber; couldn't even feel their vibrations through the thick soles of the suit's boots. How many times have I been in this suit? Gaeta asked himself. The first time was the trek across Mare Imbrium. Then the Venus plunge. And skimming Jupiter. About ten, twelve test runs for each stunt. Close to fifty times. Feels like home, almost.

'Opening outer hatch in thirty seconds,' Fritz said.

'Open in thirty.'

'No foolishness, remember.'

Gaeta shook his head inside the helmet. The perfect worry-wart, Fritz was. 'I'll just stand here like a statue,' he promised. 'No tricks.'

'Ten . . . nine . . .'

Still, Gaeta thought, it would be fun to just step out and jet around a little. Maybe do a loop around the habitat. We've got to test the suit's propulsion unit sooner or later.

'Three . . . two . . .'

Fritz would shit a brick, Gaeta chuckled to himself.

'Zero.'

The outer hatch slid slowly open. At first Gaeta saw nothing but empty blackness, but then the polarization of his visor adjusted and the stars came into view. Thousands of stars. Millions of them. Hard little points of light spangling the emptiness out there like brilliant diamonds strewn across a black velvet backdrop. And off to one side slanted the gleaming river of the Milky Way, a sinuous path glowing across the sky, mysterious and beckoning.

Gaeta was not a religious man, but every time he saw the grandeur of the real world his eyes misted and he muttered the same hymn of praise: 'The earth is the Lord's and the fullness thereof, the world and those who dwell therein.'

Rendezvous Problem

Like a lobster crawling across the sea bottom, Tavalera inched weightlessly hand over hand along the rigid buckyfiber cable connecting *Graham* to the fuel pod. Once he reached the tank, he clambered slowly from one handhold to another across the huge metal sphere. As soon as he reached the balky connector, he snapped a tether to the nearest clamp built into the tank's curving surface. It frightened him to work in empty space without a safety line, but the suit tethers were too short to span the distance between *Graham's* airlock and the jammed connector on the fuel tank. Once safely connected, he leaned forward as far as he could in the spacesuit, trying to play his helmet light on the connector that refused to unlock.

Every time he had to do an EVA he expected to feel cold, numbed by the frigid vacuum of deep space. And every time he was surprised that he got so hot inside the suit. Five minutes out here and I'm boiling like a guy in a soup pot, he grumbled to himself. He blinked perspiration out of his eyes and cursed himself for forgetting to wear a sweat band.

'Well?' The skipper's voice sounded nastier than usual in his helmet earphones.

'I'm trying to see what the hangup is,' Tavalera said. 'Gimme a couple minutes.'

'Put the camera on it, let me take a look.'

I'd like to shove the camera up your skinny ass, Tavalera growled silently. He dutifully unhooked the minicam from his equipment belt and clicked it into its slot on the left shoulder of his suit. Its light added to the light of his helmet lamp.

Shaking his head, Tavalera said, 'I can't see why it won't unlock. Everything looks normal to me.'

The skipper muttered something too low for him to make out. Then she said, 'Check the receiver.'

Tavalera instead checked his tether. He had no intention of drifting off the fuel tank and wafting off into interplanetary space. Sure, there were plenty of people from the habitat outside, but how could he be certain they'd be able to grab him? Or even try to?

'Well?' Even testier than before.

'I'm workin' on it,' he grumbled.

The receiver checked out: its battery was almost fully charged and it was receiving the command signal from the ship.

'Must be a mechanical problem,' Tavalera said.

'Try the override.'

'That won't do any good if the problem's mechanical.'

'Try the override,' the skipper repeated.

Huffing impatiently, wondering how much radiation he was absorbing by the second, Tavalera punched out the override commands on the receiver's miniature keypad, not an easy thing to accomplish in a spacesuit's gloves.

'No joy,' he reported.

'I can see that,' said the skipper. 'It must be mechanical.'

'Right.' That's what I told you, fartbrain, he added silently.

'If we don't get it loose in fourteen minutes we're going to miss the rendezvous. The habitat will be too far away from us.'

And then we can go home, Tavalera thought. Let somebody else fly the frigging fuel tank out to those dipshits. Who the hell told them to go out to Saturn in the first place?

'You'll have to disconnect it manually,' the skipper said.

'Great.'

'Get to it!'

There was no way to open the metal latch with his hands, he saw. It was made of heavy asteroidal aluminum, thick and sturdy, designed to stay closed until it received the proper electronic command. If it opened easily it could release the tank prematurely, or even cause a collision.

'Cut it off,' said the skipper. 'Use the laser.'

Tavalera looked up at the *Graham,* hanging a hundred meters or so away from the spherical tank. To him, it looked more like a thousand kilometers. Through the transparent bubble of the crew module he could see the skipper sitting in her command chair, although he couldn't make out the features of her face. Just as well, he thought. She makes a hatchet look lovable.

'Come on,' the skipper urged, 'the clock's ticking.'

He pulled the hand laser from his equipment belt, wondering if it was powerful enough to saw through the aluminum latch. Probably drain my suit batteries and I'll asphyxiate out here. A lot she cares.

'Move it!'

'I'm movin' it,' he yelled back, clicking the safety off the laser and holding its stubby snout a bare centimeter from the obstinate latch.

Grimacing, he pressed the firing stud. Harsh bright sparks leaped from the stubborn latch.

Gaeta stood in the airlock, looking out at the universe, resisting the urge to go sailing out there.

'All systems in the green,' Fritz told him. 'Four more minutes until termination of the test.'

Four minutes, Gaeta thought. I bet I could swoop all the way around the habitat in four minutes.

As he looked out, though, he saw two huge spherical tanks swing into view, and several spacesuited figures clambering on them. The fuel tanks, he realized. Better not get snarled up with those guys. Men at work. And women.

Jupiter came into view as the habitat rotated, a distant fat sphere streaked with faint colors, flattened at the poles like a beach ball that some kid was sitting on. And then another sphere, farther away than the others. Or maybe just smaller.

Another fuel tank? Gaeta remembered somebody saying there were three of them. A small spacecraft hovered near the tank. Probably the ferry ship, he thought. Then he saw sparks flashing from the tank. What the hell are they doing to it?

'Three minutes,' came Fritz's flat voice. He sounded bored.

Gaeta grinned. I've got enough juice in the propulsion tank to jet all the way around this sewer pipe, he told himself. Fritz wouldn't be bored then!

'What are you laughing about?'

Gaeta realized he must have chuckled and Fritz picked it up. 'Laughing? Who, me?'

Fritz replied, 'No, the Man in the Moon. What were you laughing about?'

'Nothing,' Gaeta said, still thinking what fun it would be to take off and do a spin around the habitat.

'Well?' the skipper demanded, testier than ever.

Tavalera clicked off the laser and peered at the latch. The beam had cut halfway through it.

'Gimme another couple minutes,' he said.

'Get with it, then. Our window closes in less than ten minutes.'

Nodding inside his fishbowl helmet, Tavalera turned on the laser again. Sparks flashed blindingly.

'What's the holdup?' demanded a new voice in his earphones.

Probably the boss of the habitat crew waiting for the third fuel tank, Tavalera realized.

'We have a malfunction on the tank's release mechanism,' the skipper answered. 'We're on it. We'll have it on its way to you in a matter of minutes,' Her tone was a half-million times sweeter than when she spoke to Tavalera, he thought.

'The attachment point is rotating out of position,' came the other voice, male, deep, irritated. 'And my crew is running out of time. We weren't scheduled to be out here this long.'

'I'll adjust the capture angle,' the skipper said, a little tenser. 'It should be no problem.'

'Time's burning.'

'Yes, yes, just be a little patient. We're working it.'

We, Tavalera grumbled silently.

'Tavalera,' the skipper yelled at him loudly enough to make him wince. 'Get it done!'

'It's almost there,' he said, angling his shoulder so she could see that the latch was nearly burned through.

Then the laser winked out.

'What's happening?' she bellowed.

'Dunno,' Tavalera muttered, shaking the stupid little gun. 'Capacitor needs to recycle, I think.'

'Bend it back!'

'Huh?'

'The latch, you stupid slug! It's almost sawn through. Bend it back with your hands! *Now!*'

Without thinking, Tavalera let the laser float off on its tether and grabbed the metal latch with both gloved hands. It wouldn't budge.

'Break it off!' the skipper screamed at him. 'Get it!'

Desperate, Tavalera grabbed the laser with one hand while he still gripped the latch with the other. Maybe the capacitor's got one more squirt, he thought, pulling the trigger.

It all happened so suddenly that he had no chance to stop it. The laser fired a set of picosecond pulses and the latch came loose in Tavalera's hand, throwing him badly off balance. He went sprawling and dropped the laser, which went spinning out to the end of its tether, then snapped back toward Tavalera and fired off another set of pulses that hit the leg of his suit.

He screamed in sudden pain as the fuel tank jerked loose of its connection with *Graham* and began drifting out into space.

'It's heading away from us!' the habitat's crew chief roared.

'I can't stop it,' the skipper yelled back.

Tavalera didn't care. The pain searing through his leg was enough to make him giddy, almost delirious. He knew he was going to die, the only question in his mind was whether it would be from loss of blood or from asphyxiation as the air leaked out of his suit.

Rescue

With nothing else to do but stand in the airlock and wait for Fritz to tell him the test was finished, Gaeta tapped at the keypad on the wrist of his suit to listen in on the chatter from the crew that was attaching the fuel pods to the habitat. Something was obviously wrong with the third tank, it was still out by the ferry ship and somebody was using a welding laser on it. More likely the laser was cutting, not welding, Gaeta thought.

'. . . stupid piece of crap,' he heard a woman's sharp-edged voice, 'how the hell did you puncture your suit?'

'I need help!' came another voice, scared. 'I'm bleeding.'

Bleeding? Gaeta wondered. Punctured suit?

Then a third voice, male, angry and aggravated, 'The tank's off course! We can't reach it!'

'There's nothing I can do,' the woman whined. 'He knocked it out of line.'

'Help me.' The bleeder's voice.

'We can't fucking reach you!' the angry male bellowed. 'You're going off in the wrong direction and you're already too far for us to get to you.'

'I'm dying . . .'

'It's your own stupid fault,' the woman screeched.

Switching back to his intercom frequency, Gaeta said into his helmet microphone, 'Turn on all the cameras, Fritz.'

'What? What do you mean?'

'Turn on all the cameras, dammit!' Gaeta snapped, launching himself out of the airlock. To himself he added silently, This looks like a job for Superman.

The suit's propulsion jets ignited smoothly and Gaeta felt

156

himself hurtling toward the errant fuel pod in the utter silence of empty space. But his earphones were far from silent.

'Come back!' Fritz yelled. 'You can't—'

Gaeta simply turned off the intercom frequency and tapped into the others' frantic chatter.

'. . . not a damned frigging thing we can do,' the crew chief was yammering.

'He'll die out there!' the woman pleaded.

Nothing from the guy who was hurt.

'Hang on,' Gaeta said into his mike. 'I'll get him.'

'Who the hell is that?'

'Manuel Gaeta,' he told them. 'I'm on my way to the injured man. Can you see me?'

'Yes!' said the crew chief and the woman simultaneously.

The fuel pod was getting bigger. Jesoo, Gaeta realized, it's huge! Despite everything, he laughed. *Huevos tremendos.*

'What's his name?' Gaeta asked as he rocketed toward the fuel tank.

'What?'

'Who said that?'

'His name, the guy who's hurt. What's his name?'

'Tavalera,' the woman replied. 'Raoul Tavalera.'

A chicano, Gaeta thought. He called, 'Hey Raoul, *habla Español?*'

No answer.

'Raoul!' Gaeta shouted. 'Raoul Tavalera! You there? You okay?'

'I'm . . . here.' His voice sounded very weak. 'Not for long, though.'

'Hang in there, man,' Gaeta said. The fuel tank was blotting out most of his vision now, a tremendous curving world of metal rushing up to meet him. 'Your suit's prob'ly sealed itself, maybe cut off the bleeding, too.'

Nothing.

'Where you hurt, man?' Gaeta asked as he slowed his approach and got ready to touch down on the massive sphere.

'Leg . . .'

'Ah, that's not so bad. You'll be okay.'

'Hey, Gay-etta or whatever your name is,' the crew chief interrupted. 'I'm bringing my gang in to replenish their air and break out a couple more flitters so we can capture that tank.'

'What about Tavalera?' the woman snapped.

Gaeta was drifting around the tank's curving surface now, looking for the injured man. 'I see him!' he shouted. 'I'll take care of him.'

Tavalera was floating a few meters off the surface of the tank, held by his tether. Gaeta could see that his left leg was dotted by three little burn holes. The hard-shell suit appeared otherwise undamaged; the emergency cuff must have sealed off the leg the way it was designed to do.

Gaeta unhooked Tavalera's tether and clicked it to his own armored suit. Then he started back for the habitat's airlock with the injured astronaut in his arms.

'You awake, man?' he asked Tavalera, rapping on his fishbowl helmet.

Tavalera opened his eyes. Groggily, he asked, 'Who the hell are you?'

Gaeta grinned. 'Your guardian angel, man. I'm your frickin' guardian angel.'

Holly watched the whole thing on Fritz's portable display monitor. Standing with the other technicians, she saw Gaeta sail back into the airlock, carrying the limp astronaut in the powerful arms of his armored suit.

He saved him, Holly thought, her heart racing. He's saved that man's life.

While the technicians cycled the airlock Holly rushed to the wallphone by the inner hatch and called for emergency medical services. Surprise showed clearly on the medic's face, even in the palm-sized screen of the wallphone, but he promised to have a team at the airlock in less than five minutes.

The inner hatch sighed open and Gaeta clumped through, still holding the injured, spacesuited man.

'Did you get it all down?' Gaeta asked, his voice booming through the suit's amplifier. 'Cameras all on?'

'Yes, yes,' said Fritz, sounding annoyed. 'You will be on all the news nets, never fear.'

Three medics in white coveralls came pounding down the corridor to the airlock, trailed by a powered gurney and a crash wagon. They quickly got the injured man's helmet off, slapped an oxygen mask over his face, pulled the suit torso off him and jabbed a hypo into his arm. Then they whisked him off toward the infirmary in the village.

Holly turned back to Gaeta, still in his massive suit.

'You saved his life,' she said, looking up at him. She could barely make out his face through the heavily-tinted visor.

'He generated good publicity,' said Fritz, a little sharply.

Holly countered, 'He risked his own life to save a man in danger.'

With an almost exasperated sigh, Fritz said, 'He risked his life, yes. He also risked the suit, which is worth several hundred millions.' Glancing up at Gaeta he added, 'We can always find another daredevil; replacing the suit would not be so easy. Or cheap.'

Gaeta laughed; it sounded like thunder echoing off the corridor's metal walls. 'C'mon, Fritz, let's get back to the shop so I can get out of this tin can.'

Holly walked beside Gaeta, still clutching her container of chili in one hand. It was ice cold now, she knew. Gaeta plodded down the corridor like a ponderous robot in a bad vid, with Fritz on his other side. The technicians trailed along behind.

At last they reached the workshop and the technicians unsealed the hatch at the suit's rear. Gaeta crawled out, stood up and stretched his arms over his head languidly. Holly heard vertebrae pop.

'Damn, that feels good,' he said, smiling.

She stepped closer to him and saw that his clothes were drenched with perspiration. He smelled like old sweat socks.

Gaeta caught her hesitant expression. 'Guess I oughtta shower, huh?'

Fritz was still unhappy with him. 'An extravehicular excursion was not planned. You shouldn't have done it. What if the propulsion unit had failed? It hasn't been properly tested for flight activity.'

Gaeta grinned at him. 'Fritz, everything worked fine. Don't be such a gloomy *fregado*. Besides, I couldn't leave the guy out there, he might have died.'

'Still, you had no right to—'

'Can it, Fritz. It's over and no damage was done to the precious suit.' To Holly he said, 'Wait there just a couple mins, kid. I gotta get outta these clothes and hit the shower.'

He ambled to the lavatory off at the workshop's rear, whistling tunelessly. Holly watched the techs clambering over the suit, checking all its systems and shutting them down, one by one.

Gaeta came back, his hair glistening and slicked back, wearing a fresh set of coveralls.

'Now, where do we eat?' he asked. 'I'm starving.'

Fritz glanced at his wristwatch. 'The restaurants are all closed by now. We'll have to eat in our quarters.'

Holly held up her plastic container. 'I've got some chili, but it's got to be reheated.'

'Chili! Great!' said Gaeta.

Glancing at Fritz and the other techs, Holly said, 'There isn't enough for all of us.'

Gaeta took her by the arm and started for the lab's door. 'There's enough for us two, right? These other clowns can get their own suppers.'

Holly let him lead her out into the corridor without a glance back at the others. But in her mind she was saying, Malcolm'll have to notice this!

Charles Nicholas was a chubby, chinless little man who had learned to wear clothes so that he somehow managed to look dapper even in a plain sports shirt and comfortable slacks. As the senior man on duty at the communications office that evening, he had watched Gaeta's heroics in fascination.

His assistant, Elinor, happened to be his wife. She was slightly taller than him, much slimmer, and wore clothes even better than he did. They always tried to have their working shifts together. They spent every waking moment together and, of course, slept in the same bed. Yet, while Charles was openly admiring of Gaeta's feat in rescuing the injured astronaut, Elinor was somewhat dubious.

'They might have staged the whole thing,' she said to her husband in her squeaky, strangely sexy voice.

Charles was rerunning the vid. 'Staged it? How could they stage it? It was an accident. That kid could've died.'

'They could have set it up weeks in advance. For the publicity.'

'Nobody was watching except us and the EVA crew.'

'But they got it all on a chip, didn't they? They'll want to beam it to the nets, back Earthside.'

Charles shook his head. 'They'll have to get permission for that. They'll have to ask Vyborg; he's in charge of news releases.'

'He'll okay it,' said Elinor. 'All they have to do is ask him. He *likes* publicity.'

'Professor Wilmot doesn't.'

'So they won't ask Wilmot. They'll ask Vyborg and he'll okay it without bucking it upstairs.'

'You think so?'

'Bet you five credits,' Elinor replied.

Charles said nothing, thinking that Elinor was probably right. She usually was. Sure enough, a call came through from somebody named Von Helmholtz, who identified himself as Gaeta's chief technician, asking permission to beam their vid of the rescue to the news nets on Earth and Selene. Charles routed the request to Vyborg's private line. In less than ten minutes Vyborg called back, gladly granting permission.

'You owe me five,' Elinor said, grinning evily at Charles.

'I never bet,' he said.

'Makes no difference,' she said loftily. 'It's a moral victory for me.'

He tried to change the subject. 'Have you made up your mind about what we should call our village?'

'Something better than Village C,' she said.

'I think we should name it after some great figure from literature. Cervantes, maybe. Or Shakespeare.'

'You know they both died the same year?'

'No.'

'Yes; 1616. You can look it up.'

'I don't believe it.'

'Bet five?'

'That I *will* bet on,' Charles said, sticking out his hand.

They shook on it, Elinor thinking, We're married more than ten years and he still doesn't realize that I only bet on sure things. She smiled kindly at her husband. It's one of the things that I love about him.

Holly and Gaeta were walking slowly along the gently climbing path that led toward her apartment building. It was well past midnight; the habitat was in its night-time mode. The solar windows were closed and everything was dark except for the small lights set atop slim poles along the edges of the path, and the windows of some of the living quarters up ahead.

'Look up at the stars,' Gaeta said, stopping in the middle of the path.

'They're not stars,' said Holly, 'they're lights from the land up there.'

'Those over there look like the petals of a flower to me,' he said, pointing overhead. 'I think I'll call it the Flower constellation.'

She giggled. 'They're just lights, Manny. See, those meandering ones over there,' she pointed too, 'those are the bike paths between the food factory and Village C. And the village itself—'

'Looks like a giant squid, doesn't it? See, there's the body and there's the tentacles stretching out.'

She was standing so close to him in the darkness that she could feel the heat of his body.

'And what's that one?' she asked, pointing up at the neat rows of lights marking one of the orchards.

'Let's see now,' he muttered. 'How about the Tic-Tac-Toe constellation?'

They laughed together and then she was in his arms and he kissed her. Jeeps, Holly thought, what am I getting into?

'He brought the man here?' Eberly asked.

Eberly was standing at his kitchen sink, a bowl of breakfast cereal in his hands. Kananga had barged in without warning, simply one sharp rap on the apartment's door and he had entered without being invited. Eberly was certain he had locked the door before retiring for the night. How did Kananga get it open? The man had been a police official back on Earth, Eberly remembered. He must be quite accustomed to getting past locked doors and entering someone's home without asking.

Kananga nodded somberly. 'He's in the hospital. Apparently the wounds on his leg were not too serious. The laser cauterized as it penetrated the flesh, so there was very little bleeding. He suffered mostly from shock.'

'How long must he remain in hospital?' Eberly asked, absently pouring flakes into a plastic bowl. 'We ought to send him back to the Jupiter station as soon as possible.'

'It's already too late for that,' said Kananga, standing on the other side of the counter that served as a partition between the kitchen and sitting room. 'We've moved too far from Jupiter for them to send a spacecraft to pick him up. It would take a special torch ship flight, and the station staff are unwilling to send for one to fetch him.'

'You mean we're stuck with this man?'

Kananga nodded again. 'The medical people have him under quarantine until they can establish that he's not carrying anything harmful in his bloodstream.'

'But he can't stay here! This habitat isn't a shelter for the homeless!'

'Do you want me to push him out an airlock?'

Eberly stared at the colonel. His question was obviously meant to be humorous, but there was no trace of a smile on his dark, utterly serious face.

'Don't be funny,' Eberly said.

'Then he's here to stay. He doesn't know it yet, by the way. Someone will have to break the news to him. He probably won't like it.'

Eberly put his cereal bowl down on the kitchen counter and came around to the sitting room.

'I'll get Holly to tell him. Or perhaps Morgenthau, she's the acting head of the human resources department. They'll have to make room for him somewhere in the habitat's population.'

'He won't like it,' Kananga repeated. 'He was due to return to Earth in a few weeks.'

'He's here to stay, unless he can afford a torch ship to pick him up.'

'He'll expect us to do that.'

With a shake of his head, Eberly said, 'There's no provision in our budget for that. Wilmot wouldn't spend the money. He couldn't. There isn't any money to spend.'

'Perhaps one of the news services,' Kananga suggested. 'The rescue made quite a sensation on the nets this morning.'

'Perhaps. I'll ask Vyborg to look into that possibility.' Eberly hesitated, rubbing his chin thoughtfully. 'On the other hand, perhaps we can use all this to our advantage.'

'How?'

'I don't know . . . yet. But there should be some way to turn this to our advantage. After all, we have a genuine hero in our midst, this stuntman, Gaeta.'

'He's an outsider. He'll be returning to Earth after he's performed his exploit.'

'Returning to Earth? Someone will send a ship for him?'

Kananga looked surprised at the idea. 'I hadn't thought about it. Perhaps he can take the refugee back with him.'

'Perhaps. But in the meantime, we should work out a way to use him. Use them both, perhaps.'

Kananga asked again, 'How?'

'Heroes are always valuable,' Eberly replied, 'if they can be manipulated. I'll have to think of a way to bring Gaeta into our camp.'

Kananga shrugged. 'At least we have one consolation.'

Eberly looked at him sharply. 'What's that?'

'It won't happen again. We won't take any more refugees aboard. The Jupiter station was the last human outpost. There's no one out this far except us.'

With that, he turned and left the apartment. Eberly realized he was right. The habitat was sailing now farther than any humans had ever gone before. Beyond the frontier, into the unknown.

Frowning, Eberly tried his front door. It was securely locked. Yet Kananga had entered and left as if it had been wide open.

Departure Plus 425 Days

Holly awoke slowly, remembering what seemed to be a dream. But it really happened, she knew. It really happened.

Manny was gone, of course. He had left her after they had made love, right here in her bed, left her drowsy and languid and warm with the touch of his hands, his lips, his body pressed against hers.

She smiled up at the ceiling. Then she giggled. I'll have to tell Don Diego what terrific chili he made. A love potion.

A glance at the digital clock on her night table told her that she ought to get up, shower and dress and get to the office. Yet she lay back on the rumpled, sweaty sheets, remembering.

But a sudden thought snapped her out of her reverie. Malcolm! What if he finds out? I just wanted to make him jealous, make him notice me. This'll make him hate me!

The phone buzzed.

'No video,' Holly said sharply. 'Answer.'

Malcolm's face appeared floating above the foot of her bed. He knows! she screamed silently. He's found out! Holly jerked up to a sitting position, clutching the sheet to her despite knowing that Eberly could not see her, waves of guilt washing over her, drowning every other emotion.

'Holly, are you there?' Eberly asked, squinting slightly, as if that would make her image appear in his apartment.

'Yes, Malcolm,' she said, straining to keep her voice level. 'I . . . I'm running a little late this morning.'

'About this man that Gaeta brought aboard the habitat last evening,' Eberly said, ignoring the tremble in her voice. 'He's going to stay aboard the habitat unless someone wants to send a ship out to fetch him.'

He doesn't know! she thought, so relieved that she nearly sagged back on the pillows. To Eberly's image she managed to utter:

'Yes?'

'I want you to interview him as soon as the medics lift his quarantine. We need a complete dossier on him.'

He doesn't know, she repeated to herself. It's all right. He doesn't know. 'I see. Of course.'

'Good. Get on it right away.'

Holly's mind began working again. 'Have you told Morgenthau about this?' Holly asked.

His brows knit slightly. 'I'm telling you.'

She nodded. 'Kay. Right. I'll inform her. She wants to be kept informed, y'know.'

'You take care of it,' he said, almost crossly.

'Kay. I'll do it.'

At last he seemed to catch the reluctance in her voice. 'Holly, would you rather I speak to Morgenthau?'

Her heart fluttered. 'Oh, Malcolm, I don't want to bother you with that.' But silently she was rejoicing, He cares! He really cares about me!

'I'll call her right now,' he said, smiling at her. 'By the time you get to the office, she'll know all about this.'

'Thank you, Malcolm!'

'It's nothing,' he said. Then he cut the connection and the screen went dark.

Leaving Holly sitting in her bed, suddenly wretched that she had made love with another man, and terrified that Malcolm might find out.

When Ruth Morgenthau arrived at her office that morning, she found Sammi Vyborg already sitting in front of her desk, waiting for her.

'I thought you'd be watching the Jupiter fly-past,' she said, sweeping around her desk and settling heavily in its padded chair.

Vyborg hunched forward in his chair. 'That stuntman's heroics have made the fly-past seem tame, by comparison. Every network is carrying the video.'

'So?' Morgenthau asked. 'Then why are you here? If it's about the refugee,' she said airily, 'I've already spoken with Eberly about it. He wants Holly to—'

'It's not about the refugee,' Vyborg snapped.

She looked at him carefully. His narrow death's head of a face was even grimmer than usual, tense with repressed anger.

'What is, then?'

'Eberly promised to make me head of the communications department. But he's done nothing to make that happen.'

Morgenthau temporized, 'That sort of thing takes time, Sammi. You know that. You must be patient.'

'He hasn't lifted a finger,' Vyborg insisted.

'Patience, Sammi. Patience.'

Strangely, Vyborg smiled. To Morgenthau it looked like the smile of a rattlesnake gliding toward its victim.

'I once saw a cartoon,' he said slowly, 'that showed two vultures sitting in the branches of a dead tree. One of them was saying to the other, "Patience, my ass! I'm going to *kill* somebody."'

Morgenthau felt her cheeks flush at Vyborg's crude language. 'And just who do you intend to kill?'

'The two people who stand between me and the top of the communications department, of course.'

'I wouldn't advise—'

'Neither one of them is a Believer. The department head is a Jew, not that he observes his own religion. The other one is a super-annuated old Mexican who spends more time gardening than he does at his desk. He should be easy to dispose of.'

'You mustn't do anything without getting Eberly's approval first.'

'Don't play games with me. We both know that Eberly is nothing more than a figurehead. You're the real authority here.'

'Don't underestimate Eberly. He can win over people. He can mesmerize crowds. I don't want you to act precipitously.'

'Yes, yes. But I believe the old adage that the Lord helps those who help themselves. I'm finished waiting. The time for action has come.'

Morgenthau pursed her lips disapprovingly. But she said nothing.

Showered, combed and dressed, Holly phoned Morgenthau before leaving her apartment.

'Dr. Eberly wants me to interview the newcomer,' she said to Morgenthau's fleshy image. 'I've checked with the medical department and they're lifting his quarantine this morning, so I'm planning to go straight there instead of to the office.'

Holly spoke the words as a declaration, not a question, not a request for permission. Eberly's name was all the permission she needed.

Morgenthau seemed to feel the same way. 'Eberly called me earlier and told me about it. But thanks for informing me, Holly. I'll see you in the office when you return from the hospital.'

Raoul Tavalera was sitting in the hospital's tiny solarium, a glassed-in bubble on the hospital's roof. Even though it was mid-morning and sunlight streamed through the habitat's solar windows, to Holly it looked like a slightly overcast day; the sunlight seemed weak, as though filtered through a layer of thin clouds. We're more than five times farther from the Sun that the Earth is, she realized. Naturally the sunlight is weaker.

Tavalera was dressed in ill-fitting gray coveralls, his long, horsy face looking glum, almost sullen. He did not get up from his chair when Holly walked over to him and introduced herself. She wore a crisply tailored dusky rose blouse over dark gray slacks: office garb.

'I'm from the human resources department,' Holly explained, once she had pulled up a chair to sit next to Tavalera. He did not move a muscle to help her. She made a smile for him and went on, 'I'm here to get your complete life story.'

He did not smile back. 'Is it true? I'm stuck here for a friggin' year or more?'

'Unless someone sends a ship to pick you up, yes, I'm afraid you're going to be with us all the way out to Saturn.'

'Who the fuck would send a ship out for me?' he muttered. 'I'm just a turd engineer, friggin' slave labor, that's all I am.'

Holly took a breath. 'Mr. Tavalera, I'm no saint, but I'd appreciate it if you notched up your language a little.'

He gave her a sidelong glance. 'A Believer?'

'Not really. I'm not a church-goer.'

'The frig— uh, I mean, it was the New Morality that sent me out here in the first place. I hadda do two years of public service. No choice.'

'I see.'

'Do ya? I only had a couple more weeks to go and they would've brought me back home. Now I'm goin' out to fri— to Saturn for chrissakes.'

Gesturing toward the rooftop view of the village and the habitat's lovely green landscape, Holly said, 'There are worse places, y'know. You might actually like it here.'

'I got family on Earth. Friends. I was gonna get my life back together . . .' His voice trailed off. Holly could see that he was struggling to keep from flying off into a rage.

'You can send them messages. We can find useful work for you to do. You'll enjoy living here, betcha.'

Tavalera glowered at her.

'I know it must seem like a bugging disaster to you,' said Holly as reasonably as she could, 'but you're here and you should try to make the best of it.'

'Easy for you to say,' Tavalera muttered.

'We'll do you everything we can to help you while you're here.'

'We?'

'The people here in the habitat. The human resources department.'

'Does that include you?'

Nodding, Holly replied, 'I'm with the human resources department, yes.'

Tavalera seemed to brigthen a little. But only a little.

Eberly paced leisurely along the path that wound around the perimeter of the lake, Morgenthau at his side.

'It's good to be out in the open air,' he was saying. 'Away from prying eyes and snooping ears.'

'They're spying on you?' Morgenthau asked. She knew how simple it was to spray molecule-thin microphones on a wall or ceiling. Cameras no bigger than a teardrop could be inserted almost anywhere.

'Probably not. Wilmot's too naïve even to understand what we're doing. But it's best to be prepared against all possibilities, don't you think?'

'We have a problem with Vyborg,' she said, as if making an announcement.

'He's impatient, I know.'

Morgenthau said, 'He's more than impatient. He's going to do something violent.'

'Violent?' Eberly felt a pang of alarm in his guts. 'What do you mean?'

Morgenthau replied calmly, 'He's not willing to wait for you to remove the two men above him in the communications department. He's ready to strike against them.'

Fighting against the fear rising within him, Eberly snarled, 'The little snake! He'll ruin everything.' Inwardly he asked himself, How can I stop him? How can I prevent him without seeming weak, indecisive? I want their loyalty, but if I try to thwart them, prevent them from acting, they'll go ahead without me. And then where will I be? When we get to Saturn they'll send me back to Earth. Back to prison!

'He's going to resort to violence, I tell you,' Morgenthau insisted.

It took an effort of will for Eberly to keep from wringing his hands. 'What can I do? How can I stop him?'

Morgenthau smiled knowingly. 'Don't stop him.'

'What?'

'Let him take action. Just make certain that whatever he does can't be traced back to us.'

Eberly stared at her, trying to understand what she was saying. Still walking along as if on a casual stroll, Morgenthau explained, 'We want Vyborg to take command of the communications department. If he's ready to take a step in that direction, why stop him?'

'What if he commits a crime? What if he's discovered, caught, arrested?'

'That's why we must have no connection with him, not until after he's succeeded.'

'But if he fails . . .'

'If he succeeds, he's one step closer to our goal. If he fails, we can honestly say we had nothing to do with it.'

'Suppose he fails,' Eberly questioned, 'and he's caught, and he blames me?'

'You can show clean hands and a pure heart,' Morgenthau replied sweetly. 'With your powers of persuasion, I'm sure you can make Wilmot and the whole population believe that you've been falsely accused. Because that will be the truth.'

Eberly walked on in silence, with Morgenthau keeping pace beside him. She *wants* Vyborg to act. Even if he commits murder, she's in favor of his acting. Why? he asked himself. And the answer came immediately: Because that will give her a stronger hold on Vyborg. And a stronger hold on me. She's allowing me to be the public figurehead because I can organize people and sway them to our side. But she's the power behind the throne. She's the real power here.

Interfaith Chapel

With ten thousand souls in the habitat and only one small chapel for them to worship in, you would think this house of God would be filled to overflowing every hour of the day and night, thought Ruth Morgenthau as she sank to her knees in the first pew. But no, it's empty except for me.

Cold anger filled her. Ten thousand people and not one of them loves God enough to kneel here in prayer. Only me. I'm the only one here.

Not so, came a stern voice from within her. God is here. Bow your head in prayer. Acknowledge your sins and beg your Maker for forgiveness.

Morgenthau prayed.

She had found God – or, rather, God had found her – when she had been a skinny fourteen-year-old prostitute in the filth-littered back streets of Nuremberg, speeding toward an early death from malnutrition, disease, and drug abuse. The Holy Disciples rescued her, healed her body and cleansed her soul.

Yet the hunger remained. She realized, in time, that the hunger was the devil's work, the insidious, inescapable hunger that would pull her down to eternal damnation unless she dedicated her every waking moment to the service of God. She prayed for relief, for the strength to overcome its constant searing need. Often she prayed for death, for she thought that only death would end the torture of her soul. She denied herself the companionship of women, slept alone in a bare monk's cell, to keep from temptation, to stave off the yearning hunger.

And then she found the substitute, the permissible passion that sublimated her forbidden hunger. Power. By working with men, by spending virtually every waking moment surrounded by the men she loathed and feared, eventually she learned to play their games of power. She deliberately allowed her body to bloat, to become unattractive physically. But she honed her mind and her instincts. She rose in the councils of the Holy Disciples. No one suspected her suppressed yearning. Women and men alike respected her growing power.

When she was asked to go on the mission to Saturn she agreed gladly.

'We have selected a man to organize a God-fearing government in the space habitat,' her superior told her, 'but he is not the most reliable of souls. He claims to be a Believer, but his past record of chicanery makes me doubt his faith.'

Morgenthau nodded. 'I understand,' she said. And she did. This was an opportunity for real power, control of ten thousand men and women. A great opportunity. And a terrible temptation.

So she knelt alone in the habitat's little chapel and prayed fervently for guidance. And power. Power was good, power in the service of God was an absolute blessing. It kept the hunger at bay. It calmed the devils that burned within her.

Morgenthau prayed for inner peace, for humility, for understanding the path that God wished her to take. But most of all, she prayed for power.

Saturn Arrival Minus 335 Days

Holly felt awkward when she saw Gaeta again, two days later. She found a good business reason to call him, yet instead of asking him to come to her office, she invited him to lunch. He easily agreed, on the condition that it was at the Bistro, not the cafeteria. When Holly hesitated, wondering if he considered that more romantic, he said:

'Don't worry, it'll be my treat.'

Despite herself, Holly laughed and agreed to meet him at the Bistro.

Yet she grew more nervous as noon approached. We spent a night together and he hasn't made a move to see me since then. I call him to talk business, but he wants to have lunch in the Bistro because it's quieter and the food's better and maybe he thinks we can go back to my place or maybe his afterwards and go to bed together. Which wouldn't be altogether a terrible thing, she thought, grinning despite her pangs of guilt. But I can't get involved with him or anybody else because Malcolm's the man I really want.

A faint voice in her head asked, 'Is that really true? Malcolm hasn't even held your hand. Are you really in love with him?'

Yes, she replied so swiftly that she did not allow herself any doubt. The faint voice said nothing more.

Gaeta was already at their table when Holly arrived at the Bistro. He shot to his feet, a bright smile on his rugged face.

The Bistro was so small that most of the tables were outside, on the grass. There was never any rain to worry about in the habitat, and the only winds were the gentle breezes that were stirred by the massive air circulation pumps set into the endcaps. Underground hoses watered the lawns and the crops, as needed, without spraying water through the air. Sensors in the ground kept track of soil moisture and nutrient levels. There were no flies or other buzzing pests in the habitat, although Holly knew that the ground was honeycombed by ants and worms and the microscopic creatures that turned inert, dead dirt from the Moon's regolith into living, productive soil.

'Sorry I'm late,' Holly said, slipping into the chair that Gaeta held for her.

'Only five minutes,' he said, sitting down again.

'Sometimes it's almost impossible to get out of the office. There's always something more to do.'

The flat-topped robot waiter trundled to their table, the menu and wine list illuminated on its touchscreen. They made their choices and the robot threaded its way through the tables and back inside the restaurant.

'We're making a nice little bundle on the rescue footage,' Gaeta said. 'It got a big play on the news nets. Outscored our fly-by of Jupiter in the ratings.'

'That's great.'

The robot rolled back to their table, bearing their drinks. As Gaeta handed Holly her frosted mug of cola he asked, 'So what did you want to see me about?' He seemed guarded, Holly thought, almost wary.

'I need to talk to you about Tavalera, the guy you rescued,' she said.

'What? He wants a percentage?'

Holly was surprised at that. 'No. Prob'ly he hasn't even thought about that. He just wants to go home.'

'Back Earthside?'

'Right.'

Gaeta made a small, careless shrug. 'He can hitch a ride with us when we leave, I guess.'

'That's what I was going to ask you.'

'Sure. No prob. Fritz'll grumble, but the guy's an engineer, isn't he? So we can carry him as a backup techie. That'll keep Fritz happy.'

176

Suddenly there was nothing left to talk about, Holly realized. Except everything.

Sammi Vyborg skipped lunch. He stayed in his office and followed Diego Romero on the surveillance cameras spotted throughout the habitat. Kananga had given him the security department's code for accessing the cameras.

The old man had spent the morning in his office, as usual, going through the motions of being second-in-command of the communications department. Then he'd left and gone to his own apartment. From the cameras atop the administration building's roof Vyborg watched Romero amble along the path to the apartment building, walking slowly, as if he hadn't a care in the world. A few minutes afterward he emerged again, dressed now in tattered, frayed work clothes, and strolled off into the woods out beyond the village, also as usual.

Morgenthau had refused to give him access to the cameras inside Romero's apartment.

'That's very sensitive,' she had said flatly. 'Only myself and a very small cadre of sworn Believers are allowed to review those records. Besides,' she added, with a dimpled smile, 'we wouldn't want to invade someone's privacy, would we?'

Simmering with frustration, Vyborg watched the views from the outdoor cameras.

Impatiently, he switched from one camera to another, keeping Romero in view on his holographic display until the old man disappeared down the slope of the culvert for the irrigation canal. There were no cameras down there. He's alone out there, Vyborg saw, except now and then that young woman from Morgenthau's department came out to help him. I can get Morgenthau to keep her busy on the day when I strike. That should be easy. But how to eliminate the old man? It must look like an accident.

Vyborg cleared his display and closed his eyes to ponder the problem. Kananga, he thought. Kananga will know how to do it. He'd even enjoy the task.

⋆   ⋆   ⋆

Eberly gazed at the document hovering above his desktop the way an art lover would admire a Rembrandt.

It's perfect, he thought, leaning back in his desk chair. A constitution that no one could possibly vote against. Every high-flown phrase from history that spoke of human freedom and dignity was in the document. And so was that tiny clause, buried deeply in all the other verbiage, that allowed the government to cancel all individual rights for the length of an emergency.

It's time to bring this before the people. Let them debate its fine points, let them argue it out, clause by clause, phrase by phrase. He laughed, alone in his apartment. Let them spend the next few months dissecting the document and then putting it back together again. Let them babble and quack at each other. In the end they will accept something very close to this document. And I will see to it that the emergency clause is untouched.

He clasped his hands together prayerfully and held them to his lips. This will make Morgenthau happy. I'll have the complete backing of the New Morality and Holy Disciples and all the other Believers scattered in among the population. They'll vote for this constitution. They'll make an effective bloc of votes that I can count on. If anything, they'll want to make it more restrictive than it is now. I can just see Wilmot and Urbain and the rest of the scientists debating against the Believers! What a show that will make! Entertainment for weeks to come.

Once the constitution is enacted, the time will come to elect the habitat's new leaders. No, not leaders, plural. There can be only one leader here and that will be me.

And once I am elected, it will be the time to clean house, the time to settle old scores, the time to make Morgenthau and those New Morality prigs grovel at my feet.

As she walked back to her office, Holly didn't know whether she should feel disappointed or relieved. Actually, she felt some of both. And puzzled.

Lunch with Manny had been pleasant, even fun. He didn't try to come on with me. Why? she asked herself. He was warm and

178

friendly, but it was like a couple of nights ago never happened. Like he has amnesia or something. Just erased from his memory bank.

Are guys all like that? Didn't it mean *anything* to him? She realized that it meant much more to her. And then there was Malcolm. Maybe it's better that Manny isn't really interested in me. He just had a fling with me, that's all. I shouldn't take it seriously. But he was so . . .

She realized she was close to tears.

Maybe I should talk to Don Diego about it, she thought. Then she shook her head. How could I tell him about it? I'd sound like a stupid dimdumb, or worse. But I've got to tell somebody. I need a friend and he's the only real friend I have.

Kananga listened to Vyborg without saying a word, without nodding or gesturing or even blinking his eyes, it seemed. He walked alongside Vyborg in the dimmed light of evening, the lamps along their path making his shaved scalp gleam darkly, and listened so intently that Vyborg wondered if the man had gone mute.

At last Vyborg asked, 'So what do you think can be done about it?'

'Why do you come to me with this problem of yours?' Kananga asked quietly.

Vyborg glowered at him. 'Because you are a man of action. Because you wouldn't be aboard this habitat if it weren't for me. I convinced the Peacekeepers to allow you to emigrate. They wanted to put you on trial for genocide.'

Kananga's dark face remained impassive. But the old fury welled up inside him once again. Genocide! The Hutu slaughtered us by the thousands and no one lifted a finger. Yet when we seized power, when we repaid the Hutu in blood just as they had done to us, the Peacekeepers come in with their satellite cameras and their laser weapons. They arrest us and put us on trial in the World Court.

Misunderstanding the rage in Kananga's eyes, Vyborg said in a more conciliatory tone, 'I need your help. No one else can do this for me. I need your strength and skill. Help me to get rid of this old man. Please.'

The tall, lanky Rwandan took a deep, calming breath. Pointing a lean finger at one of the light poles at the side of the path they were walking along, he said softly, 'That is a problem.'

Vyborg understood immediately. 'The cameras.'

Kananga nodded solemnly. 'Morgenthau has even installed cameras in the apartments.'

'Yes, I know.'

'Of course, if we do something in his apartment, I'm sure that we could get Morgenthau to suppress the video.'

'So we could take care of him in his apartment and no one would know,' Vyborg said hopefully.

'But what would we do with the body?' Kananga put the slightest of emphasis on the word 'we,' but Vyborg heard it and understood.

'Make it look like an accident. A natural death. He's an old man.'

'In excellent health. I checked his medical records.'

'People die,' Vyborg snapped.

With a low chuckle, Kananga said, 'Yes, especially when they have help.'

Feeling exasperation growing within him, Vyborg demanded, 'Well, can you help me or not?'

Kananga was silent for so long that Vyborg thought the man was going to refuse. But at last he said, 'There are no surveillance cameras down in the culverts where he spends so much of his time, are there?'

Vyborg realized he was right.

Saturn Arrival Minus 328 Days

All the department heads were seated around the oval conference table. Wilmot sat on one side, in the middle, flanked by Urbain and round-faced, dark-haired Andrea Maronella, head of the agro group. Eberly, sitting exactly across the table from Wilmot, still thought of the woman as a glorified farmer.

One by one, the department heads gave summaries of their weekly reports. Eberly felt utterly bored. *Why doesn't Wilmot record one of these meetings and simply play it back each week?* he wondered. *It would save us all an hour or two and the results would be just about the same.*

'Well, that seems to be it,' Wilmot said, once the last speaker had finished. 'Any new business?'

Eberly said, 'Raoul Tavalera has accepted a position in the maintenance department. He's now working on repair and refurbishment assignments, so I'm told.'

Tamiko O'Malley, the stubby Japanese head of maintenance, nodded vigorously. 'He's not a half bad technician, actually. Although he really wants to get back to Earth as soon as possible.'

Wilmot turned his gaze back to Eberly. 'What about that, Dr. Eberly?'

'We're making arrangements for him to leave with the video team, once they've finished their excursion to Titan.'

Urbain slapped his palm on the table top. 'They will *not* be allowed to land on Titan! Never!'

Eberly said mildly, 'Their team leader is under the impression that he will be allowed—'

'Never!' Urbain repeated, louder.

Wilmot placed a soothing hand on the scientist's arm. 'I

181

thought Dr. Cardenas was helping him solve the contamination problem.'

'With nanomachines?' Urbain snapped. 'I will believe that when I see it demonstrated, not before.'

Eberly said, 'It's going to be difficult to refuse him permission. I mean, this man Gaeta is a media hero. He rescued that injured astronaut. Everyone in the habitat respects him for that.'

Before Urbain could reply, Wilmot said, 'We must set up a demonstration of Dr. Cardenas' nanomachines. A demonstration that is done in complete safety. I don't want to take the slightest chance that nanobugs might run rampant in this habitat.'

Urbain nodded and smiled thinly. 'Zero risk,' he murmured, and his smile told Eberly that he knew zero risk was an impossibility.

'Very well,' said Wilmot. 'Are we finished, then?'

Several department heads started to push their chairs away from the table. But Eberly cleared his throat loudly and announced, 'There is one more item, if you please.'

Wilmot, halfway out of his chair, thumped down in it again, looking anything but pleased. 'What is it?' he asked peevishly.

'My committee has drawn up a draft constitution. I've reviewed it and now I think it's time for the people at large to see it and vote on adopting it.'

Something like suspicion flickered briefly in Wilmot's eyes.

One of the department heads complained, 'You've already got everyone arguing about naming things. Now you're going to start another debate?'

But Wilmot brushed his moustache with one finger and said, 'Let me see your draft document first. Then we'll have all the department heads review it. After that, we can show it to the people at large.'

'Fine,' said Eberly, with a gracious smile. It was exactly what he had expected Wilmot to do.

Several days later, Holly got up from her desk and walked to Morgenthau's door. She no longer thought of the office as Eberly's; she hadn't seen Eberly for many weeks, except for brief encounters and then always with other people present. He doesn't care about me, she told herself, desperately hoping it wasn't true, wondering how she could make him care for her as much as she cared for him.

She tapped at the door, and Morgenthau called, 'Enter.'

Holly slid the door back halfway and said, 'I'll be out of the office for the rest of the day. I'm going out to—'

Morgenthau looked apprehensive, almost startled. 'Holly, I was going to tell you earlier but it slipped my mind until this very moment. I need you to bring Dr. Cardenas' dossier up to date.'

'Up to date? I thought we had a complete file on her.'

Morgenthau tapped at the handheld resting on her desk. Cardenas' file and photo appeared above it. Morgenthau scrolled down rapidly, the words blurring before Holly's eyes. It made no difference; Holly remembered the complete file, word for word, from her first reading of it.

'There. There is a break in her record. She ran the nanolab at Selene for several years, and then abruptly quit. A few months later she went to Ceres, but she did not engage in nanotechnology research there, as far as the record shows. I want you to clear this up with her.'

Holly said, 'It doesn't seem that cosmic, does it?'

With a hardening expression, Morgenthau said, 'My dear Holly, *everything* about nanotechnology is important. Something happened to abruptly change Cardenas' career. She quit nanotech work for several years, and now she wants to resume her research here, among us. Why? What is she up to?'

'Kay,' Holly said. 'I'll call her.'

'Invite her out to lunch. If she refuses, go to her lab and don't leave until she's explained herself to you.'

'You make it sound like a police investigation.'

'Perhaps it should be.'

Wondering why Morgenthau was so worked up, Holly said, 'Kay, I'll give her a call before I go out.'

Raising a chubby finger, Morgenthau said sternly, 'Now, Holly. I want this done now. Have lunch with her now, today. I want your report about this in Cardenas' dossier first thing tomorrow morning.'

Holly's first inclination was to tell Morgenthau to jump out an airlock without a suit. But then she realized that the woman had never been so flaming insistent on anything before. She's really notched up about this, Holly realized. Maybe this nanotech stuff is scarier than I thought.

Don Diego straightened up slowly, painfully. The back is a weak spot, he told himself, trying to rub the stiffness away. If we ever get to the point where we can truly redesign the human body, much attention will have to be paid to improving the back.

He walked slowly, carefully, along the sloping embankment of the canal. The ache was in the small of his back, where his hands could not easily reach. He sighed. At least this stretch of the canal is nearly finished, he said to himself. He stopped and admired the haphazard growth of flowering bushes. Perhaps some cactus along the next stretch of the canal, he thought. I wonder if there is any cactus available in the habitat?

He had expected Holly to join him; she had said she'd be out this afternoon. He wanted her to see how well this little bit of wilderness was shaping up.

Someone stepped out from behind a tree, up at the edge of the culvert, and walked slowly down the dirt slope toward him. A tall, gangling black man with a shaved scalp and a thin beard tracing his jawline. His polished boots will be tarnished by the soil, Don Diego thought.

'Good afternoon to you,' he called to the stranger in English. 'What brings you to this quiet place?'

The stranger smiled brightly. 'You are Diego Romero, of the communications department?'

'I am he,' said Don Diego, thinking that this man must be from the office. Someone must be complaining about his long absences. Or . . .

'Might you be from the maintenance department?' he asked, almost timidly.

The black man stepped closer, still smiling. 'No. You have nothing to fear on that score.'

As ordered, Holly was having lunch with Kris Cardenas in the Bistro. But it wasn't going well.

'I know it's sort of prying,' she said apologetically. 'But my boss is cranked up about nanotech and there's this kind of gap in your dossier . . .'

Cardenas put her fork down and took a sip of lemonade. Then she looked out across the tables scattered across the grass, most of them empty, and finally returned her gaze to Holly. Her brilliant blue eyes looked sad, not angry; they seemed to be looking beyond Holly, peering into a painful past.

'I don't want it on the record,' she said. 'I'll tell you about it, but only if you promise to keep it out of my dossier.'

Holly was about to agree when she realized, 'I'll have to tell my boss about it.'

Cardenas shook her head. 'Then forget it. I'll tell you about it, Holly, but I don't want it to go any farther. If you tell your boss, they won't let me do any nanotech work here.'

'Why not?'

'Because I helped to kill a man,' Cardenas said, flat and hard and cold.

Holly felt her jaw drop open.

'I didn't do it on purpose,' Cardenas explained. 'But what I did was bad enough.'

As if an emotional dam had burst, Cardenas told Holly her entire story. How she'd been exiled at Selene, unable to return to Earth because of the nanobugs swarming inside her body. How her husband had refused to come up to the Moon, how her children turned against her, how she had never seen her grandchildren. Her anger. Her pain and tears and the bitter, searing rage against the fools and self-satisfied know-nothings who used the peoples' fear of nanotechnology to destroy her life.

She told Holly of Martin Humphries' offer. 'He said he'd get me back to Earth if I helped him sabotage a rival's spacecraft. God knows he was rich enough to buy anything. I thought he'd help me. I didn't think damaging a spacecraft would cause a man's death. So I let Humphries buy me and his biggest rival died when the spacecraft malfunctioned.'

'Did you ever get back to Earth? See your family?' Holly asked, her voice low, hollow.

'Never,' Cardenas said. 'When I heard that Dan Randolph had died because of what I'd done, I told Selene's leaders everything. I even tried to commit suicide, but I flubbed that. My punishment was to be locked out of Selene's nanotech lab. So I went out to Ceres, to the frontier, and worked with the rock rats for years. No nanotech work. I swore I'd never do any nanotech research again.'

'But you're doing it now. Here.'

Cardenas nodded, still dry-eyed but looking as if the weight of the world was crushing her. 'I decided I'd done enough penance. I can help you people here. I want to start my life over again.'

Holly murmured, 'Sort of like me.'

'We're two of a kind, in a way.'

'I guess.'

Cardenas fixed her with those bright blue eyes of hers. 'So what are you going to tell your boss?'

Holly didn't have to think for even a millisecond. 'Nothing,' she said. 'I'll just say that you decided of your own free will to go to Ceres and work with the rock rats. Which isn't really a lie, is it?'

For the first time, Cardenas smiled. 'No, it's not a lie. It's not the truth, not the whole truth, at least. But it's not a lie.'

Still smiling, Kananga stepped to within arm's reach of Don Diego. 'No, I'm not from the maintenance department,' he repeated.

'I plan to inform the maintenance department of my work here,' Don Diego said, 'but I haven't—'

With the swiftness of a pouncing leopard, Kananga punched the old man squarely in his solar plexus. Don Diego collapsed with barely a sound.

Kananga caught the old man in his arms and lifted him easily. No drag marks, he thought. No evidence of foul play.

He carried the gasping, dazed Don Diego down the dirt embankment to concrete at the edge of the canal. The old man coughed and moaned, his legs moved feebly, his eyes fluttered open.

Kananga knelt and pushed him face down into the canal, holding the back of his head carefully, almost tenderly, to keep him in the water. Don Diego sputtered a bit, flailed weakly, then went limp. The water bubbled a little, then became still. Kananga continued to hold him, counting slowly to a hundred, before he let go.

Satisfied that Diego Romero was dead, Kananga got to his feet. Not bad, he thought, looking around. No gouges in the dirt, no scuff marks on the concrete, no signs of a struggle.

No one will ever know.

Saturn Arrival Minus 323 Days

Holly discovered the body. She left Cardenas at the Bistro and headed out to the canal where Don Diego had been working. At first she saw no sign of him. Then she spotted his body sprawled down at the bottom of the embankment, half underwater.

She did not scream. She did not even cry until hours later, in the privacy of her own quarters, long after she had dragged the old man's body out of the canal and the emergency medical team had pronounced him dead.

She dreamed that night of the father she could not remember. Sometimes, in her dream, he was Don Diego; sometimes he was a shadowy, faceless figure of a man, huge and almost menacing. At one point the faceless male had his back to her and she was a little child, barely able to walk. Pancho was somewhere in the dream with her but what Holly wanted more than anything was to have her father turn around so that she could at last see his face. She tried to call to him but no sound would come from her throat. She reached out for the man and when he finally did turn to face her, she saw that it was Malcolm Eberly staring coldly down at her.

Holly sprang up in her bed, suddenly awake, the disturbing dream slowly dissolving like a cloud on a summer day. She showered and dressed quickly, skipped breakfast, and went straight to the habitat's small hospital to see the doctor who had examined Don Diego's body. She knew she should call Morgenthau and inform her that she'd be late for work, but she didn't bother.

The hospital was quiet, calm, unhurried. The habitat's personnel were mainly in good physical condition, youthful physically despite their calendar ages. The main medical problems were accidents and psychological ailments. And the sudden death of a ninety-eight-year-old man, Holly added mentally.

Dr. Yañez's normal happy smile disappeared once Holly explained that she wanted to know about Don Diego.

'Very unfortunate,' he said. 'Very sad. He was a wonderful man. We had many long talks together.'

He grasped Holly gently by the elbow and led her to the doors that opened onto the hospital's inner courtyard garden.

Holly said, 'I don't want to take you away from your work.'

'There is not that much to see today, anyway,' he said. 'Our people are disgustingly healthy.'

He walked Holly outside the two-storey hospital building and around the courtyard's carefully planted flower garden. Holly thought of how Don Diego would have made the gardens look wilder, more natural.

Pushing his hands into the pockets of his white jacket, Yañez said, 'Don Diego's death puzzles me. He must have tripped and fallen into the water and drowned.'

'Why didn't he just get up?' Holly asked.

He shrugged. 'He might have hit his head. He might have fainted – low blood pressure, a minor stroke. He was a pretty old man.'

'Were there any signs of a stroke?'

'No, but a minor stroke doesn't leave a lot of damage to be seen. We'd have to look specifically for it, and even then we might not catch it. This isn't New York or Tokyo, you know. We don't have expert pathologists on the staff.'

'I guess.'

'It's a great tragedy. A great loss.'

'You're certain it was an accident?' Holly asked.

Yañez looked startled momentarily. 'Yes. Of course. What else could it be?'

'I don't know.'

The physician looked up at Holly. 'He was my friend. If there had been foul play I would have found it, I assure you. It was an accident. Unfortunate. Regrettable. But just an accident, nothing more.'

The more the doctor talked, the more Holly wondered if it really had been an accident. But that's crazy, she said to herself. How could it be anything except an accident? Who would want to kill Don Diego?

Yet she heard herself ask, 'Can I see the record of your examination?'

Yañez said, 'It's a lot of medical jargon. Plus photos of the body.'

'I don't have any pictures of Don Diego,' Holly realized aloud. 'No mementoes at all.'

'The images of a dead man are rather grisly.'

'I don't care. I'd like to see them.'

The doctor sighed heavily. 'Very well. I'll give you the access code and you can call up the complete record at your convenience.'

'Thank you,' said Holly.

'*Da nada,*' replied Yañez automatically.

Eberly could barely control his fury. He stood behind the desk in his apartment, red-faced, almost snarling at Vyborg and Kananga.

'Murder!' Eberly raged. 'You couldn't wait for me to remove the old man, so you went ahead and murdered him.'

'No one knows about it,' Vyborg said, whispered actually. 'He's been buried and forgotten.'

'*I* know about it!' Eberly snapped. 'It's my duty to report this crime to Wilmot. What will you do if I try to do so? Murder me, too?'

Kananga said, 'No, never.'

'Murderers. My closest friends and supporters are a pair of murderers.'

'He wasn't a Believer,' Vyborg said. 'Just a lapsed Catholic.'

'And that excuses murder?'

Kananga said 'I thought it was your desire to get rid of the old man. That's what Sammi told me.'

'You agreed that he was to be removed,' Vyborg pleaded. 'I thought that—'

'You thought! You decided to act on your own, without consulting me. Without asking how your actions might impact on my master plan. I don't want you to think! I want you to follow my orders! To obey!'

'Yes, we understand,' said Vyborg, 'but—'

'No buts!' Eberly shouted. 'Either you are part of my team or you are not. There is no third possibility. Either you follow my orders explicitly or you leave me once and for all.'

Kananga glanced down at Vyborg as Eberly thought, I don't have to tell them that if they leave me I will immediately report them to Wilmot. They understand that well enough.

'Well?' he demanded. 'Make your choice.'

'I will stay with you, of course,' Vyborg said. 'I'm sorry that I acted so . . . precipitously.'

'And you, Colonel?'

It was obviously harder for Kananga to kowtow, but he visibly swallowed once, then said quietly, 'I am at your service, sir, now and forever.'

Eberly allowed himself a small smile. 'Very well then. The incident is forgotten. Vyborg, I want you to be patient enough to allow me to remove Berkowitz in my own way.'

'I will.'

'Once that is accomplished, you will take over total control of the communications department.' Turning to Kananga, he said, 'And you, my dear Colonel, will be my chief of security once we form the new government.'

Kananga began to reply, but Eberly added, 'Providing, of course, that you follow my orders and don't go striking off on your own.'

Kananga bit back a reply and nodded dumbly.

Eberly dismissed them and they walked glumly to the door and left his apartment. Then he sank back into his chair, his mind – and his insides – churning. It's not so bad, he thought. Everyone accepts the old man's death as an accident. And I have something to hold over Vyborg and Kananga, something to tie them more tightly to me. Total loyalty, based on fear. He rubbed at the ache in his stomach. And Morgenthau has me the same way. I'm riding on

191

a tiger, on a team of tigers, and the only way to keep from being eaten alive is to get them what they want.

He leaned back in the desk chair and tried to will the pain in his innards to go away. How to get rid of Berkowitz? He asked himself. Without another murder, preferably.

Who can I talk to? Holly asked herself, over and over. And the answer always came back: Malcolm. Talk to Malcolm about this.

But I can't see Malcolm without Morgenthau getting in the way. She guards my access to him like a bulldog. Holly had sent several phone messages to Eberly, asking for a private chat, only to have Morgenthau inform her that Eberly was too busy to talk to her at the moment.

'Anything you want to discuss with Eberly you can tell to me,' Morgenthau said.

'It's . . . uh, personal,' Holly temporized.

A flash of displeasure glinted in Morgenthau's eyes, quickly replaced by a sly look, almost a leer. 'My dear, he's much too busy for personal entanglements. And much too important to allow himself to be distracted.'

'But I'm not—'

'Perhaps after the new government is set up, perhaps then he'll have some time for a personal life. But not until then.'

Holly said numbly, 'Kay. I click.'

'Now then,' Morgenthau said briskly, 'how are the contests coming along? When we do move to phase two?'

Surprised that Morgenthau hadn't asked about Cardenas' dossier, pleased that her brief and incomplete addition to Cardenas' file apparently satisfied her boss, Holly began to explain the progress she'd made on the contests for naming the habitat's features.

Professor Wilmot studied the graphs hovering before his eyes.

'Astounding,' he muttered. 'Absolutely astounding.'

Despite all the efforts he and his staff had put in to keep the habitat under the protocol that had been designed before they left

Earth, the people were breaking away from it more and more. The changes were minor, he saw, most of them merely cosmetic. Some of the women had taken to adorning their clothes with homemade patches and press-on insignias, many of them of a blatantly sexual nature; it was a fad that seemed to be growing in popularity, despite Eberly's suggested dress code. A few of the men were following suit. Wilmot grunted. Youth will be served, even if some of the 'youths' are the calendar age of grandparents.

Then there was this contest business, naming every building and bush in the habitat. Incredible how much time and energy everyone seemed to be spending on it. There were reports of scuffles and even actual fistfights in the cafeteria over the naming contests. Perhaps I should cut off their liquor supplies, Wilmot mused. Then he shook his head. They'd simply cook up their own in the labs, one way or another. At least the use of narcotics seems to be low, unless the hospital staff isn't reporting drug abuse. Perhaps they're the worst offenders. He sighed. As long as it doesn't interfere with their work there's no sense trying to sniff out every recreational drug these people cook up.

There were personnel changes, Wilmot observed. People shifted from one job to another, even moved from one department to another. This Eberly chap in human resources is approving far too many changes, Wilmot thought. But he decided against interfering. Let the experiment play itself out. Don't meddle with it. The lab rats are performing some interesting tricks. I wonder what they'll do once we reach Saturn.

Then a new question formed in his mind. I wonder what they think in Atlanta about all this. Should I even report those details to them? He nodded to himself. I'll have to. I'm certain they're getting reports from other sources. For the kind of money they've invested, the New Morality must have seeded this habitat with plenty of snoops.

BOOK II

About three years ago I wrote that to my great surprise I had discovered Saturn to be three-bodied: that is, it was an aggregate of three stars arranged in a straight line parallel to the ecliptic, the central star being much larger than the others. I believed them to be mutually motionless, for when I first saw them they seemed almost to touch, and they remained so for almost two years without the least change. It was reasonable to believe them to be fixed with respect to each other, since a single second of arc (a movement incomparably smaller than any other in even the largest orbs) would have become sensible in that time, either by separating or by completely uniting these stars. Hence I stopped observing Saturn for more than two years. But in the past few days I returned to it and found it to be solitary, without its customary supporting stars, and as perfectly round and sharply bounded as Jupiter. Now what can be said of this strange metamorphosis? That the two lesser stars have been consumed, in the manner of the sunspots? Has Saturn devoured its children? Or was it indeed an illusion and a fraud with which the lenses of my telescope deceived me for so long – and not only me, but many others who have observed it with me? Perhaps the day has arrived when languishing hope may be revived in those who, led by the most profound reflections, once plumbed the fallacies of all my new observations and found them to be incapable of existing!

Galileo Galilei
Letters on Sunspots
1 December 1612

Vision of Saturn

Manny Gaeta's rugged face appeared on Holly's desktop screen.

'Hi,' he said, grinning. 'When do you close up shop?'

He called her once a week, as punctually as if he had ticked it off on his calendar. Holly kept putting him off. She had no desire to complicate her life. Since Don Diego's death Holly had buried herself in work, running the naming contests, keeping the office functioning despite Morgenthau's utter indifference to departmental duties. Her nights she spent thinking about Don Diego, going over the medical record time and again, picturing in her mind every detail of the scene down at the culvert when she first came across the old man's dead body. It wasn't an accident, Holly convinced herself. It couldn't be an accident. There's no evidence of any physical trauma: his heart was sound, he didn't have a stroke, he didn't even have a bump on his head or a bruise anywhere on his body. But he drowned. How? Why?

She hardly saw anyone except Kris Cardenas now and then. They had lunch together every few days. Holly asked Kris to help her go over Don Diego's medical records. Cardenas looked them over and then told Holly she could find nothing amiss.

'You've got to accept the fact that people die, Holly,' Cardenas told her over lunch in the bustling cafeteria. 'It doesn't happen often, but it happens. People die.'

'It doesn't make any sense,' Holly insisted.

'Give it up, Holly,' Cardenas said gently. 'He was a sweet old man, but he's dead and you can't bring him back.'

'Someone killed him.'

Cardenas' eyes went wide. 'Murder?'

Holly nodded, knowing she was being cosmically stupid about this but unable to back away from it.

'I think you need to get your mind off this, kid,' said Cardenas. 'You're getting . . . well, you're getting almost paranoid about it.'

'But he couldn't have just walked down the embankment and stuck his head in the water and drowned. That's impossible!'

'Get off it, Holly. This is consuming too much of your time and energy. Go out tonight and have a good time. Take your mind off it. Have some fun for yourself.'

Holly saw that Cardenas was in earnest. 'Momma Kris,' she murmured. And smiled.

'There must be plenty of young men who'd be happy to take you out for the evening,' said Cardenas.

Trying to push Don Diego out of her mind, Holly replied, 'Manny Gaeta's been calling me.'

'There you go. He's a chunk of grade-a beef.'

Holly nodded.

'Do you like him?'

'I went to bed with him once,' Holly blurted.

'Really?'

'That night he rescued the injured astronaut.'

'Oh yeah,' Cardenas said, remembering. 'He must've been on an emotional high. Pumped up with adrenaline.'

'I guess.'

'And testosterone.'

Despite herself, Holly laughed. 'Plenty of that.'

'And he's been calling you?'

'Uh-huh. But I don't want to get involved with him. I don't think I do, but if I go out with him I guess he'll expect me to do it again.'

Cardenas glanced down at her salad, then said, 'You don't have to do what he expects. You can have dinner and nothing more. Just don't give him the wrong signals.'

'Signals?'

'Be pleasant, but no touchy-feely.'

'I don't know if that would work,' Holly said uncertainly.

'Meet him at the restaurant. Stay in public places. Walk yourself home.'

'I guess.'

'Unless you want to go to bed with him again.'

'I don't! Well, not really. It's like, I want him to like me, but not too much.'

With a shake of her head, Cardenas dug her fork into the salad. 'Men aren't subtle, Holly. You have to set the rules clearly. Otherwise there'll be a problem.'

'See,' Holly confessed, feeling confused, 'I really want Malcolm to notice me. I mean, he's the reason I signed up for this habitat in the first place but I've hardly even seen him in the past few months and Manny's flaming nice and all but I don't want to get myself involved and . . .' She didn't know what more to say.

'Malcolm?' Cardenas asked. 'You mean Dr. Eberly?'

'The chief of human resources, yes.'

Cardenas looked impressed. 'You're interested in him.'

'But he's not interested in me.' Holly suddenly felt close to tears.

'Isn't that always the way?'

'I don't know what I should do.'

Cardenas glanced around the busy cafeteria, then said firmly, 'Have as much fun as you can with the stunt stud. Why not?'

'You think it'll make Malcolm jealous?'

With a huff that was almost a grunt, Cardenas replied, 'No, I don't think he'll pay any attention to it. But why shouldn't you have some fun? Manny seems to be a nice guy.'

'F'sure.'

'Then have some fun with him while you can. He'll be leaving for Earth after he's done his stunt so you won't have to worry about a long-term commitment.'

'But I *want* a long-term commitment,' Holly blurted, surprising herself. She immediately added, 'I mean, maybe not right now, and not with Manny, I guess, but sometime.'

'With Eberly?'

'Yes!'

Cardenas shook her head. 'Good luck, kid.'

Nadia Wunderly had dieted stringently, exercised regularly, and lost four kilos. Her tireless work on her research proposal had paid off, too: Dr. Urbain had approved her study of Saturn's rings. His approval was reluctant, she knew; Wunderly was the only scientist on the staff interested in the rings. All the others were focused on Titan, as was Urbain himself.

She was in Urbain's office, pleading for an assistant and some time on the habitat's major telescope.

'I can't do it all by myself,' she said, trying to walk the fine line between requesting help and admitting defeat. 'My proposal called for two assistants, if you remember.'

'I remember perfectly well,' Urbain said stiffly. 'We simply do not have the manpower to spare.'

The chief of the planetary sciences department sat tensely behind his desk as if it were a barricade to protect him against the onslaughts of revolutionaries. Yet all Wunderly wanted was a little help.

'The main telescope is completely engaged in observing Titan,' Urbain went on, as if pronouncing a death sentence. 'This is an opportunity that we must not fail to use to our advantage.'

'But the rings are—'

'Of secondary importance,' said Urbain.

'I was going to say, unique,' Wunderly finished.

'So are the life forms on Titan.'

Wondering how to convince him, she said, 'I wouldn't need much time on the 'scope. An hour or so each day to compare—'

'An hour?' Urbain looked shocked. His trim little dark beard bristled. 'Impossible.'

'But we should use this time as we approach the planet to do long-term studies of the ring dynamics. It'd be criminal not to.'

Nervously running a hand over his slicked-back hair, Urban said, 'Dr. Wunderly, this habitat will be in orbit around Saturn for many, many years. Indefinitely, in fact. You will have ample opportunity to study the dynamics of your rings.'

He almost sneered at those last words. Wunderly knew that behind her back the other scientists called her 'the Lord of the Rings,' despite the gender inaccuracy.

She pulled out her trump card. 'I thought that if we could study the rings during the months of our approach, do a synoptic study, a thorough one, then we could publish our findings before we established orbit around Saturn, before the university teams fly out to take over our research work. With your name as the lead investigator, of course.'

Instead of snatching at the bait she offered, Urbain stiffened even more at the mention of the university teams that would supersede him.

Visibly trembling, his face ashen, he said in a low, hard voice, 'Every resource I have at my disposal will be used to study Titan. All my other staff personnel are working overtime, working nights as well as days, to complete the rover vehicle that we will send to Titan's surface. That moon bears life! Unique forms of life. You are the only member of my staff who is not working on Titan, you and your precious rings! I leave you undisturbed to study them. Be grateful for that and don't bother me again with demands that I cannot meet.'

The threat was hardly veiled, Wunderly realized. Leave him alone or he'll put me to work on Titan, along with everybody else.

She pushed herself to her feet, feeling defeated, empty, helpless. And angry. The man's fixated on almighty Titan, she grumbled to herself as she left Urbain's office. He's so doggone narrow-minded he could look through a keyhole with both eyes.

Precisely at 17:00 hours, Gaeta rapped once on the frame of Holly's open door and stepped into her office.

'Quitting time,' he announced. 'Come on, I've got something to show you.'

Despite her inner turmoil, Holly laughed and told her computer she was leaving for the day. The holographic image blinked once and winked off.

'What's this all about?' Holly asked as she let him lead her out of the building.

'I thought you'd enjoy a good long look at where we're going,' Gaeta said.

'Saturn?'

'Yeah. You can see it pretty easy now with the naked eye.'

'Really?'

He chuckled. 'Just like I thought. You haven't taken a peek at it, have you?'

'Not for a while,' Holly admitted.

He had a pair of electrobikes waiting outside the office building. Holly followed him, pedaling along the winding bike path across the park, through the orchard and farmlands, out toward the endcap. They left the bikes in racks that stood at the path's terminus and headed up a narrow footpath, through flowering shrubbery and a few young trees.

'I'll never get used to this,' Gaeta muttered.

'What?'

'The way gravity works in here. We're walking uphill but it feels like we're going downhill.'

Holly put on a superior air. ' "The habitat's spin-induced gravity," ' she quoted from the orientation manual, '"decreases as one approaches the habitat's centerline." Which is what we're doing now.'

'Yeah,' he said, sounding unconvinced.

At last they came to a small building with a single door marked TO ENDCAP OBSERVATION UNIT. Inside, a flight of dimly lit metal stairs led downward. As their softboots padded quietly on the steel treads Holly realized that it felt as if they were climbing up, not down.

'We're not in Oz anymore,' Gaeta muttered as they made their way along the shadowy stairwell. His voice echoed slightly off the metal walls.

'Oz?' Holly asked.

'It's an old story. I'll get the vid beamed up from Earthside for you.'

Holly really didn't understand what he was talking about. The stairs ended and they walked along a narrow passageway, a tunnel lined with pipes and conduits overhead and along both walls. Although the tunnel looked straight and level, it felt as if they were trudging up an incline. At last they reached a hatch marked ENDCAP OBSERVATION UNIT: USE CAUTION IN ENTERING. Gaeta tapped on the entry pad and the hatch sighed open.

An automated voice said, 'Caution, please. You are about to enter a rotating enclosure. Please proceed with care.'

An open cubicle stood on the other side of the hatch. Its walls, floor and ceiling were softly cushioned.

Gaeta laughed as they stepped in. 'Great. They finally got me into a padded cell.'

'Rotation beginning,' announced the computerized voice.

Holly suddenly felt lightheaded, almost woozy.

'It's like an amusement park ride,' Gaeta said, grasping Holly around the waist.

The computer voice announced, 'Ten seconds to hatch opening. Use caution, please.'

The padded wall they were facing slid open and Gaeta, still holding Holly by the waist, pulled her through. Holly gasped and forgot the slightly wobbly feeling in her legs. A million stars were spread across her view, hard unblinking pinpoints of light, the eyes of heaven staring back at her.

'Cosmic,' she breathed.

'That's a good word for it,' Gaeta said in a hushed voice.

Then Holly realized that someone was already there in the dimly lit blister, her back to them, staring out at the stars. She looked short and stocky; in the muted light the color of her spiky hair was difficult to determine; Holly thought it might have been red.

The woman stirred as if coming out of a trance, turned slightly and whispered, 'Hi.'

'Hello,' Holly whispered back. It was like being in a cathedral; nobody raised their voices.

Gaeta said softly, 'This whole compartment counter-rotates against the habitat's spin, so you can see everything without having it revolve all around you.'

Holly knew that from the orientation vids, but it didn't matter. The sight of the universe spread out before her blotted everything else from her awareness. So many stars! she thought. Millions and zillions of them. Red stars, blue stars, big bright ones, smaller dimmer ones.

Gaeta leaned over her shoulder and pointed. 'That blue one, there. That's Earth.'

'And that bright yellow one?'

'Jupiter.'

'So where's Saturn?' she asked.

The other woman pointed down toward the lower edge of the big curving window. 'There.'

Holly stared at a bright pinkish star. No, not a star; she could see that it was a disk, flattened at the poles.

Then it hit her. 'Where's the rings? There's no rings!'

Ring World

The woman smiled at Holly. 'Galileo felt just the way you do. The doggone rings disappeared on him.'

'What do you mean?' Holly asked, looking back and forth from the pink disk of the planet to the round, owl-eyed face of the woman, half-hidden in the shadows of the dimly lit observation blister.

The woman smiled, a little sadly, Holly thought. She said, 'Galileo was the first to see that Saturn had something strange about it, back in 1609, 1610, somewhere in there. His dinky little telescope couldn't resolve the rings; all he saw was what looked like a pair of stars hovering on either side of Saturn's disk.'

'And they disappeared?' Holly asked.

'Ah-yup. He laid off observing Saturn for a while, and when he looked again – around 1612 or so, this was – the doggone rings were gone.'

'What happened to them?'

'They didn't go anyplace. They were still there. But every fifteen years or so Saturn's tilt comes around to a position where the rings are edge-on to an observer on Earth. They're so doggone thin they seem to disappear. You can't see them in low-power telescopes. Not even in some pretty darn big 'scopes, really.'

'So we're looking at them edge-on right now,' Gaeta said.

'That's right. Poor Galileo. He didn't know what was going down. Must have driven him half crazy.'

Holly stared at the disk of Saturn, as if she could make the rings reappear of she just tried hard enough.

'You can see 'em in the 'scopes over at the astronomy blister,' the woman said. She seemed on the verge of saying more, but stopped herself.

'Are you an astronomer?' Holly asked.

'Sort of. Nadia Wunderly's my name.' She put out her hand, fingers splayed and thumb sticking straight up. Holly took it and introduced herself and Gaeta. Wunderly shook hands with him, too, her expression serious, as if meeting people was a chore that had to be done correctly.

'What do you mean, you're sort of an astronomer?' Gaeta asked.

Wunderly's face became even more somber. 'I'm with the planetary sciences team,' she explained, 'but they're mostly astro-biologists. They're all hotted up about Titan.'

'You're not?'

'Naw. I'm interested in Saturn's rings. I'm really a physicist by training; a fluid dynamicist.'

Within an hour they were all in Holly's apartment, munching leftovers from her refrigerator while Wunderly explained that Saturn's rings could be thought of as a fluid, with each individual chunk of ice in the rings acting as a particle in that dynamic, ever-changing fluid.

'So the ice flakes are speeding around Saturn like they're on a race track,' Wunderly was saying, making a wobbly circle with the spear of celery she held in one hand, 'and banging into one another like people jostling in the New Tokyo subway trains.'

'All the time?' Gaeta asked.

'All the time,' Wunderly replied, then crunched off a bite of celery.

Holly was on the other side of the counter that partitioned off the kitchen, waiting for the microwave to defrost a packaged dinner. 'And they have these little moons going around, too?'

'Ay-yup. Sheep dogs. The moons keep the rings from spreading out and mixing into one another.'

Gaeta, sprawled over the living-room sofa with a bowl of chips resting on his flat stomach, seemed deep in thought.

'Then there's the spokes, too,' Wunderly went on. 'Magnetic field levitates the smaller ice flakes.' She waved her free hand up and down like a snake's sinuous undulations.

'Everything's bumping into everything else,' Holly said, just as the microwave finally pinged.

'And not all of the particles are little flakes, either. Some of 'em are big as houses. The moons, of course, are a few kilometers across.'

'Sounds confusing,' Holly said, carrying the steaming-hot dinner tray into the living room. She put it down on the coffee table in front of Wunderly.

'Sounds dangerous,' said Gaeta, hauling himself up to a sitting position.

'It's only dangerous if you stick your nose in,' Wunderly said. 'I just want to study the rings from a safe distance.'

'Nobody's been there, huh?' he asked.

'To the rings? We've sent automated probes to Saturn, starting with the old *Cassini* spacecraft darn near a century ago.'

Gaeta was sitting up straight now, his eyes kindled with growing excitement. 'Any of them go *through* the rings? I mean, from one side to the other, top to bottom?'

Wunderly was poking at the dinner tray with the stub of her celery stalk. 'Through the ring plane, you mean?'

'Yeah, right.'

Holly sat down beside Gaeta on the sofa.

'They've sent probes through the gaps between the rings, of course. But not through a ring itself. That'd be too danged dangerous. The probe would be beaten up, abraded. It'd be like going through a meat grinder.'

Holly said, 'Manny, you're not thinking of doing that, are you?'

He turned to her, grinning. 'It'd make a helluva stunt, *chiquita*.'

'Stunt?' Wunderly looked puzzled.

'That's what I do for a living,' Gaeta explained. 'I go where no one has gone before. The more dangerous, the better.'

'Within reason,' Holly said.

He laughed.

Recognition dawned on Wunderly's face. 'You're the guy who scaled Mt. Olympus! On Mars. I saw the vid.'

'That was me. And I skiboarded halfway down the slope, too,' Gaeta said, with pride in his voice.

'Yes, but you can't go skydiving through Saturn's rings.'

'Why not?'

'You'll get killed.'

'There's always an element of risk in a stunt. That's what makes people watch.'

Holly said, 'They pay money to see if you get killed.'

He laughed. 'Like the Roman gladiators. Only I don't hafta kill anybody. I just risk my own neck.'

Wunderly said, 'Not in the rings. It's suicide.'

'Is it?' Gaeta mused. 'Maybe not.'

Holly wanted to stop him before he got to like the idea too much. 'Manny . . .'

'I mean, Wilmot and the science guys don't want me going down to Titan. Maybe the rings would be a better stunt. Nothing else like them in the whole solar system.'

'All the big planets have rings, don't they?' Holly said. 'Jupiter and Uranus and Neptune.'

'Yeah, but they're just puny little ones. *Pobrecitos.*'

'The real question is,' said Wunderly, her eyes beginning to sparkle, 'how come Saturn has such a terrific set of rings while the other giant planets just have those dinky little ones.'

Gaeta looked at Holly, then back to Wunderly. He shrugged.

Wunderly went on, 'I mean, you'd think that the bigger a planet is, the bigger its ring system would be. Right? Then how come Saturn's is bigger than Jupiter's? And those rings are dynamic, they don't just sit there. Particles are falling into the planet all the time, new particles abraded off the moons. Why is Saturn's system so big? Are we just lucky enough to see Saturn at precisely the right time when its ring system is big and active? I don't believe in luck. Something's different about Saturn. Something important.'

'So what is it?' Holly asked. 'What makes Saturn so special?'

'GOK,' said Wunderly.

'What?' Holly and Gaeta asked in unison.

'God Only Knows,' Wunderly replied, with a grin. 'But I intend to find out.'

Wunderly talked about the rings for more than an hour, growing

208

more excited with each word. When Gaeta asked about flying through the rings, Wunderly stressed the danger. 'It's impossible, I tell you,' she said. 'You'll get yourself killed.' Which only made Gaeta more excited about the stunt.

Finally she left, but not before Gaeta got her to promise that she would let him see all the vids and other data she had amassed. He told her he would bring his chief technician to take a look, too.

Holly saw Wunderly to the door, and when she closed and turned back to Gaeta, she realized they were alone and he was grinning from ear to ear. Don't get involved with him, she warned herself. He's going to get himself killed, sooner or later. Prob'ly sooner.

Yet she went to the sofa and sat beside him and leaned her head on his strong, muscular shoulder and within minutes they were kissing, their clothes vanishing, and he carried her into the bedroom like a conquering hero and she didn't think of Malcolm Eberly at all. Hardly.

Saturn Arrival Minus 317 Days

Wilmot felt like a harried schoolmaster confronted by a gaggle of unruly students.

'A punch-up?' he bellowed, furious. 'The two of you actually struck one another?'

The two young men standing before his desk looked sheepish. One of them had a blue-black little bruise swelling beneath his left eye. He was red-haired and pink-cheeked; Irish, Wilmot guessed. The other was taller, his skin the color of milk chocolate; a crust of blood stained his upper lip. Neither of them spoke a word.

'And what was the reason for this brawl?'

They both remained mute.

'Well?' Wilmot demanded. 'Out with it! What caused the fight?'

The one with the black eye muttered, 'We disagreed over the name for Village B.'

'Disagreed?'

The other guy said, 'He wanted to call the village Killarney.'

His antagonist said, 'It's a proper name. He said it was stupid.'

'And this led to fisticuffs? A disagreement over naming the village? What on Earth were you drinking?'

Alcoholic beverages were not sold in the cafeteria, where the scuffle had occurred, although the habitat's two restaurants did have liquor as well as wine and a homebrewed beer supplied by one of the farms.

'It's my fault,' said the one whose nose had been bloodied. 'I had a drink in Nemo's before going to the cafeteria.'

Wilmot glared at them. 'Must I suspend all alcohol? Is that what you want?'

They both shook their heads. Wilmot studied their hangdog expressions. At least they look properly repentant, he thought. A logistics analyst and a communications technician, brawling like schoolboys.

With the sternest scowl he could produce, Wilmot said, 'One more incident like this and I will suspend your personal drinking privileges altogether. And put you to work in the recycling facility. If you want to act like garbage, I'll set you to handling garbage six hours a day.'

The one with the black eye turned slightly toward the other and extended his hand. 'I'm sorry, bud.'

His erstwhile opponent clasped the hand in his own. 'Yeah. Me too.'

'Get out of here, the two of you,' Wilmot growled. 'And don't *ever* behave so idiotically again.'

The communications tech hurried from Wilmot's office to his own quarters, where he dabbed a wet cloth to clean off the scabbed blood on his lip and then put in a call to Colonel Kananga.

'I started a fight in the cafeteria,' he said to Kananga's image in his phone screen.

The Rwandan said, 'I've already heard about it, through channels. What did Wilmot have to say to you?'

'Nothing much. He seemed more puzzled than angry.'

Kananga nodded.

'What do you want me to do next?'

'Nothing at present. Just go about your duties and behave yourself. I'll call you when the time comes.'

'Yessir.'

With a population that included people of many faiths, there was no Sabbath aboard the habitat that everyone adhered to, so election day for phase one of the naming contests was declared a holiday for everyone.

Malcolm Eberly sat in his living room, looking gloomy, almost sullen, as he watched the newscast on the hologram projector. The image showed the polling center in Village A. People filed in and voted, then left. It was about as rousing as watching grass grow.

Ruth Morgenthau tried to cheer him. 'The turnout isn't as bad as my staff predicted. It looks as if at least forty percent of the population will vote.'

'There's no excitement,' Eberly grumbled.

Sammi Vyborg, sitting on the other side of the coffee table, shrugged his bony shoulders. 'We didn't expect excitement at this phase. After all, they're only choosing categories for naming, not the names themselves.'

Eberly gave him a sharp glance. 'I want the people worked up. I want them challenging Wilmot's authority.'

'That will come,' said Kananga. He was leaning back on the sofa, his long arms spread across its back. 'We've been testing different approaches.'

The hint of a frown clouded Eberly's face. 'I heard about the fistfight in the cafeteria.'

'Before the next election day we can create a riot, if you like.'

Eberly said, 'That's not the kind of excitement that we need.'

'A riot would be good,' said Vyborg. 'Then we could step in and quell the fighting.'

'And you could stand as the man who brought peace and order to the habitat,' Morgenthau said, smiling at Eberly.

'Maybe,' he said, almost wistfully. 'I just wish—'

Morgenthau interrupted, 'You wish everyone would listen to you and fall down in adoration.'

'If I'm going to be their leader, it's important that they trust me, and like me.'

'They'll love you,' said Vyborg, his voice dripping sarcasm, 'once you have the power to determine life or death for them.'

At the end of election day, Holly sat at her desk tabulating the results of the voting. Villages would be named after cities on Earth, the voters had decided. Individual buildings would be named for famous people. The farms and orchards and other open areas would get names from natural features on Earth or from mythology: that particular vote was too close to call a clear winner.

Her phone announced that Ruth Morgenthau was calling. Holly told the computer to accept the call, and Morgenthau's face appeared, hovering alongside the statistics.

'Do you have the results?'

Nodding, Holly said, 'All tabbed.'

'Forward them to me.'

With a glance at the phone's data bar beneath her caller's image, Holly saw that Morgenthau was calling from Eberly's apartment. She felt nettled that Morgenthau was with Malcolm and she hadn't been invited. Maybe I can fix that, she thought.

'I've got to send them to Professor Wilmot first,' she said. 'Official procedure.'

'Send them here as well,' said Morgenthau.

Holly replied, 'If I do, there'll be an electronic record that I violated procedure.' Before Morgenthau could frown, Holly went on, 'But I could bring you a copy in person; there'd be no record of that.'

Morgenthau's fleshy face went crafty for a moment, then she dimpled into a smile. 'Very good, Holly. Good thinking. Bring the results to me. I'm at Dr. Eberly's quarters.'

'I'll be there FTL,' Holly said.

The instant Holly stepped into Eberly's apartment she felt tension in the air; the room was charged with tight-coiled emotions. Morgenthau, Vyborg and Kananga were there: Holly thought of them as the hippo, the snake and the panther, but there was no humor in the characterizations. Kananga, in particular, made her edgy the way he watched her, like a hunting cat tracking its prey.

Eberly was nowhere in sight, but before Holly could ask about him, he entered the living room and smiled at her. The tension that she felt dissolved like morning mist melting under warm sunlight.

'Holly,' he said, extending both arms toward her. 'It's been too long since we've seen you.'

'Mal—' she began, then corrected herself. 'Dr. Eberly. It's wonderful to see you again.'

213

Morgenthau said, 'Holly's brought us the election results.'

'Fine,' said Eberly. 'That's very good of you, Holly.'

Pulling her handheld from her tunic pocket, Holly projected the tabulations on one of the living room's bare walls. Malcolm doesn't have any decorations in his apartment, she saw. Just like his office used to be: empty, naked.

For hours the five of them studied the voting results, dissecting them like pathologists taking apart a corpse to see what killed the living person. Kananga disappeared into the kitchen for a while and, much to Holly's surprise, eventually placed a tray of sandwiches and drinks on the bar that divided the kitchen from the living room. Eberly kept digging deeper into the statistics, trying to break down the voting by age, by employment, by educational background. He wanted to know who voted for what, down to the individual voter, and why.

Vyborg, his tunic unbuttoned and hanging loosely from his spindly shoulders, rubbed his eyes, then took a sandwich from the tray.

'The scientists voted pretty much as a bloc,' he said, gesturing with the sandwich in his hand. 'That's surprising.'

'Why are you surprised?' Morgenthau asked. She had nibbled at a sandwich and left most of it uneaten on the coffee table. Holly wondered how she kept her size if she ate so delicately.

'Scientists are contentious,' Vyborg said. 'They're always arguing about something or other.'

'About scientific matters,' said Eberly. 'But their *interests* are something else. They voted as a bloc because they all have the same interests and the same point of view.'

'That could be a problem,' Kananga said.

Eberly smiled knowingly. 'Not really. There's nothing to worry about.'

Holly followed their ruminations, fascinated, looking from one to another as they surgically dismembered the voting results. She realized that Morgenthau had designed the ballot to include information on the department the voter worked in and the voter's specific occupation. Secret ballots, Holly thought, were secret only

214

as far as the individual voter's name was concerned. Each ballot carried enough information for detailed statistical analyses.

'We're going to need a counterweight for them,' Vyborg said, between bites of his sandwich.

'For the scientists?' asked Kananga.

'Yes,' Eberly snapped. 'It's already taken care of.'

Morgenthau gave Holly her crafty look again. 'What about this stuntman that you've been seeing?'

Holly blinked with surprise. 'Manny Gaeta?'

'Yes,' said Morgenthau. 'He's had his arguments with the scientists, hasn't he?'

'He wants to go down to the surface of Titan and they won't allow that until they—'

'The surface of Titan?' Eberly interrupted. 'Why?'

Holly explained, 'He does spectacular stunts and sells the VR rights to the nets.'

'He's extremely popular on Earth,' Morgenthau pointed out. 'A vid star of the first magnitude.'

'A stuntman,' Vyborg sneered.

Eberly asked, 'And he's in conflict with the scientists?'

'They're afraid he'll contaminate the life forms on Titan,' said Holly. 'Dr. Cardenas is trying to help him—'

'Cardenas?' Vyborg snapped. 'The nanotech expert?'

'Right.'

'How well do you know this stuntman?' Eberly asked her.

Holly felt a pang surge through her. 'We're pretty good friends,' she said quickly.

'I want to meet him,' said Eberly. 'Make it a social occasion, Holly. I want to have dinner with the two of you. Invite Cardenas also. We'll make it a foursome.'

Holly tried to mask the rush of emotions she felt. Jeeps, she thought, I finally get to go out to dinner with Malcolm but I've got to bring along the guy I've been sleeping with!

Saturn Arrival Minus 312 Days

Of the two restaurants in the habitat, Nemo's was by far the more spectacular. Where the Bistro was small and quiet, with most of its tables out on the lawn, Nemo's was plush and ambitious. The restaurant was designed to resemble the interior of a submarine, with curved bare metal walls and large round portholes that looked out on holograms of teeming undersea life. The proprietor, a former Singapore restaurateur whose outspoken atheism had gotten him into trouble, had sunk a fair share of his personal assets into the restaurant. 'If I'm going to fly all the way out to Saturn,' he told his assembled children, grandchildren, and more distant relatives, 'I might as well spend my time doing something I know about.' They were not happy to see the head of the family leave Earth – and take so much of their inheritance with him.

Holly felt distinctly nervous as she followed the robot head waiter to the table for four that she had reserved. Gaeta had offered to pick her up at her apartment, but she thought it better that they meet at the restaurant. She was the first to arrive, precisely on time at 20:00 hours. The squat little robot stopped and announced, 'Your table, Miss.' Holly wondered how it decided she was a Miss and not a Ma'am. Did it pick up the data from her ID badge?

She sat at the chair that allowed her to look across the room at the entryway. The restaurant was not even half filled.

'Would you care for a drink?' the robot asked. Its synthesized voice was warm and deep. 'We have an excellent bar and an extensive wine list.'

Holly knew that that was an exaggeration, at best. 'No thanks,' she said. The robot trundled away.

Eberly appeared at the entryway, and Kris Cardenas came in

216

right behind him. She wore an actual dress, a knee-length frock of flowered material, light and summery. Holly suddenly felt shabby in her tunic and tights, despite the sea-green shawl she had knotted around her waist.

She stood up as the two of them approached. Neither of them realized they were both heading to the same table, at first, but Eberly caught on quickly and gallantly held Cardenas' chair for her as she sat down. As Holly introduced them to one another she found herself hoping that Manny wouldn't come. Maybe he got tied up on something, some test or whatever. She barely paid attention to the conversation between Eberly and Cardenas.

Then Gaeta appeared, wearing a form-fitting mesh shirt and denims. No badge. No decorations of any kind, except for the stud in his earlobe. He didn't need finery. Heads turned as he strode to their table well ahead of the robot headwaiter.

Except for the fluttering in her stomach, the meal seemed to go easily enough. Gaeta knew Cardenas, of course, and Eberly acted as their host, gracious and charming. Conversation was light, at first: they talked about the recent voting and Gaeta's previous feats of daring.

'Soaring through the clouds of Venus,' Eberly said admiringly, over their appetizers. 'That must have taken a great deal of courage.'

Gaeta grinned at him, almost shyly. 'You know what they say about stunt people: more guts than brains.'

Eberly laughed. 'Still, it must take a good deal of both guts and brains.'

Gaeta dipped his chin in acknowledgement and turned his attention to his shrimp cocktail.

By the time the entrees were served, the topic had turned to Gaeta's intention to get to the surface of Titan.

'If Kris here can convince Urbain and his contamination nuts that I won't wipe out their *chingado* bugs,' Gaeta complained.

Cardenas glanced at him sharply.

'Pardon my French,' he mumbled.

'I thought it was Spanish,' said Holly.

Eberly skillfully brought the conversation back to Urbain and his scientists. Gaeta grumbled about their worries over contaminating Titan, while Cardenas shook her head as she talked about their fears of runaway nanobugs.

'I can understand where they're coming from, of course,' she said, 'but you'd think I'm trying to create Frankenstein's monster, the way they're hemming me in with all kinds of safety regulations.'

'They're overly cautious?' Eberly asked.

'A bunch of little old ladies,' Gaeta said.

Holly asked, 'Manny, have you thought any more about going through the rings?'

With a shake of his head he replied, 'I haven't heard anything from that Nadia. She said she'd look into it.'

'I'll call her,' Holly said. 'Maybe she forgot.'

By the time dessert was being served, Eberly was suggesting, 'Perhaps I can help you with Dr. Urbain. I have direct access to Professor Wilmot; I can make your case for visiting Titan's surface.'

Then he added, turning to Cardenas, 'And for easing some of the restrictions on your nanotechnology lab.'

'It's not the restrictions, so much,' Cardenas said earnestly. 'I can live with them. I understand why they're scared, and I even agree with them, up to a point.'

'Then what is your problem?' Eberly asked.

'Manpower, pure and simple,' said Cardenas. 'I'm all alone in the lab. I've tried to recruit assistants, but none of the younger scientific staff will come anywhere near nanotech.'

Glancing at Holly, Eberly asked, 'Hasn't the human resources department been able to help?'

Cardenas looked surprised at the thought. 'I've asked Urbain,' she said. 'What I need is a couple of lab assistants. Youngsters who have basic scientific training. But the scientists run in the opposite direction when I ask them for help.'

'I see,' Eberly murmured.

Smiling, Cardenas said, 'Back when I was on Earth, in the Stone Age, the professors ran their labs with grad students. Slave labor. Cheap and plentiful.'

Eberly steepled his fingers. 'We don't have many grad students among us, or even undergraduates, I'm afraid. And everyone has a job slot; that was a requirement for being accepted aboard the habitat.'

'We don't have any unemployed students,' Holly said.

'I figured that out right away,' said Cardenas. 'But I thought I'd be able to talk a couple of the younger people on Urbain's staff to come over and help me.'

'He won't allow them to,' Eberly guessed.

Cardenas' expression hardened. 'He won't let me talk to them anymore. And he's got them frightened of even meeting me socially. I'm being frozen out.'

Eberly turned to Holly and placed a hand on her wrist. 'Holly, we've got to do something to correct this.'

She glanced at Gaeta before replying, 'If that's what you want, Malcolm.'

He looked back at Cardenas as he answered, 'That's what I want.'

Dinner ended and the four of them went outside into the twilight atmosphere. Holly's heart was thumping. What happens now?

Eberly said, 'Holly, why don't we go up to your office and see what we can do to help Dr. Cardenas?'

She nodded. 'If I knew what skills you need, Kris, I could pull up a list of possible candidates for you.'

Cardenas said, 'I'll shoot the requirements to you as soon as I get home.'

Gaeta said, 'I'll walk you home, Kris. It's on my way.'

Holly stood frozen to the spot as Gaeta and Cardenas said goodbye and started along the path that led to her quarters. Eberly had to touch her shoulder to break the spell.

'We have work to do, Holly,' he told her.

But she kept staring at Cardenas and Gaeta, walking side by side down the dimly lit path. Cardenas turned and looked over her shoulder at Holly, as if to say, *don't worry, nothing's going to happen.* At least, Holly hoped that's what she was signifying.

She's my friend, Holly told herself. She knows Manny and I

have made out together. She wouldn't do anything with him. It was his idea to walk her home. She won't let him do anything.

Still, Eberly had to tell her again, 'Holly, come on. We have work to do.'

The Second Rally

Eberly prided himself on never making the same mistake twice. The first public speech he'd given, to announce the naming contests, had been good enough, as far as it went, but a miserable failure in the eyes of Morgenthau and Vyborg. The crowd at the cafeteria had been sparse, and despite their rousing response to his oratory they made it clear that they considered the whole affair as nothing better than a learning experience, at best.

He intended to profit from that.

With phase one of the naming campaign finished, and categories for each type of feature in the habitat settled by the first round of voting, Eberly carefully prepared for his second public appearance.

It's impossible to please everyone, he realized, but it *is* possible to split people up into small, distinct groups and then find out what each group desires and promise it to them. Divide and conquer: a concept as old as civilization, probably older. Eberly learned how to use it. He was pleased, almost surprised, at how easy it was to use the natural antipathy between the stuntman and Urbain's scientific staff.

For weeks he had Vyborg build up the stuntman's presence in the habitat with vids and news releases that showed how heroic, how exciting Gaeta was: the conqueror of Mt. Olympus on Mars, the man who trekked across Mare Imbrium on the Moon. Vyborg cleverly played up the scientific information that Gaeta had harvested during each of his feats. Now he wanted to be the first human being to set foot on the murky, forbidding surface of Titan. Will the scientists allow him to do it? Humans will land on Titan someday, sooner or later. Why not allow this intrepid hero to take the risks he is so willing to endure? At Eberly's insistence, no mention was made of Dr. Cardenas and her effort to create nanobugs to attack the contamination problem. 'There will be no publicity about nanotechnology,' he decided.

Kananga's people helped to divide the general populace. It was pathetically simple to set individuals against one another. Eberly himself hit on the idea of using vids from Earthside sporting events to create organized fan clubs, clannish factions who placed bets on 'their' teams and watched each game in boozy uproarious exuberance. When Wilmot and his administrators tried to control the distribution of alcoholic drinks, even beer, the fans spontaneously began meeting in private apartments. A lively commerce in homebrew began, and it wasn't unusual for fights to break out when one fan club clashed with another.

Morgenthau saw to it that Eberly was apprised of each group's special interests. The machinists complained that their salary level was kept artificially lower than that of the lab technicians. One group of farmers wanted to expand their acreage and plant tropical fruits that Wilmot's administrators had disallowed because they would require more water and an extensive hothouse to create a warmer, wetter environment than in the rest of the habitat. A bitter rivalry was simmering between the fans of two football teams that were heading for the World Cup back on Earth. The brawls between them were getting so serious that even Kananga suggested they be toned down.

Through all this, Holly's work was an invaluable asset to Eberly. She ran the human resources department and faithfully brought to Eberly the statistics he needed to determine all the inner group dynamics. She was earnest, honest, and had no idea that the fractures within the habitat's social structure were being eagerly fomented by Eberly's clique.

'We need to do something to bring people together again,' she told Eberly, time and again. 'We need some way of unifying everybody.'

Wilmot watched the growing disharmony with a mixture of fascination and dread. The carefully knit society that had been created for this habitat was unraveling. Coming apart at the seams. People were splitting up into tribes, no less. Clans, even. As an anthropologist he was enthralled by their behavior. As the leader of the expedition, however, he feared that the growing chaos would lead to mayhem, perhaps even murder. Yet he resisted the urge to interfere or clamp down with new regulations and enforcements. Let the experiment continue, he told himself. Let them play out their little games. The end result will be more important than any individual's life; in the final analysis it could be more important than the success or failure of this mission.

Ultimately, Holly urged Eberly, 'You've got to do something, Malcolm! You're the only one who has the vision to bring everybody together again.'

He allowed Morgenthau to back Holly's increasingly insistent pleading with similar suggestions of her own. At last he told them to organize a rally.

'I'll speak to them,' he said. 'I'll do my best.'

Holly worked sixteen and eighteen hours a day to organize a rally that would bring out everyone in the habitat. She set it up in the open park along the lake outside Village A. She saw to it that the cafeteria and both restaurants closed down at 18:00 hours that afternoon; no one was going to have dinner until after Eberly's speech was finished.

At Morgenthau's suggestion, Holly organized parades. The sports fans' clubs easily agreed to march to the park, each of them carrying makeshift banners in their club's colors. The musicians among the populace formed impromptu bands and even agreed to play one at a time, rather than competing in cacophony. The farmers put together a march of sorts, not that they walked in any discernible order. So did the other workers, each organized by their specialty.

Still, when the music played and the people marched, only a few thousand showed up. Most of the population stayed home. Holly consoled herself with the thought that they all would watch the rally on video. At least, she hoped so.

Even so, some three thousand people formed a considerable

crowd. Eberly looked delighted as they assembled raggedly in front of the band shell where he sat on the stage, watching and smiling at them.

Morgenthau looked pleased, too. Holly heard her say into Eberly's ear, 'This is a big enough minority to give us the power we need, Malcolm. The ones who've stayed home will be swept up in the tide, when the time comes.'

The atmosphere was like an old-fashioned summertime picnic. Music played. People marched, then stood shoulder to shoulder, facing the little band shell and stage that stood at one end of the park.

Manuel Gaeta was the first speaker. Morgenthau introduced him and the crowd roared and whistled as he slowly, shyly, climbed the steps of the stage.

He motioned for quiet, grinning out at a sea of expectant faces. 'I'm no public speaker,' he began. 'I've done a lot of scary things in my life, but I think this is scarier than any of them.'

People laughed.

'I don't have all that much to say. I hope to be able to get down to the surface of Titan, and when I do, I'd like to dedicate the mission to you folks, the people of this habitat.'

They roared their delight. Holly, sitting beside Eberly at one side of the stage, looked around the crowd, searching for the faces of scientists that she knew. She spotted only a few of them. Neither Dr. Urbain nor Professor Wilmot was in the crowd.

'My real job today,' Gaeta went on, 'is to introduce the main speaker. I think you all know him. Malcolm Eberly is director of the human resources department, and the one man among the habitat's top staff who's tried to help me. I think he can help all of us.'

With that, Gaeta turned and gestured toward Eberly, who slowly, deliberately got up from his chair and walked to the podium. The crowd's applause was perfunctory.

'Thank you, Manny,' Eberly said, gripping the sides of the podium with both hands. Looking out into the crowd, he went on, 'And thank *you*, each and every one of you, for coming to this rally this evening.'

He took a breath, then lowered his head, almost as if in prayer. The crowd went silent, waiting, watching.

'We have before us a task of awesome magnitude,' Eberly said. 'We must face new and unknown dangers as we sail farther into unexplored space than any human beings have gone before.'

Holly was struck by the pitch of his voice. He was a different man on the platform, she saw: his eyes blazed, his voice was deeper, stronger, more certain than she had ever heard before.

'Soon now we will be reaching Saturn. Soon our real work must begin. But before we can start, we have the responsibility of creating a new order, a new society, a new government that will represent us fairly and justly and accomplish all that we want to achieve.

'The first step in creating this new order is the naming of names. We have the opportunity, the responsibility, of choosing the names by which our community will be known. It may seem like a trivial task, but it is not. It is of primary importance.

'Yet what do we see all around us? Instead of unity, there is strife. Instead of clear purpose, there is confusion and struggle. We are divided and weak, where we must be united and strong.'

Holly listened in growing fascination, feeling herself drawn into his web of words. It's enthralling, she realized. Malcolm is mesmerizing all these thousands of people.

'We are the chosen ones,' he was telling them. 'We few, we chosen few, we who will establish human purpose and human dignity at the farthest outpost of civilization. We who will bring the banner of humanity to the cold and hostile forces of nature, we who will show all the universe that we can build a strong and safe haven for ourselves, a paradise of our own creation.

'The naming of names is merely the first step in this quest. We then must create a new government and elect the leaders who will serve us as we begin to create the new society that we desire.

'Instead of rivalry, we must have cooperation. Instead of struggle, we must have unity. Instead of weakness, we must have strength. Let each man and woman here firmly resolve that this society shall be strong and united. Ask not what gain you as an individual will obtain. Ask rather what strength you can contribute to help create a free and flourishing new order. We can build a paradise with our own hands! Will you help to do it?'

They bellowed, 'YES!' They clapped and cheered and whistled. Eberly stood at the podium, head bowed, soaking up their adulation the way a flower drinks in sunlight.

The crowd quieted, watched his silent form up on the podium. Slowly Eberly raised his head, looked out on them with an almost beatific smile on his lips.

'Each of you – each man and woman here – must pledge yourselves to the unity and cooperation we need to create the new order. I want each of you to reach out and clasp hands with the person next to you. Friend or stranger, man or woman, take your neighbor's hand in your own and swear that we will work together to build our new world.'

The crowd murmured, heads turned, feet shuffled. Then, slowly at first, people turned to each other and clasped hands. Holly watched as more and more people embraced, their differences forgotten for the moment, many of them openly sobbing. Holly realized that Malcolm was the only person in the entire habitat who could bring the people together like this.

She was proud to have helped this great man achieve this moment of unity, this powerful emotion of loving friendship.

Urgent Communication

To: Dr. Professor E. Urbain
Habitat *Goddard*

From: H. H. Haddix
Chair, IAA Executive Board

Subject: Titan contamination risk

In response to your request, the Executive Board initiated a thorough assessment of policy in regard to human exploration of the Saturnian moon, Titan. After review by the astrobiology and planetary protection committees of the International Astronautical Authority, it has been unanimously decided that any human excursion upon the surface of Titan is strictly forbidden. Protection of the indigenous life forms of Titan takes precedence over all other goals, including scientific investigation. Robotic exploration of Titan's surface is permitted, providing existing planetary protection decontamination procedures are strictly adhered to.

H. Harvey Haddix
Chair, IAA Executive Board
Rev. Calypso J. C. Abernathy
Imprimatur

Saturn Arrival Minus 288 Days

Ruth Morgenthau hated these nature walks that Eberly insisted upon. He's absolutely paranoid, she thought as she trudged reluctantly along the path that led through the park from Village A toward the orchards. He worries that someone might be bugging his apartment the way we're bugging everyone else's.

It's no longer Village A, she reminded herself. It's Athens now. And the orchard is officially the St. Francis of Assisi Preserve. Morgenthau almost giggled aloud. What a name! What arguments they had had, real shouting battles between herself, Vyborg and Kananga. Even the normally moderate and reserved Jaansen had raised his voice when it came to naming the habitat's various laboratory buildings.

The months-long campaign to produce actual names for the habitat's villages, buildings and natural features had been little more than a farce. Every vote had a scatter factor larger almost than the number of votes. *Everyone* in the habitat had an opinion about what the names should be, and hardly two votes agreed with each other. It was a grand mess, but Eberly came through with a magnificent solution.

'Since there is no unanimity among the voters,' he told his inner cadre of confidants, 'we will have to make the decisions ourselves.'

That set the four of them wrangling, with Kananga insisting that African names be just as numerous as European or Asian, Vyborg holding out for names that had powerful psychological connotations among the populace, and Jaansen firmly – sometimes stubbornly – proffering his own list of famous scientists' names. Eberly had stayed above the fray, listening to their squabbles with cold disdain. Morgenthau found the whole affair disgusting; she hadn't cared what names were chosen, as long as they were not blatantly secular. She had flatly refused to allow the biology facility to be named after Charles Darwin, of course.

In the end, Eberly resolved most of their disputes. When they could not agree, he made the decision. When they wrangled too long, he stepped in and told them to stop acting like children. Morgenthau watched over him carefully, though, and he knew it.

Village A got a European name: Athens. Village B went to the Asians: Bangkok. Village C became Cairo; D became Delhi and E was named Entebbe. The Americans – North and South – complained bitterly, but Eberly stared them down by solemnly proclaiming those were the names that the habitat's residents had voted for. After all, he pointed out, Americans actually were a minority in the habitat's population.

Since the votes were secret ballots, Eberly refused to allow anyone to recount them. In a great show of seeming impartiality, he erased all the votes – 'so that no one can tamper with them, or use them to cause unrest in the future,' he announced.

There were some grumbles, but the people by and large accepted the names that the voters allegedly chose. Eberly saw to it that there were plenty of American and Latino names sprinkled among the buildings and natural features, to keep everyone reasonably satisfied.

It was a strong, masterful performance, Morgenthau felt. Yet a tendril of worry troubled her. Perhaps Eberly was too strong, too determined to have his own way, too hungry for power. We are agents of God, she reminded herself. We seek power not for ourselves, but for the salvation of these ten thousand lost souls. She wondered if Eberly felt the same way. In fact, she was almost certain that he did not. Yet authorities higher than her own had chosen Eberly to lead this mission; her job was to support him – and keep him from straying too far from the path the New Morality and Holy Disciples had chosen for him.

So Morgenthau walked beside him along the Washington Carver pathway, which led from Athens to the St. Francis Orchard and beyond, over the little ridge of knolls that bore the incongruous name of the Andes Hills toward the farmlands of the Ohio region. She desperately hoped that Eberly would not decide to walk all the way to California, the open region up by the endcap. Her feet hurt enough already.

'You're very quiet this afternoon,' Eberly said as they walked along the meandering brick path. Those were the first words he himself had spoken in many minutes.

Morgenthau could feel sweat beading on her brow. 'I'm just happy that the names have been settled on,' she said. 'You did a masterful job, a brilliant job.'

He allowed a wintry smile to curve his lips. 'Just as long as the actual votes have been totally erased.'

'Totally,' she swore.

'And no one outside our inner circle knows about how the names were chosen.'

'No one.'

'Not even Holly? She's very bright, you know.'

Morgenthau agreed with a nod. 'She asked why the votes should be erased. Once I told her that it was your decision, though, she put up no resistance.'

Eberly nodded. 'I'll probably have to take her to bed, sooner or later. That will ensure her loyalty.'

Morgenthau gaped at him, shocked. 'She's quite loyal enough now. There's no need—'

He cut her short. 'The next steps we take will be more and more distasteful to her. I'll have to keep her bound to me personally. Otherwise she might balk, or even rebel against us.'

'But bedding her. That's sinful!'

'It's in a good cause. We must all be prepared to make sacrifices.'

She caught his sarcastic tone. 'Well, at least she's rather attractive.'

'A bit dark for my liking,' Eberly said, almost as casually as if he were discussing his preferences in clothing or food. 'I favor blonds, with fuller figures.'

Morgenthau felt her cheeks reddening. And yet . . . . Is he toying with me? she wondered. Testing me? She had no desire to pursue this line of discussion. She had no fantasies about her own attractions, or her own preferences.

'You didn't ask me out on this walk to discuss your plans for romance, did you?'

'No,' he answered, quite seriously. 'Hardly that.'

'Then what?'

Without changing his leisurely pace, Eberly looked up at the light poles and the miniature cameras atop them, then out to the green and flowering parkland spread about them.

'Offices can be bugged too easily. There are always prying eyes and ears to worry about.'

She understood. 'Out here, it simply looks as if we're taking in some exercise together.'

'Precisely.' He nodded.

Morgenthau considered that the fact the two of them were walking together might start some tongues wagging, although hardly anyone would suspect her of having a romantic interest in Eberly, or of being of any physical attraction to him. Or any man, for that matter. They all see me as a short, dumpy, over-weight loser, Morgenthau knew. I'm no threat to any of them. How little they know!

'Sooner or later we're going to have to confront Wilmot,' Eberly said, his eyes still scanning for eavesdroppers. 'Vyborg is constantly nagging me about removing Berkowitz and installing himself as the chief of communications. I've decided that the way to get to Berkowitz is through Wilmot.'

'Through Wilmot?'

'Berkowitz is an innocuous former network executive. He doesn't appear to have any obvious vices. He runs the communications department so loosely that Vyborg is actually in charge of virtually the entire operation.'

'But Sammi wants the title as well as the responsibility,' Morgenthau said. 'I know him. He wants the respect and the power.'

'Yes. And he's impatient. If what he did to that old man Romero is ever discovered . . .'

'It won't reflect on you,' she assured him. 'It can't.'

'Perhaps. But still, Berkowitz should be removed.'

'And to do that, you want to go through Wilmot?' Morgenthau asked.

'That's not the only reason, of course,' Eberly went on. 'Wilmot believes he is in charge of the habitat. The day will come when I'll have to disabuse him of that notion.'

'We can't have a godless secularist ruling these people!' Morgenthau said fervently.

'I'll need some ammunition, something to hold over Wilmot.'

'A carrot or a stick?' Morgenthau asked.

'Either. Both, if possible.'

'We'll need someone to review all his personal files and phone conversations.'

Eberly nodded. 'This must be kept totally secret. I don't want even Vyborg to know that we're going through Wilmot's files.'

'Then who should do the work?'

'You,' said Eberly, so clearly and precisely that there was no room to argue. Morgenthau's heart sank; she saw long dreary nights of snooping into the professor's phone conversations and entertainment vids.

She lapsed into silence, thinking hard as they walked slowly along the path.

'Well?' Eberly prodded.

'It might be very boring. He's nothing more than an elderly academic. I doubt that there's much there to use.'

Eberly did not hesitate a microsecond. 'Then we'll have to manufacture something. I prefer to find a weakness that he actually has, though. Drumming up false accusations can be tricky.'

'Let me talk to Vyborg about it.'

'No,' Eberly snapped. 'Keep this between the two of us. No one else. Not yet, at least.'

'Yes,' she agreed reluctantly. 'I understand.'

All the time during the long walk back to their offices in Athens, Morgenthau thought about Eberly's commitment to their cause. He's seeking nothing more than his own personal aggrandizement, she thought. But he has the charisma to be the leader of these ten thousand people. I'll have to put up with him. Wilmot, she told herself, is an out-and-out secularist: an atheist or an agnostic, at best. Find something that will hang him. I've got to find something that will hang him.

Saturn Arrival Minus 287 Days

'I haven't slept with him, if that's what's worrying you,' said Kris Cardenas.

Holly looked into her cornflower blue eyes and decided that Kris was telling the truth. She was spending an awful lot of time with Manny Gaeta, but it was strictly business, she insisted. On the other hand, Manny hadn't asked Holly out or dropped into her office or even phoned her since the night he had walked Kris home.

And Malcolm was as cool and distant as ever. All business, nothing but business. Some love life, Holly thought. It's all in tatters.

'I'm telling you the truth, Holly,' Cardenas insisted, misinterpreting Holly's silence.

'I know, Kris,' she said, feeling more confused than unhappy. 'Point of fact, I wouldn't blame you if you did. He's a dynamo.'

The two women were having a late lunch in the nearly empty cafeteria, well after almost everyone had cleared out of the place.

Cardenas leaned closer to Holly and confided, 'He hasn't come on to me at all. If you weren't interested in him, I'd be kind of disappointed. I mean, I'm a lot older than he is in calendar years but I'm not repulsive, am I?'

Holly giggled. 'Kris, if you're interested, go right ahead. I've got no claims on him.'

'Yes you do.'

'No, not really. In fact, I think I'm better off without him on my scanner screen.'

Cardenas raised a disbelieving eyebrow.

'Really,' Holly said, wondering inwardly if she were doing the right thing, 'his only interest in me was purely physical.'

'A lot of relationships have started that way.'

'Well this one's over. It isn't really a relationship, anyway. It never was.' Holly was surprised that it didn't hurt to admit it. Not much, anyway.

Cardenas shrugged. 'It's a moot point. He's nothing but business with me.'

'Prob'ly in awe of you.'

Cardenas laughed. 'I'll bet.'

'Sure.'

'Never mind,' she said, waving one hand as if brushing away an annoying insect. 'You said you've got a possible lab assistant for me?'

'Maybe,' Holly said. 'I haven't raised the idea with him, yet. But he's got some of the qualifications you're looking for. An engineering degree—'

'What kind of engineering?'

'Electromechanical.'

'How recent?'

Holly pulled her handheld out of her tunic pocket. Raoul Tavalera's three-dimensional image appeared in the air above their table, together with the facts and figures of his dossier.

Cardenas scanned through the data. 'Whose department is he working in?'

'Maintenance,' Holly replied. 'But he's just putting in time there; he doesn't officially belong to any department. He's the astronaut that Manny fished out.'

'Oh.' She went through the dossier again, more slowly this time. 'Then he'll only be with us until Manny packs up and leaves.'

'I guess. But he's available now and you said you needed help right away.'

'Beggars can't be choosy,' Cardenas agreed. 'I'll have to talk to him. Has he agreed to work with me?'

'He doesn't know anything about it yet. I can set up a meeting for you, though.'

'Good enough.'

'In my office, kay?'

Cardenas thought a moment. 'That's probably better than inviting him to my lab. He might be scared of having nanobugs infect him.'

Tavalera looked suspicious as he sat down in front of Holly's desk. He arrived promptly on time, though; that was a good sign, she thought. She had asked him to come to her office fifteen minutes before Cardenas.

'What's this all about?' he asked, almost sullenly.

'Job op,' said Holly brightly.

'I've got a job, with the maintenance crew.'

'Like it?'

He scowled. 'Are you kiddin'?'

Holly made a smile for him. 'I'd be worried if you said you did.'

'So what've you got for me?'

'It's in a science lab. You'll be able to use your engineering education, f'sure.'

'I thought all the science slots were filled. That's what you told me when I first came aboard here.'

'They are. This is with Dr. Cardenas, in her nanotech lab.'

His eyes widened momentarily. Holly could sense the wheels churning inside his skull.

'Nanotech,' he muttered.

Holly nodded. 'Some people are clanked up about nanotechnology, I know.'

'Yeah.'

'Are you?'

Tavalera hesitated a moment, then replied, 'Yeah, kinda. Guess I am.'

'You'd be foolish not to be,' Holly agreed. 'But working with Dr. Cardenas, you'll be working with the best there is. It'll look cosmically good on your résumé, y'know.'

'The hell it will. I wouldn't want anybody back on Earth to know I'd been within a zillion lightyears of any nanobugs.'

'Well,' Holly said, 'you don't have to take the job if you don't want to. We're not going to force you. You can always stay with maintenance.'

'Thanks a bunch,' he groused.

He was still wary about the idea when Cardenas arrived. She seemed uncertain about him, as well.

'Mr. Tavalera, I can't work with somebody who's frightened to be around nanomachines.'

'I'm not scared of 'em. I'm just scared they won't let me go back home if anybody finds out I've been workin' with you.'

'You can demand a complete physical,' Cardenas said. 'Then they'll see you're not harboring any nanobugs in your body.'

'Yeah,' he reluctantly admitted. 'Maybe.'

Holly suggested, 'We can keep your employment with Dr. Cardenas completely off the record. As far as the authorities Earthside will know, you worked in maintenance all the time you were aboard this habitat.'

'You can do that?' Even Cardenas looked incredulous.

'I can do it for special cases,' Holly said, thinking about how she would have to keep Morgenthau from poking her fat face into Tavalera's official dossier.

'You'd do it for me?' Tavalera asked.

'Sure I would,' said Holly.

He looked unconvinced, but he abruptly turned to Cardenas and said, 'Well, I guess if you screw up and let killer bugs loose everybody in this tin can is gonna get wiped out anyway. I might as well work with you. Beats overhauling farm tractors.'

Cardenas glanced at Holly, then started laughing. 'You certainly are enthusiastic, Mr. Tavalera!'

His long, horsy face broke into a awkward grin. 'That's me, all right: Mr. Enthusiasm.'

'Seriously,' Holly said to him, 'do you want to work with Dr. Cardenas or not?'

'I'll do it. Why not? What have I got to lose?'

Turning to Cardenas, Holly asked, 'Are you satisfied with him?'

Still smiling at her new assistant, Cardenas said, 'Not yet, but I think we can work it out.'

She got to her feet and Tavalera stood up beside her, smiling shyly. Holly thought, He looks so much better when he smiles.

Cardenas put out her right hand. 'Welcome to the nanolab, Mr. Tavalera.'

His long-fingered hand engulfed hers. 'Raoul,' he said. 'My name's Raoul.'

'I'll see you at the nanolab at eight a.m. sharp,' Cardenas said.

'Eight hundred. Right. I'll be there.'

Cardenas left. Tavalera stood uncertainly before Holly's desk for a moment, then said, 'Thanks.'

'*Da nada*,' said Holly.

'You meant it, about keeping this out of my dossier?'

'Certainly.'

He fidgeted for a few heartbeats more, then said, 'Uh . . . would you like to have dinner with me tonight? I mean, I 'preciate what you did for me—'

Holly cut him off before he spoiled it. 'I'd be happy to have dinner with you, Raoul.'

Two weeks later, Cardenas invited Edouard Urbain to her laboratory, to show him what she had accomplished in decontaminating Gaeta's suit. Tavalera sat at the master console, set against the wall opposite the door to the corridor.

'Remember, Raoul,' Cardenas said, 'we want to be completely honest with Dr. Urbain. We have nothing to hide.'

He nodded, and a small grin played across his face. 'I got nothing to hide because I don't know anything.'

Cardenas smiled back at him. 'You're learning fast, Raoul. I'm very impressed with you.' To herself, Cardenas thought, He's been a lot brighter than I thought he'd be. Maybe having a couple of dates with Holly has helped him to cheer up about being stuck here.

When the chief scientist stepped through the door, more than ten minutes late, he looked as tense and guarded as a man walking into a minefield. Cardenas tried to put him at his ease by showing him through her small, immaculately neat laboratory.

'This is the assembly area,' she said, pointing to a pair of stainless steel boxlike structures resting atop a lab bench. Gauges and control knobs ran across the face of each. 'The nanomachine prototypes are assembled in this one,' she patted one of the breadbox-sized enclosures, 'and then the prototype reproduces itself in here.'

Urbain kept a conspicuous arm's length from the apparatus. When Cardenas lifted the lid on one of the devices he actually flinched.

Cardenas tried not to frown at the man. 'Dr. Urbain, there is nothing here that can harm you or anyone else.'

Urbain was clearly not reassured. 'I understand, in my head. Still . . . I am nervous. I'm sorry, but I can't help it.'

She smiled patiently. 'I understand. Here, come over to the main console.'

For more than an hour Cardenas showed Urbain how the nanomachines were designed and built. How they reproduced strictly according to preset instructions.

'They're machines,' she stressed, over and over. 'They do not mutate. They do not grow wildly. And they are deactivated by a dose of soft ultraviolet light. They're really quite fragile.'

With Tavalera running the scanning microscope from the main console, Cardenas showed how the nanomachines she had designed broke up the contaminating molecules on the exterior of Gaeta's suit into harmless carbon dioxide, water vapor and nitrogen oxides.

'The suit is perfectly clean within five minutes,' she said, pointing to the image from the console. 'The residues outgas and waft away.'

Urbain appeared to be intrigued as he leaned over Tavalera's shoulder and peered intently at the data and imagery. 'All the organics are removed?'

Nodding, Cardenas said, 'Down to the molecular level there's not a trace of them remaining.'

'And the nanobugs themselves?'

'We deactivate them with a shot of UV.'

'But they are still on the surface of the suit? Can they reactivate themselves?'

'No,' said Cardenas. 'Once they're deactivated they're finished. They physically break down.'

Urbain straightened up slowly.

'As you can see, we can decontaminate the suit,' Cardenas said.

'Not merely the suit,' Urbain said, his eyes looking past her. 'This process could be used to decontaminate every piece of equipment we send to Titan's surface.'

'Yes it could,' Cardenas agreed.

For the first time since entering the nanotechnology laboratory, Urbain smiled.

Saturn Arrival Minus 273 Days

'This man Berkowitz has got to go!' Eberly insisted.

Wilmot sank back in his comfortable desk chair, surprised at the vehemence of his human resources director's demand.

Softly, he asked, 'And what gives you the right to interfere with the working of the communications department?'

Eberly had stoked himself up to a fever pitch. For weeks Vyborg had been pressuring him, threatening to act on his own if Eberly could not or would not get rid of Berkowitz. Vyborg wanted to be head of communications, and his scant patience had reached its end. 'Either you get him removed or I will remove him myself,' the grim little man said. 'In a few months we'll be entering Saturn orbit. I want Berkowitz out of the way before then. Long before then!'

Eberly knew this was a test of his power. Vyborg would never challenge him so unless he felt that Eberly was deliberately procrastinating. Now, Eberly knew, if I don't deliver Berkowitz's head, Vyborg will stop believing in me, stop obeying me. So, like it or not, he had to confront Wilmot.

Morgenthau hadn't come up with a thing that he could use against Wilmot. Although she swore that she spent every night faithfully plowing through his phone conversations and his computer files, she had found nothing useful so far.

I can do it without her help, Eberly told himself as he arranged to meet the chief administrator. A man can do anything, if he has the unbreakable will to succeed.

Yet now, as he sat before Wilmot's desk and saw the professor's steel-gray eyes assessing him coolly, Eberly wondered which of them had the stronger will.

'After all,' Wilmot said, 'your position as head of human resources doesn't give you the right to meddle in other departments, does it.'

'This is not meddling,' Eberly snapped. 'It's a matter of some urgency.'

Wilmot thought, he had a big success with the naming contest and the voting connected with it. That rally he held out in the park was a rather rousing event. It's gone to his head. He thinks he's already in charge of every department. He thinks he's going to replace me as chief of the entire habitat. Well, my lad, you have another think coming.

'Urgency?' he asked, deliberately calm and methodical. 'How so?'

'Berkowitz is incompetent. We both know that.'

'Do we? I thought the communications department was running rather smoothly.'

'Because Dr. Vyborg is doing all the work,' Eberly said.

'Vyborg. That little reptilian fellow.'

Eberly stifled an angry reply. He's deliberately trying to goad me, he realized. This old man is trying to make me angry enough to make a mistake.

He took in a breath, then said more calmly, 'Vyborg is a very capable man. He is actually running the communications department while Berkowitz sits on his laurels and does nothing.'

'Much as Ms. Morgenthau is running your office, I should imagine,' said Wilmot, with the trace of a smile.

Eberly smiled back at the older man. You're not going to make me lose my temper, he said silently. I'm not going to fall into your trap.

'Vyborg is ambitious,' he said aloud. 'He's come to me to ask my help. He feels frustrated, unappreciated.'

'Why doesn't he come to me? You can't help him.'

'I agreed to speak to you about the situation,' Eberly said. 'Vyborg feels he shouldn't go over Berkowitz's head and speak directly to you. He's afraid that Berkowitz will hold it against him.'

'Really?'

'Berkowitz is a drone, and we both know it. Vyborg does all the work for him.'

'As long as the communications department runs well, I have no reason for removing Berkowitz from his position. This discussion is actually over the man's management method. To his underlings he may seem like a drone, but as long as the department hums along, he's doing his job effectively as far as I'm concerned.'

Eberly sat back, thinking furiously. This is a test, he realized. Wilmot is testing me. Toying with me. How should I answer him? How can I get him to do what I want?

Wilmot, meanwhile, studied Eberly's face carefully. Why is he so worked up about the communications department? Does he have some personal grudge against Berkowitz? Or some personal relationship with Vyborg? I wish old Diego Romero were still with us; he kept the department's different factions working together smoothly enough, before he died.

Eberly finally hit upon a new ploy. 'If you find it impossible to remove Berkowitz, perhaps you could promote him.'

Wilmot felt his brows rise. 'Promote him?'

Hunching forward on his chair, Eberly said, 'Apparently this man Gaeta is going to be allowed to go to the surface of Titan after all.'

'That stuntman?'

'Yes. Dr. Cardenas has convinced Urbain that she can decontaminate Gaeta's suit so well that the man can go to Titan's surface without harming the life forms there.'

'Urbain hasn't told me of this,' Wilmot said sharply.

Eberly held back a snicker of triumph. You sit in your office and expect everyone to come to you, he sneered inwardly at Wilmot. The real life of this habitat swirls around you and you know almost nothing of it.

'You're certain that Urbain has approved of this . . . this stunt?' Wilmot asked.

'The approval isn't official yet, but Cardenas has worked out an understanding with him.'

Wilmot nodded. 'Urbain will notify me when he makes his approval official.'

'Why not ask Berkowitz to join Gaeta's team, as their full-time publicity manager?'

'Ahh. I see.'

Eberly went on, 'Berkowitz would enjoy that, I think.'

'And while he's enjoying his special assignment, your friend Vyborg can run the communications department.'

'He can be given the title of acting director,' said Eberly.

'Very neat. And what happens when Gaeta has performed his stunt and it's all finished?'

Eberly shrugged, 'We'll cross that bridge when we come to it.' To himself, though, he said, By the time Gaeta's done his stunt we'll have the new constitution in effect and I'll be the elected leader of this habitat. Berkowitz, Vyborg – even you, old man – will have to bow to my wishes.

But as he left Wilmot's office, his satisfaction melted away. He was playing with me, Eberly realized, like a cat plays with a mouse. Like a puppeteer pulling my strings. He let me have my way with Berkowitz because he intended to do it all along; he was just waiting to see how I jumped. Berkowitz doesn't mean a thing to him. It's all a game he's playing.

I've got to get control over him, Eberly told himself. I've got to find some way to bend the high and mighty Professor Wilmot to my will. Make him jump through my hoops.

When is Morgenthau going to find something I can use? There must be *something* in Wilmot's life that I can use for leverage. Some weakness. I've got to get Morgenthau to work harder, concentrate on his files, his phone conversations, everything he says or does, every breath he draws. I want him in my grasp. That's vital. If I'm to be the master here, Wilmot's got to bow down to me, one way or the other.

Holly saw Raoul Tavalera sitting alone in the cafeteria, bent over a sizable lunch. She carried her tray to his table.

'Want some company?' she asked.

He looked up at her and smiled.

'Sure,' he said. 'Sit right down.'

Tavalera had invited her to dinner at least once a week since starting work at the nanotechnology lab. Holly enjoyed his company, although he could get moody, morose. She tried to keep their dates as bright and easy as possible. So far, he'd worked up the nerve to kiss her goodnight. She wondered when he would try to go farther. And what she would do when he did.

'How's it going in the nanolab?' Holly asked as she removed her salad and iced tea from her tray.

'Okay, I guess.'

'Dr. Cardenas treating you well?'

He nodded enthusiastically. 'She's easy to work with. I'm learnin' a lot.'

'That's good.'

'None of it'll be any use when I go back to Earth, though.'

For a moment, Holly didn't know why he would say that. Then she remembered, 'Ohh, nanotech's banned on Earth, isn't it?'

Tavalera nodded. 'They'll probably quarantine me until they're certain I don't have any nanobugs in my body.'

'There's a nanotech lab in Selene.'

'I'm not gonna live underground on the Moon. I'm goin' back home.'

They talked about home: Holly about Selene and Tavalera about the New Jersey hills where he had grown up.

'A lotta the state got flooded out when the greenhouse cliff hit. All the beachfront resorts . . . people go scuba diving through the condo towers.'

'That's something you don't have to worry about in Selene,' Holly pointed out.

Tavalera grinned at her. 'Yeah. The nearest pond is four hundred thousand kilometers away.'

'We have a swimming pool in the Grand Plaza!'

'Big fr— uh, big deal.'

Ignoring his near lapse, Holly went on, 'It's Olympic-sized. And the diving platforms go up to thirty meters.'

With a shake of his head, Tavalera said, 'You wouldn't get me up there, low gravity or no low gravity.'

He just wants to go home, Holly saw. He wants to get back home. It made her sad to realize that she had no home to go back to. This is my home, she told herself. This habitat. Forever.

Saturn Arrival Minus 266 Days

If it must be done, Wilmot said to himself. 'twere best done quickly.

It was a dictum that had served him well all during his long career in academe. He often coupled it with Churchill's old aphorism: if you're going to kill a man, it costs nothing to be polite about it.

So he invited Gaeta and Zeke Berkowitz to dine with him, in the privacy of his own apartment. Berkowitz was an old friend, of course, and Wilmot was delighted when he showed up precisely on time, before the stuntman.

As Wilmot poured a stiff whisky for the news director, Berkowitz grinned amiably and said, 'Must be pretty bad news, to make the first drink so tall.'

Wilmot smiled, a little sheepishly, and handed the glass to Berkowitz. 'You still have your nose in the wind, don't you, Zeke?'

Berkowitz shrugged. 'I'd be a lousy newsman if I didn't know what was going on.'

Wilmot poured an even stiffer belt for himself.

'Rumor is,' Berkowitz said, still standing by the apartment's compact little bar, 'that you're going to kick me upstairs.'

With a slight nod, Wilmot admitted, 'I'm afraid so.'

Before Berkowitz could ask another question, they heard a rap at the door. 'That will be Gaeta,' said Wilmot, heading for the door.

Gaeta wore a denim work shirt and jeans, about as formal an outfit as he possessed. He looked serious, almost somber, as Wilmot introduced him to Berkowitz and asked the stuntman what he wanted to drink.

'Beer, if you have it,' said Gaeta, still unsmiling.

'Would Bass ale do?' Wilmot asked.

Gaeta broke into a grin. 'It'll do very well, thanks.'

Wilmot steered his two guests to the sitting room chairs. Once they were comfortably settled, he said to Gaeta, 'I've asked you here because I want to assign Zeke to be your full-time publicity man.'

Berkowitz nodded knowingly. The stuntman looked surprised.

By the time Wilmot carried the dinner tray to the table, though, the two men seemed to be getting along well enough.

'So if Urbain or the IAA or whoever prevents me from going down to Titan, I'll take a spin through the rings,' Gaeta was saying.

Berkowitz twirled his fork in the air. 'Through the rings? Wow. That'd be spectacular.'

'You think you could get me some coverage, huh?'

'A brain-dead librarian could get you coverage for that. I mean, everybody's seen footage from the automated probes they've sent to Titan's surface. Fascinating stuff, yeah, but it's been *done*. Nobody's been to the rings.'

'No human has set foot on Titan,' Wilmot pointed out.

'I know. But the rings! They'll salivate over that. I could run an auction right now and gin up enough cash to pay for your whole crew and then some.'

Gaeta leaned back in his chair, looking contented. Wilmot saw that Berkowitz was as happy as a child with a new toy. The professor felt relieved. I can give Eberly and that Vyborg creature what they want without hurting anyone's feelings. A win–win situation. All to the good.

Pancho Lane could feel her face tightening into a frown as she watched Manuel Gaeta's message to her.

'So even if I can't get to Titan, this stunt with the rings oughtta pay you back for the trip with interest.'

Yeah, but what about my sister? Pancho demanded silently.

Gaeta rambled on about his possible stunts while Pancho sat fuming behind her desk. What about Susie? she wondered. Holly, I mean.

At last Gaeta said, 'Your sister's fine, Ms. Lane. She's a very bright young woman. Very intelligent. And very attractive, too. She has lots of friends and she seems very happy here. Not to worry about her.'

But Pancho focused on his 'And very attractive, too.' Gaeta had something of a reputation. Handsome chunk of beef, Pancho had to admit. I wouldn't throw him out of my bed. Is he making it with my sister?

Pancho sighed. If he is, there's not much I can do about it. I just hope Susie enjoys it. I hope he doesn't hurt her. If he does, this'll be his last stunt. Ever.

Professor Wilmot rocked slightly in his desk chair as he dictated his status report to Atlanta.

'It's interesting to observe the different motivations of these people. Eberly isn't after power so much as adulation, it seems to me. The man wants to be adored by the people. I'm not certain what Vyborg wants; I haven't been able to work up the stamina to get close to the man. Berkowitz is happy to be rid of the responsibilities of heading the communications department. He's back to being an active newsman. I understand there's some friction between him and Gaeta's technical crew, but that's perfectly understandable. Quite normal.

'Gaeta himself is fascinating, in his own way. He actually wants to risk his hide on these stunts he does. He enjoys it. Of course, it brings him money and fame, but I believe he'd do them anyway, merely for the sheer adrenaline rush it gives him. In a strange way, he's rather like a scientist, except that scientists enjoy the intellectual thrill of being the first to discover new phenomena, while this stuntman enjoys the visceral excitement of being the first man on the scene.'

Saturn Arrival Minus 205 Days

Night after night Holly spent in her apartment, alone, calling up programs on forensic medicine from Earth. She recalled with perfect clarity the way Don Diego's crumpled body had looked when she discovered it lying headfirst in the water of the irrigation culvert. She remembered every detail of the medical examination report: no heart attack, no major stroke, nothing unusual except that the heels of his hands seemed slightly abraded, and his lungs were full of water.

What would roughen his hands, Holly wondered. The concrete surface of the culvert, she decided. Then she began to search for a reason *why* his hands were bruised. Eventually she came to the conclusion that he was trying to push his head out of the water, trying hard enough to scrape the skin off the heels of both hands.

And why, if he was trying so hard to get up, why couldn't he lift his head out of the water? Because something – or some*one* – was holding his head down. Drowning him. Murdering him.

Not trusting her memory, good as it was, Holly called up the medical report and studied it for several nights in a row. No sign of violence. Only the abrasions on his hands.

It wasn't much to go on. But Holly doggedly pursued that one clue. She thought of it as a clue. She was convinced Don Diego had been murdered.

Why? By whom?

Closing her eyes, she envisioned once again the scene when she found the old man's body. No signs of a struggle. Nothing disturbing the slope that led down to the concrete except some footprints in the dirt. Boot prints, actually.

★   ★   ★

Professor Wilmot also spent his evenings watching video displays, as usual. The business of the habitat faded into oblivion as he sat in his favorite chair, swirling his glass of whisky in his right hand, watching his collection of vids about naked women undergoing torture. Sometimes, when a scene was particularly revolting, he felt a twinge of guilt. But that passed quickly enough. It's all make-believe, he told himself. They wouldn't produce such vids unless there was a market for them. I'm not the only one who enjoys this sort of thing.

He had run through the collection he'd brought aboard the habitat, seen each of them twice and his favorites more than that. For weeks he fretted about ordering more from Earth. They made new ones all the time, he knew. Fresh faces. New young bodies.

There was a certain danger in calling a supplier on Earth and ordering more vids. Even if he routed his order through a middle-man at Selene, sooner or later it would be traced to the habitat. But there are ten thousand people here, he told himself. How would they know it's me, and not some clerk or farm worker? Besides, I'd wager there are others aboard who have similar tastes and make similar orders.

After weeks of arguing with himself, and watching the same old vids, he sent an order to Earth by the habitat's tight-beam laser communications link. It was all in code, of course. No one will know, Wilmot reassured himself. After all, who would be tapping the comm links? It's not as if I'm using my personal phone line. Someone would have to tap every outgoing and incoming message to find my one brief little order. Who would be fanatical enough to do that?

Saturn Arrival Minus 87 Days

'It's remarkable, really,' Wilmot was saying to his computer. 'They have drafted a constitution and are preparing for elections. By the time we establish ourselves in orbit about Saturn, they'll be ready to transfer power to their new government.'

The computer was automatically encrypting his words for transmission to Earth, to the headquarters of the New Morality in Atlanta, the covert financial backers of the Saturn mission. Wilmot was the only person in the habitat who knew where the funding for this experiment had come from, and he intended to keep the secret entirely to himself. His reports back to Atlanta were private, coded, and sent toward Earth by the automated laser system, not by the habitat's regular communications links.

'The man Eberly has formed something of a clique around himself,' Wilmot continued, 'which is more or less what I had expected. The scientists have formed a countervailing political force, led by Dr. Urbain. Frankly, Urbain seems more interested in personal flattery than politics, but he seems to be the acknowledged leader among the technical types.

'Even the engineers have organized a political bloc, of sorts. Their leader seems to be a Russian exile named Timoshenko, although he insists that he has no interest in politics. Yet he's allowed the engineers to bruit his name about as a candidate for the chief administrator's position. Frankly I doubt that he has one chance in a million.

'There have been a few scuffles here and there, but by and large the political campaigning has been remarkably free of the usual hooliganism, which is little short of extraordinary when one considers that the bulk of our population is made up of dissidents and freethinkers who got themselves into trouble on Earth. I believe the reason is that most of the population doesn't care a fig about this political campaigning. Most of the people here have absolutely no interest in their own government. In fact, they try rather hard to avoid any commitments of any sort.'

Wilmot leaned back in his comfortable swivel chair and reread his words from the image displayed above his desk. Satisfied with his report so far, he continued:

'In three weeks we will have the general elections that will bring our new constitution into power and elect the individuals who will form the new government. Eberly is the odds-on favorite. I shall have to install him as the new chief administrator and gracefully retire to the ceremonial role of president. I suspect that Eberly will name Urbain to some important-sounding but innocuous position: probably deputy administrator or some such. I have no idea of how he'll handle the engineer, Timoshenko.

'Some of the people around Eberly frankly give me the willies. He's surrounded himself with nonentities who believe themselves to be quite important, such as this Vyborg person who's now running the communications office. I know that the Morgenthau woman is a high official in the Holy Disciples. Why she volunteered for this mission is beyond me. And this Kananga fellow! He's positively frightening.' Wilmot talked on, bluntly giving his opinions on each of the major players in the habitat's coming elections. He would have been much less free with his judgments if he had known that every word he spoke was being picked up by molecular-film microphones and recorded for Eberly's perusal.

Late in the afternoon the cafeteria was quiet, nearly empty; most of the lunchtime crowd had left, and the dinner rush hadn't started yet. Manuel Gaeta sat with three others at a table near the holowindow that showed a view of a pristine lake in the Rockies, a picture from distant Earth taken long before the greenhouse warming had driven millions from their flooded cities to makeshift refugee camps in such regions.

Of the four people talking intently together over the remains of their lunches, Gaeta was the only one who looked anywhere near happy.

'We can do it,' Gaeta said firmly.

'It would be awfully dangerous, Manny,' said Kris Cardenas.

Nadia Wunderly nodded her agreement. 'It'd be like trying to walk past a firing squad that uses machine guns.'

Gaeta shrugged carelessly. 'All I gotta do is go in between the bullets.' He turned to von Helmholtz. 'What do you think, Fritz?'

Von Helmholtz cast a cold eye at him. 'Isn't it enough to do what we came here to do?'

Gaeta said, 'We'll do the Titan gig if we can get the scientists to allow it. But while we're out here, why not do a spin through the rings?'

'Because you could get killed,' von Helmholtz snapped.

Spreading his hands as if he'd proven his point, Gaeta countered, 'That's why people watch, Fritz. They're waiting to see if I get killed.'

'What is worse, you'll ruin the suit.'

Gaeta laughed.

'There's a really strong chance that you would be killed,' Wunderly said.

'Not if you can pick out the right spot in the rings for me to traverse. A spot without so many big chunks.'

With a sigh, Wunderly explained, 'I'd have to study the rings close-up for months, Manny. Years, maybe.'

'We've still got a few weeks before we go into orbit around Saturn. Won't that be enough?'

'I'd need all the computer time we've got on board to make any reasonable computations,' she said. 'Plus I'd need time on the big 'scopes and Urbain won't let me near them.'

Von Helmholtz looked surprised. 'He won't allow you to use the telescopes in the astronomy pod?'

Wunderly shook her head. 'Urbain won't let me have any time on the big 'scopes. They're all being used full-time on Titan.'

'All of them?'

'All of them,' said Wunderly.

'Maybe we can talk him into letting you use one,' Gaeta suggested.

'He won't. I've asked, more than once. Besides, I'd need a ton of computer time.'

'Maybe somebody else should ask him,' said Gaeta.

'Who?' Cardenas asked.

'Wilmot. Or if not him, maybe Eberly can swing it.'

Again she shook her head. 'Urbain won't listen to Eberly. He won't even talk to him. They're running against each other in the elections, remember?'

Eberly, meanwhile, was sitting tensely in the living room of his apartment, which had become the command center for his election campaign. A bank of computers lined the wall where the sofa had once been, each machine humming with continuous recording of the conversations in every public space in the habitat and quite a few private apartments and offices, including Wilmot's and Urbain's.

'I don't like this constitution,' Morgenthau was saying. 'I never did, and the closer we get to putting it into action, the less I like it.'

Eberly studied her fleshy face as she sat in the upholstered chair on the opposite side of the oval coffee table. Her usual smile was gone; she was deadly serious.

'Why didn't you voice your objections when we were drafting it?' he asked sharply.

'I thought Vyborg and Jaansen were thrashing everything out satisfactorily, and then you made it clear that you wanted an end to their arguing.'

With growing impatience, Eberly said, 'I've explained it to all of you time and again. As long as the emergency-powers clause is in the constitution all the rest of it doesn't matter.'

'I still don't like it,' Morgenthau insisted.

Eberly thought he knew what the problem was. Morgenthau was no fighter; she was an agent planted on the habitat ostensibly to help him, but actually to keep watch on him and report back to the Holy Disciples. Someone high up in the hierarchy must have

255

finally reviewed the new constitution and told her that it didn't suit the stern moral standards of the Disciples. She would never oppose me like this, Eberly said to himself. Not unless she's under pressure from her superiors back on Earth.

'It's too late to change it now,' he said, trying to keep his voice calm, even. 'The people vote on it in three weeks.'

Morgenthau said, 'You could withdraw it. Say it needs further work.'

'Withdraw it?' Despite his self-discipline, Eberly nearly shouted the words. 'That would mean we'd have to postpone the election.'

Morgenthau said nothing.

How can I get her back on my side? Eberly asked himself. How can I make her see that she'd be better off following my orders than the stupid commands from Earth?

'Listen to me,' he said, leaning forward in his chair, bending his head closer to hers. 'In three weeks the people will vote. They'll accept this constitution for the very same reasons that you distrust it: because it promises individual freedom and a liberal, relaxed government.'

'Without any rules for population control. Without any moral standards.'

'Those will come later, after the constitution is adopted and we are in power.'

Morgenthau looked totally unconvinced.

'As I've explained more than once,' Eberly said, straining to hold on to his swooping temper, 'once I'm in power I'll declare a state of emergency and suspend all those liberal laws that bother you.'

'How can you declare a state of emergency if everyone is satisfied with the constitution?'

'We'll need a crisis of some sort. I'll think of something.'

Morgenthau's face looked as hard as steel. 'You were taken out of prison and placed in this habitat to form a proper, God-fearing government. You are not living up to your end of the agreement.'

'That's not true!' he protested. Inwardly, a panicky voice whined, they can't send me back to prison. They can't!

'All we need to do is generate a crisis,' he said aloud. 'Then Kananga and his security teams can clamp down.'

'It won't be that simple,' Morgenthau said. 'The more power you give Kananga the more he will seize control of everything. I don't trust him.'

'Neither do I,' Eberly admitted, silently adding, I don't trust *anyone*.

'And then there's this Cardenas woman, working with nano-machines. They're the devil's spawn and yet you allow her to go right ahead and do her evil in our midst.'

'Only until I'm in power,' Eberly said.

'She's got to go. Get rid of her.'

As Eberly nodded somberly, the solution to his problems suddenly struck him with the blinding force of a revelation. Yes! he said to himself. That will solve everything!

He made a warm smile for the still scowling Morgenthau and, leaning forward, patted her chubby knee. 'Don't worry about it. I'll take care of everything.'

Her frown faded somewhat, replaced by curiosity.

'Trust me,' Eberly said, smiling still more broadly.

Laboratory *Lavoisier*

Kris Cardenas wondered why Urbain had asked her to meet with him. Not in his office, not even in the astronomy pod, where the big telescopes were housed. Here in the science building, in his main laboratory, which had been named for the eighteenth-century French founder of modern chemistry, Antoine Laurent Lavoisier.

Cardenas' own lab (named after the American physicist Richard P. Feynman) was in a separate building, up at the top of the ridge on which Athens was built, as far away from the other labs as possible. As she made her way down the bricked path that curved past the low, white-walled apartment buildings and shops of the village, Cardenas felt the old resentment against the unreasoning fear of nanotechnology still simmering deep within her.

Keep it under control, she warned herself. Keep everything in perspective. Remember that Lavoisier was beheaded during the French Revolution. Idiots and bastards have always been in our midst.

So she put on a sunny smile as she entered the lab complex and saw Edouard Urbain standing in the doorway to his laboratory, waiting for her. He looked nervous. No, Cardenas decided, not nervous. Excited. Expectant. Almost like a little boy standing in front of the Christmas tree, eager to tear into the brightly wrapped packages.

'Dr. Cardenas!' Urbain greeted her. 'How good of you to come.'

'It was good of you to invite me,' she replied.

He ushered her into the lab. Cardenas was slightly taller than Urbain, her sandy blond hair and bright blue eyes a sharp contrast to his dark, slicked-back hair and eyes of mahogany brown.

The lab was two stories tall, its bare metal ceiling the underside of the building's roof. A tall screen stood just inside the doorway, cutting off the main area of the lab from view. The place felt to Cardenas like an airplane hangar or an empty warehouse. With a slight gesture, Urbain led Cardenas along the screen toward its end.

'I wanted you to see this,' he said, his voice brimming with anticipation. She thought his moustache would start quivering any moment. 'I am very proud of what we have accomplished.'

They reached the end of the screen. With a flourish, Urbain turned the corner and pointed to the massive object standing in the middle of the laboratory floor.

The first thing that Cardenas noticed was that the lab had been cleaned, the floor swept. Not a scrap of paper or piece of equipment in sight. No wires snaking across the floor or dangling from overhead mounts. He's spiffed up his lab, Cardenas thought. He's got it looking like an old automobile showroom.

'There it is,' Urbain said, aglow with pride. '*Titan Alpha*.'

A spacecraft, Cardenas realized. More than two meters tall; nearly three, she estimated. Standing on a pair of caterpillar treads, like an old-fashioned tank. Massive. Silvery-gray. Titanium, she guessed. Its oblong body was studded with projections.

'It has been built here, completely,' Urbain said, almost in a whisper. 'It did not exist when we left Earth. None of it. My staff and I constructed it.'

Cardenas became aware that half a dozen men and women were standing off along the far wall of the lab, like students who had been lined up and told to remain quiet and respectful.

'You'll go to the surface of Titan in this,' Cardenas said.

'Not in person, of course,' said Urbain. '*Alpha* is designed to be tele-operated from here in the habitat. It is a mobile laboratory that will explore the surface of Titan for us.'

'I see.'

Urbain snapped his fingers; one of the technicians across the lab whirled and began tapping out instructions on a desk-sized console. The spacecraft seemed to stir. A loud electrical hum filled the lab and a pair of long, skeletal arms unfolded from one side of its body. Pincer-like claws opened and shut. Cardenas instinctively moved back a couple of steps.

Urbain laughed. 'Don't be afraid. She won't harm you. Those grippers can handle the most delicate biological samples without damaging them.'

'It's . . . very impressive.'

'Yes, isn't it? *Alpha* is equipped with a complete array of sensors. She can take samples, store them in insulated capsules and send them back to us, here in the habitat, for analysis.'

'Won't it return after it's finished its mission?'

'No. Never. She remains on Titan. We will send replenishments of fuel and supplies for its sensors.'

'Isn't it nuclear powered?' Cardenas asked.

'Of course! The fuel is necessary for the sample-return rockets.'

'I see.'

Urbain sighed contentedly. 'I haven't had as much time to spend on this project as I would have liked. My hours are consumed with this political campaign, you know.'

Cardenas nodded. 'Yet you've completed the job. It's a great accomplishment.'

'I am blessed with a fine staff.'

Afraid that Urbain would order the bulky spacecraft to start trundling across the laboratory floor, Cardenas said, 'I'm very grateful that you asked me to see it.'

She started toward the door, slowly. Urbain caught up with her in two strides.

'My motivation was not entirely from pride,' he said, looking a little less animated now. 'I have a favor to request of you.'

Still walking along the screen, feeling somehow oppressed by the massive spacecraft, almost threatened by it, Cardenas replied with, 'A favor?'

Urbain hesitated, as if he didn't know how to choose the right words. 'It concerns *Alpha's* self-repair capabilities.'

Cardenas glanced sharply at him.

'I was wondering,' Urbain said as they turned around the end of

260

the screen, 'if nanomachines might be able to repair *Alpha* while she is on the surface of Titan.'

Cardenas nodded, thinking, So that's it. They're all terrified of nanobugs until they come up against something where nanomachines can help them.

'I mean,' Urbain went on, 'you yourself have nanomachines in your body, don't you? They're constantly repairing your tissues, aren't they?'

With a slight laugh of relief, Cardenas answered, 'And you'd like to have a nanotech immune system built into your spacecraft.'

'Nanomachines that could continuously repair any equipment failures or damage.'

'Or wear and tear,' Cardenas added.

'Yes! Precisely.'

She stopped at the open doorway, thinking swiftly. 'It would take time, Dr. Urbain. When do you plan to send the spacecraft to Titan?'

'As soon as we establish orbit around Saturn. Within a few days of that, at the most.'

'I certainly can't come up with a set of therapeutic nanos that soon.'

'But perhaps they could be sent to A*lpha* after she is on Titan, once you produce them.'

'Perhaps,' Cardenas conceded.

'Will you look into the possibilities?' he asked eagerly.

Cardenas saw in his eyes that he regarded this machine of his almost like a human being, a woman he loved and cherished and wanted to protect, keep from harm. A kind-hearted Dr. Frankenstein, she thought, worried about the creature he's created. Then a sharp pang of memory hit her. How many times have you been called Frankenstein? she asked herself.

'Can you do it?' Urbain pressured.

'I can try.'

'Good! Excellent!'

'Under one condition,' she added.

His brows rose toward his receding hairline. 'Condition? If you mean you want me to allow that . . . that *stuntman* to go down to the surface— '

Cardenas said, 'But we've tested the decontamination procedure several times now. I've sent you the reports.'

'Tests in the airlock. Yes, I've scanned your reports.'

'So you know that we can clean his suit to your satisfaction.' Suddenly Cardenas got a new inspiration. 'We can decon your spacecraft the same way.'

'*Alpha* can be decontaminated the normal way.'

'Yes, but if you use nanomachines you won't have to subject the spacecraft to such high levels of radiation. Won't that be better for its electronics systems?'

Urbain started to reply, stopped himself, then admitted, 'Yes. Definitely.'

'I can set that up for you in a couple of days. By the time we're in Saturn orbit I'll be able to decon your craft as clean as new-fallen snow.'

'But that doesn't mean that I can allow the stuntman to go down to the surface. The IAA forbids it. My hands are tied.'

Don't push it any farther, Cardenas told herself. You've got a toe in the door. Let it rest there, for now.

Yet she heard herself say, 'There is one other thing.'

Urbain's brows went up again.

'It's rather minor . . .'

'What is it?'

'One of your staff people, Dr. Wunderly—'

'Wunderly?'

'She needs some telescope time to study the rings.'

'Impossible. I've told her—'

'Surely you can spare some time at one of the telescopes for her,' Cardenas said, more as a declaration than a request. 'After all, you're going to have your spacecraft operating on Titan's surface in a few weeks, won't you?'

Urbain hesitated. 'Yes, that's true enough.'

'And you want to be able to use nanomachines to keep it in good shape.'

His face showed clearly that he understood Cardenas' threat. 'I see. Yes. Very well, I will attempt to get some time for Wunderly on one of the telescopes so she can study her wretched rings.'

'Fine,' said Cardenas. 'And I'll attempt to develop a set of nanomachines that can auto-repair your spacecraft while it's on Titan.'

'And to decontaminate *Alpha*,' Urbain reminded her.

Cardenas nodded her agreement and started for the door. Then she turned back. 'By the way, how is the political campaign going?'

Urbain took in a sharp breath, as if surprised by her sudden change of subject. Then he shrugged. 'It takes too much of my time. I must give speeches, prepare position papers on everything from medical care to garbage recycling. Every person in the habitat feels free to ask me pointless questions and to give me their own vapid opinions.'

'That's politics, I guess,' Cardenas said, chuckling.

'I fear it will be even worse after I am elected.'

'You expect to win?'

'Of course. This is a scientific mission, isn't it? The whole purpose of our flight to Saturn is scientific.'

'But the scientists are only a small part of the population,' Cardenas pointed out.

'Yes, of course. But the others will vote for me. It is the only logical choice they can make. Eberly is the only other major candidate, and he has no scientific background at all.'

'What about the engineer, Timoshenko?'

Urbain made an unpleasant face. 'He is nothing. A posturer. The engineers and technicians will vote for me, overwhelmingly.'

Cardenas held back the comment she wanted to make. Better not to disillusion the man, she thought. He'll find out soon enough on election day. It'll bruise his ego, but in the long run he'll probably be relieved to get out of politics and give all his attention to his clunky *Alpha*.

Saturn Arrival Minus 45 Days

The three women met for breakfast in the cafeteria, so early that the place was hardly half filled. Holly thought the cafeteria seemed different this early in the morning, quieter, subdued, as if the people shuffling through the lines weren't fully awake yet.

She found Kris and Nadia Wunderly already at a table, heads leaning together, pleased grins on their faces.

Holly unloaded her tray of melon slices, bran cereal, soymilk and faux coffee and sat down.

Wunderly looked happy, her big gray eyes sparkling. 'I still can't thank you enough for getting me some telescope time. You should see the dynamics of those rings! It's . . . it's . . .'

Cardenas laughed lightly. 'Words fail you?'

Wunderly looked a little embarrassed. 'I'd like you to see the imagery I've been getting.' Turning to Holly, Wunderly said, 'You too, Holly.'

Holly smiled at her. 'Sure. I'd love to.'

Wunderly asked Cardenas, 'I still can't understand how you got Urbain to let me use the 'scope.'

Still grinning, Cardenas said, 'Trickery and deceit. And a little blackmail.'

'Whatever works, I guess,' Holly said.

Wunderly dipped into her bowl of soy-yogurt. 'Thanks to you, Kris, I can feed Manny the data he needs.'

Holly's innards twitched. 'Manny?'

'He wants to dive through the rings,' Wunderly explained. 'But he can't do it without my help.'

Looking across the table to Cardenas, Holly said, 'I haven't seen Manny in weeks. How is he?'

Wunderly answered, 'Terrific.'

Cardenas looked surprised. 'Come to think of it, the last time I saw him was our final test of the decon nanos.'

Wunderly glanced from Holly to Cardenas and then back again. 'I see him almost every day,' she said. A little smugly, Holly thought.

'Do you see him nights?' asked Cardenas, raising her teacup to her lips.

Wunderly said, 'Sure. Sometimes.' Very smugly, as far as Holly was concerned.

'He's pretty good, isn't he?' said Cardenas.

Wunderly nodded with pleasure.

Suddenly aware, Holly blurted, 'Kris, have you maxed out with Manny?'

Cardenas actually blushed. Nodding behind her teacup, she said in a small voice, 'A couple of times. You said you didn't mind, remember?'

'I *don't* mind,' Holly insisted, knowing from the turmoil inside her that it wasn't really true.

Wunderly's owl eyes went even wider than usual. 'You mean he's slept with both of you?'

Cardenas put down her teacup. 'Actually, we didn't do all that much sleeping.'

Holly burst into laughter. The pain inside her dissolved. 'He's a flamer, all right.'

Wunderly looked hurt, though. 'Both of you,' she whispered. It was no longer a question.

Cardenas reached across the table to touch Wunderly's hand. 'He's just a man, Nadia. It doesn't mean anything to him. Just fun and games. Recreational.'

'But I thought . . .'

'Don't think. Just enjoy. He'll be heading back to Earth soon. Have fun while you can.'

'Gather ye rosebuds,' Holly quoted, wondering where she remembered the line from.

Forcing a halfhearted smile, Wunderly said, 'I suppose you're right. But still . . .'

'Just don't get pregnant.'

'Oh, I'd never!'

Holly was thinking, though. 'He slept with me when he needed help from the administration. And he slept with you, Kris, when he found out you could help him with nanobugs.'

'And now he's sleeping with me,' Wunderly chimed in, 'because I can help him with the rings.'

'That sonofabitch,' Cardenas said. But she was grinning widely.

'You know what they'd call a woman who did that,' Wunderly said.

Holly didn't know if she should be angry, amused, or disgusted.

'It's a good thing he'll be leaving soon,' Cardenas said. 'Otherwise he might get murdered.'

'He's getting away with murder right now,' said Wunderly, with a tinge of anger.

'Well,' Cardenas said, 'he's good at it.'

Holly asked, 'Nadia, are you going to keep on with him?'

'I couldn't! Not now.'

'Why not?' Cardenas asked. 'If you enjoy being with him, why not?'

'But he's . . . it's . . . it's not *right*.'

With a shake of her head, Cardenas said, 'Don't let the New Morality spoil your fun. There's nothing wrong with recreational sex, as long as you understand that it's recreational and nothing more. And you protect yourself.'

Holly wondered, how do you protect your heart? How do you let a man make love to you and then just walk away and let him go do it with someone else? With your friends, for god's sake.

Wunderly nodded slightly, but she looked just as unconvinced as Holly felt.

'It's not like the old days,' Cardenas went on, 'when you had to worry about AIDS and VD.'

'I read about AIDS in history class,' Wunderly said. 'It must have been terrible.'

'Just don't get yourself pregnant.'

'I won't. I can't. The habitat's regulations won't allow it.'

Cardenas was no longer grinning. 'I can remember a time, back before either one of you were born, when religious fundamentalists were against abortion. Against any kind of family planning.'

'Really?' Holly was surprised.

'Yes. It wasn't until they dropped their "right to life" position that the New Morality began to gain real political power. Once the Catholics got an American Pope, even the Vatican caved in.'

For several moments all three of the women were silent. The cafeteria seemed to be waking up. There were more people coming in, more chatter and clatter as they lined up for their breakfasts before heading off to their jobs.

Wunderly pushed her chair back from the table and stood up. 'I've got to make a progress report to Dr. Urbain.'

'And Manny?' Cardenas asked.

She shrugged. 'I don't know. He can be . . . well, attractive, you know.'

'Seductive,' said Cardenas.

'Charming,' Holly added. 'Like a snake.'

Wunderly just shook her head and walked off, leaving her half-finished breakfast on the table.

'What do you think she'll do?' Holly asked.

Cardenas chuckled. 'She'll go to bed with him but feel bad about it.'

'That's brutal.'

'Yep.'

'Would you go to bed with him again?'

Cardenas gave her a guarded look. 'Would you?'

Holly felt her lips curling upward into a rueful smile. 'Only if he asks me.'

They both laughed.

'The sonofabitch is getting away with murder, all right,' Cardenas said.

Suddenly serious, Holly said softly, 'I wonder if somebody else has gotten away with murder.'

'Huh? Who?'

'I don't know. I just wonder about Don Diego.'

'You're still gnawing on that?'

'They didn't find anything wrong with him.'

'Except that he drowned.'

'But how could he drown?' Holly wondered. 'How could a man fall into a few centimeters of water and drown himself?'

'He was pretty old,' Cardenas said.

'But his health was fine. They didn't find any heart failure or any sign of a stroke.'

'You think someone pushed him into the water and deliberately drowned him?'

The scene appeared in Holly's mind, every detail, just as she had seen it that day. 'I don't know. Maybe.'

'Who? Why?'

Holly shrugged. 'I don't know. I wish I did.'

Campaign Speeches

The political debate was held in the habitat's outdoor theater, a big concrete shell that curved gracefully to focus the sound waves produced on its stage out into the rows of seats set up on the grass.

It's a fairly good crowd, Eberly thought as he looked out over the audience. Must be more than a thousand out there, and a lot more watching by vid. Seated on the stage three meters to his left was Edouard Urbain, looking stiffly elegant in an old-fashioned dove gray suit over a sky-blue turtleneck. Next to him sat Timoshenko, sour and gruff; he wore gray coveralls as a symbol of pride in his profession. Eberly thought he looked like a janitor. Eberly himself wore a charcoal-grey tunic and comfortable slacks of lighter gray, true to the dress code he had promulgated.

Wilmot stood at the podium in his usual tweed jacket and shapeless trousers, explaining the rules of the debate.

'. . . each candidate will begin with a five-minute summary of his position, to be followed by another five minutes apiece for rebuttal. Then the meeting will be opened to questions from the audience.'

Eberly kept himself from smiling. Vyborg and Kananga had 'seeded' the audience with dozens of supporters, each of them armed with questions that would allow Eberly to dominate the Q&A period. He had no intention of allowing Urbain or Timoshenko to say a single word more than absolutely necessary.

'So without further ado, allow me to introduce Dr. Edouard Urbain, head of our scientific section,' said Wilmot. He began reading Urbain's *curriculum vitae* from the display on the podium.

What a bore, thought Eberly. Who cares what scientific honors he won in Quebec?

At last Urbain got up and went to the podium to the accom-

269

paniment of scattered applause. There are only a few scientists in the audience, Eberly realized. So much the better. He saw that Urbain limped, ever so slightly. Strange I'd never noticed that before, he said to himself. Is that something new, or has he always walked with a little limp? Looking out over the audience, Eberly recognized several of his own people, including Holly and the stuntman, Gaeta, sitting in the front row. Good. Just as I ordered.

Urbain cleared his throat and said, 'As you know, I am not a politician. But I am a capable administrator. Managing more than one hundred highly individualistic scientists and their assistants has been compared to attempting to make a group of cats march in step.'

He stopped, waiting for laughter. A few titters rose from the audience.

Looking slightly nettled, Urbain went on: 'Allow me to show you how I have managed the scientific programs of this habitat. In this first image we see . . .'

AVs! Eberly could hardly keep himself from whooping with glee. He's showing audiovisuals, as if this was a scientific meeting. The audience will go to sleep on him!

Holly felt distinctly uncomfortable sitting next to Gaeta, but Eberly had told her to bring the stuntman to the meeting and she had followed his orders.

Gaeta had smiled his best when Holly called him. 'Go to the rally with you? I'm not much for listening to speeches.'

'Dr. Eberly has asked specially that you come,' Holly had said to his image, from the safety of her office. 'It would be a favor to him.'

'Eberly, huh?' Gaeta mulled it over for a moment. 'Okay, why not? Then we can have dinner together afterward. Okay?'

Despite everything she knew about Gaeta, Holly wanted to say yes. Instead, 'I'm sure Dr. Eberly would like to have dinner with you.'

'No, I meant you, Holly.'

'I don't think I'll be able to.'

'Why not?'

270

She wanted to say, Because you've bedded every woman who's been able to help you. Because you just think of me as a convenience, because you're an insensitive macho bastard. Because I want you to care for me and all you care about is getting laid.

But she heard herself say, 'Well, maybe. We'll see.'

From his seat on the stage, Eberly saw Urbain's audiovisuals in a weird foreshortening as they hovered in the air behind the speaker's podium. Urbain was explaining them in a flat, unemotional monotone.

An organization chart. Then some quick telescope images of Titan that showed a blurry orange sphere. Urbain used a laser pointer to emphasize details that had no interest for Eberly. Or the rest of the audience, Eberly thought.

'And the final holo,' said Urbain. Eberly wanted to break into applause.

What appeared in three dimensions above the stage looked like a silver-gray tank.

'This is *Alpha*,' said Urbain, his voice taking on a glow of pride. 'She will descend to the surface of Titan and begin the detailed exploration of that world, directed in real time by my staff of scientists and technicians.'

The tank lurched into motion, trundling back and forth on caterpillar treads, extending mechanical arms that ended in pincers or shovel-like scoops. Urbain stood to one side of the podium watching the machine, looking like a proud father gazing fondly at his child as it takes its first steps.

Wilmot, who had been sitting in the first row, climbed the steps onto the stage and advanced to the podium.

'A very impressive demonstration, Dr. Urbain, but I'm afraid your five minutes are up,' he said, his voice amplified for everyone to hear by the pin mike clipped to the lapel of his jacket.

A grimace of disappointment flashed across Urbain's face, but he immediately turned off his palm-sized projector and made a smile for the audience.

'Thank you for your patience,' he said, then turned and took his seat on Eberly's left. Not one person clapped his hands.

Wilmot, at the podium, said, 'And now we have Mr. Ilya Timoshenko, from the engineering department. Mr. Timoshenko was born in Orel, Russia, and took his degree in electrical engineering . . .'

Eberly tuned out Wilmot's drone and watched the crowd. There were lots of men and women out there who had also dressed in gray coveralls. My god, he realized, it's like a team uniform. And almost half the crowd is wearing gray coveralls!

Timoshenko ambled up to the podium, nodding his thanks to Wilmot and then looking out at the audience. He tried to smile, but on his dour face it looked more like a grimace.

'I won't need five minutes,' he said, his voice rough, gravelly. 'What I have to say is very simple. Dr. Urbain says you should vote for him because he's a scientist. Dr. Eberly is going to tell you to vote for him because he's not a scientist.'

A few people laughed.

'I ask you to vote for me because I'm a working stiff, just as most of you are. I'm not a department head. I'm not a boss. But I know how to get people to work together and I'm one of you. I'll look out for your interests because I'm one of you. Remember that when you vote. Thank you.'

And he turned and went back to his seat. No applause. The audience was too surprised at the abruptness of his presentation.

Wilmot looked startled for a moment, but then he rose and went purposefully to the podium.

'Thank you, Mr. Timoshenko,' Wilmot said, looking over his shoulder at the engineer. Turning back to the audience he said, 'I think we should give Mr. Timoshenko a hearty round of applause, for being so brief, if for no other reason.'

Wilmot started clapping his meaty hands together and the crowd quickly joined in. The applause was perfunctory, Eberly thought, and it quickly faded away.

'Our final candidate,' said Wilmot, 'is Dr. Malcolm Eberly, head of the human resources section and chief architect of the proposed constitution that we will vote on, come election day.'

Without a further word of introduction, he turned halfway toward Eberly and said simply, 'Dr. Eberly.'

Several dozen people scattered through the audience got to their feet, applauding loudly, as Eberly rose and stepped to the podium. Others looked around and slowly, almost reluctantly, got up from their seats, too, and began to clap. By the time Eberly gripped the edges of the podium half the audience was on their feet applauding. Sheep, thought Eberly. Most people are nothing better than stupid sheep. Even Wilmot was standing and clapping half-heartedly, too polite to do otherwise.

Eberly gestured for silence and everyone sat down.

'I suppose I should say that I'm not a politician, either,' he began. 'Or at least, I wasn't one until I came into this habitat.

'But if there is one thing that I've learned during our long months of travel together, it is this: our society here must not be divided into classes. We must be united. Otherwise we will fragment into chaos.'

He turned slightly to glance at Urbain. Then, looking squarely at his audience again, Eberly said, 'Do you want to be divided into scientists and non-scientists? Do you want a small, self-important elite to run your government? What makes these scientists believe that they should be in charge? Why should you have to take orders from an elite group that puts its own goals and its own needs ahead of yours?'

The audience stirred.

Raising his voice slightly, Eberly said, 'Did the scientists help to draft the constitution that you will vote on? No. There was not a single scientist on the drafting committee. They were all too busy with their experiments and observations to bother about the way we're going to live.'

Urbain began to protest, 'But we were not asked—'

Wilmot turned off Urbain's lapel mike. 'Rebuttals will come after the first position statements,' he said firmly.

Urbain's face went red.

Suppressing a satisfied grin, Eberly said, 'Our new government must be managed by people from every section of our population. Not only scientists. Not only engineers or technicians. We need the factory laborers and farmers, the office workers and maintenance technicians, butchers and bakers and candlestick makers. Everyone should have a chance to serve in the new government. Everyone should share in the authority and responsibility of power. Not just one tiny group of specialists. Everyone.'

They got to their feet with a roar of approval and applauded like thunder. Eberly smiled at them glowingly.

Wilmot stood up and motioned for them to stop. 'Your applause is eating into Dr. Eberly's allotted time,' he shouted over their clapping.

The applause petered out and everyone sat down.

Eberly lowered his head for a moment, waiting for them to focus their complete attention on him. Then he resumed.

'I'll tell you one other thing we need in our new government. A person at its head who understands that we must be united, that we must never allow one elite group to gain power over the rest of us. We need a leader who understands the people, a leader who will work tirelessly for everyone, and not merely the scientists.'

'Damn right!' came a voice from the audience.

Eberly asked, 'Do you want an elite group of specialists to impose their will on you?'

'No!' several voices answered.

'Do you want a government that will work for everyone?'

'Yes!'

'Do you want a leader who can control the scientists and work for *your* benefit?'

'Yes! Yes!' they shouted. And Eberly saw that his own people were only a small part of those who rose and responded to him.

He let them cheer and whistle until Wilmot came to the podium to announce that his initial five minutes were up.

Eberly went placidly back to his seat, noting with pleasure that Urbain looked upset, almost angry, and Timoshenko's scowl was even darker than usual.

Q&A Session

Urbain sputtered through the rebuttal period, defending the importance of the habitat's science mission, denying that he would put the scientists' needs above those of all the others. The more he denied, Eberly thought, the more firmly he fixed in the audience's mind the fact that he considered the scientists to be separate and apart – above, really – everyone else.

Timoshenko hammered on his theme of being a simple, ordinary working man who understood the needs of the common people. Eberly noted with pleasure that neither candidate attacked him.

When it came to his time for a rebuttal statement, Eberly walked slowly to the podium and said:

'We have a choice that reminds me of the three bears in the tale of Goldilocks. One of our candidates has too little experience at management. He tells you that he is an ordinary guy. This is quite true, but for the leader of this great society we are struggling to create we need someone who is not ordinary; we need someone with experience, and courage, and skill.'

He hesitated a heartbeat, then said, 'The other candidate has too much experience at management. He's been managing scientists for so long that he's completely out of touch with what the rest of us need. Charts and equations and fancy mechanical toys that will explore the surface of Titan have nothing to do with our needs and our future here in this habitat.'

The brought a round of applause. Eberly stood at the podium, his head bowed slightly, soaking up the adulation.

At last Wilmot got up and said, 'Now we will open the meeting to questions from the floor, and from those who are watching these proceedings in their homes.'

Eberly snapped his attention to the professor. Wilmot hadn't told him that people would be able to call in questions from their homes, and Vyborg hadn't even warned him of the possibility. We don't have anyone ready with prepared questions from home, he thought. The crowd is seeded, but not the home audience.

'He makes some sense,' Gaeta said to Holly as they sat down again. 'I mean, Urbain is deadset against letting me go to Titan, even though Kris has shown him she can clean my suit with nanobugs.'

Holly nodded and said, 'Why don't you ask about that?'

Gaeta nodded back at her. 'Good idea!'

The questions were all for Eberly. The people Vyborg had planted in the crowd dominated the Q&A period, and even those who weren't plants addressed their questions to Eberly, not to Urbain or Timoshenko. Eberly stood at the podium, ignoring his opponents sitting a few meters away. Wilmot stood beside him, choosing the questioners from the hands raised in the audience and the incoming calls lighting up his handheld.

The questions were all so predictable, Eberly realized with some relief. Even those calling in from their homes asked the kind of routine, boring questions that he could have answered in his sleep.

'Yes, I will review all applications for babies. I believe we can allow a modest growth in our population.

'No, I will not permit any religious group to attain control of the government.' He saw Morgenthau's cheek twitch at that answer, but it was the answer they had agreed to give. 'We have to get voted into power first,' he had told her, time and again, 'before we can even hint at our true affiliations.'

'Of course I will pay personal attention to the needs of the farmers', he said to a caller who refused to identify himself. 'Without the farms we will quickly starve.'

He recognized Manuel Gaeta when the stuntman rose to his feet to ask, 'Will you permit me to go to the surface of Titan?'

Everyone knew Gaeta and his beat-up handsome face. All attention in the outdoor theater turned to him.

Eberly couldn't help smiling. 'If you can satisfy the scientists that you won't contaminate the life forms on Titan I don't see any reason to prevent you from going.'

Wilmot turned and motioned Urbain to come up to the podium. 'Dr. Urbain, what is your position on this?'

Slicking his hair back with one hand, Urbain said without hesitation, 'The threat of contamination to the microbial organisms of Titan is much too serious to allow any human exploration of that world for the foreseeable future. Besides, we have no choice in the matter. The IAA forbids any human intervention on Titan's surface.'

Gaeta called from the first row, 'But Dr. Cardenas has shown you that she can clean my suit.'

Wilmot said to the audience, 'Mr. Gaeta is referring to the work of Dr. Kristin Cardenas, who has developed nanomachines that may be capable of decontaminating Mr. Gaeta's spacesuit.'

'The decontamination appears to be acceptable,' Urbain conceded, looking a little flustered, 'but appearances can be deceiving. Besides, we should not take the risk of having nanomachines infect Titan's ecology.'

Eberly nudged Urbain away from the podium and looked out at the sea of faces watching them. 'This is a good example of why we can't allow the scientists to have control of the government. Why shouldn't this man be allowed to carry out his adventure, if it's been proven that he won't hurt the bugs down there?'

'It has not been proven!'

'Dr. Cardenas says that it has been,' Eberly countered.

'Not to my satisfaction,' snapped Urbain.

'*Your* satisfaction!' Eberly shouted. 'In other words, you make the decision and everyone else has to obey you – even a Nobel prize winner like Dr. Cardenas.'

'It is my decision to make,' Urbain insisted.

'I thought you said the International Astronautical Association made the decision.'

'Yes, of course, that's true' Urbain stammered, 'but if necessary

I could override their decision. After all, I am the director of all scientific efforts here.'

'You want to be a dictator!' Eberly exclaimed, pretending shock.

Wilmot jumped between them. 'Wait a moment. There is another issue here. What about the dangers of nanotechnology?'

'Nanotechnology is a tool,' Urbain said. 'A tool that must be used carefully, but nothing more than a tool, nonetheless.'

Eberly was surprised at that. All he could add was, 'Yes, I agree.'

Timoshenko rose from his chair. 'Wait. There are dangers with nanotechnology. The bugs can get out of control—'

'Bullshit!' came a screaming voice from the audience. Kris Cardenas shot to her feet, her face white with anger. 'Show me one instance where nanomachines have gotten out of control. They've been using nanobugs at Selene and the other lunar communities for decades now, and there's been no trouble at all. Not one incident.'

Timoshenko scowled at her. 'Nanobugs killed several people, back when it was still called Moonbase.'

'That was deliberate murder. You might as well outlaw hammers because they've been used to smash people's skulls.'

Wilmot spread his hands to calm things down. 'No one is thinking of outlawing nanotechnology,' he said flatly. 'We recognize Dr. Cardenas as the solar system's acknowledged expert on the subject, and we have agreed to use nanomachines – but under the strictest safety procedures.'

Before either of the other candidates could say anything, Eberly stepped in. 'Nanotechnology can be very helpful to us, and I have every confidence in Dr. Cardenas' ability to develop nanomachines safely.'

'I too,' said Urbain.

They all turned to Timoshenko. He grimaced, then said, 'With all respect to the admired Dr. Cardenas, I believe nanomachines can be very dangerous in a closed environment such as ours. They should be banned.'

Eberly seized the moment. 'Most of us are here in this habitat,' he said, 'because of laws and regulations that stifled our lives. Most of us are educated, knowledgeable, unafraid of new ideas and new capabilities. We have all suffered under governments that restricted our freedoms.'

He saw several heads nodding agreement.

'All right then,' he asked the audience, 'how many of you are in favor of banning nanotechnology altogether?'

The people hesitated, glanced at each other. A few hands went up. Very few. Down on the floor, Kris Cardenas looked around, smiled, and sat down.

Eberly nodded, satisfied. Turning to Timoshenko, he said, 'There you are. Vox populi, vox dei.'

Saturn Arrival Minus 20 Days

Holly saw that it would be senseless to try to talk with Malcolm after the debate ended. He was immediately surrounded by admirers, including Morgenthau and that dark little man, Vyborg.

Kris Cardenas pushed her way through the departing throng, a bright grin on her face. 'I think we might get you down to Titan after all,' she said to Gaeta.

He grinned back at her. 'Maybe. If Eberly wins the election.'

Holly suddenly felt like a third wheel on a bicycle, standing between Kris and Manny. The crowd was thinning out, little knots of three or four people heading for home or one of the restaurants. Eberly came down from the stage, enveloped in well-wishers and sycophants. As he walked past Holly he nodded to her and smiled, but he did not invite her to join his group.

Before she could feel any reaction, Gaeta said, 'Come on, Holly, we'll walk you home.'

Surprised, Holly glanced at Cardenas. She arched one brow, as if to remind Holly of what they had learned about the stuntman's activities.

Holly nodded back and the three of them started across the grass and up the lakeside path toward the village of Athens.

'I didn't see Nadia here,' Cardenas said as they climbed toward the apartment buildings.

'She's probably working,' Gaeta said. 'Urbain's given her some time on a telescope; she always up in the observatory now.'

'I thought she'd come with you,' said Holly.

He actually looked surprised. 'With me?'

Holly let it pass. They reached Cardenas' building and said

goodnight, then Gaeta walked with Holly to the next building, where her apartment was.

'You've been seeing Nadia a lot, haven't you?' she asked.

Gaeta nodded. 'If this Titan gig falls through, I've got to do something to keep my investors happy. She's helping me plan a jaunt through the rings.'

'Sure.'

The dawn finally shed its light on Gaeta's face. 'Ohh,' he said. 'She told you, didn't she.'

'It came up in conversation, yes,' said Holly.

They were at the door to her apartment building. As Gaeta stopped there, the habitat's lighting flicked from its evening mode to the nighttime system. His face fell into shadow, but Holly could see him well enough.

'Okay,' he admitted, 'it happened.'

'More than once.'

He grinned sheepishly. 'Christ, you sound like a priest at confession: "How many times?"'

'It's not funny, Manny.'

'You didn't take our times together seriously, did you?'

She thought a moment, then half-lied, 'No, not all that seriously, I guess.'

'I mean, I know I was supposed to look out for you, but, well . . . it just sort of happened.'

'It happens a lot with you.'

'You seemed to enjoy it at the time,' he said softly.

Holly suddenly realized what he had just said. 'What do you mean, you were supposed to look out for me?'

He took a deep breath. 'That's why I'm here, Holly. Your sister wanted me to keep an eye on you.'

She felt her jaw drop open. 'Pancho? Panch *hired* you?'

Shuffling from one foot to another like a little boy caught in a place where he shouldn't have been, Gaeta said, 'It's not that simple, Holly. She didn't exactly hire me.'

'She thought I needed a bodyguard,' Holly groused. 'My big sister didn't trust me out here on my own.'

'I was trying to raise the funding for the Titan gig,' he tried to explain, 'and this guy from Astro Corporation came up with an offer.'

Suddenly the absurdity of it hit Holly like a bucketful of ice-cold water. She broke into laughter.

Perplexed, Gaeta asked, 'What's so funny?'

'You are. And my big sister. She hired you to protect me, and you pop me into bed. My faithful watchdog. When she finds out she'll want to castrate you.'

'She wanted me to keep you away from Eberly and that's what I did.'

Holly's laughter choked off like a light switch being thrown. 'Panch hired you to keep me away from Malcolm?'

He nodded sheepishly.

'And that's why you took me to bed?'

'No! I didn't plan that. You . . . I . . . it just—'

'Just sort of happened. I know.'

'I didn't hurt you.'

'The hell you didn't,' Holly snapped. 'And then you go off and screw Kris, and then Nadia. You'll be lucky if you live long enough to get to Titan.'

'Oh Christ. Does Kris know about all this?'

'Kris? Sure she knows. So does Nadia.'

'So my name's mud with her, eh?'

'With Nadia?'

'With Kris.'

'Why don't you ask her?'

In the shadowy lighting it was hard to make out the expression on Gaeta's face, but the tone of his voice came through clearly enough, 'Because I'd . . . *mierda!* I really like Kris.'

'More than Nadia?'

'More than anybody. I guess I hurt her feelings, didn't I? I guess she's pissed off at me.'

Holly couldn't resist the opportunity. 'I don't think she's really mad at you. Of course, she's working up some nanobugs that eat testicles, but other than that I don't think she's sore at you at all.'

Gaeta mumbled, 'Guess I can't blame her.' Then he turned away and started walking down toward his own quarters, head hung low. Holly almost felt sorry for him. Almost.

They're all trying to keep me away from Malcolm, Holly thought as she undressed for bed. Pancho, Manny, Morgenthau, they're all trying to keep Malcolm and me apart.

As she slipped into bed and commanded the lights to turn off, she wondered if she still wanted Malcolm the way she did when she first came aboard the habitat. He's been so bugging distant; he doesn't care about me. He hardly even knows I'm alive. But he's been so busy. This political stuff takes all his time. It was different when we first met, different when we started out in this habitat. I could see him all the time then, and he liked me, I know he did.

How can he like me, how can he even think about me, when he never sees me? He's always surrounded by Morgenthau and that Vyborg snake. And Kananga, he scares me.

How can I get past them? How can I get to be alone with Malcolm, even for a few minutes?

Her thoughts drifted to her sister. She *hired* Manny. She's paying him big bucks to keep me away from Malcolm. He made love to me for money, the dirty . . . Holly tried to think of the masculine equivalent of the word 'whore.'

Lying in bed, staring into the darkness, she thought, So Pancho wants to keep me away from Malcolm, does she. I'll show her. I'll get to Malcolm. I'll get past the Hippo and the Snake and even Kananga, the panther.

And suddenly, like a bright light clicking on, she knew how to accomplish that.

Midnight – I

Holly got out of bed and dressed swiftly. She didn't have to check a directory to know where Eberly's quarters were; she had the complete map of the habitat in her head, every square centimeter, every assigned apartment, laboratory, workshop, airlock, even the maze of underground tunnels and conduits.

Yet she hesitated before leaving her own apartment. The clock said three minutes before midnight, but she thought that Eberly would probably still have a throng of admirers and well-wishers crowding his quarters. Better to wait. Wait until they all leave.

So she went instead to her office and pulled up a display from the outdoor surveillance camera that looked at Eberly's building. Sure enough, people were still milling around out on the grounds. His apartment must be jammed with them, Holly thought.

Drowsily she watched as the crowd slowly thinned away. She fell asleep, then woke with a start. The digital clock said 02:34. The apartment building looked dark and silent. He's prob'ly asleep by now, Holly thought. For several moments she debated inwardly about awakening him. He works so hard, she thought; he needs his rest.

But you'll never get to see him alone otherwise, Holly told herself. She commanded the phone to call Eberly.

'You have reached the residence of Dr. Malcolm Eberly,' his phone answered. 'Please leave your name and Dr. Eberly will return your call.'

Screw that! Holly said to herself. She got up from her desk chair and headed for his apartment.

There was a perfunctory security lock on the building's main door. Holly had memorized all the combinations long ago, and tapped on the keypad. The door popped open. As she went up the stairs, a sudden thought shook her. Maybe he's not alone! Maybe he's got somebody with him.

With a shake of her head Holly told herself, Better to find out now. She marched down the shadowy hallway, lit only by the glow of fluorescent nameplates on each door. Eberly's apartment was at the end of the hall.

She took a breath and rapped on the door. No response. Holly banged on it with the flat of her hand, worrying that the noise would wake the neighbors but determined to get Eberly to answer her.

She heard someone cough on the other side of the door. Then Eberly's muffled voice demanded, 'Who is it?'

'Holly,' she said, standing squarely in front of the peep hole.

Eberly slid the door back. He had a dark-colored robe pulled around him, his hair looked slightly tousled.

'There is a doorbell,' he said crankily.

'I've got to talk to you,' she said. 'It's urgent.'

As if he were slowly remembering his manners, Eberly gestured her into his sitting room. A snap of his fingers and the glareless overhead lights came on. Now Holly could see that his robe was deep maroon. And his feet were bare.

'What is it, Holly? What's wrong?'

'I'm sorry to bother you at this hour, Malcolm, but I can't get past Morgenthau and all your other assistants and I've got to have your help and the only way I could see you alone was like this.'

He smiled a little and slicked back his hair with one hand. 'All right. You're seeing me. What's the problem?'

'Diego Romero. He was murdered.'

'Murdered?' The strength seemed to leak out of Eberly's legs. He sank down onto the sofa.

Taking the closest chair to him, Holly said, 'I'm positive. It wasn't an accident. He was trying to push himself out of the water and somebody held him down.'

Eberly swallowed visibly, then asked, 'You have proof of this?'

'I have evidence. The abrasions on his hands. They couldn't

have happened any other way.' Picturing the scene in her mind once again, she added, 'And there were boot prints in the dirt, too many prints for one person to make.'

'But who would want to kill that gentle old man? Why would someone want to murder him?'

'I don't know,' Holly said. 'That's why I need your help. There ought to be an investigation.'

He sat in silence for a moment, obviously thinking furiously. 'Holly, this is a matter for the security department. You should tell them about your evidence.'

'Security? That means Kananga, doesn't it?'

'He's in charge of security, yes.'

Holly wrung her hands. 'I don't think he'd take me seriously. He's . . . he wouldn't think my evidence is enough to start a real investigation.'

Eberly leaned back in the sofa. 'Colonel Kananga is an experienced police officer. He'll know what to do.'

'Malcolm, he scares me,' she confessed.

He said nothing for several heartbeats, looking at Holly with those startling blue eyes of his. Then he smiled gently. 'Holly, would you like me to go with you to Kananga?'

Her heart clutched within her. 'Would you?'

'For you, Holly, of course.'

'Oh, great. Cosmic!'

Eberly's smile grew warmer. 'I'll call Kananga first thing in the morning.' His eyes shifted to the digital clock across the room. 'Which is only a few hours from now.'

She shot to her feet. 'Oh, jeeps, I'm so sorry to bother you at this time of night, Malcolm. It's just that I can't get to see you anytime else, you've always got so many people around and—'

Eberly rose and grasped her shoulder lightly. 'I know. I've been so terribly busy. Too busy. But I'll always make time for you, Holly. Simply call me here at my quarters. Leave a message and I'll get back to you so we can meet together, in private.'

She didn't know what to say, except utter an awed, 'Cosmic.'

Eberly guided her to the door. 'I don't want you to worry about a thing, Holly. We'll meet with Kananga tomorrow. And from now on, whenever you want to see me, simply leave a message on my private line, here.'

'I will, Malcolm. I surely will.'

As she walked homeward, feeling almost lightheaded, Holly realized how wrong, how stupid, Pancho had been. Malcolm could've taken me to his bed and I'd hopped in like a rabbit on aphrodisiacs, she thought. But Malcolm was too much of a gentleman to even think about that. And the guy Panch hired to protect me screws me whenever he feels like it. Some bodyguard.

Midnight – II

Manuel Gaeta did not go to sleep, either. By the time he reached his own quarters he had decided he should call Kris Cardenas and tell her everything.

'Can I see you, Kris?' he asked to her image floating in the middle of his one-room apartment. She was still wearing the slacks and blouse from earlier in the evening. Then Gaeta realized she wasn't in her apartment; the phone had tracked her to her laboratory.

Cardenas looked slightly bemused. 'Sure, Manny. When?'

'Tonight. Now.'

'Now?' She seemed to think it over for a few moments. 'Okay. Come on over to my lab. I'll wait for you.'

'Great!'

Halfway there, Gaeta remembered Holly's crack about Kris developing nanobugs that ate testicles. He laughed to himself. Hey man, he said to himself, you live with danger. That's the life you've chosen.

Cardenas wasn't laughing, though, when she opened the locked door to her lab. She looked bright and perky, despite the late hour, but utterly serious.

'What's on your mind, Manny?' she asked as she led him past a row of lab benches and spotless, gleaming plastic and metal equipment.

'You are,' he said.

Cardenas perched herself on a high swiveling stool and pointed to a hard straight-backed chair for Gaeta. He remained standing.

'So you're thinking about me at,' she glanced at the clock on the far wall, 'twenty-eight minutes before one o'clock in the morning.'

Gaeta folded his arms across his chest. 'Come on, Kris, cut the crap. Holly told me that you know about her and about Nadia.'

'I imagine you're bragging to all your buddies about your hit parade.'

'I haven't said a word to anybody. You grow up where I did, you learn to keep your mouth shut.'

She eyed him, clear disbelief in her expression. And something else, he thought. Curiosity? Maybe even regret?

'I just want you to know,' he said, 'that you're the only one who means anything to me. You're the one I don't want to lose.'

That shocked her. 'You're joking!'

'No joke, Kris,' he said. 'I've never said this to anybody else in my life. I think I love you.'

Cardenas started to reply, then closed her mouth, pressed her lips together tightly.

'I mean it,' Gaeta said. 'I never said that to anybody before.'

At last she replied, so softly he could barely hear her, 'I never thought I'd hear anyone say that to me again.'

Ruth Morgenthau wanted to sleep, but she had hours and hours of vids to watch and phone taps to listen to. Eberly was pressing her for results, and she was determined to go through all of the material that Vyborg had amassed on Professor Wilmot's communications. So she sat in her padded recliner, resisting the urge to crank it all the way back and drift off to sleep. I've let this material pile up so much, she realized. I've got to wade through it; otherwise it will just get worse.

Why not let Vyborg do this? she asked herself wearily as the hours ground on. He's put the taps in place, his people have set up the cameras in Wilmot's quarters and office. Why not let him drudge through all this drivel? She knew the answer: it was because if Vyborg found something, Vyborg would get the credit in Eberly's eyes. Morgenthau shook her head ponderously. No, that will never do. If anyone is going to bring Wilmot low, it must be me. Eberly must see that I did it. No one else but me.

She worried about Eberly's devotion to their cause. He seems more interested in being admired than in furthering the reach of the Holy Disciples. He's an American, of course, and they're all infatuated with their own individuality, but still he's subject to the judgments of their New Morality.

Another reason to see this job through, she thought. If I can bring him something to use against Wilmot, it will make Eberly see that he needs me. Vyborg and that murderous Kananga can help him in some ways, but I must make him realize that he is dependent on me. One word from me can put him back in prison, yet he treats me as just another of his underlings. He's smart enough to call my bluff on that. If I send him packing, our whole mission here will be destroyed. Urbain or that growling Russian will be elected leader of this habitat and I'll have failed miserably.

Eberly has no respect for my abilities. He thinks I'm lazy, incompetent. Well, let me bring him the goods on Wilmot and his opinion of me will have to change.

Silently Morgenthau prayed for help, for success. Let me find something that we can use against Wilmot, she prayed. For the greater glory of God, let me find a way to bring the Professor to his knees.

The only answer she received was hour after hour of watching Wilmot at his desk, listening to his phone conversations, reading the reports he wrote before he encoded them to send back to Earth. Each evening the professor sat watching vids for hours. Morgenthau fast-forwarded and skipped past them. She could not see them clearly from the vantage point of the camera set in Wilmot's sitting room ceiling, and she couldn't hear the sound tracks because he listened to the vids through a miniature plug he wormed into his ear. Hour after hour, he watched the indecipherable vids.

And hour after hour, Morgenthau skimmed past them, looking for something tangible, something sinful or illegal or merely embarrassing, something that could hurt Professor Wilmot.

Utterly bored and weary, Morgenthau yawned and rubbed her heavy-lidded eyes. I can barely stay awake, she said to herself. Enough is enough.

She turned off the display, still showing Wilmot staring at his entertainment vid in rapt concentration, and started to push herself up from her recliner when she remembered to check if Wilmot had sent any messages out of the habitat, to Earth. Each week he sent a coded report to somewhere in Atlanta, she knew. Very cryptic, even once the computer decoded them. A strange coincidence that whoever Wilmot was reporting to resided in the same city as the headquarters of the New Morality. Morgenthau shrugged it off as merely a coincidence.

Already half asleep, she pulled up the file of his outgoing messages. Aside from the usual brief report to Atlanta, there was an even shorter message to some address in Copenhagen. And he had sent it not through the usual radio channel, but by a tight-beam laser link.

Suddenly Morgenthau was wide awake, calling the same number in Copenhagen, tracing Wilmot's message.

'She knows?' Vyborg asked, startled.

Eberly, walking along the curving path between Vyborg and Kananga, replied, 'She suspects.'

To a casual observer the three men seemed to be ambling slowly along the flower-bordered pathway out beyond the edges of Athens. Late morning sunlight streamed through the habitat's solar windows. Bees hummed among the hyacinths and hollyhocks. Butterflies fluttered. Vyborg, short and spare, hunching over slightly as he walked, was scowling like a man who had just swallowed something vile. Even tall, regal Kananga, on Eberly's other side, looked displeased, perhaps even worried.

'And she came to you for help,' Kananga said.

Eberly nodded slowly. 'I have volunteered to bring her to your office.'

'Not my office,' said Kananga. 'Too many eyes watching there. We'll have to meet somewhere more secluded.'

'Where?' Eberly asked.

Vyborg suggested, 'How about the scene of the crime?'

Kananga smiled gleamingly. 'Perfect.'

Eberly glanced from one man to the other. They're drawing me into their crime, he realized. They're going to make me a party to another murder. What alternative do I have? How can I keep clear of this?

Aloud, he said, 'I'll tell her to meet me at the scene of the old man's death, but I won't be there when she arrives.'

'I will,' said Kananga.

'She's got to disappear entirely,' Eberly said. 'We can't have another dead body to explain.'

Vyborg said, 'In a habitat as large as this, there must be thousands of places where she could run off to.'

'I don't want her body found,' Eberly repeated.

'It won't be,' said Kananga. 'That's what airlocks are for.' Looking past Eberly to Vyborg, he said, 'You'll be able to erase the airlock security camera record, won't you?'

Vyborg nodded. 'And replace it with perfectly normal footage that will show absolutely nothing.'

'Good,' Kananga said.

Eberly drew in a deep breath. 'Very well. When shall we do it?'

'The sooner the better.'

'This afternoon, then.'

'Fourteen hundred hours,' Kananga suggested.

'Make it earlier,' said Vyborg, 'while most of the people are at lunch.'

'Yes,' Kananga agreed. 'Say, twelve-thirty hours.'

'Good.'

Vyborg smiled, relieved.

'I don't like any of this,' Eberly said.

'But it's got to be done.'

'I know. That's why I'm helping you.'

'Helping us?' Vyborg challenged. 'What will you be doing to help us? The colonel here is doing what needs to be done. You'll be in your office, establishing an alibi.'

Eberly looked down at the smaller man coldly. 'I'll be in my office amending Holly Lane's dossier to show that she is emotionally unstable, and has attempted suicide in the past.'

Kananga laughed aloud. 'Good thinking. Then her disappearance won't look so suspicious.'

'Just be certain that her body isn't found,' Eberly snapped.

'It won't be,' said Kananga, 'unless someone wants to get into a spacesuit and search a few million kilometers of vacuum.'

Saturn Arrival Minus 19 Days

Holly and Eberly walked past the orchard's neat rows of trees, heading for the spot along the irrigation canal where Don Diego had drowned. Holly didn't need a map or a marker; she remembered the exact location perfectly.

'But what did Kananga find?' she asked.

Eberly shrugged his rounded shoulders. 'I don't know. He said he didn't want to talk about it on the phone.'

'Must be something important,' she said, quickening her pace.

'Must be.' Eberly touched his comm, in the breast pocket of his tunic. *Vyborg was supposed to call him, give him an excuse to leave Holly and head back to his office. Why hasn't he called? Is he trying to make certain I'm involved personally in this? Trying to make me a witness to Holly's murder? An accomplice?*

Holly was oblivious to his nervous behavior. 'Wonder what it could be?'

'What what could be?' Eberly asked, with growing impatience.

'Whatever it is that Kananga found.'

Your death, he replied silently. *He's going to kill you, and make me a party to it.*

'Wait,' said Eberly, reaching out to grasp Holly's arm.

'What is it, Malcolm?'

He stood there, feeling cold sweat beading his upper lip, his forehead, trickling down his ribs. *I can't do it,* he realized. *I can't let them draw me in this deep.*

'Holly, I . . .' *What to say? How can I get out of this without telling her everything?*

His comm buzzed. Almost giddy with relief, Eberly fished it out of his tunic pocket and fumbled it open.

Instead of Vyborg's dark, sour face, Morgenthau appeared on the miniature screen. She was smiling broadly. 'I've found it,' she said, without preamble. 'His entertainment vids. They're—'

'I'm out here in the orchard with Holly,' he interrupted, his voice as strong and imperative as he could make it without shouting. 'What is it that you've found?'

Morgenthau looked flustered for a moment, then she seemed to understand what he was trying to tell her. 'It's an important breakthrough,' she temporized. 'Too complicated to discuss over the phone. I must show you all the details, so that you can then discuss them with Professor Wilmot.'

'Is it urgent?' he prompted.

'Oh, yes, quite urgent.' Morgenthau took her cue. 'I suggest you come to my office immediately. This can't wait.'

'Very well,' he said sharply. 'I'll meet you at your office.'

He clicked the handheld shut and looked up at Holly. 'I'm afraid I'll have to go back. You go on to your meeting with Kananga. I'll join you as soon as I can.'

Holly was clearly disappointed, but she nodded her understanding. Without another word, Eberly turned around and started walking quickly back toward the village, practically loping through the trees. Puzzled, Holly turned back and headed for the irrigation culvert. Then she realized she would have to see Kananga by herself. The prospect didn't please her, but she was determined to find out what the security chief had learned about Don Diego's death.

No, not death, Holly reminded herself. Murder.

For one of the rare times in his life, Manuel Gaeta felt awkward. As he walked down the corridor toward Nadia Wunderly's cubbyhole office, he actually felt nervous, like a teenager going out on his first date. Like a guilty little kid going to confession.

The door marked PLANETARY SCIENCES STAFF was wide open. The area inside looked like a maze constructed of shoulder-high partitions, filled with quietly intense scientists and their assistants. Gaeta had been there often enough to know the way, but this particular morning he got confused, lost, and had to ask directions. Everybody seemed to know who he was and they smilingly pointed him in the right direction. The women seemed to smile especially warmly, he noticed.

None of that now, he told himself sternly.

Feeling a little like a mouse in a psychologist's maze, Gaeta finally made it to Wunderly's cubbyhole, which was about as far from the front door as it could be.

'Good morning, Manny,' she said, barely looking up as he hesitated by the entryway.

'Hi,' he said as brightly as he could manage. 'You got the results for me?'

She nodded without smiling. Unasked, Gaeta took the squeaky little plastic chair at the side of her desk. *Suma friadad,* he thought. A man could freeze to death in here.

Wunderly projected a set of tables on the blank partition that formed the back wall of her cubicle. 'These are the frequencies of particles bigger than ten centimeters in the brightest belt, the B ring,' she said, her voice flat, as unemotional as a machine. 'And here are the deviations that they—'

'I don't blame you for being sore at me,' he interrupted.

She blinked her big gray eyes slowly, solemnly.

'I know you and Kris talked.'

'Holly, too.'

He conceded with a shrug and a weak attempt at a boyish smile. 'Yeah, and Holly too.'

'And god knows who else.'

'Now wait,' he said, raising a hand defensively. 'It's bad enough, don't go making it worse than it is.'

'I don't want to talk about it,' Wunderly said.

'I owe you an apology.'

She glared at him for a moment. Then, 'I don't want to talk about it. Ever again.'

'But I—'

'Never again, Manny!' Her eyes flashed. She meant it, he realized.

Wunderly took a breath, then said, 'Our relationship from now on is strictly business. You want to go skydiving through the rings and I want to draw public attention to the rings. We'll work together on this strictly as professionals. No personal involvement. Understood?'

'Understood,' he said weakly.

'With any luck, I'll get a big fat grant to study the rings and you'll break your ass.'

Despite himself, Gaeta grinned at her. 'With any luck,' he agreed.

Holly made her way along the culvert to the spot where Don Diego's murder had taken place. As she made her way down the dirt embankment she looked for Kananga. He was nowhere in sight.

He's not here? she wondered. What's going on?

Then she saw his tall, lanky form, maybe a hundred meters up the embankment, standing there, waiting for her. As usual, he was dressed completely in black: tunic, slacks, boots, all dead black.

'Hello,' she called.

Kananga started toward her.

'This is the spot, right here,' Holly shouted. 'By the peach trees up there.'

Kananga called back, 'Are you certain?'

'I remember every detail.'

He stopped once he was within arm's reach. 'You have an excellent memory.'

'Photographic,' Holly said. She tried to hide her nervousness, with Kananga towering over her. She noticed that his boots left prints in the dirt just like the ones at the murder scene.

'And I suppose that spot, there,' he stretched out a long arm, pointing, 'is where you found the old man's body.'

Holly pointed slightly more leftward. 'Over there. That's where it was.'

'I see.' And he grabbed Holly, one big hand clamped over her face, covering her nose and mouth, the other arm wrapped around her waist, pinning her arms to her sides and lifting her completely off her feet.

Fight Or Flee

Can't breathe! Kananga's big hand was clamped over Holly's face, smothering her. She flailed her feet, trying to kick him, but her softbooted feet merely bounced off his long, muscular legs.

Holly's arms were pinned to her sides as Kananga carried her down along the culvert. She was desperately gasping for air but his hand was gripping her painfully, tighter and tighter.

Holly's right hand brushed against Kananga's slacks. Without conscious thought she felt for his crotch, grabbed and squeezed as hard as she could. He yowled and dropped her. Holly landed on the balls of her feet and whirled to face him. Kananga was doubled over, his face contorted with pain. She kicked him in the side of his head with every gram of strength she could muster.

Kananga went sprawling. Holy jeeps! Holly said to herself. I must have had martial arts training back on Earth. Kananga was staggering to his knees, groaning. Holly kicked him again and then took off, racing as fast as she could along the sloping concrete wall of the culvert, splashing along the edge of the stream, getting as far away from Kananga as fast as she could.

By the time Eberly got back to the administration building, most of his nervousness had abated. Kananga's killed her. It's on his head, not mine. Nobody knows that I led Holly to him. Not even Morgenthau knows. If Kananga gets caught, I can distance myself from him.

He entered the human resources section of the building and walked past the four clerical types working at their desks. The door to Morgenthau's office was closed; he slid it open without knocking.

She looked up sharply from her desk, recognized who had invaded her privacy, and put on a smile for Eberly.

He glanced around before sliding the door shut again and taking the chair in front of the desk. This used to be my office, he thought, noting how Morgenthau had tricked up the walls with holoviews of Monet's paintings of cathedrals.

'You found something of Wilmot's?' he asked, without preamble. It was important to make Morgenthau understand who was the chief here and who the underling. Otherwise she'd flaunt her connections to the Holy Disciples and try to control him.

'Something that can destroy him,' Morgenthau said, smiling devilishly.

Eberly hiked his eyebrows dubiously. 'Really?'

'Really.' Morgenthau projected a list of titles against a bare spot on the wall. Each title had a still picture image alongside it.

Eberly gaped at the pictures.

'Pure filth,' Morgenthau said. 'He watches these disgusting vids every night before he goes to bed.'

'You're sure?'

She nodded, grim-faced. 'Every night. I have it all on camera.'

Eberly broke into laughter. 'We have him!' he crowed. 'We have Wilmot in our grasp.' And he clenched both his hands into tight, painful fists.

'I may have a concussion.' Kananga lay stretched out on the sofa in Vyborg's apartment, long legs dangling over the sofa's edge, his head thundering with pain. The side of his face was swollen.

Vyborg carried a cold towel to the colonel, biting his lips to keep from screaming curses at the blundering idiot. Allowing a little slip of a girl to beat him up! To get away! Now she knows for certain that Rivera was murdered. He kept silent, though. In the foul mood he's in, Kananga might decide to throttle me if I tell him what I actually think of him.

'Where did she go? Where is she now?' Vyborg said, his voice low, sibilant. 'That's the important question.'

'You've got to tell Eberly.'

'I've got to? Why not you? You're the one who allowed her to get away.'

'You tell him,' Kananga said, his face hard, determined.

Vyborg didn't try to suppress the angry disdain he felt. Puffing a disgusted breath from his nostrils he called, 'Phone! Connect me with Dr. Eberly, wherever he is. Emergency priority.'

Within ten seconds Eberly's face appeared hovering in the air above the coffee table. He was smiling happily. Vyborg immediately saw that he was in Morgenthau's office.

'I'm glad you called,' Eberly said. 'I have important news for you both.'

'I'm afraid I have news, also,' said Vyborg. 'Bad news.'

Eberly's smile faded. Behind him, Morgenthau looked suddenly concerned.

No sense prolonging the agony, Vyborg decided. Come right out with it. 'Holly Lane escaped.'

'Escaped? What do you mean?'

'Apparently she is a martial arts champion. She got away from our good colonel here,' Vyborg gestured toward Kananga, still supine on the sofa, 'and we have no idea of where she is.'

Eberly stared at the three-dimensional image that filled half of Morgenthau's office: Vyborg standing tense and obviously angry while Kananga lay on the sofa pressing a cold towel to his head.

He glanced at Morgenthau, whose expression was gradually changing from puzzlement to understanding. She's piecing it together, Eberly realized. Now she knows that I'm involved in the attempt on Holly's life.

Shaking inside with a mixture of fury and fear, Eberly managed to say, 'I want you both at my apartment in five minutes.'

Holly ran blindly along the culvert until her lungs burned with exertion. She stopped, bent over, puffing hard. A glance backward showed nothing. He's not following me, she decided with some relief. Prob'ly unconscious, the way I kicked him. Jeeps, maybe he's dead. She straightened up and headed up the embankment,

301

into the dappled shadows of the orchard. Serve him right, she thought. He tried to kill me. He must've killed Don Diego.

Kay, she told herself. Kananga killed Don Diego. Why? She had no idea. Who do I tell about it? Malcolm?

Then she realized that Malcolm had led her to this meeting with Kananga. Had suggested it in the first place. Malcolm knew what was going down. He's part of it, whatever 'it' is, she realized.

She wanted to cry. Malcolm's involved in Don Diego's murder. He wanted Kananga to murder me!

Who could she trust? Who could she turn to? I can't go back to my apartment, they might be waiting for me there. Kris! I'll call Kris. Or maybe Manny. She thought about it as she hurried through the apples trees at the far end of the orchard. Ahead lay rows of berry bushes and, beyond that, the endcap.

Not Manny, she decided. I won't go running to him like some helpless little girl asking the big, strong hero to protect her. He prob'ly wouldn't believe me, anyway. Kris would. Kris'll believe me. But should I get her involved in this?

She kept on walking toward the endcap, trying to sort out her options and finding there weren't all that many options open to her. If Eberly is part of this, whatever it is, that means Morgenthau and that slimy Vyborg snake are part of it too.

Under the stand of elms at the endcap, Holly sat tiredly on the grass and tried to think. Looking down the length of the green landscape, the habitat seemed exactly the same as it had been the day she and Kris Cardenas had stopped here. But nothing was the same, Holly thought, her insides suddenly hollow. Her whole world had crashed and burned. I wish Pancho was here, she admitted to herself. Panch would know what to do.

Holly pulled out her comm unit and stared at it in her hand. No sense calling Pancho; it'd take the better part of an hour for a message to get to her. And what could I say to her? Help, somebody's just tried to murder me? What good would that do?

Kris. I'll call Kris. She said to the comm unit, 'Kris Cardenas.'

Nothing happened. Holly saw that the screen was flat and dark. The unit wasn't working.

They've deactivated my phone! Why? she asked herself. And answered, Because they want me to use a wallphone, so then they'll know where I am. They're after me! They want to locate me and grab me.

For the first time, Holly felt truly afraid.

Nanotech Laboratory

'We'll go on the day after we establish orbit around Saturn,' Gaeta said.

Sitting at her desk in her office cubicle, Kris Cardenas looked far from pleased. 'Why so soon? Why not wait and get more data first?'

Gaeta smiled at her. 'This isn't science, Kris, it's show biz. We go right away, we get a lot more attention, much bigger audience. We wait until the *chingado* scientists have all the data they want, we'll be old and gray and nobody'll give a damn anymore.'

Her cornflower blue eyes snapped. 'I'm one of those *chingado* scientists, Manny.'

Pursing his lips, Gaeta answered, 'You'd be a *chingada,* feminine. But you're not. It's not a nice word and you're a nice person.'

Cardenas was not amused. 'Isn't it dangerous enough without plunging in there as soon as we arrive at Saturn?'

'Kris, I love you, but I don't think you're ever gonna understand my business. The more danger the better.'

'Until you kill yourself.'

'I'm not gonna kill myself. Fritz won't let me. It'd ruin the damned suit. He'd kill me if I did that.'

Despite herself, Cardenas laughed.

Raoul Tavalera popped his head over the edge of the cubicle's partition. 'I'm goin' home now. Okay?'

'That's fine, Raoul,' said Cardenas.

An uncertain expression clouded Tavalera's long face. 'You heard from Holly this afternoon?'

'No.'

'She said she'd call me. We were goin' to go out for dinner. But I haven't heard from her all day. And she's not answering her phone.'

Before Cardenas could reply, Gaeta said, 'I thought we'd go out to Nemo's tonight, Kris.'

'All right by me.' Turning back to Tavalera, 'I haven't heard a thing from Holly, Raoul.'

'Funny,' he said. 'That's not like her, not calling when she said she would.'

'It is a little strange,' Cardenas agreed.

'Whatever,' Tavalera said. 'I'm goin'. The main processor is still working on the assemblers for Dr. Urbain.'

She nodded. 'I know. Switch on the UVs before you leave, okay?'

'Yeah.'

'Well, where is she?' Eberly demanded.

Kananga was sitting up on Vyborg's sofa now. He had put the cold towel away, but his left cheek was slightly puffy. 'I have my whole staff searching for her. We'll find her within an hour or two.'

Eberly paced past Vyborg, who was sitting in the armchair on the other side of the coffee table. 'She's got to be found. And silenced.'

'She will be,' Kananga said.

'She can't go far,' Vyborg offered. 'This habitat is big, but it's not that big.'

Eberly frowned at him. His mind was racing. *They've dragged me into this. Now I'm a party to their crime, whether I want to be or not. Two blundering oafs; they couldn't even take care of one woman, a girl, a child really.* He glared at Kananga as he paced across the room. *Or maybe they're smarter than I think. Maybe they planned it all this way precisely to pull me into their orbit. How can I hold the old man's murder over their heads now?*

Abruptly he stopped and jabbed a finger at Kananga. 'As soon as she's found I want her brought to me. Do you understand that? No more violence. I'll take care of her.'

Kananga's brows knit. 'What do you have in mind?'

'That's my business. I'll handle it.'

'She can accuse me of murder,' Kananga said.

'And assault, perhaps attempted murder,' said Vyborg. 'Certainly attempted rape.'

'You,' Eberly pointed at Vyborg, 'get every phone in the habitat checked out. I want to know where she is when she calls, who she's calling, and what she's telling them.'

Vyborg nodded and got up from his chair.

Eberly headed for the door.

'Where are you going?' asked Kananga.

'To see Wilmot. If we're going to hunt down this woman we must prevent him from getting in our way.'

Holly ducked through the hatch and clambered down a steel ladder to the utilities tunnel that ran the length of the habitat. Maybe they won't think of looking for me down here, she thought. And even if they do, I can hide out in this maze for days and days. Long as I have to. Like Jean Valjean in the sewers. As she headed down the silent, dimly lit tunnel, she tried to remember when she'd read *Les Miserables*. Pancho had made her read a lot of old stuff after she had been reborn from the cryonics tank. Panch called it literature. Most of it was pretty boring. But Holly remembered vividly the scene in the sewers that ran beneath the Paris streets. Did I see a vid of it? she wondered. Maybe before I died?

With a puzzled shake of her head she felt thankful that the habitat's tunnels were dry and there were no rats. No sewer smell, either. Holly sniffed and smelled nothing. Maybe some dust, and the faint trace of machine oil or something. Water gurgling through some of the pipes. The ever-present hum of electrical machinery.

The tunnel's automatic lights turned on as she walked and off as she left a section. She saw a wallphone.

I could call Kris, she thought. Or Manny. He'd help me. He'd beat the crap out of Kananga.

But she hesitated in front of the phone. Kananga's in charge of security. He's got the whole warping security force under his command. And Malcolm's in with him. They could say whatever they want about me, say I'm under arrest or something. Jeeps! They could even say that I murdered Don Diego!

And if I call Kris or anybody else I'd be getting them into trouble. Holly felt panic surging in her gut. What should I do? What can I do?

She sagged against the tunnel's metal wall and slumped to the floor. Don't do anything, she told herself. You're pretty safe here, at least for the time being. Nobody knows where you are. You can stay down here until you figure things out.

Or starve to death. She looked up and down the tunnel, darkness in both directions. Good. If anybody was coming after her, the lights would be flicking on and off.

Food. I was supposed to go to dinner with Raoul tonight. He'll think I stood him up.

She pushed herself up to her feet. Sorry Raoul, she apologized silently. Then she grinned. Food. Holly closed her eyes briefly, picturing the layout of the tunnels. The food processing plants were further down this tunnel. But if I take the cutoff and head back under Athens I can get under the storage lockers for the cafeteria. Plenty of food there.

She started off in that direction.

Saturn Arrival Minus 18 Days, Six Hours

'What's so important that you have to interrupt my dinner?' Wilmot asked testily.

Eberly smiled at the older man. He had spent the past two hours watching Morgenthau's recordings of Wilmot's evening activities. Morgenthau had been disgusted by the professor's choice of entertainment, but Eberly had watched snatches of the vids, fascinated by their mixture of eroticism and savagery. Now he stood in Wilmot's living room, facing the professor's sternly disapproving frown.

'We have a serious situation on our hands, Professor,' said Eberly.

'Well, what is it?'

'One of the human resources staff members has disappeared. I have reason to believe she's suffered a mental breakdown.'

'What?' Wilmot looked startled. 'Who is this person?'

'Holly Lane. You've met her.'

'Have I?'

Eberly was keenly aware that Wilmot had still not offered him a chair. The two men were still standing, facing each other, barely a meter inside Wilmot's front door. Inwardly, Eberly was amused. He knew he was keeping the professor from his evening's entertainment.

'I suppose I'm partially to blame,' Eberly said, trying to sound contrite. 'I've been protecting her all these months. But she's finally snapped.'

Wilmot looked puzzled, and more than a little annoyed.

Eberly fished his handheld from his tunic and projected Holly's dossier on the wall above Wilmot's sofa.

The professor recognized Holly's face. 'She's the one you brought with you a while back.'

'Yes.' Eberly shook his head sadly. 'As you can see, she has a history of emotional dysfunction.' He had spent hours carefully rewriting Holly's dossier. 'As long as she takes her medication she's perfectly normal. But once she stops . . .'

Wilmot studied the dossier briefly, then asked, 'Why'd she go off her meds?'

'It's this Diego Romero business. Holly became obsessed by the old man's death. She convinced herself that he was murdered.'

'Murdered?'

'It's nonsense, of course. But this afternoon she attacked Colonel Kananga. She tried to kill him, at exactly the same site as the old man's death.'

'Good lord! And where is she now?'

'Disappeared, as I told you. Kananga has organized a search for her.'

Wilmot nodded, as if satisfied. 'Very well. It seems that Kananga is doing what he should. But why have you bothered me about this?'

'Because I want you to appoint me deputy administrator.'

'Deputy? I don't need a deputy.'

'I think you do. You will appoint me deputy administrator so that you can retire from running the habitat.'

'Retire? And put you in charge? Hah!'

'It's not such a ridiculous idea,' Eberly said softly. 'You will retire and I will take over your duties.'

'Nonsense!'

'Once retired,' Eberly went on, 'you can spend all your time watching your filthy vids, instead of merely the evenings.'

Wilmot staggered back a step. The color drained from his beefy face.

'This habitat needs strong leadership,' said Eberly. 'Especially with the elections coming up and our impending arrival at Saturn. You've done your job quite well, Professor. Now it's time for you to step aside.'

'And turn everything over to you? Never!'

Eberly shrugged. 'In that case, we'll have to make your choice of entertainment known to the entire population of the habitat.'

'We? Who do you mean?'

'We don't want to embarrass you, Professor. Simply step aside and allow me to take control and no one will ever know about your little perverse entertainments.'

Wilmot sank down into the nearest chair, speechless.

Kris Cardenas lay in her bed, trying to decide if she was making another mess of her life. What will I be this time? she asked herself: a hard-hearted bitch or a romantic idiot?

Her relationship with Gaeta has started out as a passionate fling, all glands and heat. Once Holly had stepped out of the way she allowed Manny to bed her; she hadn't had so much fun in decades. But then she found out about Nadia. It wasn't that Gaeta had been unfaithful to her, neither one of them had promised anything except fun and games. But the thought that Manny used women that way, slept with a woman who could help him and then moved on to the next, that angered her. Then came his sudden declaration of love. True love! Cardenas almost laughed aloud at the thought. But whatever it was, she was overjoyed by it. At my age, she thought, stifling a giggle. Score a real triumph for nanotechnology!

As she turned to face her love, though, her thoughts sobered. He's going to get himself killed, she feared. That's the business he's in, taking constantly bigger risks. Cardenas hated the public, the audience of vicarious thrill-seekers who pushed Manny to riskier and riskier stunts until he tried the one stunt that would kill him.

He lay on his back, blissfully asleep, his rugged, expressive face relaxed, almost boyish. Cardenas studied the slight scars on his brow and along his jawline, the slightly pushed-in aspect of his nose.

Stop it! she commanded herself. You're getting soft as a grape. Even if he lives through this rings stunt he'll be leaving afterward. Then what will you do? Go traipsing after him like some overaged groupie?

Gaeta opened his eyes, turned toward her, and smiled. Cardenas felt her heart melt for him.

'What time is it?' he mumbled, raising his head enough to see the digital clock.

'Early,' Cardenas whispered. 'Go back to sleep.'

'Big test today,' he said. 'The snowball fight.'

'Not yet. Go back to sleep.'

'Nah. I'm up.'

Cardenas reached for him. 'Why, so you are,' she said, with an impish grin.

The phone buzzed.

'Aw, *mierda*,' he groaned.

'Audio only,' Cardenas told the phone.

Holly's face took shape at the foot of the bed. 'Can't talk long. Just gotta tell you Kananga tried to kill me and I'm on the run. I'll buzz later when I can.'

And her image winked out, leaving the two of them staring at emptiness.

Snowball Fight

'Pay attention!' Fritz snapped.

Inside the massive suit, Manny blinked. Fritz was right, his thought had wandered. That's the dangerous part of this love thing, it makes it hard to concentrate on the business at hand. We'll be at Saturn in a few days and I'll do the rings. If it clears enough profit, then fuck Titan and Urbain and all those uptight *cositas*. I'll just take the money and run home.

With Kris? Will she come with me? Do I have the guts to ask her to? He almost laughed: the most fearless stuntman in the whole solar system and I'm scared to death she'd turn me down. Where's your *cojones*, tough guy?

The banging on his suit startled him. Fritz was whacking at the suit's armored chest with the flat of his hand, as high up as he could reach.

'Wake up in there!' Fritz hollered.

'I'm awake,' said Gaeta.

'These days you spend too much time in bed and not enough time sleeping.'

'I'm awake,' Gaeta repeated peevishly.

From inside the suit, Fritz looked like a cranky little guy standing out there scowling at him, not even as tall as Gaeta's shoulder. Together with the four other technicians, they were standing in a sealed-off section of corridor that led to one of the habitat's major airlocks, big enough to handle bulky equipment. Gaeta had marched in and, at Fritz's order, turned his back to the airlock hatch. Now he could see, down where they had sealed the corridor from the rest of the habitat, half a dozen fans that the techs had set up. Three of the techs were lugging heavy plastic jugs of water and placing them in precisely marked spots on the corridor's floor of metallic squares. Beside each of the fans stood a dark metal tube encased in a copper-colored magnetic coil, looking to Gaeta like a cross between a laboratory contraption and a shotgun. The fourth tech was loading them with ball bearings.

'This simulation will last only a few seconds,' Fritz said, 'but it is designed to give you a feeling for what you will encounter in the ring.'

'I know all that, Fritz,' Gaeta said impatiently. 'Let's get on with it.'

As unperturbed as if he had heard not a syllable, Fritz went on, 'The water will vaporize into ice crystals and the fans will blow them at you. The electromagnetic guns will fire the pellets that simulate larger pieces of ice at approximately Mach one point three.'

'And I stand here and take it all in the face,' said Gaeta.

'I trust the suit will not be penetrated,' said Fritz.

'The self-sealing gunk will stop any leaks.'

'Temporarily.'

'Long enough for this test.'

'But not long enough to save you once you are out in the ring.'

'Which is why we're running this sim, to see if the suit holds up. So let's get on with it.'

Fritz gazed up at him, his expression somewhere between discontent and anxiety.

'Come on, Fritz,' Gaeta urged. 'Let's get it over with.'

With a shake of his head, Fritz led the other techs past the airtight door that sealed off the end of the corridor section. Gaeta saw it close.

'Pumping down the chamber,' Fritz's voice said in his helmet earphones.

'Pump away,' said Gaeta.

The only aspect of his flight through Saturn's B ring that this test couldn't simulate was the lack of gravity. Gaeta didn't think that was important; he had experienced microgee many times, it wasn't a problem for him. But standing in the middle of a superblizzard and allowing himself to be pelted by supersonic stainless steel ball bearings, that was something else. Like facing a firing squad. Yeah, he said to himself, but I'm inside an armored suit. Like Superman. Those bullets'll just bounce off my chest.

He hoped.

James Coleraine Wilmot sat alone in his living room, staring into infinity. Ruined. Tripped up by my own stupidity.

He sighed heavily. I could fight him. Most of the population here is in this habitat because they couldn't stand the rules and regulations that were strangling them. So I have a rather bizarre taste in entertainment. I could offer to take counseling, even psychotherapy. I don't have to knuckle under to this snotty Eberly and his clique. Not unless I want to.

He thought about that. Not unless I want to. Why should I go through the embarrassment and stress of public revelation, public ridicule? Accusations and defenses, excuses, pleading for under-standing? No, I won't subject myself to all that. I can't.

In a way, actually, this is better than ever. Now I'm totally removed from any semblance of control, any hint of responsibility. The experiment is completely free now from any possible inter-ference. I'll have to inform Atlanta about that.

He hesitated, frowning. Eberly's been watching every move I make. Every communication. Even what I do here in the supposed privacy of my own quarters. He's watching me now.

What to do? Nothing. Absolutely nothing. Atlanta will find out about this powerplay of Eberly's soon enough. They must have plenty of spies scattered through the population.

Holly had debated for hours about calling Kris. At last she decided she would do it from a phone up topside. She didn't want Kananga or anyone else to know that she was using the underground tunnels as her hiding place. So, just before the habitat's solar windows opened for 'sunrise,' she climbed up the ladder that opened into the cafeteria's storeroom. She could hear people stirring in the kitchen, just beyond: pots clanging and voices calling back and forth. A robot trundled in from the kitchen, rolled right past her and went to a shelf where it grasped a carton of preserved fruit in its gripper-tipped arms, then turned a precise one hundred and eighty degrees, rolled past her again, and pushed through the double doors to the kitchen.

Holly tiptoed to the wallphone near the kitchen door and made her hurried call to Kris. Somebody's got to know that I'm alive and being hunted by Kananga, she told herself.

After her swiftly spoken message to Kris, she went back to the trapdoor, down the ladder, and ran nearly a kilometer along the main tunnel before slumping down to the floor, panting.

You flaming dimdumb, she said to herself. You were in the warping storeroom and you never thought to get something to eat. Stupid!

Her stomach agreed with a growl.

'She made a call?' Kananga asked eagerly. 'When? From where?'

His aide, wearing the black tunic and slacks that Kananga demanded for his security staff, replied, 'From the cafeteria storeroom, sir. About an hour ago.'

'An *hour* ago?' Kananga snarled, rising from his desk chair.

The woman glanced at her handheld. 'Actually fifty-two minutes ago, sir.'

'And you're just telling me now?'

'We only had a skeleton staff on at the time, sir. They can't monitor every phone in the habitat in real time. It's—'

'I want an automated program set up immediately. Use her voiceprint as the key to trigger an automatic alarm. Immediately!'

'Yessir.'

'This woman is a dangerous psychopath. She's got to be apprehended before she kills someone else!'

The aide scampered from Kananga's office and his baleful glare.

He slowly settled himself back in his chair. The cafeteria. Of course. She's got to eat. We'll simply stake out teams at the cafeteria and the restaurants. She'll be drawn to the food, sooner or later. And once she is, we'll have her.

*   *   *

Gaeta had never been in a blizzard, never tried to trudge through drifts of snow while a cold wind battered at him and drove flakes of ice stinging against his face.

For nearly half a minute, though, he faced the fiercest maelstrom that Fritz's ingenuity could devise. Ice crystals flew all around him, enveloping him in a blinding whirl of gleaming, glinting white. Steel pellets peppered him, rattling against his armored suit so loudly that Gaeta knew it was going to crack. He worried especially about the faceplate. It was bulletproof, he knew, but how bulletproof could it be? He was being machine-gunned, strafed by supersonic pellets of stainless steel.

Yet he stood it. He remained on his feet and even took a few plodding steps upstream, into the blinding whiteout blowing at him. The rattling of the pellets was so loud, though, that he had trouble hearing Fritz's voice counting down the time in his helmet earphones.

All he could do was stand and take it. And look at the lighted displays splashed across the inside of his visor. Every damned light was green, every monitor was showing that the suit was functioning normally. Whoops! One went yellow. Nothing important, he saw; one of the knee joints had suddenly lost lubrication. The backup came on and the light switched back to green.

The noise was damned near deafening. Like a thousand crazy woodpeckers attacking the suit. Why the hell do I put up with this crap? Gaeta wondered. Why am I spending my life getting the shit kicked out of me? Why don't I take whatever money I make out of this and retire while I've still got all my arms and legs.

The classic answer rang in his head: What, and quit show business? He laughed aloud.

And then it was over. As suddenly as it had started, it all disappeared, leaving Gaeta standing there inside the cumbersome suit, his ears ringing from the pounding bombardment.

'What are you laughing about?' Fritz demanded.

Gaeta replied, still grinning, 'I laugh at danger, Fritz. Don't you read my media releases? I think you wrote that line yourself.'

It took the better part of half an hour for them to refill the corridor section with air and for Gaeta to crawl out of the suit.

Fritz inspected it minutely, going over every square centimeter of the hulking suit with a magnifying glass.

'Dimpled, but not penetrated,' was Fritz's estimation.

'Then we can go as planned.'

'Yes, I believe we can.'

Gaeta's handheld buzzed. He flicked it open and saw Nadia Wunderly's face on the minuscule screen.

'If you're worried about the test—'

'No, no, no!' she said, brimming with excitement. 'I just had to tell you right away. You're the luckiest guy in the solar system!'

'Whattaya mean?'

'There's going to be a capture event!' Wunderly was almost shouting. 'Three days after we arrive in orbit Saturn's going to capture an asteroid from the Kuiper Belt.'

'What? What do you mean? Slow it down a little.'

'Manny, a small chunk of ice-covered rock is approaching Saturn from deep in the Kuiper Belt, out beyond Pluto. It's already fallen into Saturn's gravity well. I've done the calculations. It's going to fall into orbit around Saturn smack in the middle of the A ring! Three days after we arrive in orbit outside the rings!'

'Three days?' Fritz asked, looking over Gaeta's shoulder at Wunderly's ecstatic face.

'Yes! If you delay your excursion for three days, you can be there when the capture takes place!'

Book III

I agree . . . in regarding as false and damnable the view of those who would put inhabitants on Jupiter, Saturn and the moon, meaning by 'inhabitants' animals like ours, and men in particular . . . If we could believe with any probability that there were living beings and vegetables on the moon or any planet, different not only from terrestrial ones but remote from our wildest imaginings, I should for my part neither affirm it nor deny it, but should leave the decision to wiser men than I.

Galileo Galilei
Letters on Sunspots
1 December 1612

Saturn Arrival Minus 4 Days

Controlled frenzy, Eberly decided. That's what this is, controlled frenzy.

Since being named deputy director of the habitat, Eberly had moved his election campaign headquarters out of his apartment and into a vacant warehouse space in the Cairo village. It was large enough to house his growing staff of campaign volunteers and their even-faster-growing sets of computers and communications equipment.

He seldom visited the headquarters, preferring to stay aloof from his foot soldiers. The less they see of me, he reasoned, the more they appreciate my rare visits to them.

This evening before election day was one of those rare visits. Sure enough, the dozens of volunteers swarmed around Eberly as soon as he stepped through the warehouse's big double doors. They were beaming at him, especially the women.

He allowed himself to be shown around the makeshift workbenches and shook hands with each and every volunteer. He wore his best smile. He assured them that tomorrow's election would be a smashing triumph for them. They smiled back and agreed that 'we can't lose' and 'by this time tomorrow you'll be the top man.'

Eberly disengaged from them at last, and let Morgenthau lead him to the small private office that had been partitioned off in the far corner of the warehouse space. He had specified that the office should be enclosed by true walls that reached the high ceiling, not merely shoulder-high dividers. And the walls should be soundproofed.

Vyborg was sitting behind the desk in the office when Morgenthau shut the door behind Eberly, Kananga in the chair next to a bank of computer consoles. Both men got to their feet.

'It's going well,' Vyborg said as Eberly approached the desk.

'Never mind that,' he snapped. 'What about Holly? Have you found her?'

'Not yet,' Kananga replied.

'It's been two weeks!'

'This habitat is very large and I have only a limited number of people to search for her.'

'I want her caught.'

'She will be. I've staked out all the places where she can obtain food. We'll find her sooner or later.'

'Make certain she's dead,' Vyborg said.

Eberly frowned at that, thinking, They all profess to be Believers but they don't even blink at the thought of murder. And they want to make me a party to their crimes. Then they'll have an even stronger hold over me.

Morgenthau wondered, 'What if she surrenders herself in some public place? She might be clever enough to show up at the cafeteria at lunchtime and offer to turn herself in.'

Eberly actually shuddered. 'If she starts talking, everything we've worked for could be ruined.'

'But she's been neutralized,' Vyborg countered. 'I've seen to it that everyone believes she's a dangerous lunatic.'

With a shake of his head, Eberly replied, 'No matter what the people believe, if she decides to start blabbing in public it could upset the election. It could throw the election to Urbain. Or even Timoshenko.'

'Tonight is the critical time, then,' Morgenthau said. 'By this time tomorrow the election will be over.'

'I want her found tonight.'

'It would be good,' Vyborg said, almost in a whisper, 'if she were found dead.'

Kananga nodded. 'I'll put the entire security force on it.'

'Has she any allies?' Eberly asked. 'Any friends that she might turn to for help?'

Vyborg said, 'She phoned Dr. Cardenas.'

'That was two weeks ago,' said Morgenthau.

'And only once,' added Kananga. 'It was too brief for us to catch her.'

'Cardenas?' Eberly suddenly saw the way to catch Holly. 'She phoned the nanotech expert?'

'Yes.'

Morgenthau saw the gleam in his eye. 'Do you think . . . ?'

'A nanobug threat,' said Eberly. Turning to Vyborg, he commanded, 'Put out the news that Holly might be harboring dangerous nanomachines. Make it sound as if she's a threat to the entire habitat. A nanoplague! Then every person in the habitat will be on the lookout for her. Kananga, you'll have ten thousand people searching for her!'

The Rwandan laughed delightedly. Vyborg nodded and scampered to the desktop comm unit. As he began dictating a news bulletin, Eberly turned to Morgenthau.

'So much for our fugitive. Now, what are the latest election predictions?'

He expected her to give him a rosy forecast for the election. Instead, her smile faded and a cloud of doubt darkened her chubby face.

'We may have created a Frankenstein monster in this engineer, Timoshenko,' Morgenthau said, turning toward the computer bank.

She called up the latest projection, and a multicolored chart appeared against the bare office wall.

'The blue represents our votes,' said Morgenthau, 'the red is Urbain's and the yellow is Timoshenko's.'

'We're well ahead,' said Eberly.

'Yes, but there's a disturbing trend.' The chart shifted, colors melting or growing. 'If Timoshenko's people throw their support to Urbain, they could beat you.'

'Why would they do that?'

Morgenthau shrugged heavily. 'I don't know why, but it's happening. Urbain has picked up nearly twenty percent of the voters who were solidly in Timoshenko's camp only a few days ago.'

'According to your analyses,' said Eberly.

'Which are based on extensive polls by our volunteers out there.' She pointed toward the door. 'I may be overly alarmist, but it might be possible for Urbain to pick up enough of Timoshenko's votes to win tomorrow.'

Eberly stared hard at the chart, as if he could force the numbers to change by sheer force of will. He kept his face immobile, trying to hide the anger and terror churning in his gut. *I could lose! And then where would I be? They'll take me back, put me back in prison!*

He barely heard Morgenthau's voice. 'Cancel the election. You're deputy administrator now. Wilmot's been neutralized. Cancel the election and set up the government on your own authority.'

'And have three-quarters of the population rebel against me?' Eberly snarled at her.

'If they do,' said Kananga, 'you'll have the perfect excuse to establish martial law.'

'Then we could control everyone,' Morgenthau agreed. 'I had the blueprints for neural probes beamed here from Earth. Once martial law is established we could arrest the troublemakers and implant them with the neural controllers. It would be just what we want.'

Except that the people would hate me, Eberly thought. *They would scheme against me. They'd work night and day to overthrow me.*

'No,' he said flatly. 'I can't rule these people by force. Or by turning them into useless zombies.'

'You wouldn't need neural implants,' said Kananga, drawing himself up to his full height. 'I could make certain that they obey you.'

And make me dependent on you, Eberly answered silently. *I want these people to respect me, to follow me out of admiration and respect. I want them to love me the way those volunteers outside love me.*

'No,' he repeated. 'I must win this election legally. I want the people to elect me freely. Otherwise there will be nothing but turmoil and resistance to my rule.'

Morgenthau looked genuinely alarmed. 'But if the election goes against you? What then?'

'It won't go against me.'

'How can you be sure?'

'The rally tonight. I'll win them over. I'll split Timoshenko's supporters away from Urbain's.'

'How?'

'You'll see.'

Despite the fear that constantly gnawed at her, Holly was almost enjoying her exile. It's like camping out, she thought. Not that she could remember camping out from her first life, back on Earth. Yet she felt strangely free, unattached to anyone or any duties except what she felt like doing. There were plenty of unoccupied areas up topside in the habitat, she knew; two whole villages had been set aside for population growth. And when she got tired of prowling through the tunnels she could always climb up into the orchards or farms and sleep undisturbed on the soft, warm ground.

As far as she could tell, no one was watching her, no one was tracking her. She had made that one call to Kris from the cafeteria's storeroom, and sure enough, a squad of Kananga's security goons had converged on the wallphone within minutes. Holly had watched them from the nearly shut trapdoor in the storeroom's rear. Flatlanders, she thought. They haven't tumbled to the idea that somebody could live beneath the ground, in the tunnels. And there's a gazillion kilometers of tunnels down here, she told herself. I could stay for years and they'd never find me.

But always the realization that Kananga had murdered Don Diego stuck in her memory like a cold knife. And Malcolm's in on it, somehow. How and why she didn't know, but she knew she couldn't trust Malcolm or anyone else. Well, you can trust Kris, she thought. But that would bring trouble down on Kris' head. They murdered Don Diego and Kananga tried to kill me. Would they try to murder Kris if they thought she was helping me? Flaming yes, she decided swiftly.

As the days spun along, though, Holly realized she was accomplishing nothing. Kay, it was fun hiding out in the tunnels and living off the farms and all that. But how long do you want to go on this way? You can't let them get away with it, she told herself. And the election's coming up. Once Malcolm's elected chief of the habitat things'll only get worse, not better.

You've got to find some way to nail them, she kept thinking. Kananga and fat Morgenthau and the little snake Vyborg. Yes, and Malcolm, too. But how? You can't do it by yourself. You need somebody . . . but who?

At last it came to her. Of course! Professor Wilmot. He's in charge of everything. At least, until the election is over. Once I tell him what it's all about, he'll know what to do.

Jeeps! she realized. The election's tomorrow! I've got to visit the professor tonight.

Planning Session

Gaeta sat flanked by Kris Cardenas on one side and Fritz von Helmholtz on the other. Berkowitz sat on Fritz's left. Nadia Wunderly stood before them, waving a laser pointer in one hand. We should've worn safety glasses, Gaeta thought. She's gonna zap somebody's eye with that thing if she's not careful.

Wunderly was practically bouncing with excitement.

'Here's the real-time position of the iceball,' she said, pointing at the computer display with the laser. 'Right on track for capture.'

Gaeta saw Saturn floating lazily in the dark infinity of space, its rings bright and splendid. A greenish oval marked the habitat's current position, heading toward an orbit outside the rings. The tiny red dot of the laser pointer was on a speck of light that was farther from the planet than their own habitat.

'And here's what's going to happen over the next four days,' Wunderly said.

They saw the habitat moving slowly into orbit, as planned. The iceball swung past the planet and almost completely out of the picture, but then Saturn's gravity pulled it back. The iceball skimmed past the rings once, went behind the planet, then swung around again and pulled in tighter.

'Here we go,' Wunderly said breathlessly.

The iceball entered the wide, bright B ring from the top, popped through to the other side, circled behind Saturn's massive bulk once more. When it reappeared it was noticeably slower. Gaeta saw it settle into the B ring almost like a duck landing gently on a pond.

'And that's it,' Wunderly said, freezing the image. 'Saturn

acquires a new moon smack in the middle of the B ring. Nobody's ever seen anything like this before.'

Berkowitz breathed an awed, 'Wow. Every network will carry the capture event.' Leaning past Fritz slightly, he said to Gaeta, 'What a terrific set-up for your gig!'

Gaeta grinned at him.

'How will it affect the rings?' Cardenas asked.

Wunderly shrugged. 'It's too small to have any major effect. It's only eight klicks across. Tiny, really.'

'But it will jostle the particles that are already in the ring, will it not?' asked Fritz.

She nodded. 'Ay-yup, but it won't affect the ring dynamics much. No changes in the Cassini division or anything like that. I've done the sims; the only strong effects will be very local.'

'So that's where we want to be when it happens,' said Gaeta.

'No!' Wunderly and Cardenas said in unison.

'It's too dangerous,' Cardenas added.

'I agree,' Wunderly said. 'You should wait a day or two, give everything a chance to settle down.'

'Won't hurt to wait a little,' Berkowitz agreed. 'But not more than a day or two. We want to go while people are still focused on Saturn and the rings.'

Gaeta looked at Fritz, who was intently studying the three-dimensional image hanging before them.

'What do you think, Fritz?'

'It would be dangerous, but I think within our capabilities. The suit should hold up sufficiently. And it would give us spectacular footage.'

Wunderly said, 'I don't think—'

'Wouldn't it be a help to you,' Gaeta interrupted her, 'to get real-time footage of the capture from inside the ring itself?'

'I can do that with a few remotes,' she said. 'You don't have to risk your neck for the sake of science.'

'Still . . .'

'No, Manny,' said Cardenas, quite firmly. 'You do what Nadia tells you. Nobody wants to see you get killed over this. Waiting a day or two won't make the stunt any less spectacular.'

Fritz agreed with a glum, 'I suppose they are right.'

'You really want to wait?' Gaeta asked his chief technician.

'No sense destroying the suit.'

Gaeta grinned at him, then shrugged. Looking squarely at Cardenas, he said, 'Okay, we'll wait until the next day.'

'Will that be time enough for the ring to settle down?' Cardenas asked.

Wunderly said, 'Two days would be safer.'

'One day would be better,' said Berkowitz, 'publicity-wise.'

'The next day,' Gaeta said, thinking, I can't let Kris run this stunt. I can't let her worries control my work.

'The next day, then,' Cardenas agreed reluctantly. She got up from her chair. 'I'm going to the big rally. Anybody else want to see the fireworks?'

'I've got too much work to do,' said Wunderly.

Gaeta stayed in his seat as he said gently, 'Nadia, if you're finished with the pointer, would you mind turning it off?'

Only after she did so did Gaeta get up and head for the door with Cardenas.

Gaeta walked with Cardenas up the village street.

'Are you sure you're not taking too big a chance by going the day after the new moon's captured?' she asked.

He saw the concern on her face. 'Kris, I don't take risks I can't handle.'

'That's how you broke your nose.'

'The ice sled hit a rock and I banged my beak on the helmet faceplate,' he said, with a grin. 'Could've happened in my bathroom, for god's sake.'

'Your bathroom is on Mars?'

His grin faded. 'You know what I mean.'

'And you know what I mean,' she replied, utterly serious.

'I'll be okay, Kris. I'll be fine. Fritz won't let me take chances with the suit.'

329

She fell silent, while Gaeta thought, Jezoo, I can't be thinking about her and her fears while I'm out there. I've gotta concentrate on getting the job done, not worry about what she's thinking. Surest way to get yourself killed is to let your attention drift away from the job at hand.

They walked up the gently rising street in silence toward the apartment building where both their quarters were. Through the spaces between the buildings on their left, Gaeta could see a crowd already starting to gather by the lakeside, where the big election-eve rally was scheduled to take place. Eberly expects me there, he remembered.

'Maybe we oughtta get a quick bite in the cafeteria,' he said to Cardenas, 'before we go to the rally.'

'I've got some snacks in the freezer. You can nuke them while I change.'

Gaeta nodded and smiled. Women have to change their clothes for every occasion. Then he thought about his own pullover shirt and form-fitting denims. I'm gonna be on the platform with Eberly, he realized. What the hell, this is good enough. I'm a stunt guy, not a vid star.

Raoul Tavalera was sitting on the doorstep of their apartment building, head hanging low, looking more morose than usual. He rose slowly to his feet as he saw Cardenas and Gaeta coming up the walk toward him. Gaeta thought he saw the younger man wince with pain.

'Raoul,' Cardenas said, surprised. 'What are you doing here?'

'They closed down the lab,' he said.

'What?'

'About an hour ago. Four big goons from security came with their damned batons in and told me to shut down everything. Then they locked everything up. Two of 'em are still there, guarding the door.'

Cardenas felt a flush of rage race through her. 'Closed the lab! Why? Under whose authority?'

Rubbing his side, Tavalera answered, 'I asked but they didn't

330

answer. Just whacked me in the ribs and muscled me out into the hall. Big guys. Four of 'em.'

Pushing through the building's front door, Cardenas whipped out her handheld as she started up the stairs. 'Professor Wilmot,' she snapped at the phone.

Gaeta and Tavalera followed her up the stairs and into the sitting room of her apartment. Tavalera looked gloomy. Gaeta thought idly that he could change his clothes in Kris' bedroom; he had almost as much of his wardrobe in her closet as he had in his own.

Cardenas projected Wilmot's gray-haired face against the far wall of the sitting room.

'Professor,' she said, without a greeting, 'someone from security has shut down my laboratory.'

Wilmot looked startled. 'They have?'

'I want to know why, and why this was done without consulting me first.'

Brushing his moustache with one finger, Wilmot looked pained, embarrassed. 'Um, I suggest you ask the deputy director about that.'

'The deputy director?'

'Dr. Eberly.'

'Since when does he have the authority to shut down my laboratory?'

'You'll have to ask him, I'm afraid. Actually, I know nothing about it. Nothing at all.'

'But you can tell him to let me re-open my lab!' Cardenas fairly shouted. 'You can tell him to call off his dogs.'

His face slowly turning red, Wilmot said, 'I really think you should talk to him directly.'

'But—'

'It's his show. There's nothing I can do about it.'

Wilmot's image abruptly winked out. Cardenas stared at the empty air, open-mouthed. 'He hung up on me!'

Gaeta said, 'I guess you'll have to call Eberly.'

Fuming, Cardenas told the phone to contact Eberly. Ruth Morgenthau's image appeared, instead.

'Dr. Eberly is busy preparing his statement for this evening's rally,' she said smoothly. 'Is there something I can help you with?'

'You can call off the security officers posted at my laboratory and let me get back to my work,' Cardenas barked. 'Right now. This minute.'

'I'm afraid that can't be done,' Morgenthau said, completely unflustered. 'We have a dangerous situation on our hands. There's a fugitive loose, and we have reason to believe she might try to break into your laboratory and release nanobugs that could be very dangerous to everyone in the habitat.'

'A fugitive? You mean Holly?'

'She's psychotic. We have reason to believe she murdered a man. We know she attacked Colonel Kananga.'

'Holly? She attacked somebody?'

Gaeta said, 'Holly's never been violent before. What the hell's going on?'

Morgenthau's face took on a sad expression. 'Apparently Miss Lane has stopped taking her medication, for some reason. She is decidedly unbalanced. I can send you her dossier, if you want proof of her condition.'

'Do that,' Cardenas snapped.

'I will.'

'But I don't see what this has to do with my lab,' Cardenas said.

Morgenthau sighed like a teacher trying to enlighten a backward child. 'We know that she's been friendly with you, Dr. Cardenas. We can't take the chance that she might get into your lab and release dangerous nanobugs. That would be—'

'There aren't any dangerous nanobugs in my lab!' Cardenas exploded. 'And even if there were, all you have to do is expose them to ultraviolet light and they'd be deactivated.'

'I know that's how it seems to you,' said Morgenthau patiently. 'But to the rest of us nanomachines are a dangerous threat that could wipe out everyone in this habitat. Naturally, we must be extremely careful in dealing with them.'

Seething, Cardenas started to say, 'But don't you understand that—'

'I'm sorry,' Morgenthau said sternly. 'The issue is decided. Your laboratory will remain closed until Holly Lane is taken into custody.'

Saturn Arrival Minus Three Days, Six Hours, 17 Minutes

Gaeta could see that Cardenas was livid, furious. Even Tavalera, who usually seemed passively glum, was glaring at the empty space where Morgenthau's image had been.

'Holly's not a nutcase,' Tavalera muttered.

'I don't think so either,' said Cardenas.

'But Morgenthau does,' Gaeta pointed out. 'And so does Eberly and the rest of the top brass, I guess.'

Cardenas shook her head angrily. 'And Wilmot won't do a damned thing about it.'

Gaeta said, 'This is serious, Kris. They're saying Holly might've killed somebody.'

'Who?' asked Tavalera.

Striding toward the kitchen, Cardenas said, 'The only person who's died recently was Diego Romero. Drowned.'

'And they're sayin' Holly did it?' Tavalera said.

Cardenas didn't answer. She went behind the kitchen counter and started yanking packages from the freezer.

Gaeta noticed the message light blinking on her desktop unit. 'You got incoming, Kris.'

'Take it for me, will you?'

It was Holly's dossier. The three of them studied it, displayed against the sitting-room wall.

'She's bipolar, manic-depressive,' Gaeta said.

'But that doesn't mean she'd become violent,' said Cardenas.

Tavalera made a sour face. 'I don't believe it. She's not like that.'

Cardenas looked at him for a long moment, then said, 'Neither do I.'

'Could somebody have faked her dossier?' Gaeta asked. 'Framed her?'

'There's one way to find out,' said Cardenas. She commanded the phone to locate Holly's dossier in the files of the New Morality headquarters in Atlanta.

'This is gonna take an hour or more,' said Gaeta.

'Let's grab a bite to eat while we wait,' Cardenas suggested.

'Are we going to the rally?' Gaeta asked.

'After we have Holly's Earthside dossier in our hands,' Cardenas replied.

Holly was waiting for the evening news report while eating a dinner composed of fresh fruits taken from the orchard and a package of cookies from the underground warehouse that cached the specialty foods brought from Earth.

She sat cross-legged on the floor of the utility tunnel that ran beneath the orchard. She planned to go later out to the endcap and sleep in the open, beneath the trees, safely hidden by the flowering bushes that grew in profusion there. Don Diego would've loved the area, she thought, its unorganized roughness, a little bit of wilderness in all this planned-out ecology.

The phone screen on the wall opposite her showed an educational vid beamed from Earth: something about dinosaurs and the comet-born microbes that wiped them out. Holly thought that it was safe enough to watch the program; no one could trace a passive use of the phone. It was only if she made an outgoing call that they could track her location.

The ed program ended as she munched on the cookies. A three-note chime announced the evening news.

Holly's eyes went wide when the newscaster announced that she was not only a hunted fugitive, but a dangerously unbalanced mental case, wanted in connection with the drowning of Don Diego, who might try to unleash a nanoplague on the habitat.

'You bastards!' Holly shouted, jumping to her feet.

Then the newscast showed a prerecorded interview with Malcolm Eberly, who was identified as the deputy director of the habitat. With convincing sorrow, Eberly said:

'Yes, Miss Lane worked in the human services department when I served as its chief. She seemed perfectly normal then, but apparently once she goes off her medication she becomes . . . well, violent.'

'You're flaming right I'm violent!' Holly screeched. 'Wait till I get my hands on your lying face!'

Dressed in a sky-blue blouse and slacks, Cardenas came back into the sitting room where Gaeta and Tavalera were talking together.

'Has her dossier come in from Atlanta yet?' Cardenas asked.

Gaeta shook his head. 'Your message is probably just reaching them Earthside by now. We're a long way from home, Kris.'

Tavalera got to his feet. 'The rally's due to start in half an hour.'

'Sit down, Raoul,' said Cardenas. 'I want to see Holly's dossier before we go.'

'We'll miss—'

'The candidates won't be making their final statements for another hour, at least,' Gaeta said. 'All we'll miss is a lot of noise: the marching bands and all that crap.'

Sitting back on the sofa, Tavalera said, 'I'm worried about Holly. Those goons from security can be rough.'

'Where could she be?' Cardenas wondered aloud, going to the sofa and sitting beside Tavalera.

Gaeta, in the armchair across the coffee table from the sofa, suddenly lit up. 'I bet I know.'

'Where?'

'The tunnels. She liked to explore the tunnels that run under the ground.'

'Tunnels?'

'There must be a hundred kilometers of 'em. More. They'd never be able to find her down there. And she knows every centimeter of them; has it all memorized.'

'Then how could we find her?' Cardenas asked.

'I'll look for her,' said Tavalera, getting up again.

Gaeta reached out and grasped his wrist. 'Raoul, there's just too much of the tunnels to search. You'll never find her. Especially if she doesn't want to get found.'

Tavalera pulled free of his grip. 'It beats sitting around here doin' nothing,' he said.

'If you do find her,' Cardenas said, 'bring her here. We'll keep her safe until this all gets sorted out.'

'Yeah. Okay.'

With nothing else to do after Tavalera left, Cardenas and Gaeta watched the news broadcast that showed the crowd building up at the rally site beside the lake. The speaker's platform was empty, but several small bands paraded through the gathering throng, blasting out march tunes and working up the crowd. They noted that there were plenty of empty chairs spread out on the grass.

'We won't have any trouble getting seats,' Cardenas murmured.

Gaeta got up from the armchair to sit beside Cardenas, on the sofa. They watched the video, close enough to touch. Despite everything else, Cardenas thought that within a week, two at most, Gaeta would be packing up and preparing to leave the habitat. His torch ship might be already on the way here, she said to herself. Should I go with him? Would he want me to?

The phone chimed. Cardenas displayed the message. It was the dossier of Susan Lane, from the files of the New Morality head-quarters in Atlanta.

'They got the wrong Lane,' Gaeta said.

But then the file photo of Holly came up, unmistakable.

'She must've changed her name,' murmured Cardenas.

'Is that a sign of instability?'

They read the dossier, every word and statistic.

'No mention of mental or emotional problems,' Gaeta said.

'Or of medications.'

'The sons of bitches have faked her dossier. They're framing her.'

Cardenas recorded the entire file into her handheld. Then she popped to her feet.

'Let's go to the rally and confront Eberly with this,' she said.

'Right,' said Gaeta.

But when he slid the front door open, four burly men and women in the dead black tunics of the security force were standing in the hallway, slim black batons hooked into their belts.

'Colonel Kananga wants to talk to you,' said one of the women, who seemed to be their leader. 'After the rally. He asks that you stay here until he can get to you.'

Wordlessly, Cardenas slid the door shut and went back to the sofa.

'They must know what we've done,' Gaeta said.

'They've bugged this apartment,' said Cardenas, dropping back onto the sofa. 'They can hear every word we say. And they know about Holly's dossier from Atlanta.'

Feeling dazed, helpless, Gaeta said, 'Then they know that Tavalera's gone to the tunnels to find her.'

The Final Rally

It was hard to talk with so many people pressing around them. Eberly and Morgenthau were walking side by side along the path that led down to the lakeside rally site. Vyborg was slightly behind them, Kananga and a pair of his biggest men up ahead, clearing a path through the thick crowd of people who lined the path, shouting and smiling and reaching for Eberly to shake his hand, touch him, get a smile from him.

He wanted to shake their hands, smile at them, bask in the glow of their adulation. But instead he virtually ignored them as he talked with Morgenthau.

'She's in the tunnels?' he shouted over the crowd's meaningless hubbub.

Morgenthau nodded, puffing hard despite the fact that the press of the crowd slowed their pace to little more than a snail's pace.

'Cardenas' assistant has entered the tunnels to search for her,' she yelled into Eberly's ear.

'I hope he has better success than Kananga's oafs.'

'What?'

'Nothing,' he said louder. 'Never mind.'

'We've detained Cardenas and the stunt man. They have Holly's original dossier.'

A shock of alarm hit Eberly. 'How did they get it?'

'From Atlanta. The New Morality has dossiers on everyone aboard the habitat, apparently.'

Wringing his hands in frustration, Eberly said, 'I should have doctored those files, too.'

'Too late for that.'

'This is getting out of hand. We can't keep Gaeta and Cardenas locked up. I've been pushing Gaeta's stunt as a campaign issue.'

'Vyborg thought it best to keep them quiet until after the election tomorrow.'

Eberly glanced over his shoulder. Vyborg. That sour little troll has been the cause of all this trouble, he told himself. Once I'm firmly in power, I'll get rid of him. But then he thought, the little snake knows too much about me. The only way to be rid of him is to silence him permanently.

A brass band came blaring up to him, surrounded his little group and escorted it to the speaker's platform. They were amateur musicians, making up in enthusiasm what they lacked in talent. They blew so loudly that Eberly couldn't think.

Urbain and Timoshenko were already seated on the platform, he saw as they approached. The crowd was cheering wildly, already worked up to a near frenzy. Wilmot was nowhere in sight. Good. Let him remain in his quarters, as I instructed. I want these people to see me as their leader, no one else.

He climbed the stairs and took his chair between Timoshenko and Urbain. The several little bands clumped together into one large conglomeration in front of the platform and played a faltering rendition of *Now Let Us Praise Famous Men*. Eberly wondered how the women of the habitat felt about the sexist sentiment. The band was so poor that it didn't matter, he decided.

The blaring music finally ended and an expectant hush fell over the crowd. Eberly saw that fully three thousand of the habitat's population was standing on the grass, facing him. It was the biggest crowd of the campaign, yet Eberly felt disappointed, dejected. Seventy percent of the population doesn't care enough about this election to attend the rally. Seventy percent! They sit home and do nothing, then complain when the government does things they don't like. The fools deserve whatever they get.

The crowd sat on the chairs that had been arranged for them. Eberly saw that there were plenty of empties. Before they could begin to get restless, he rose slowly and stepped to the podium.

'I'm a little embarrassed,' he said as he clipped the pinhead

340

microphone to his tunic. 'Professor Wilmot isn't able to be with us this evening, and he asked me to serve as moderator in his place.'

'Don't be embarrassed!' came a woman's voice from somewhere in the throng.

Eberly beamed a smile in her general direction and went on, 'As you probably know already, we are not going to bore you with long-winded speeches this evening. Each candidate will make a brief, five-minute statement that summarizes his position on the major issues. After these statements you will be able to ask questions of the candidates.'

He hesitated a heartbeat, then went on, 'The order of speakers this evening was chosen by lot, and I won the first position. However, I think it's a little too much for me to be both the moderator and the first speaker, so I'm going to change the order of the candidates' statements and go last.'

Dead silence from the audience. Eberly turned slightly toward Urbain, then back to the crowd. 'Our first speaker, therefore, will be Dr. Edouard Urbain, our chief scientist. Dr. Urbain has had a distinguished career . . .'

Holly watched the newscast of the rally from the tunnel. Professor Wilmot's not there, she thought. I wonder why.

Then she realized that this was the perfect opportunity to get to Wilmot without Kananga or anyone else interfering. Holly got to her feet. Just about everybody's at the rally, she saw, eyes still on the screen. I'll bet Wilmot's in his quarters. I could sneak in there and tell him what's going down.

She turned off the wallscreen and started striding purposively along the tunnel, heading for Athens and Wilmot's quarters.

After a few minutes, though, she turned off into a side tunnel that provided access for maintenance robots to trundle from one main utility tunnel to another. No sense marching straight to the village, she told herself. Go the roundabout way and look out for any guards that might be snooping around.

So she missed Raoul Tavalera, who came down the utility tunnel from the direction of Athens, looking for her.

★　　★　　★

341

Urbain and then Timoshenko spent their five minutes reviewing the positions they had stressed all through the campaign. Urbain insisted that scientific research was the habitat's purpose, its very *raison d'etre,* and with him as director the habitat's exploration of Saturn and Titan would be a great success. Timoshenko had taken up part of Eberly's original position, that the scientists should not become an exalted elite with everyone else in the habitat destined to serve them. Eberly thought that Timoshenko received a larger and longer round of applause than Urbain did.

As Timoshenko sat down, Eberly rose and walked slowly to the podium. Is Morgenthau right? he asked himself. Are Timoshenko's voters switching to Urbain? Are the engineers lining up with the scientists?

It makes no difference, Eberly told himself as he gripped the edges of the podium. Now is the time to split them. Now is the time to swing the overwhelming majority of votes to me.

'Now is the time,' he said to the audience, 'for me to introduce the final speaker. I find myself in the somewhat uncomfortable position of introducing myself.'

A few titters of laughter rippled through the crowd.

'So let me say, without fear of being contradicted, that here is a man who needs no introduction: me!'

They laughed. Vyborg and several of his people began to applaud, and most of the crowd joined in. Eberly stood at the podium soaking up their adulation, real or enforced, it didn't matter to him as long as the people down there performed as he wanted them to.

Once they quieted down, Eberly said, 'This habitat is more than a playground for scientists. It is more than a scientific expedition. This is our home, yours and mine. Yet *they* want to tell us how we should live, how we should serve them.

'*They* take it for granted that we will maintain strict population controls, even though this habitat could easily house and feed ten times our current population.

'But how will we be able to afford an expanding population? Our ecology and our economy are fixed, locked in place. There is

342

no room for population growth, for babies, in *their* plans for our future.

'I have a different plan. I know how we can live and grow and be happy. I know how each and every one of you can get rich!'

Eberly could feel the crowd's surge of interest. Raising an arm to point outward, he said:

'Circling around Saturn is the greatest treasure in the solar system: thousands of billions of tons of water. Water! What would Selene and the other lunar cities pay for an unending supply of water? What would the miners and prospectors in the Asteroid Belt pay? More than gold, more than diamonds and pearls, water is the most precious resource in the solar system! And we have control of enough water to make us all richer than Croesus.'

'No!' Nadia Wunderly screamed, leaping to her feet from the middle of the audience. 'You can't! You mustn't!'

Saturn Arrival Minus Three Days, Three Hours, 11 Minutes

Eberly saw a stumpy, slightly plump woman with spiky red hair pushing her way to the front of the crowd.

'You can't siphon off the ring particles!' she shouted as the people moved away to clear a path for her. 'You'll ruin the rings! You'll destroy them!'

Holding up a hand for silence, Eberly said dryly, 'It seems we've reached the question-and-answer part of this evening's rally.'

Once she got to the front of the crowd, at the edge of the platform, Wunderly hesitated. Suddenly she looked embarrassed, unsure of herself. She glanced around, her cheeks reddening.

Eberly smiled down at her. 'If the other candidates don't mind, I'd like to invite this young woman up here to the podium to state her views.'

The audience applauded: lukewarm, but applause nonetheless. Eberly glanced at Urbain and Timoshenko, sitting behind him. Urbain looked uncertain, almost confused. Timoshenko sat with his arms crossed over his chest, an expression somewhere between boredom and disgust on his dark face.

'Come on up,' Eberly beckoned. 'Come up here and state your views so that everyone can hear you.'

Wunderly hung back for a couple of heartbeats, then – her lips set in a determined grim line – she climbed the platform stairs and strode to the podium.

As Eberly clipped a spare microphone to the lapel of her tunic, she said earnestly, 'You can't mine the rings—'

Eberly stopped her with a single upraised finger. 'Just a moment. Tell us your name first, if you please. And your affiliation.'

344

She swallowed once, then looked out at the audience and said, 'Dr. Nadia Wunderly. I'm with the planetary sciences group.'

'A scientist.' I thought so, Eberly said to himself. Here's my chance to show the voters how self-centered the scientists are, how righteous they are, not caring an iota about the rest of us.

'That's right, I'm a planetary scientist. And you can't start mining the rings. You'll destroy them. I know they look big, but if you put all of the ring particles together they'd only form a body of ice that's no more than a hundred kilometers across.'

Turning to Urbain, Eberly said, 'Would you care to join this discussion, Dr. Urbain?'

The Québécois got up from his chair and approached the platform, while Timoshenko sat unmoving, his arms still folded across his chest, his face still scowling.

'The rings are fragile,' Wunderly said earnestly. 'If you start stealing tons of particles from them you might break them up.'

Eberly asked, 'Dr. Urbain, is that true?'

Urbain's face clouded momentarily. Then, with a little tug at his beard, he replied, 'Yes, of course, if you continue to remove particles from the rings at some point you will destabilize them. That is obvious.'

'How many tons of ice particles can we remove without destabilizing the rings?'

Urbain looked at Wunderly, then gave a Gallic shrug. 'That is unknown.'

'I could calculate it,' Wunderly said.

'How many tons of ice are there in the rings?' Eberly probed.

Before Urbain could answer, Wunderly said, 'A little over five times ten to the seventeenth metric tons.'

'Five times . . .' Eberly made a puzzled face. 'That sounds like a lot, to me.'

Urbain said, 'It is five with seventeen zeroes after it.'

'Five hundred thousand million million tons,' said Wunderly.

Eberly pretended to be amazed. 'And you're worried about our snitching a few hundred tons per year?'

A few snickering laughs rose from the crowd.

345

'But we don't know what effect that would have on the ring dynamics,' Wunderly said, almost pleading.

Urbain added more forcefully, 'You say a few hundred tons per year, but that number will grow.'

'Yes, but there's five hundred million *million* tons available,' said Eberly.

Nostrils flaring, Urbain said, 'And once all of Canada was covered with trees. Where are they now? Once the oceans of Earth were filled with fish. Now even the plankton are dying. Once the jungles of Africa were home to the great apes. Today the only chimpanzees or gorillas in existence live in zoos.'

Turning to the audience, Eberly said in his strongest, most authoritative voice, 'You can see why scientists must not be allowed to run this habitat. They care more for apes than they do for people. They want to keep five hundred million *million* tons of water ice out of our hands, when just a tiny amount of that water could make all of us wealthy.'

Wunderly burst, 'But we don't know enough about the rings! At some point you could upset the ring dynamics so badly that they'll all go crashing down into the planet!'

'And what would happen to any organisms living beneath the clouds?' Urbain added. 'It would be an environmental catastrophe beyond imagining. Planetary genocide!'

Eberly shook his head. 'By taking a hundred tons or so, out of five hundred million million.'

'Yes,' Urbain snapped. 'I will not allow it. The International Astronautical Authority will not allow it.'

'And how will they stop us?' Eberly snapped back. 'We're an independent entity. We don't have to follow the dictates of the IAA or any other Earthbound authority.'

Turning again to the audience, he said, 'I will establish our government as independent of all Earthbound restrictions. Just like Selene. Just like the mining communities in the Asteroid Belt. We will be our own masters! I promise you!'

The audience roared its approval. Urbain shook his head in bafflement. Tears sprang to Wunderly's eyes.

Professor Wilmot's Quarters

Instead of his usual evening's entertainment, Wilmot watched the final rally. Eberly's a rabble-rouser, nothing less, he thought. Mining the rings and making everyone rich. What an extraordinary idea. Ecologically unwise, perhaps, but the short-term gains will wipe out any fears of long-term problems.

The scientists are unhappy, of course. But what can they do? Eberly's got this election sewed up. Timoshenko's people will vote their pocketbooks and go for Eberly. So will a good many of the scientists, I wager.

He leaned back in his comfortable upholstered chair and watched the crowd boil up onto the platform and carry Eberly off on their shoulders, leaving Urbain, Timoshenko, and that pathetic little red-haired woman standing there like forlorn children.

Holly knew there was no exit from the utilities tunnel that opened directly into the apartment building where Professor Wilmot lived. Since she'd gone into hiding she'd been able to sneak into office buildings in the dead of night and use their lavatory facilities. She had even gone clothes shopping in the main warehouse without being detected. But now she would have to risk coming up in the village and scurrying along the streets of Athens in full view of the surveillance cameras atop the light poles.

How can I do that without being seen? she asked herself as she made her way along the tunnel. I need a disguise.

Or a diversion, she realized. She stopped and sat on the floor, thinking hard.

★   ★   ★

Tavalera walked for kilometers along the main utility tunnel running from Athens out under the orchards and farms and all the way to the endcap. No sign of Holly.

He passed a sturdy little maintenance robot swiveling back and forth across a small patch of the metal flooring, its vacuum cleaner buzzing angrily.

Tavalera stopped and watched the squat, square-shaped robot. From his weeks spent with the maintenance department, Tavalera knew that the robots patrolled these tunnels, programmed to clean any dust or leaks they found, or to call for human help if they came across something beyond their limited means of handling. There was some kind of crud at this one spot, Tavalera reasoned. He couldn't see any dirt or an oil smear. Could it have been crumbs? Could Holly have been eating here?

He looked up and down the tunnel. The robot, satisfied that the area was now clean, trundled off toward the endcap, deftly maneuvering around Tavalera, its sensors alert for anything amiss.

'Holly!' Tavalera yelled, hoping she was close enough to hear him. No answer except the echo of his own voice bouncing down the tunnel.

Sitting side by side, Cardenas and Gaeta watched the rally, too, from the enforced confinement of her apartment.

'Mine the rings?' Cardenas gasped at the idea. 'Nadia's going to have a stroke over that.'

Gaeta made a grudging grunt. 'I dunno. Maybe he's onto something. Ten to the seventeenth is a big number.'

'But still . . .' Cardenas murmured.

'You know what the going price is for a ton of water?'

'I know it's more precious than gold,' said Cardenas, 'but that's because the price of gold has collapsed since the rock rats started mining the asteroids.'

'Mining the rings.' Gaeta scratched at his jaw. 'Might be a workable idea.'

'What are we going to do about Holly?' Cardenas asked, her voice suddenly sharp.

Gaeta said, 'There's not much we can do, is there? We're stuck here.'

'For the time being.'

'So?'

'There's the phone,' Cardenas said.

'Who do you want to call?'

'Who can help us? And help Holly?'

'*Quïen sabe?*'

'What about Professor Wilmot?'

'He wasn't at the rally,' said Gaeta.

'So he's probably at home.'

Cardenas told the phone to call the professor. No image formed, but Wilmot's cultured voice said, 'I cannot speak with you at the moment. Please leave a message.'

Before Gaeta could say anything, Cardenas said, 'Professor, this is Kris Cardenas. I'm concerned about Holly Lane. I've taken the liberty of accessing her dossier from the Earthside files, and it doesn't match the dossier that Eberly claims is hers. There's no record of mental illness or emotional stability. Something is definitely wrong here, and I'd like to discuss it with you as soon as possible.'

Once the phone light winked out, Gaeta said, 'That's assuming Eberly lets us out of here.'

Cardenas replied tightly, 'He can't keep us under lock and key forever.'

'Well, he's got us under lock and key right now.'

'What can we do about it?' she wondered aloud.

Gaeta reached for her. 'Well, you know what they say.'

She let him pull her into his arms. 'No, what do they say?'

Grinning, 'When they hand you a lemon, make lemonade.'

She thought about the bugs that Eberly's people must have planted in the apartment. 'They've probably got cameras watching us.'

He grinned wickedly. 'So let's give 'em something to see.'

Cardenas shook her head. 'Oh no. But we could stay under the blanket. I doubt that they've got infrared sensors planted.'

★   ★   ★

Holly came up in the administration building and slipped along its empty corridors to her own office. There was no window in her cubicle so she went to Morgenthau's office and looked out at the street. Empty. Everybody's either at the rally or at home watching the rally, she thought. She hoped.

But there are security goons watching the surveillance cameras. Worse, there are computers programmed to report any anomalies that the cameras pick up, she knew. I bet my description is on their list of anomalies. People can be distracted or lazy or even bribed; the warping computers never blink.

What I need is a distraction. It won't fool the computers but it'll keep the security people busy.

A distraction.

Holly closed her eyes, picturing the schematics of the habitat's safety systems that she had memorized. For several minutes she sat at Morgenthau's desk, her face twisted into a grimace of concentration. Then at last she smiled. She activated Morgenthau's desk computer and, recalling the access code for the fire safety system, began instructing the computer to create a diversion for her.

Tavalera trudged wearily back along the tunnel he had come down. At least, he was pretty certain it was the same tunnel. He had taken a couple of turns out near the endcap, where several tunnels joined together.

No sign of Holly. Maybe those security goons got her. He felt anger welling up inside him. Anger and frustration and fear, mixed and churning inside his guts. And the sullen ache in his side where they had whacked him with their batons.

The bastards, he thought. Holly never hurt anybody. Why are they out to get her? Where could she be? Is she safe? Have they got her? Where could she be?

He stopped walking and looked around the dimly lit tunnel. Pipes and electrical conduits ran along the overhead and both walls.

'Christ,' he muttered, 'where the hell am I?'

★   ★   ★

Monitoring the security cameras was easy duty. Gee Archer had his back to the double row of surveillance screens as he tapped a stylus against his teeth, planning his next move.

'You sleeping?' asked Yoko Chiyoda, grinning impishly.

'Thinking,' said Archer.

'It's hard to tell the difference.'

She was a big woman, with a blocky torso and thick limbs well muscled from years of martial arts training. Archer was slim, almost delicate, with slicked-back blond hair and soft hazel eyes. The tabletop screen between them showed the battle dispositions of the Russian and Japanese fleets at the Tsushima Straits in May 1905. Just to devil Archer, she had taken the Russian side, and was beating him soundly nevertheless.

'Gimme a minute,' Archer mumbled.

'You've already had—'

Several things happened at once. The sprinklers set in the ceiling began spraying them with water. The intercom loudspeakers blared, 'FIRE. EVACUATE THE BUILDING AT ONCE.' Archer jumped to his feet, banging his shin painfully against the play table. Chiyoda sputtered as she got up, blinking against the spray of ice-cold water drenching her. She grabbed Archer's hand and dragged him limping toward the door.

Unseen behind them, one of the surveillance screens showed a lone woman walking swiftly along the empty street in Athens that led from the administration building to the complex of apartment buildings further up the hill. The security computer's synthesized voice was saying, 'Ninety-three percent match between the person in camera view and the fugitive Holly Lane. Notify security headquarters at once to take appropriate steps to apprehend the fugitive Holly Lane. She is wanted for questioning . . .'

But neither Archer nor Chiyoda heard the security computer. They were already halfway out of the building, drenched, rushing blindly to escape the fire that did not exist, except in the circuits of the safety computer.

*   *   *

Computers are so smart, Holly thought, and so dumb. A human person would've looked to see if there really was a fire in the building. But give a computer the right set of instructions and it'll act as if a fire had truly broken out.

She grinned as she skipped up the steps in front of the apartment building and tapped out its security code. The door sighed open and she stepped in, out of range of the surveillance cameras at last, and hurried up the stairs to the second level, where Wilmot's apartment was.

And ran almost into the arms of the two security officers standing in the corridor outside Wilmot's door.

'Nobody's allowed to see Professor Wilmot,' said the first one.

'But I—'

'Hey!' snapped the second guard, recognition dawning on his face. 'You're Holly Lane, aren't you?'

Holly turned to run, but the guard grasped her arm. She swung on him but the second guard grabbed her other arm in mid-swing.

'Come on, now. We don't want to hurt you.'

Holly saw it was useless. She relaxed and glowered at them.

The first guard banged on Wilmot's door hard enough to rattle it against its frame while the second one spoke excitedly into his handheld:

'We've got her! Holly Lane. The fugitive. She's here at Wilmot's quarters.'

A tinny voice replied, 'Excellent. Hold her there until we arrive.'

Wilmot opened his door, a fuzzy robe of royal blue wrapped around him and tightly tied at the waist. His eyes widened with surprise as he saw Holly in the grip of the guard.

'Got a visitor for you, Professor,' the guard said, pushing Holly past the startled old man and into his sitting room. Then he slid the door shut again.

'I suppose I shouldn't be astonished that you're here,' Wilmot said, standing by the door. 'The remarkable thing is that you've managed to elude the security people for so long.'

'Not long enough,' Holly said ruefully.

'Well . . . do sit down. We might as well be comfortable. Would you like something? Sherry, perhaps?'

'No thanks.' Holly perched on the edge of one of the twin armchairs. She glanced at the closed door. No other way out of here, she knew. Wilmot sank down into the other armchair with a pained sigh.

'Whatever brought you here, to me?' he asked.

'I wanted your help,' Holly said. 'Colonel Kananga murdered Don Diego and he's after me now.'

'Diego Romero? I thought his death was an accident.'

'It was murder,' said Holly. 'Kananga did it. He tried to kill me when I found out about it.'

'And Eberly is on it, is he?'

'You know about that?' Holly asked, surprised.

His face showing distaste, Wilmot said, 'He's put out a dossier that purports to show you are dangerously unbalanced.'

Holly bit back the anger and remorse that surged within her. 'Yes. Malcolm's protecting Kananga.'

'A little earlier this evening Dr. Cardenas sent me your dossier from the files on Earth. Eberly's done some creative lying about you.'

'Then you'll help me?'

Wilmot shook his head. 'I'm afraid I'm not even able to help myself, actually. He's got me locked in here.'

'Locked up? You? How could he do that? I mean, you're—'

'It's a long, sad story,' said Wilmot wearily.

'Well, now he's got me, too,' Holly said.

'Yes, I'm afraid so.'

Saturn Arrival
Minus Three Days, 45 Minutes

Eberly frowned as Kananga shooed the last of the well-wishers out of his apartment. He had enjoyed his triumph at the rally, gloried in the crowd's adulation. Carried off on their shoulders! Eberly had never known such a moment.

Now, as midnight approached, Kananga officiously shoved the last starry-eyed young woman out into the corridor and slid the apartment's front door firmly shut. Morgenthau sat on the sofa, nibbling at one of the trays of the finger food that had been set out. Vyborg hunched by a three-dimensional image of the newscast, already showing a rerun of Eberly's minidebate against the red-haired scientist.

'You've got them,' Vyborg said. 'They all want to get rich. Most of them, at least.'

'It was a brilliant stroke,' Morgenthau agreed.

Still leaning against the door, Kananga snapped, 'Turn that thing off. We've found her.'

A surge of sudden fear cut through the elation Eberly had been feeling. 'Found her? Holly?'

Smiling grimly, Kananga said, 'Yes. She tried to sneak into Professor Wilmot's quarters. Looking to him for help, I suppose.'

'Where is she now?'

'Still there. My people have the apartment sealed off. I told them to cut Wilmot's phone off, too.'

'What are you going to do with her?' Morgenthau asked.

The euphoria ebbed out of Eberly like water swirling down a drain. Morgenthau had asked Kananga, not him.

'We'll have to eliminate her. Permanently.'

'Tricky,' said Vyborg. 'If she's with Wilmot you can't just go in there and snap her neck.'

'She can always be killed trying to escape,' Kananga said.

'Escape how?'

Kananga thought a moment. Then, 'Perhaps she runs away from my guards and goes to an airlock. She puts on a spacesuit and tries to go outside, to hide from us. But the suit is defective, or perhaps she didn't seal it up properly.'

Morgenthau nodded.

Spreading his hands in a *fait accompli* gesture, Kananga said, 'Poor girl. She panicked and killed herself.'

With a mean chuckle, Vyborg said, 'She always was unbalanced, after all.'

The three of them turned to Eberly. This is getting out of control, he thought. They're making me a party to their murders. They're forcing me to go along with them. They'll be able to hold this over my head forever.

And after tomorrow, when I'm the elected head of the government, they'll still have power over me. I'll be a figurehead, a puppet dancing to their tune. They'll have the power, not me.

Kananga slid the door open. Eberly could see that the corridor outside was empty now. It was late. All his adoring crowd had gone to their own homes.

'Shall we go pick her up?' Kananga said.

'I'll go,' said Eberly, trying to sound firmer, more in control, than he really felt. 'Alone.'

Kananga's eyes narrowed. 'Alone?'

'Alone. It would be more believable if she escaped from me than from two of your thugs, wouldn't it?'

Before Kananga could reply, Vyborg said, 'He's right. We've got to make the story as plausible as possible.'

Morgenthau eyed Eberly carefully. 'This young woman is a definite threat to us all. Whether we like it or not she's got to be eliminated. For the greater good.'

'I understand,' said Eberly.

'Good,' Morgenthau replied.

Kananga looked less agreeable. He obviously wanted to take care of this himself. Eberly pulled himself up to his full height and stepped to the door. He had to look up to see into Kananga's eyes. The Rwandan tried to face him unflinchingly, but after a few heartbeats he moved away from the door. Eberly walked past him and out into the corridor. Not daring to look back, he strode down the hallway toward the outside door.

Standing in the apartment doorway watching him, Kananga muttered, 'Do you think he's strong enough to carry this out?'

Morgenthau pushed herself up from the sofa. 'Give him a few minutes. Then you go to Wilmot's building and take the guards away from his apartment door. Wait for him and the girl outside the building. When Eberly brings her out, you and the guards can take over.'

Vyborg agreed. 'That way he's not party to the killing. Good.'

Morgenthau cast him a contemptuous glance. 'He's party to it. We're all party to it. I want to make certain that the girl is taken care of properly.'

Holly came out of Wilmot's bathroom and sat tiredly on the sofa. The digital clock showed it was past midnight.

'My phone doesn't work,' the professor grumbled. 'They really want to keep us incommunicado.'

'What's going to happen now?' she wondered.

With a sigh that was almost a snort, Wilmot replied, 'That's in the lap of the gods. Or Eberly and his clique, rather.'

'I wish there was some way I could talk to Kris Cardenas.'

'Dr. Cardenas lives in this building, doesn't she?'

'Yes.'

Wilmot glanced at the door. 'With those two guards outside, I don't suppose we'd be able to get to her.'

'Guess not.' The sofa felt very comfortable to Holly. She leaned back into its yielding softness.

'It's rather late,' said the professor. 'I'm going to bed. You can stretch out on the sofa if you like.'

Holly nodded. Wilmot got up from his armchair and walked slowly back to his bedroom.

356

He hesitated at the bedroom door. 'You know where the bathroom is. If you need anything, just give a rap.'

'Thank you,' said Holly, suppressing a yawn.

Wilmot went into his bedroom and shut the door. Holly stretched out on the sofa and, despite everything, fell into a dreamless sleep as soon as she closed her eyes.

Thinking furiously, Eberly walked slowly along the path that led from his apartment building to Wilmot's.

The voting starts in a few hours, he said to himself. In twelve hours or so I'll be the head of the new government. I'll have it all in my grasp.

But what good will that be if Kananga and the rest of them can hold their murders over my head? They'll be able to control me! Make me jump to their tune! I'll just be a figurehead. They'll have the real power.

It was almost enough to make you weep. Here I've struggled and planned and worked all these months and now that the prize is at my fingertips they want to keep it from me. It's always been that way; every time I reach for safety, for success and happiness, there's someone in my way, someone in power who puts his foot on my neck and pushes me back down into the mud.

What can I do? What can I do? They've put me in this position and they'll never let me out of it.

As he came up the walk in front of Wilmot's building he saw that one of Kananga's guards was standing outside the front door, waiting for him.

Of course, Eberly thought. Kananga's already talked to him, told him that I'd be coming. Kananga and the others are probably coming up behind me.

And then it hit him. He stopped a dozen meters in front of the black-clad guard. The revelation was so powerful, so beautiful, so perfect that a lesser man would have sunk to his knees and thanked whatever god he believed in. Eberly had no god, though. He simply broke into a wide, happy smile, grinning from ear to ear. His knees still felt a little rubbery, but he strode right up to the guard, who

357

opened the building's front door for him. Without a word, without even a nod to the man, Eberly swept past him and started up the steps to Professor Wilmot's apartment.

The knock on the door startled Holly awake. She sat up like a shot, fully alert.

'Holly, it's me,' came a muffled voice from the other side of the door. 'Malcolm.'

She got up from the sofa and went to the door. Sliding it open, she saw Eberly. And only one guard in the corridor.

Turning to the guard, Eberly said, 'You can go now. I'll take charge here.'

The guard touched his right hand to his forehead in a sloppy salute, then headed toward the stairs.

'Holly, I'm sorry it's come to this,' Eberly said as he stepped into the sitting room and looked around. 'Where's Professor Wilmot?'

'Asleep,' she replied. 'I'll get him.'

Wilmot came into the room, wearing the same fuzzy robe. Otherwise he looked normal, wide awake. Not a hair out of place. His face, though, was set in an expression that Holly had never seen on the old man before: wariness, apprehension, almost fear.

'May I sit down?' Eberly asked politely.

'I imagine you can do anything you bloody well like,' said Wilmot, irritably.

Instead of sitting, though, Eberly took an oblong black box from his tunic pocket and swung it across the room in a full circle, then swept it up and down, from ceiling to floor and back again.

'What're you doing?' Holly asked.

'Exterminating bugs,' said Eberly. 'Making certain our conversation isn't overheard by anyone else.'

Wilmot bristled. 'You've had my quarters bugged for some time, haven't you?'

'That was Vyborg's doing,' Eberly lied smoothly, 'not mine.'

'Indeed.'

358

'I want to get this all straightened out before there's any more violence,' Eberly said as he finally sat in the nearer of the two armchairs.

'So do I,' said Holly.

Wilmot sank slowly into the armchair facing Eberly. Holly went to the sofa. She sat down and tucked her feet under her, feeling almost like a little mouse trying to make herself seem as small and invisible as possible.

'You're in danger, Holly. Kananga wants to execute you.'

'What do you intend to do about it?' Wilmot demanded.

'I need your help,' Eberly replied.

'*My* help? What do you expect me to do?'

'In eighteen hours or so I'll be the elected head of the new government,' said Eberly. 'Until then you are still the director of this community, sir.'

'I'm under house arrest and threatened with scandal,' Wilmot grumbled. 'What power do I have?'

'If you ordered those guards away, they would obey you.'

'Would they?'

Eberly nodded. 'Yes, providing I second your command.'

'I see.'

Holly swiveled her attention from Eberly to Wilmot and back again. Scandal? she wondered. House arrest? What's going on between these two?

She said to Eberly, 'Kananga killed Don Diego, didn't he?'

'Yes.'

'And he wants to kill me.'

'He certainly does.'

'How are you going to stop him?'

'By arresting him,' Eberly said, without hesitation. But his face looked worried, doubtful.

'Suppose he doesn't want to be arrested?' Wilmot said. 'He's the chief of the security forces, after all.'

'That's where you come in, sir. You still have the legal power and the moral authority to command the security officers.'

'Moral authority,' Wilmot mumbled.

'We'll need to arrest Morgenthau and Vyborg as well. They were parties to Kananga's crime.'

'Easier said than done. If Kananga wants to resist, I'll warrant most of the security force will follow his lead, not mine.'

Holly said, 'But the security force is only about three dozen men and women.'

'That's a dozen for each of us,' Wilmot pointed out.

'Yes,' said Holly. 'But there are ten thousand other men and women in this habitat.'

Election Day

Kananga looked at his wristwatch, then up at the apartment building. He'd been waiting out in the street with a half-dozen of his best people for nearly an hour.

'I don't think she's coming out, sir,' said the team's leader. 'We could go in and get her.'

'No,' Kananga barked. 'Wait.'

He yanked his handheld from his tunic pocket and called for Eberly.

'What's going on?' he demanded as soon as Eberly's face appeared on the miniature screen.

'Miss Lane is going to stay here in Professor Wilmot's quarters for the time being,' Eberly said smoothly.

'What? That's not acceptable.'

'She'll remain here until after the election is finished. We don't want to have anything disturb the voting.'

'I don't see why—'

'I've made my decision,' Eberly snapped. 'You can post guards around the area. She's not going anywhere.'

His image winked out, leaving Kananga staring angrily at a blank screen.

'What do we do now?' the team leader asked him.

Kananga glared at her. 'You stay here. If she tries to leave the building, arrest her.'

'And you, sir?'

'I'm going to try to get a few hours' sleep,' he said, stalking off toward his own quarters.

The phone woke Kris Cardenas. She sat up groggily and called out, 'No outgoing video.' Glancing at Gaeta sleeping peacefully beside her, she thought that the man could probably snooze through the end of the world.

Holly's face appeared at the foot of the bed. 'Kris, are you there?'

'Holly!' Cardenas cried. 'Where are you? Are you okay?'

'I'm in Professor Wilmot's apartment, upstairs from you. Can you come up here right away?'

Cardenas saw that it was a few minutes past seven a.m. 'There's a couple of security goons outside my door, Holly. They won't—'

'That's okay. They'll let you come up here. Professor Wilmot's already spoken to them.'

Oswaldo Yañez woke bright and cheerful. He heard his wife in the kitchen, preparing breakfast. He showered and brushed his teeth, whistling to himself as he dressed.

Breakfast was waiting for him on the kitchen table, steaming hot and looking delicious. He kissed her lightly on the forehead and said, 'Before I eat, I must do my duty as a citizen.'

He called to the computer as he sat across the table from Estela.

'Who will you vote for?' she asked.

Grinning, he replied, 'The secrecy of the ballot is sacred, my darling.'

'I voted for Eberly. He makes more sense than the others.'

Yañez's jaw dropped open. 'You voted? Already?'

'Of course. As soon as I awoke.'

Yañez felt all the excitement of the day drain out of him. He wanted to be the first to vote. It was unfair of his wife to sneak in ahead of him. Then he sighed. At least she voted for the right candidate.

'You're really okay?' Cardenas asked as soon as she entered Wilmot's apartment. Gaeta was right behind her, looking a little puzzled.

'I'm fine,' said Holly. Turning to Eberly and Wilmot, she said, 'You know everybody, don't you?'

'Of course.'

362

Gaeta fixed Eberly with a pugnacious stare. 'What's the idea of cooping us up in the apartment? What's going on?'

'We are trying to save Miss Lane's neck,' Eberly said.

'Yes,' Wilmot added. 'We want to avoid violence, but there are certain steps we must take.'

Holly told them what she had planned, and what she needed them to do.

Cardenas blinked, once she understood. '*Posse comitatus?*' she asked, unbelieving.

Gaeta broke into a nervous laugh. 'Holy Mother, you mean a posse, like in the old Westerns?'

'It won't work,' Cardenas said. 'These people are too independent to form a posse just because you ask them to. They'll want to know why and how. They'll refuse to serve.'

'I was wondering about them myself,' said Wilmot.

Eberly smiled, though. 'They'll do it. They merely need a bit of persuasion.'

After a few hours of sleep, Kananga stormed into Eberly's apartment. 'What are you doing? We agreed that the Lane woman would be put into my custody.'

Sitting bleary-eyed at his desk, watching the three sets of numbers from the early voting returns, Eberly said, 'I've been up all night, working on your problem.'

'My problem? She's your problem, too. I want her delivered to me immediately.'

Eberly said blandly, 'She will be. Don't get upset.'

'Where is she? Why isn't she in my hands?'

Trying to control the tension that was tightening inside him, Eberly said, 'She's in Wilmot's apartment. She's not going anywhere.'

'What's going on? What are you up to?' Kananga loomed over Eberly like a dangerous thundercloud.

'Wait until the election returns are in,' Eberly said, jabbing a finger toward the rapidly changing numbers. 'Once I'm officially the head of this habitat I'll be able to act with real authority.'

Kananga scowled suspiciously.

Hoping he had at least half-convinced the Rwandan, Eberly got up from his desk chair. 'If you'll excuse me, I've got to get some sleep.'

'Now? With the voting still going on?'

'There's nothing I can do to affect the voting now. It's all in the lap of the gods.'

Despite himself, Kananga smiled tightly. 'Better not let Morgenthau hear you speaking like a pagan.'

Eberly forced himself to smile back. 'I must sleep. It wouldn't do for the newly elected head of this habitat to have puffy eyes when he accepts the authority of office.'

Saturn Arrival
Minus One Day, Seven Hours

Edouard Urbain watched the final few minutes of the voting in the privacy of his quarters with a strange mixture of disappointment and relief. Eberly had clearly won, that much was certain early in the afternoon. But Urbain waited until the voting ended, at 17:00 hours, before finally accepting the fact that he would not be the director of the habitat.

He almost smiled. *Now I can get back to my real work*, he told himself. *I will no longer be distracted by these political monkey-shines.*

Yet he felt close to tears. *Rejected again. All my life I have been turned away from the top position. All my life I have been told that I am not good enough to be number one. Even Jeanne-Marie turned against me, in the end.*

And more, he realized. *Now I must face this crazy stuntman and his demand to go to the surface of Titan. Eberly will support his demand, of course. I will have to ask the IAA to inform Eberly that they will not permit it. I will have to show everyone back on Earth that I am not strong enough to keep a simple adventurer from contaminating a pristine new world.*

Tears blurred his eyes as he commanded the phone to contact Eberly. *I must congratulate him and concede my defeat*, Urbain thought. *Another defeat. With more to come.*

Ilya Timoshenko had no difficulty making his concession message. Sitting at the bar in the Bistro surrounded by a gaggle of supporters – mostly engineers and technicians – he used his handheld to call Eberly.

'You've won and I'm glad,' he said to Eberly's pleased image. 'Now let's get this bucket into its proper orbit around Saturn.'

Eberly laughed. 'Yes, by all means. We're all counting on you and the technical staff to bring us into Saturn orbit tomorrow.'

While Eberly's supporters celebrated his victory with an impromptu picnic out by the lake, Holly was still in Wilmot's apartment, using his computer to comb through the habitat's personnel files. It took several hours, but at last she had a list of fifty men and women whom she thought could serve as her posse.

As she sent the list to Eberly at his quarters, she wondered how good her idea really was. Would the people she had selected actually agree to serve as a posse? It was so hard to pinpoint attributes such as loyalty and responsibility from a person's dossier. Most of the people aboard the habitat were far from being 'establishment' types. They weren't misfits, as Pancho had called them, but they were definitely freethinkers, self-starters, unwilling to accept discipline imposed by others.

I hope this works, Holly thought. She realized that her very life depended on it.

The victory party was getting rowdy. Several of Eberly's supporters had brought coolers of homebrewed beer to the lakeside picnic and now the celebrants were getting noisier and more obstreperous, laughing uproariously at almost anything, sloshing beer over one another's heads, even wading into the lake fully dressed, giggling and staggering like college students.

Normally, Eberly would have basked in the adulation of his supporters. He didn't drink, and no one dared to douse him with beer or anything else, but still Eberly would have enjoyed every millisecond of the hours-long picnic. Except that he knew what was coming after the party ended.

So despite the smile he wore, in the back of his mind he was thinking that he would have to deal with Kananga, and that was going to be far from pleasant. Dangerous, more likely.

Morgenthau seemed rather pleased, despite the drunken antics of the staggering, boisterous crowd. Even snaky little Vyborg chatted happily with a few of the glowing-eyed young women that clustered about him, Eberly noted. Power goes to some people's heads; in other people, power goes straight to the groin.

Morgenthau shouldered her way through a throng of well-wishers crowding Eberly, a plastic cup in her chubby hand. Nonalcoholic, Eberly was certain. Probably lemonade. The crowd melted away. Are they being respectful, Eberly wondered, or do they realize that she views all this frivolity with infinite distaste.

Once the others had moved out of earshot, she quietly asked Eberly, 'Enjoying your triumph?' A knowing smile dimpled her broad face.

He nodded soberly. He had been careful to drink nothing stronger than iced tea all through the picnic.

'Now our true work begins,' she said, in a lower voice. 'Now we bring these people under control.'

Eberly nodded again, less enthusiastically. He knew that she meant that he too would be under control, as well. Her control. I've done all this work and she thinks she's going to be the true power.

He wondered if Wilmot and Holly would turn out to be strong enough to help him.

The following morning, fifty puzzled men and women crowded into the largest conference room in the administration building.

Holly, escorted by Gaeta and Cardenas, left Wilmot's quarters to join them, after a detour to their own apartments for a shower and change of clothes. They could see Kananga's security officers following them at some distance, hanging back but watching their every move as they spoke into their handhelds for instructions from Kananga. Holly thought of vids she had seen of hyenas tracking a herd of gazelles, waiting for a weak one to falter so they could pounce.

Eberly met them at the building's front door and together they walked past the Human Resources offices, where Morgenthau should have been, to the conference room.

There weren't enough chairs in the conference room for everyone, and the fifty people Holly had selected were mostly on their feet, making the packed room feel hot and sweaty with the press of too many bodies. And they were decidedly unhappy.

'What's going on?' one of the men demanded as soon as Eberly stepped through the door.

'Yeah, why do you want us here?'

'We're not gonna miss the orbit insertion, are we? It's set for a few hours from now.'

Eberly made a placating gesture with both hands as he squeezed through the group and up to the head of the table. Holly, with Gaeta and Cardenas still flanking her, waited near the door.

'Hey, isn't that the fugitive?' someone said, pointing at Holly.

'The security people want her.'

'She must've turned herself in.'

Holly said nothing, but it frightened her to be considered a fugitive, a criminal who has to be turned over to the authorities.

'What's she doing here?'

'Maybe Eberly's got her to give herself up.'

'Then why're we here? What's he want with us?'

Gradually, they all turned toward Eberly, who stood in silence behind the unoccupied chair at the head of the table, his hands gripping the chair back, waiting for their mutterings to cease.

At last he said, 'I've asked you here because I need your help.' Pointing down the table to Holly, he said, 'Miss Lane has been falsely accused. Colonel Kananga is the one who should be arrested.'

'Kananga?'

'But he's the chief of security!'

'That's why I need you,' Eberly said. 'I want you to form a committee, a posse. We will go to Kananga's office and arrest him.'

'Me?'

'Us?'

'Arrest the chief of security?'

'This has gotta be some kind of joke, right?'

'What about the rest of the security staff? You think those goons are gonna stand by and let us arrest their boss?'

Eberly said, 'The fifty of you should be enough to discourage the guards from interfering. After all, they aren't armed with anything more dangerous than their batons.'

'I heard they're all martial arts specialists.'

'I don't see why I have to get involved in this. You're the chief administrator now. You do it.'

'As chief administrator, I am drafting you to serve—'

'The hell with that! I'm not going to get my face punched in just because you've got a gripe with the security chief. Get some other suckers to do your dirty work!'

One of the women said, 'Anyway, you're not really the chief administrator yet, not officially. Not until Professor Wilmot swears you in.'

'But I *need* you to arrest Kananga,' Eberly pleaded. 'It's your duty as citizens!'

'Duty my ass! You wanted to be head of this community. *You* do your duty. Leave me out of it.'

'Do it yourself,' a bellicose red-faced man thundered. 'We didn't ride all the way out here to Saturn to help you set up a dictatorship.'

'But—'

They turned away from Eberly and began filing past Holly through the door, grumbling and muttering.

'Wait,' Eberly called uselessly.

Hardly any of them even hesitated. They hurried by, leaving the conference room, most of them avoiding Holly's eyes as they left.

Eberly stood at the head of the table, watching them leave. Morgenthau has all the offices bugged, he realized. Kananga will know about this failure before the last of them leaves the room.

Saturn Orbit Insertion

Unheeding of politics, uncaring of human aspirations and activities, oblivious to the hopes and fears of the ten thousand people aboard the habitat, *Goddard* fell toward the ringed planet, gripped in Saturn's massive gravity well, sliding down into its preordained orbit just outside the ring system.

Half a million kilometers away, a jagged chunk of ice-covered rock half the size of the habitat was also falling into an orbit that would bring it squarely into Saturn's brightest, widest ring.

In the tidy, efficient command center, Timoshenko scowled at the data his console screen showed him.

'We're picking up more dust than predicted,' he said.

Captain Nicholson nodded, her eyes fixed on her own screens. 'Not to worry.'

'It's causing abrasion of the hull.'

'Within acceptable limits. Once we're in orbit we'll be moving with the dust and the abrasion level will go down.'

Timoshenko saw that the navigator and first mate both looked more than a little worried, despite the captain's calm assurance.

'If the abrasion causes a break in one of the superconducting wires,' the first mate said, 'it could cause our radiation shielding to fail.'

The captain swiveled her chair toward him. She was a small woman, but when her square jaw stuck out like that she could be dangerous.

'And what do you want me to do about it, Mr. Perkins? We're in freefall now. Do you expect me to put her in reverse and back out of Saturn's gravity well?'

'Uh, no, ma'am. I was just—'

'You just attend to your duties and stop being such an old maid. We calculated the abrasion rate before we left lunar orbit, didn't we? It's not going to damage our shielding.'

The first mate bent his head to stare at his console screens as if his life depended on it.

'And you,' she turned on the navigator, 'keep close track of that incoming iceball. If there's any danger here, that's where it is.'

'It's following the predicted trajectory to within five nines,' said the navigator.

'You watch it anyway,' snapped Captain Nicholson. 'Astronomers can make all the predictions they want; if that thing hits us we're dead meat.'

Timoshenko grinned sourly. She's a tough old bitch, all right. I'll miss her when she leaves.

And then he realized, when she and the other two leave I'll be the senior man of the crew. Senior and only.

Vyborg hissed, 'He's sold us out. The traitor has sold us out.'

Kananga, watching the real-time display of Eberly's failed meeting with his unwilling posse, laughed aloud. 'No,' the Rwandan said. 'He *tried* to sell us out. And failed.'

They were in Morgenthau's office. From behind her desk she turned off the spy-camera's display, then hunched forward in her creaking chair. 'So what do we do about him?' she asked.

'He's a traitor,' Vyborg insisted. 'An opportunistic turncoat who'd sell his mother's milk if he thought he could make a penny out of it.'

'I agree,' said Morgenthau, her expression grim. 'But what do we *do* about him?'

Still smiling, Kananga said, 'That's what airlocks are for. Him, and the girl as well.'

'And Cardenas?' Morgenthau asked. 'And the stuntman? And Wilmot and anyone else who opposes us?'

Kananga started to nod, then realized what she was saying. He rubbed his chin thoughtfully.

Vyborg said, 'We can't execute everyone who disagrees with us. Unfortunately.'

'Yes,' said Kananga. 'Even my best people would draw the line somewhere.'

'So we have to control them, rather than execute them,' Morgenthau said.

'Can we control Eberly now? In a few hours he'll be installed as leader of this community.'

'It means nothing,' Morgenthau assured him. 'You saw how those people reacted to his plea for their help. These malcontents and freethinkers aboard this habitat won't raise a finger to support him against us.'

'They elected him.'

'Yes, and now they expect him to run things without bothering them. They don't want to get involved in the messy work of being active citizens.'

'Ahh,' said Kananga. 'I understand.'

'As long as we don't bother the people, they'll let us have a free hand to run things as we see fit.'

'So Eberly has the title, but we make certain he has no power.'

'Exactly. He'll have to jump to our tune, or else.'

'And Wilmot?'

'He's already out of the way.'

'Cardenas? The stuntman?' Vyborg asked.

'The stuntman will be leaving after his performance. He'll go out on the ship that's bringing the scientists from Earth.'

'Cardenas,' Vyborg repeated. 'I don't like having her here. Her and her nanomachines.'

'And the Lane girl,' said Kananga, touching his once-swollen cheek. 'She has got to be put away. Permanently.'

'She should be executed for Romero's murder,' Morgenthau said.

'Better that she kills herself trying to escape,' said Kananga.

'Yes, probably so.'

'What about Cardenas?' Vyborg insisted.

Morgenthau took a deep, sighing breath. 'I don't like her, either. She could become a troublemaker.'

Then her face lit up. 'Nanotechnology! Suppose we find that Dr. Cardenas is cooking up dangerous nanobugs in her lab?'

'She's not.'

'But the people will believe she is. Especially if we find that Romero was murdered by nanomachines.'

Despite her reliance on Newtonian mechanics, despite her assurances to Timoshenko and the other two men of her minuscule crew, Captain Nicholson felt her insides tensing as the countdown clock ticked off the final seconds.

The screens were all boringly normal. Nothing seemed wrong with their trajectory. The dust abrasion was a worry, but it was only slightly above predicted limits. The approaching iceball was following its predicted path, a safe two hundred thousand kilometers away from the habitat.

Still . . .

'Thirty seconds to orbital insertion,' said the computer's synthesized voice.

I know that, Nicholson replied silently. I can read the countdown clock as well as you, you pile of chips.'

'Abrasion level rising,' Timoshenko called.

It was still within acceptable limits, the captain saw. Yet it was worrisome, despite her assurances.

'Ten seconds,' said the computer. 'Nine . . . eight . . .'

Nicholson glanced up from her screens. The three men looked just as tense as she felt, all of them hunched over their consoles.

What if something breaks down? she asked herself. What could I do about it? What could anyone do?

'Three . . . two . . . one. Orbital insertion.'

The navigator looked up from his console, his worried frown replaced by a wide grin. 'That's it. We're in orbit. On the nose, to five nines.'

Timoshenko called out, 'The abrasion rate is decreasing rapidly.'

Nicholson allowed herself a tight grin. 'Congratulations, gentlemen. We are now the forty-first moon of Saturn.'

Then she got up from her chair, noticing the perspiration that made her blouse stick to her back, flung her arms over her head and bellowed a wild, ear-splitting, 'YAHOO!'

Like most of the other residents of the habitat, Manuel Gaeta watched the final orbital maneuver on his video. With Kris Cardenas beside him.

'It's really gorgeous, isn't it?' she murmured, staring at the image of Saturn with its bands of many hues swirling across the planet's disc, and its rings hanging suspended above the equator, shining brilliantly in the light from the distant Sun, casting a deep shadow across the planet's face.

The rings were tilting as they watched, almost as if they were coming up to meet the approaching habitat, becoming narrower and foreshortened with each passing second until they were nothing more than a knife edge slashing across Saturn's bulging middle.

STABLE ORBIT ACHIEVED: the words flashed out over the planet's image. 'That's it,' Gaeta said. He turned and gave Cardenas a peck on the lips.

'We should do something to celebrate,' Cardenas said, without much enthusiasm.

'They're going to have a big blowout right after Eberly's installed in office,' Gaeta said, equally glum.

'I don't feel like going out.'

'I know. Having those security mugs tracking us is a pain. Gimme a couple of beers and I'll knock them both on their asses.'

'No you won't,' Cardenas said firmly. 'No alcohol for you. Tomorrow you're going out to the rings.'

'Yeah. Tomorrow.'

Neither one of them mentioned it, but they both knew that after Gaeta's stunt in Saturn's ring system, he would be leaving the habitat and heading back to Earth.

Inauguration

'She's got to be eliminated,' Morgenthau said firmly. 'And the Cardenas woman, too.'

Eberly walked beside her at the head of the procession that wound along the central footpath of Athens down to the lakeside, where the inauguration ceremony would be held. Behind them, at a respectful few paces, strode the tall, long-limbed Kananga and Vyborg, looking like a hunchbacked gnome beside the Rwandan. Behind them marched several hundred of their supporters. Even though every member of the security, communications and human resources departments had been told to attend the inauguration, hardly half of their staffs had bothered to show up.

'Eliminated?' Eberly snapped, trying to hide the fear that was making his inside flutter. 'You can't eliminate someone of Cardenas' stature. You'll have investigators from Earth flying out here in torch ships to see what happened.'

Morgenthau cast him a sidelong glance. 'Neutralized, then. I don't want her working on those damnable nanomachines here.'

Without breaking stride, Eberly said, '*You* don't want? Since when are you giving the orders here?'

'Since the very beginning. And don't you forget it.'

'I'm the one being inaugurated,' Eberly said, with a bravado he did not truly feel. 'I'm going to be installed as the leader of this community.'

'And you will do as I tell you,' Morgenthau countered, her voice flat and hard. 'We know you tried to sell us out. You and your posse.' She broke into a low chuckle.

'That was a necessary tactical maneuver. I never had any intention—'

'Don't add another lie to your sins. I could have you removed from this habitat and sent back to your prison cell in Vienna with just a single call back to Amsterdam.'

Eberly bit back the reply he wanted to make. They had reached the lakeside recreation area, where hundreds of chairs had been set in neat rows facing the band shell stage. A few dozen people were already seated there. Professor Wilmot sat alone up on the stage, looking somewhere between weary and bored. The band musicians that were lounging off at one side of the stage picked up their instruments and arranged themselves into a ragged semblance of order.

Eberly stopped at the edge of the last row of mostly empty chairs. Everything was as he had planned it. This was the moment he had worked for ever since that meeting in Schönbrunn Prison. He had planned out every detail of this inauguration ceremony. The only thing he could not control was the yawning indifference of the habitat's people. That, and Morgenthau's hardening attitude toward him. All the details are perfect, Eberly said to himself, but the day is an utter failure.

Turning to Morgenthau, he said, 'You'll have to walk three paces behind me.'

'Of course,' she said, with a knowing smile. 'I know how to play the role of the subservient woman.'

Eberly took a deep breath. It's going to be like this forever, he realized. She's going to make my life a hell on wheels.

Outwardly, though, he appeared to smile and pull himself up to his full height. He hesitated at the last row of chairs until he caught the bandleader's eye. With a nod, Eberly started marching down the central aisle between the empty chairs. Halfway between his second and third steps the band broke into a half-hearted rendition of 'Hail to the Chief.'

Holly watched the inaugural ceremony from her own apartment, deeply uncertain about what her future had in store. Malcolm had tried to go against Kananga and got nowhere. What will he do once he's officially installed in office?

What will Kananga do?

Holly decided she couldn't wait for them to make up their minds. She grabbed a few clothes, stuffed them into a tote bag, and headed for the door of her apartment. I'd better be where they can't find me, she told herself, until I know what they're really going to do.

Her phone buzzed. She put the bag down and pulled out the handheld.

Raoul Tavalera's face appeared on the tiny screen. He looked bone-weary, disheveled.

'Holly? You okay?'

'I'm fine, Raoul,' she replied, nodding. 'But I can't really talk with you now.'

'I'm worried about you.'

'Oh, for . . .' Holly didn't know what to say. She felt genuinely touched. 'Raoul, you didn't have to worry about me. I can take of myself.'

'Against that Kananga guy and his goons?'

She hesitated. 'You shouldn't get yourself involved in this, Raoul. You could get into deep trouble.'

Even in the minuscule screen she could see the stubborn set of his jaw. 'If you're in trouble, I want to help.'

How to get rid of him without hurting his feelings? Holly blurted, 'Raoul, you're really a special guy. But I've got to run now, See you later.'

She clicked the phone off, tucked it back into her tote, picked up the bag and left her apartment. I don't want to hurt him, she told herself. He's too nifty to get himself tangled up in this mess.

There were only two security people following her as she walked down the empty path: a chunky-looking guy and a slim woman who was either Hispanic or Oriental, it was hard for Holly to tell which, at the distance from which they followed her. Both wore black tunics and slacks, which made them stand out against the village's white buildings like ink blots on a field of snow.

She grinned to herself. I'll lose those two clowns as soon as I pop down into the tunnels.

She never noticed the third security agent moving far ahead of her. But he tracked her quite clearly. Every item of Holly's clothes had been sprayed with a monomolecular odorant that allowed the agent to track her like a bloodhound.

'You're missin' the inauguration,' Gaeta said.

Cardenas shrugged. 'So I miss it.'

Gaeta's massive armored suit stood like a grotesque statue in the middle of the workshop floor. The chamber hummed with the background buzz of electrical equipment and the quiet intensity of specialists going about their jobs. Fritz and two of his technicians were using the overhead crane to slowly lower the bulbous suit to a horizontal position and place it on its eight-wheeled transport dolly. It looked to Cardenas like lowering a statue. A third technician had crawled inside the suit: Cardenas could see his sandy-brown mop of hair through the open hatch in its back. Off at a console against the workshop wall, Nadia Wunderly was tracing the trajectory of the ice-covered asteroid that was making its last approach to the main ring before falling into orbit around Saturn. Berkowitz shuttled nervously from one to another, recording everything with his handcam.

Gaeta walked slowly to the diagnostic console and bent over it to study rows of steady green lights intently.

He's really trying to get away from me, Cardenas said to herself. I shouldn't be here. I shouldn't be distracting him now. I should leave him to focus completely on his job.

Yet she stayed, shuffling uneasily, uncertainly, as the men around her went through their final tasks before wheeling the suit down to the airlock where they would stow it aboard the shuttle craft that would take Manny to the rings.

As Gaeta watched them gently lowering the suit, Cardenas realized that the contraption would be his home for the next two days. He'll have to live inside it, work inside it . . . maybe die inside it.

Stop it! she commanded herself. No blubbering. He's got enough to worry about without you crying all over him.

It took an enormous effort of will, but finally Cardenas heard herself say, 'Manny, I'd better get back to my apartment. I—' She stopped, then touched his strong, muscular shoulder and kissed him lightly on the lips. 'I'll see you when you get back,' she said.

He nodded, his face deadly serious. 'In two days.'

'Good luck,' she said, barely able to move her hand from his shoulder.

'Nothing to worry about,' he said, making a smile for her. 'This is gonna be a walk in the park.'

'Good luck,' she repeated, then abruptly turned away from him and started walking toward the workshop door. Her mind kept churning, He'll be all right. He's done more dangerous stunts than this. He knows what he's doing. Fritz won't let him take any unnecessary chances. He'll be back in two days. In two days it'll be all over and he'll be safe.

Yes, said a voice in her mind. And then he'll leave the habitat, go back to Earth, leave you for good.

'Therefore,' Professor Wilmot was saying, 'in accordance with this community's Principles of Organization, I declare the new Constitution to be the deciding law of this habitat. I further declare that you, Malcolm Eberly, having been duly elected by free vote of the population, are now officially the Chief Administrator of this habitat.'

The few hundred people scattered among the chairs spread across the grass rose to their feet and applauded. The band broke into 'Happy Days Are Here Again.' Wilmot gripped Eberly's hand limply and mumbled, 'Congratulations, I suppose.'

Eberly grasped the podium's edges and looked out at the sparse audience. There sat Morgenthau, in the front row, eying him like an elementary school teacher waiting for her pupil to recite the speech she had forced him to write. Kananga and Vyborg sat behind her.

Eberly had composed an inauguration speech, liberally cribbed from the words of Churchill, Kennedy, both Roosevelts and Shakespeare.

He looked down at the opening lines, in the podium's display screen. With a shake of his head that was visible to everyone in the audience, he looked up again and said, 'This is no time for fancy speeches. We have arrived safely at our destination. Let those who are Believers thank God. Let all of us understand that tomorrow our real work begins. I intend to file a petition with the World Government, asking them to recognize us as a separate and independent nation, just as Selene and Ceres have been recognized.'

There was a moment of surprised silence, then everyone jumped to their feet and applauded lustily. Everyone except Morgenthau, Kananga and Vyborg.

Launch

Raoul Tavalera watched the orbital insertion and Eberly's inauguration from his apartment, although he barely noticed what the images displayed. He was thinking about Holly. She was in trouble, and she needed help. But when he had offered to help her, she had turned him down flat.

The story of my life, he grumbled to himself. Nobody wants me. Nobody gives a friggin' damn about me. Mr. Nobody, that's me.

He was surprised at how much pain he felt. Holly had been kind to him, more than kind, since he had first come aboard the habitat. He remembered the dates they had had. Dinners at the Bistro and even Nemo's, once. That picnic out at the endcap, where she told me about old Don Diego. She likes me, he told himself. I know she does. But now she doesn't want me to be with her. Why?

He tried phoning her again, but the comm system said her phone had been deactivated. Deactivated? Why? Then it hit him. She's on the run again. She's trying to hide from Kananga and his apes. That's why she deactivated her phone, so they can't track her.

Slowly, Tavalera got up from the chair in which he'd been sitting most of the day. Holly's in trouble and she needs help, whether she thinks so or not. My help. I've got to find her, help her, show her she's not alone in this.

For the first time in his life, Raoul Tavalera decided he had to act, no matter what the consequences. It's time for me to stop being Mr. Nobody, he told himself. I've gotta find Holly before Kananga's baboons do.

★   ★   ★

Focus, Gaeta told himself. Blot out everything from your mind except the job at hand. Forget about Kris, forget about everything except getting this stunt done.

He stood at the inner hatch of the airlock, surrounded by Fritz, Berkowitz and Timoshenko, who would pilot the shuttlecraft to the rings. The other technicians were behind him, checking out the suit for the final time.

Berkowitz had microcams mounted on the walls around the airlock enclosure, inside the airlock chamber, even clipped to a headband that matted down his stylishly curled and tinted brown hair.

'How does it feel to be undertaking the first human traverse through Saturn's rings?' Berkowitz asked, almost breathless with eager intensity.

'Not now, Zeke,' said Gaeta. 'Gotta concentrate on the work.'

Fritz stepped between them, a stern expression on his face. 'He can't do interviews now.'

'Okay, okay,' said Berkowitz amiably enough, although disappointment showed clearly in his eyes. 'We'll just record the preparations documentary-style and put in the interviews over it afterward.'

Gaeta turned to Timoshenko. 'It's going to be just you and me out there.'

'Not to worry,' Timoshenko said, totally serious. 'I'll get you to the B ring, then swing through the Cassini division and pick you up on the other side of the ring plane.'

Gaeta nodded. 'Right.'

'Suit's all primed and ready to go,' said one of the technicians.

'Any problems?' Gaeta asked.

'The pincer on your right arm is a little stiff. If we had a couple hours I'd break it down and rebuild it for ya.'

'You won't be needing the pincers,' Fritz interjected.

'It works good enough,' the tech said. 'Just isn't as smooth as it oughtta be.'

Gaeta thought, if it's good enough for Fritz it'll be okay.

But Fritz said, 'I'm going in for a final check.'

Gaeta smiled and nodded. He had expected that. There were three standards of acceptability in this world: average, above average, and Fritz. His chief technician's keen eye and finicky demands had saved Gaeta's life more than once.

Sure enough, Holly eluded her trackers after less than half an hour in the tunnels. She had ducked through an access hatch, clambered down a ladder, and then scooted light-footedly along the lower tunnel until she came to the big valve on the water line. Holly knew that this pipeline was a backup and not in use except when the main line was down for inspection or repair. So she tapped out the combination code on the hatch's electronic lock and crawled into the dark pipe, closing the hatch after her without making a sound.

She couldn't stand up inside the pipe; couldn't even get up to a kneeling posture. She slithered along on her belly almost effortlessly. The pipe was dry inside, its plastic lining smooth and easy to slide along. Her only problem was estimating distance in the dark, so she used a penlight to show her where the hatches appeared. Holly knew to the centimeter the distances between hatches. When she had crawled half a kilometer, she stopped and broke open one of the sandwich packs she had brought with her.

As she munched on the sandwich in the faint glow from the penlight, she felt almost like a little mouse down in its burrow. There are big cats out there, she knew. But I'm safe enough here. Unless somebody decides to divert the main water routing through this backup pipeline. Then I'd be a drowned little mouse.

The two black-clad security officers stood uncertainly in the tunnel, gazing up and down along the pipes and conduits.

'She just disappeared on us,' the man said to the third tracker, who wore a gray running suit. He was tall, rangy, not a gram of fat on him; he looked like an athlete who trained hard every day.

He held the chemical sniffer in one hand, a small gray oblong box, the same shade as his running suit.

'She came this way, definitely,' he said.

'But where's she gone?' asked the woman.

'That's not your problem. I'll take over from here. You can go back and report to the boss.'

They were reluctant to leave, not so much because they were zealous about their jobs, as a decided lack of enthusiasm for the prospect of facing Kananga empty-handed.

'You sure you don't need help?' the man asked.

The gray-clad tracker smiled and hefted the electronic sniffer. 'I've got all the help I need, right here.'

Gaeta had been in the shuttlecraft before. Fritz insisted that the stuntman familiarize himself with the vehicle that would carry him from the habitat to the rings. Manny had found the craft to be pretty much like dozens of others he had seen: utilitarian, austere, built more for efficiency than comfort. The cockpit had two seats shoehorned in among all the flight controls. Behind that was a closet-sized 'amenities' area with a zero-g toilet built into the bulkhead right next to the food storage freezer and microwave oven. The sink was there, too. Two mesh sleeping bags were pinned against the opposite bulkhead.

The cargo bay was pressurized, so while Timoshenko ran through his final checkout of the craft's systems, Gaeta ducked through the hatch to look over his suit.

It stood looming in the bay, so tall that the top of the helmet barely cleared the bay's overhead. Gaeta looked up into the empty faceplate of the helmet. Some people saw the suit for the first time and got the shudders. Gaeta always felt as if he were meeting his other half. Alone, each of them were much less than they were together: the suit an empty shell, the man a helpless weakling. But together – ahh, together we've done great things, haven't we? Gaeta reached up and patted the suit's upper arm. Some of the dents from the simulation test they'd done hadn't been smoothed out of the suit's armored chest, he noticed. Shaking his head, he thought he should speak to Fritz about that. He should've treated you better, Gaeta said to the suit.

'Launch in five minutes,' Timoshenko's voice came through the open cockpit hatch. 'You'll have to strap down.'

Gaeta nodded. With a final look at the suit, he turned and went back into the cockpit to start his journey through the rings of Saturn.

Kris Cardenas tried to keep busy during the last hours before Gaeta's launch. Eberly had lifted the ban on her nanolab, so she had gone to the laboratory, where she had real work to do. It was better than sitting in the apartment trying to keep herself from weeping like some helpless female who was supposed to stand by bravely while her man went out to do battle.

It annoyed her that Tavalera wasn't at his job, until she realized that he probably didn't know the lab had been allowed to reopen. She tried to phone him, but the comm system couldn't find him and his personal handheld had been deactivated.

That's not like Raoul, she thought. He's always been reliable.

She went through the motions of designing repair nanos for Urbain's Titan lander, then finally gave it up altogether and turned on the vid.

'There is the shuttlecraft,' Zeke Berkowitz's voice was poised on the edge that separated authoritative self-assuredness from excited enthusiasm. 'In precisely fifteen seconds it will separate from the habitat and begin the journey that will carry Manuel Gaeta into the rings of Saturn.'

Cardenas saw a view from the exterior shell of the habitat. She knew that Berkowitz's newscast was being beamed to all the media networks on Earth. She could hear the computer's voice counting down the final seconds.

'Three . . . two . . . one . . . launch.'

The shuttlecraft detached from the habitat's huge, curved surface, looking like a squarish metallic flea hopping off the hide of an elephant. Against the iridescent glowing disc of many-hued Saturn, the shuttlecraft rose, turned slowly, and then began dwindling out of sight.

'Manuel Gaeta is on his way,' Berkowitz was announcing

ponderously, 'to be the first man to traverse the mysterious and fascinating rings of Saturn.'

'Goodbye Manny,' Cardenas whispered, certain that she would never see him again.

Into The Rings

Even though she knew that the backup pipeline was perfectly safe, Holly began to get a little edgy about staying in it. In her mind's eye she saw some maintenance engineer casually switching the habitat's main water flow from the primary pipeline to the backup. Just a routine operation, yet it would send a flood of frothing water cascading down the pipe toward her, engulfing her, sweeping her along in its irresistible flow, drowning her as she tumbled over and over in the roaring, inescapable flood.

Dimdumb! she snapped at herself. You're scaring yourself like some little kid afraid of monsters under the bed. Yet, as she crawled along the perfectly dry pipeline, she kept listening for the telltale rush of water, feeling with her fingertips for the slightest vibration of the pipe. And the pipe wasn't perfectly dry, at that: here and there small damp patches and even actual puddles told her that water had been flowing not so long ago.

She had thought she'd stay in the pipeline until it made its big U-turn, up near the endcap. Well, maybe not all the way. It'd be good to get out and stretch, be able to stand up again. So she slithered further along the pipe, even though the lingering fear of drowning still gnawed at her.

The tracker reached the hatch where Holly had entered the pipeline easily enough. The electronic sniffer in his hand followed the scent trail she had left quite easily. My faithful bloodhound, he thought, with a crooked smile.

Now he had a decision to make. Should I go into the pipe and follow her, or stay outside? He decided to remain outside. He could make better time walking, or even jogging, than he could crawling inside the dark pipe. She has to come out sooner or later, and when she does the sniffer will tell me which hatch she used.

But which direction did she go? She was heading away from the village, toward the endcap, he knew. I'll follow that vector. The chances that she'd double back toward the village are pretty scarce. Still, he phoned Kananga to report the situation and advise him to have a few people standing by at the pipeline hatches near the village.

'I'll do better than that,' Kananga said, grinning fiercely. 'I'll order maintenance to run the main water flow through the line. That'll flush her out.'

Tavalera bicycled out to the endcap along the path that meandered through the orchards and farmlands. He left the bike at the end of the path, then followed the walking trail that led through the woods at the endcap. It felt strange: he could see he was climbing a decent slope yet it felt as if he were going downhill; the gravity diminished noticeably with every step he took.

At last he reached the little spot in the woods where he and Holly had once picnicked. I can't search the whole habitat for you, Holly, he said silently, so you'll have to come to me.

Tavalera sat down and began to wait for her to show up. It was the best course of action he could think of.

Gaeta felt the same pulse of excitement that always hit him once he was sealed inside the suit, with all the systems turned on and working. Not merely excitement. What he felt was *power*. In the suit he had the strength of a demigod. The suit protected him against the worst that the universe could throw at him. He felt virtually invulnerable, invincible.

Keep thinking like that, pal, and you'll end up dead, he warned himself. Take a deep breath and get to work. And remember that it's damned dangerous out there.

Still, he felt like a superman.

'Approaching insertion point.' Timoshenko's raspy voice came through the helmet earphones.

Gaeta nodded. 'I'm sealed up. Open the cargo bay hatch.'

'Opening hatch.'

Gaeta had been through this many times. He always felt a thrill when the hatch slid open and he could look out at the universe of endless black void and countless brilliant stars.

But this time was different. As the hatch opened the cargo bay was flooded with light, overpoweringly brilliant light. Gaeta looked up at an endless field of gleaming, dazzling white, as far as his eyes could see, nothing but glittering sparkling light. It was like looking out at a titanic glacier or a field of glistening snow that extended forever.

No, he realized, it's like looking out at a whole world made of diamonds: sparkling, glittering diamonds. They're not just white, they gleam and glow like diamonds, hundreds of millions of billions of bright, beautiful gems spread out from one end of the universe to the other.

His breath caught in his throat. 'Jesus Cristo,' he muttered.

'What was that?' Timoshenko asked.

'I'm going out,' Gaeta said.

'Your trajectory program is operative?'

Gaeta called up the trajectory program vocally. It splashed its colored curves on the inside of his faceplate.

'Operative.'

'Ready for insertion in eight seconds. Seven . . .'

Gaeta had to make a conscious effort to concentrate on the task ahead. His eyes kept wandering to the endless field of dazzling gems stretching out before him.

They're just flakes of ice, he told himself. Nothing more than bits of dust with ice covering them.

Yeah, answered a voice in his mind. And diamonds are nothing more than carbon. And the *Mona Lisa* is nothing more than some dabs of paint on a chunk of canvas.

'. . . one . . . zero. Launch,' said Timoshenko.

The suit's master computer ignited the thrusters in the backpack and Gaeta felt himself pushed gently out of the cargo bay. Now he was looking down on the endless field of gleaming gems and beginning to drift toward them.

How fucking beautiful, he thought. How incredibly fucking beautiful!

'Say something!' came Berkowitz's voice, relayed from the habitat. 'We need some words from you for posterity.'

Gaeta licked his lips. 'This is the most incredibly beautiful sight I've ever seen. It's . . . it's . . . beyond description. Words just can't capture it.'

For some minutes Gaeta just drifted along above the ring plane, allowing the computer to guide him automatically along the preset trajectory. He knew the cameras in his helmet were recording it all, there wasn't much for him to do at this point in the trajectory. He simply gaped, awed by the splendor that surrounded him.

'It's like something out of a fairy tale,' he said, hardly realizing he was speaking aloud. 'A field of diamonds. A whole world of diamonds spread out below me. I feel like Sinbad the Sailor and Marco Polo and Ali Baba, all rolled into one.'

'That's great,' Berkowitz's voice answered. 'Great.'

'Have any particles hit you?' Fritz asked.

'No, nothing that the sensors have picked up,' Gaeta replied. 'I'm still too high above the ring.' Good old Fritz, he thought. Trying to bring me back to reality.

Another gentle push of thrust at his back and Gaeta began to come closer to the ring. Within minutes he would be going through it. That would be the dangerous part of the stunt, barging in there among all those bits and chunks while they're whipping around the planet in their orbits.

He could see now that the ring wasn't a solid sheet. It was clearly made of separate, individual rings, braiding together and unwinding even while he watched. He could see stars through the ring, and the ponderous curve of Saturn with its colorful bands of clouds.

'Looks like a cyclonic storm down in the southern tropics,' he reported.

'Never mind that,' Fritz said. 'Pay attention to the rings.'

'Yes, master.'

'What about the spokes?' Wunderly's voice, trembling with exhilaration. 'I can see them in your camera view. One of them is approaching you.'

Gaeta realized that there were darker regions in the ring, undulating like a wave made by fans at a sports arena.

'Yeah, heading my way,' he said.

Looking closer, he saw that it was almost like a cloud of darker bits of dust rising up from the ring plane and sweeping along the brighter stuff of the ring's main body. And he was approaching it at a fairly rapid clip.

'I'm going to duck into it,' he said.

Fritz warned, 'Wait. Let us examine it first.'

'It'll pass me; I'll miss it.'

'There will be others.'

Gaeta didn't want to wait for another spoke to swing by. He pulled his right arm out of the suit sleeve and tapped in a maneuver command for the navigation program.

'Here we go,' he said as the suit tilted and dove into the approaching cloud.

Fritz muttered something in German.

'It's dust,' Gaeta saw. 'Sort of gray, like there's no ice coating the particles.'

'Adjust your approach vector,' Fritz snapped. 'Don't go plunging headlong into the cloud.'

'I'll just skim along it,' said Gaeta, enjoying himself now. 'Doesn't look thick enough to cause any problems. I can see right through it.'

Wunderly said, 'See if you . . .' Her voice broke up into crackling static.

'Say again,' Gaeta called. 'You're breaking up.'

No answer except hissing electronic interference. Gaeta was barely touching the cloud as it swept along the ring. He called for a systems check and the displays on his faceplate showed everything in the green, including the radio.

Outside interference, he said to himself. Something in the dust cloud screws up radio communications.

The cloud raced past him, swinging along the ring far faster than Gaeta's leisurely pace.

'. . . off the scale!' Wunderly was shouting excitedly. 'That proves the spokes are driven by electromagnetic interactions.'

'I can hear you again,' Gaeta said. 'Whatever it was that blocked the radio is gone now.'

'It's the spokes!' Wunderly said. 'We've just proved that high-powered electromagnetic fields drive them!'

'And interfere with radio links,' Fritz added calmly.

'It didn't mess up anything else in the suit,' Gaeta said.

'The suit is heavily shielded,' said Fritz.

'Yeah.' Gaeta saw that he was approaching the ring particles pretty fast now. Like diving into a field of diamonds, he thought, chuckling.

'What is funny? Fritz demanded.

'I was thinking I shoulda brought a big bucket to haul back some of these diamonds.'

'They are not diamonds. They are dust particles covered with ice.'

'But the ones in the spokes don't seem to have ice on 'em.'

'That is a mystery for Dr. Wunderly to ponder. For you, you should be adjusting your velocity vector to make it as close to that of the ring particles as possible. That will minimize impacts and abrasion problems.'

It was all in the automated nav program, Gaeta knew, but he checked his approach velocity against the ring particles' and saw that he could notch down his approach a hair. That'll give me more time in the ring itself, he thought. Good.

Then he saw a bigger chunk of ice tumbling slowly through the ring, glittering brilliantly.

'Hey, see that one? It's big as a house.'

'Stay away from it,' Fritz commanded.

'Can you get close enough to measure its size precisely?' Wunderly asked.

Gaeta laughed again. 'Right. Stay away and get close. No sweat, folks.'

Captured

Crawling along the pipe on all fours, Holly's right hand splashed into a shallow little puddle at precisely the same instant that her left hand felt a slight vibration along the pipe's curved interior surface.

She froze for an instant, listening for the rush of water, then decided, By the time I hear it it'll be too late to do anything about it.

She had passed a hatch about five minutes earlier. That meant the next hatch would be roughly five minutes ahead. Which way is the water coming? she asked herself. Doesn't matter, came the answer. You've got to get your butt out of here. *Now!*

She scurried forward, feeling like a mouse in its burrow, scampering as fast as her hands and knees would carry her. She heard a rumble from somewhere behind her, thought it might be her imagination over-reacting, then felt the unmistakable shudder of water rushing along the pipe. By the time she reached the hatch she could hear the flood roaring down toward her. With trembling fingers she opened the hatch, crawled out of the pipe, and slammed the hatch shut again. Water thundered past, some of it splashing through the hatch before she could seal it properly.

That was close!

Holly's legs wouldn't hold her up. She slid to the metal flooring of the tunnel and sat in the puddle beneath the hatch.

They knew I was in the pipe! she realized. They knew and they tried to drown me.

The tracker was loping along the tunnel, running easily alongside the pipeline. He could hear the water gushing through it but, careful man that he was, he jogged down the tunnel on the chance that his prey had gotten out in time. Take no chances, don't give the prey a chance to get away.

He was an Ethiopian who had dreamed of winning Olympic gold medals for long-distance running until the Olympic Games were indefinitely postponed. He supported himself, his parents and his younger siblings on a policeman's meager salary. Even that failed, however, when a relative of a politician from the capital was handed his position and salary. Faced with starvation, he accepted a position on the outbound Saturn habitat, on the condition that his salary be sent each month to his parents. Once aboard the habitat, he was befriended by Colonel Kananga and given a soft post with the security department.

This job of tracking was his first important duty for the colonel, after so many months of routine security patrols in a habitat where there were no real criminals, only spoiled, independent-minded sons and daughters of the wealthy who acted like children who didn't have to grow up.

He had no intention of failing this assignment. He wanted to please Colonel Kananga.

'I'm getting pinged,' Gaeta said.

He was still a considerable distance above the ring, but particles of dust were already hitting on his suit, according to the sensors on its outer shell. No problem, Gaeta told himself. Not yet. It'll get worse in a coupla minutes.

It was hard to estimate distances. He was looking down at a dazzling field of white, glaring light, like floating down in a balloon to the top of an enormous glacier. Yet the ring wasn't solid; it was composed of millions upon millions of particles, like all the shiny bright marbles in the universe had gathered themselves together here. The house-sized chunk of ice had passed by, tumbling end over end, visibly banging into the smaller particles that swarmed around it.

Fritz's voice, calm and assured, said, 'Your velocity vector is good. The impacts should be at minimal energy.'

'Yeah,' Gaeta agreed, drifting closer to the vast sea of glittering particles. 'I don't feel anything yet.'

'We're getting size estimates for the particles,' said Wunderly. 'There doesn't seem to be anything above a few millimeters now.' She sounded disappointed.

'You want me to look for bigger stuff?'

'You just stick to the planned trajectory,' Fritz said stiffly. 'No adventures, please.'

Gaeta laughed. No adventures. What the hell do you call this?

Wunderly came back on. 'The new moon has settled into its permanent orbit.'

'Can't see it from here.'

'No, it's on the other side of Saturn. I'm getting video from the minisat in polar orbit.'

The particles were noticeably thicker now. Gaeta felt as if he were slowly sinking into a blizzard: whirling snowflakes glistening all around him, swirling, dancing on an invisible wind. They seemed to be moving away from him slightly, making room for him in their midst.

'I know this is crazy,' he said, 'but these flakes are moving away from me, looks like.'

He could sense Fritz shaking his head. 'It's merely your perspective. They're moving around Saturn in their own orbits, just as you are.'

'Maybe, but I could swear they're keeping their distance from me.'

'Can you grab any of them?' Wunderly asked.

Gaeta worked his keyboard, then wriggled his arms back into the suit's sleeves. 'I've opened the collection box, but I don't think any of 'em are getting caught in it.'

He heard Fritz chuckle dryly. 'Do you think they're avoiding you? Perhaps they don't like your smell.'

'I don't know what to think, pal. It's as if—' Gaeta stopped as a red warning light suddenly flared on the inner surface of his faceplate. A shock of alarm raced through his nerves.

'Got a red light,' he said.

'Sensors down,' Fritz said, his voice abruptly brittle, tense. 'No immediate problem.'

Scanning his helmet displays swiftly, Gaeta saw that four of the sensors on the suit's skin had gone blank. Two on the backpack and two more on his left leg. He knew it was impossible to see his legs from inside the suit but he tried anyway. All he could see through the faceplate was the tips of his boots. They seemed to be rimed with ice.

He raised both arms and saw that they too were covered with a thin layer of ice. As he watched, he saw the ice moving along each arm.

'Hey! I'm icing up. They're covering me with ice.'

'That shouldn't happen,' Wunderly said, sounding almost annoyed.

'I don't give a shit what *should* happen. These little *cabrons* are covering me up!'

More red lights flashed on his faceplate. One by one the sensors on the skin of the suit were going down. Covered with ice.

'Can you still move your arms and legs?' Fritz asked.

Gaeta tried. 'Yeah. The joints are running a little stiff but they still – oh, oh.' Several particles of ice attached themselves to his faceplate.

'What's the matter?'

'They're on my faceplate,' Gaeta said. He stared at the particles, more fascinated than frightened. The little *fregados* are crawling across my faceplate, he realized.

'They're moving,' he reported. 'They're walkin' across my faceplate!'

'They can't walk,' Wunderly said.

'Tell it to them!' Gaeta answered. 'They're covering up my faceplate. The whole suit! They're wrapping me up in ice!'

'That's impossible.'

'Yeah, sure.'

Whatever they were, the tiny particles were crawling over his faceplate. He could see it. More of them were coming in, too, covering more and more of the visor. Within minutes Gaeta could see nothing of the outside. His suit was completely encased in ice.

396

Prisoners

Wunderly was in her own cubbyhole office, a pair of video monitors on her desk, trying to watch Gaeta on one display screen and the new moon that had joined the main ring on the screen beside it.

All she was getting from Gaeta was his data from his suit's interior sensors and his own excited report that the ice particles were encasing the suit. They can't move, she told herself. They're not alive, not motile. They're just flakes of dust covered with ice.

But what's making them cover Manny's suit? Electromagnetic attraction? Temperature differential?

She was running through possibilities that grew more and more fanciful while she absently switched to the spectrographic sensor from the minisatellite that was watching the newly arrived moonlet on the other side of the ring. Wunderly frowned at the display. It didn't look right. She called up the spectrograph's earlier data. The moonlet was definitely icy, but laced with dark carbonaceous soot. Yet the real-time spectrogram showed much less carbon: it was practically all ice. Where did the carbon get to?

Intrigued, she switched back to the minisat's visual display. And sank back in her little chair, gasping.

The moonlet was in the center of what looked like a maelstrom. A whirlpool of ice flakes was swirling around the moonlet, like a huge family engulfing a newly arrived member.

'My god almighty, they're alive!' Wunderly shouted, leaping out of her chair. 'They're alive!'

★   ★   ★

Gaeta had learned long ago that panic was the worst enemy. Even with his faceplate covered so thickly that he could see nothing outside, he kept calm as he checked the suit's systems. Life support okay, power okay, communications in the green, propulsion ready. No need to push the red button yet.

'Try rubbing the ice off your faceplate,' came Fritz's voice, also calm, methodical.

Fritz'll keep on recommending different fixes until I go down in flames, Gaeta knew.

'I've done that,' he said, raising his left arm to wipe at the faceplate again. The arm felt stiffer than it had just a few moments earlier. 'They just come back again.'

As he spoke, Gaeta rubbed the pincers of his left arm across the faceplate. They scraped some of the ice off enough so that he could see more particles rushing toward him. Within seconds the faceplate was covered up again.

'No joy,' he said. 'They just swarm in and cover everything. It's like they're alive. I can see them crawling across my faceplate.'

'They *are* alive!' Wunderly broke in, her voice shrill with exhilaration. 'Get some in the sample box!'

Gaeta huffed. 'Maybe they're gonna get me in *their* sample box.'

He wondered how much thickness of ice it would take to block his antennas and cut off communications. I'm getting freeze-wrapped like Christmas turkey and she's worried about getting samples to study. He checked the temperature inside the suit. The display was normal, although Gaeta thought it felt chillier than normal. Just my imagination, he told himself. Yeah. Sure.

He called to Fritz, 'I think maybe I oughtta light off the jets and get outta here.'

'Not yet!' Wunderly pleaded. 'Try to collect some samples!'

Fritz's voice, icy calm, said, 'Your suit functions aren't being impaired.'

'Not yet,' Gaeta agreed. 'But what *chingado* good am I sitting out here, blind as a bat and covered with ice?'

Wunderly asked, 'Can you at least wait until the minisat swings over to your side of the planet, so I can get spectrographic readings on the ice that's covering you?'

'How long will that take?' Fritz asked.

A pause. Then Wunderly answered, her voice much lower, 'Eleven hours and twenty-seven minutes.'

'The suit is designed for a forty-eight-hour excursion,' said Fritz. 'But if the ice covering continues to build up, his communications and propulsion functions might be disabled.'

Before Wunderly could reply, Gaeta said, 'I'm okay for now, Fritz. Let's see what happens.'

Berkowitz spoke up. 'This is terrific stuff, people, but all your suit cameras are covered up. We're getting nothing but audio from you, Manny. If we can get outside video from the minisat, we'll be golden.'

Gaeta nodded inside his helmet, thinking sardonically, 'And if I get killed, the ratings'll be even better.'

Feeling shaky after her near drowning, and even shakier knowing that somehow Kananga's people were tracking her, Holly walked as fast as she could to the end of the tunnel, climbed the metal ladder that led up to the surface, and pushed open a hatch disguised to look like a small boulder. She was at the endcap; she paused for a moment and took a deep breath of air. It seemed fresh and sweet. The entire habitat spread before her eyes, green and wide and open.

She pulled herself up from the hatch, swung the plastic boulder shut again, and started across the springy green grass toward the grove of young elms and maples sprouting farther up toward the centerline.

Somebody was already there, she saw as she approached the woods. Lying stretched out on the mossy ground in among the trees.

Holly froze, feeling like a deer that's spotted a mountain lion. But the man – she thought it looked like a man – seemed to be asleep, or unconscious or even dead. He wasn't wearing the black outfit of the security department, either; just tan coveralls.

Cautiously, Holly approached near enough to make out his face. It's Raoul! she realized. What's he doing out here? A thought stopped her in her tracks. Is he working for Kananga? Is he part of some search group, looking for me?

Then she realized she was standing out in the open, perfectly visible to anyone within a kilometer or more. Raoul wouldn't go over to Kananga, she decided. He's a friend.

She went to him, feeling a little safer once she was within the shadows of the trees.

Tavalera stirred as she approached him, blinked, then sat up so abruptly it startled Holly.

He blinked again, rubbed his eyes. 'Holly? Is it you, or am I dreaming?'

She smiled warmly. 'It's me, Raoul. What are you doing all the way out here?'

'Lookin' for you,' he said, getting to his feet. 'Guess I dozed off. Some searcher, huh?' He grinned sheepishly.

'You're just going to get yourself in trouble, Raoul. Kananga's people are following me. I've been trying to stay a jump ahead of them.'

Tavalera took in a deep breath. 'I know. I came to help you.'

Holly thought that if Raoul knew enough about her to wait for her here at the endcap, Kananga's people must have figured out her habits, too.

'We've got to find someplace to hide,' she said. 'Someplace where we'll be safe.'

'It's too late for that,' said a new voice.

They turned and saw a tall, lanky young man whose skin was the color of smooth dark chocolate. In his hand was the small electronic sniffer.

'Colonel Kananga wants to see you, Miss Lane,' he said, his voice soft, non-threatening.

'I don't want to see Colonel Kananga,' said Holly.

'That's unfortunate. I'm afraid I must insist that you come with me.'

Tavalera stepped in front of Holly. 'Run, Holly,' he said. 'I'll hold him off while you get away.'

The black man smiled. Pointing out beyond the trees to a trio of black-clad people approaching them, he said, 'There's no need for violence. And there's no place to run to.'

Ring Creatures

Wunderly could barely contain her excitement. She was bouncing up and down in her little chair as she watched the ring particles swarming over the new moonlet.

It's *food* for them! she told herself as she switched from visual to infrared and then to the spectrographic display. She wished there had been room in the minisat for ultraviolet and gamma ray sensors. What we need is an active laser probe, she thought, then immediately countered, but that might kill the particles. Particles? No, they're living creatures. Ice creatures, surviving at temperatures of minus two hundred Celsius and lower. Extremophiles that thrive in a low-temperature environment.

The mystery of Saturn's rings is solved, she thought. The rings aren't just passive collections of ice flakes. They're made of active, living creatures! They grab anything that falls into their region and take it apart. Asteroids, little ice chunks, it's all food for them. That's how Saturn can maintain its ring system. It's alive.

Let's see, she thought. Saturn has forty-two moons that we know of. Every so often an asteroid or an ice chunk from the Kuiper Belt wanders into the ring system and these creatures chew it up. The rings are constantly losing particles, having them sucked down into Saturn's clouds. But the rings keep renewing themselves by devouring the incoming moonlets that stray into their grip.

Suddenly she looked up from the displays. Manny! They'll try to chew up Manny's suit. They could kill him!

She yelled into her comm link, 'Manny! Get out of there! Now! Before they chew through your suit!'

Fritz's voice replied coldly, 'I don't know if he can hear us. I haven't had any word from him for nearly half an hour. The ice must have built up too thickly over his antennas.'

Holly watched the three black-clad figures approaching, climbing the grassy rise toward the copse where she and Tavalera stood with the Ethiopean tracker. He had his comm unit to his ear, nodding unconsciously as he listened to his orders.

At last he said, 'Colonel Kananga is on his way. He wants to meet you by the central airlock, here at the endcap.'

Tavalera suddenly lunged at the tracker, shouting wildly, 'Run, Holly!' as he tackled the Ethiopean.

The two men went down in a tangle of arms and legs. Holly hesitated an instant, long enough to see that Raoul was no fighter. The Ethiopean quickly recovered from his surprise and threw Tavalera off his back, then scrambled to his feet. Before he could do anything, Holly launched herself in a flying kick that caught the tracker in the ribs and knocked him down again. Tavalera got up and grabbed for her hand.

The bolt of a laser beam knocked him down again. Tavalera grabbed his leg with both hands as he rolled on the ground in pain. 'Shit! The same friggin' leg!'

Holly froze into immobility. Raoul's leg wasn't bleeding much, but a pinprick of a black hole smoldered halfway up his thigh.

The Ethiopean got slowly to his feet as the three other security officers ran across the grassy rise toward them.

'How'd they get weapons into the habitat?' Holly asked, sinking to her knees beside the writhing, cursing Tavalera.

'Cutting tools,' Tavalera grunted, grimacing. 'They must've adapted laser tools into sidearms.'

The leader of the three newcomers looked over the situation. 'Good work,' he said to the Ethiopean. Gesturing to his two underlings, he said, 'Haul this one to his feet and drag him along.'

They grabbed Tavalera, not gently at all.

'Come along,' the leader said to Holly. 'Colonel Kananga wants to see you at the central airlock.'

★　　★　　★

403

The only thing that truly worried Gaeta was being cut off from communicating with Fritz. The suit was holding up all right, although the interior temperature had definitely dropped nearly three degrees.

Gaeta was thinking of his possible alternatives as he drifted, wrapped in ice, mummified cryogenically. Wunderly thinks the ice particles are alive. Maybe she's right. They sure looked like they were crawling across my faceplate. So maybe they're trying to eat me, eat the suit. Can they eat cermet or organometallics? Jezoo, I hope not!

Wait for another eleven hours, so they can get video of me? I could be dead by then.

But if I bug out now, there won't be any video to show the nets.

Funny, he thought, how the mind works. Right here in the middle of this *mierda* what does my brain come up with? *He who fights and runs away lives to fight another day.* These rings have existed for thousands of years, millions, more likely. They're not going away. I can come back. With better preparation, better equipment. And better video coverage.

That decided him. Gaeta pulled his right arm out of its sleeve and set up the thruster program. I'll be flying blind, he realized. He had lost all sense of where he was in relation to the habitat or to Timoshenko, waiting for him in the shuttlecraft. The suit's navigation program was useless now. Better take it slow and easy. First priority is to get your butt out of this blizzard. But don't go blasting off to Alpha Centauri.

He touched the keypad that fired the thruster jets. Nothing happened.

Eberly had taken over Professor Wilmot's old office, now that he was officially the habitat's chief administrator. His first official act was to send Wilmot's stuffy old furniture to storage and replace it with sleek modernistic chrome and plastic bleached and stained to look like teak.

He had hardly sat at his gleaming desk when Morgenthau pushed open the door to his office and stepped in, unannounced.

Dressed in a flamboyant rainbow-hued caftan, she looked around the office's bare walls with a smug, self-satisfied smile that was close to being a smirk.

'You'll need some pictures on these walls,' she said. 'I'll see that you get some holowindows that can be programmed—'

'I can decorate my own office,' Eberly snapped.

Her expression didn't change at all. 'Don't be touchy. Now that you have the power you should surround yourself with the proper trappings of power. Symbols are important. Just ask Vyborg, he knows all about the importance of symbolism.'

'I have a lot of work to do,' Eberly said.

'You have to meet with Kananga.'

Eberly shook his head. 'It's not on my agenda.'

'He's waiting for you at the central airlock, out at the endcap.'

'I'm not going—'

'He has Holly in custody. He wants you there for her trial. And execution.'

Drumhead

Blinded by the ice coating his suit, his communications antennas blocked, the temperature inside the suit dropping, Gaeta mulled over his options. The thrusters won't fire, he realized, and I don't know why. The diagnostic display splashed on the inside of his faceplate showed the propulsion system was in the green.

'Engineer's hell,' he muttered to himself. 'Everything checks but nothing works.'

The suit's diagnostics were bare-bones. Fritz had a better idea of what was going on than he did, Gaeta knew. He's got the details. He's even got the positioning data that feeds my nav program; all I've got is a comm link that doesn't work.

Gaeta had one last trick in his repertoire. If this doesn't work I'll be a frozen dinner for these *chingado* ice bugs, he told himself. He popped the suit's emergency antenna. The spring-loaded Bucky-ball wire cracked through the ice shell and whizzed out the full length of its hundred meters. Gaeta felt the vibration inside the suit, like the faint buzz of an electric razor.

'Fritz! Can you hear me?' he called.

'Manny!' Fritz's voice replied immediately. 'What's your situation? The diagnostics here are a blur.'

'Suit antennas iced over,' Gaeta replied, slipping automatically into the clipped, time-saving argot of pilots and ground controllers. 'Thrusters won't fire.'

'Life support?'

'Okay for now. Thrusters, man. I gotta get outta here.'

'Have you tried the backup?'

'Of course I've tried the backup! It's like everything's frozen solid.'

Wunderly's voice interrupted, 'Crank up your suit's heaters.'

'The heaters?'

'Run them up as hot as you can stand it,' she said. 'The ice bugs probably don't like high temperatures.'

'*Probably* doesn't sound like much help,' Gaeta said.

'Try it,' Fritz commanded.

Gaeta knew the suit's electrical power came from a nuclear thermionic generator: plenty of electricity available for the heaters.

Reluctantly he said, 'Okay. Going into sauna mode.'

Holly was more worried about Tavalera's leg than her own prospects. Two of the black-clad security people were dragging Raoul up the slope toward the central airlock. He looked to be in shock, his face white, his teeth gritted. It was foolish of him to try to help me, Holly thought. Foolish and very brave.

With the Ethiopean in the lead, they climbed the gentle rise, feeling the odd decrease in gravity as they got closer to the habitat's centerline. Holly wondered if she could use the confusing loss of gravity as a weapon, but there were four of Kananga's people and only herself and the wounded Tavalera to counter them. She couldn't leave Raoul in their clutches, no matter what lay ahead.

'Why are you taking us here?' Holly demanded.

'Just following orders,' said the burly leader of the security team.

'Orders? Whose orders?'

'Colonel Kananga's. He wants to meet you at the central airlock.'

Eberly groused and grumbled, but he realized he had no choice but to accompany Morgenthau to this meeting with Kananga. What else can I do? he asked himself. I'm nothing more than a figurehead. She holds the real power, she and Kananga and that viper Vyborg. If it hadn't been for him and his stupid ambition, none of this would have happened. I've won power for them, not myself.

He meekly followed Morgenthau to the bike racks outside the administration building and mounted one of the electrically powered bicycles. From the rear, Morgenthau looked like a hippopotamus riding the bike. He noted that she hardly pedaled at all, even on the flat; instead she let the quiet little electrical motor propel her along. I hope she runs out of battery power by the time we have to start climbing, Eberly thought viciously.

But she made it all the way to the endcap and the hatch that led to the central airlock, Eberly dutifully following behind her. They left the bikes in the racks at the hatch and entered the cold, dimly lit steel tunnel that led to the airlock.

As the hatch swung shut behind them, Eberly looked over his shoulder, like a prisoner taking his last glimpse of the outside world before the gates close on his freedom. He saw a small group of people trudging up the slope toward the hatch. Three of them were in the black tunics of the security forces. The tall slim figure in their midst looked like Holly. He didn't recognize the even taller man in a tan outfit walking up ahead of the others. Two of the security people were dragging a man who was clearly injured.

Then the hatch closed, and Eberly felt the chill of the cold steel tunnel seep into his bones.

'Come along,' said Morgenthau. 'Kananga's waiting for us at the airlock. Vyborg is there, too.'

Wondering what else he could do, Eberly followed her like a desperately unhappy little boy being dragged to school.

Gaeta blinked sweat from his eyes. He had reeled in the emergency antenna and fired it out again, twice. Each time it had given him about five minutes of clear communications before the ice creatures coated it so thickly that the radio link began to break up.

His faceplate displays were splashed with yellow as he diverted electrical power from the suit's sensors and even the servomotors that moved its arms and legs to pour as much energy as possible into the heaters. The arms were getting too stiff to move even with the servomotors grinding away. Christ knows how thick the ice is packing up on them.

Trouble is, he knew, the suit's skin is thermally insulated too damned well. The suit's built to keep heat in, not to let it leak outside.

That gave him an idea. It was wild, but it was an idea. How long can I breathe vacuum? he asked himself. It was an old daredevil game that astronauts and stuntmen and other crazies played now and then: vacuum breathing. You open your suit to vacuum and hold your breath. The trick is to seal up the suit again before you pass out, or before your eyes blow out from the loss of pressure. A lot of people claimed the record; most of 'em were dead. Pancho Lane had a reputation for being good at it, he remembered, back in the days when she was an ass-kicking astronaut.

The real question, Gaeta realized, is: how much air does the suit hold? And how fast will it leak out if I pop one of the small hatches, like the one in my sleeve?

He wished he could check it out with Fritz, but even the emergency antenna was out now; the last time he'd used it, it had got too thickly coated with ice to reel it back in.

You're on your own, *muchacho*. Make your own calculations and take your own chances. There's nobody left to help you.

Kananga looked calm and pleased, standing tall and smiling in front of the inner hatch of the airlock. It was an oversized hatch, wide and high enough to take bulky crates of machinery or other cargo, as well as individuals in spacesuits.

Vyborg was fidgeting nervously, obviously anxious to get this over with, Eberly thought.

On the other side of the steel-walled chamber stood Holly, trying to look defiant but clearly frightened. A young man who identified himself as Raoul Tavalera lay at her feet, grimacing in pain and anger. Eberly remembered him as the astronaut who had been rescued during the refueling at Jupiter. The Ethiopian tracker and the three security team people were further down the tunnel, blocking any attempt to run away.

'I'm pleased,' said Kananga, 'that our newly installed chief administrator could take the time away from his many duties to join us here at this trial.'

'Trial?' Eberly snapped.

'Why, yes. I'd like you to serve as the chief judge.'

Eberly glanced uneasily at Holly, then quickly looked away.

'Who is on trial? What's the charge?'

Extending a long pointing finger, Kananga said, 'Holly Lane stands accused of the murder of Diego Romero.'

'That's bullshit!' Tavalera shouted.

Kananga stepped toward the wounded young man and kicked him in the ribs. The breath rushed out of Tavalera's lungs with a painful grunt. Holly's hands balled into fists, but Kananga turned and struck her with a vicious backhand slap that split her lip open. She staggered back a few steps.

'This court will not tolerate any outbursts,' Kananga said severely to the gasping, wincing Tavalera. 'Since you have aided and abetted the accused, you stand accused along with her.'

'If I'm the judge here,' Eberly said, 'then I'll determine who can speak and who can't.'

Kananga made a mock bow. 'Of course.'

'I assume you are the prosecutor,' Eberly said to the Rwandan. Kananga dipped his chin once.

'And who is the defense attorney?'

'The accused will defend herself,' Morgenthau answered.

'And the jury?'

Vyborg said, 'Morgenthau and I will serve as the jury.'

Eberly thought bleakly, A drumhead military trial. They're making me part of it. I'll never be able to deny that I took part in Holly's execution; they've seen to that. The best I can do is see to it that this drumhead trial follows some kind of legal order. The result is as clear as the fear in Holly's eyes.

He sighed deeply, wishing he could be somewhere else. Anywhere else, he thought, except my old prison cell back in Vienna.

'Very well,' he said at last, avoiding Holly's eyes. 'This trial is called to order.'

Execution

Using the suit's internal computer, Gaeta made some rough calculations. The temperature inside the suit was still sinking even though he had the heaters up full blast. *Make up your mind while you've still got some heat inside the suit. Otherwise you're dead.*

He made his decision. Gaeta pulled both arms out of the suit sleeves. Getting his legs out of the suit's legs was more difficult. *Shoulda taken those yoga lessons they were offering last year,* he told himself as he strained to pull out one leg and fold it beneath his buttocks. The other leg was even more difficult; Gaeta yelped with pain as something in the back of his thigh popped. Cursing in fluent Spanglish, he finally managed to pull the other leg up into the suit's torso. Panting from the exertion, feeling his thigh muscle throbbing painfully, he sat inside the suit's torso in a ludicrous parody of a lotus position.

'Okay,' he said to himself. 'Now we see how long you can breathe vacuum.'

'I didn't kill Don Diego,' Holly insisted, dabbing at the blood from her split lip. With her other hand she pointed at Kananga. 'He did. He admitted it to me.'

'Do you have any witnesses to that?' Eberly asked, stalling for time. He didn't know why. He knew there was no hope. Kananga was going to 'convict' Holly of the murder and execute her, with Tavalera alongside her. Airlock justice.

Holly shook her head dumbly.

Kananga said, 'She's lying, of course. She was the last one to see Romero. She claims she discovered the body. I say she murdered the old man.'

'But why would I do that?' Holly burst. 'He was my friend. I wouldn't hurt him.'

'Perhaps he made sexual advances at you,' Eberly suggested, clutching at straws. 'Perhaps the killing was self-defense. Or even accidental.'

Morgenthau, standing to one side beside Vyborg, muttered, 'Nonsense.'

'You're the jury,' Eberly said. 'You shouldn't make any comments.'

'She's guilty,' Vyborg snapped. 'We don't need any further evidence.'

Let the heat out of the suit and maybe it'll drive 'em away, Gaeta told himself. If it doesn't, I'm dead. So what've I got to lose?

He nodded inside the ice-covered helmet. So do it. What're you waiting for?

He reconfigured the control board inside the suit's chest to pop the access panels in both the suit's arms and both legs. The four keypads glowed before his eyes. The four fingers of his right hand hovered above them.

Do it! he commanded himself.

Squeezing his eyes shut and blowing hard to make his lungs as empty as possible, Gaeta jammed his fingers down onto the keypad.

And counted: One thousand one, one thousand two, one thousand three . . .

In his mind's eye he saw what was happening. The suit's heated air was rushing out of the open access panels. The ice creatures should feel a sudden wave of heat. Maybe it would kill them. Certainly it should make them uncomfortable.

. . . one thousand eight, one thousand nine . . .

Gaeta's ears popped. He couldn't hold his breath much longer. He didn't dare open his eyes yet. He remembered tales of guys who'd been blown apart by sudden decompression. The whole suit's insides'll be dripping with my blood and guts, he thought.

. . . one thousand twelve, one thousand . . .

He banged the keyboard and felt the access panels slam shut. Opening his eyes a slit he hit the air control and heard the hiss of air from the emergency tank refilling the suit.

But his faceplate was still completely iced over. In final desperation he banged on the thruster firing key again.

It was like lighting a firecracker under his butt. The thrust of the jets caught him completely unaware. He yowled in a mix of surprise, delight, and pain as the suit jetted off. He was flying blind, but at least he was flying.

Morgenthau and Vyborg didn't even have to look at each to agree on their verdict.

'Guilty,' said Morgenthau.

'Guilty as charged,' said Vyborg. 'And her accomplice, too.'

'Accomplice?' Tavalera blurted.

Kananga kicked him again.

'The jury has found you guilty,' Eberly said to Holly. 'Is there anything you wish to say?'

'Plenty,' Holly spat. 'But nothing you'd want to hear.'

Morgenthau stepped in front of Holly. Pulling a palmcomp from her gaudy caftan, she said, 'There is something I would like to hear. I want you to confess that you and your friend here were working with Dr. Cardenas to develop killer nanobugs.'

'That's not true!' Holly said.

'I didn't say it had to be true,' Morgenthau replied, with a sly smile on her lips. 'I merely want to hear you say it.'

'I won't.'

'Neither will I,' Tavalera said.

Kananga looked down at the wounded, beaten engineer, then turned to face Holly. Smiling wolfishly, he said, 'I think I can convince her.'

He punched Holly in her midsection, doubling her over. 'That's for the kick in the face you gave me,' he said, fingering his jaw. 'There's a lot more to come.'

*　　*　　*

Fritz had been sitting tensely at the main control console for hours, not speaking, not moving. The other technicians tiptoed around him. With their communications link to Gaeta inoperative, there was nothing they could do except wait. The mission-time clock on Fritz's console showed Gaeta still had more than thirty hours of air remaining, but they had no idea of what shape he was in.

Nadia Wunderly came into the workshop and immediately sensed the funeral-like tension.

'How is he?' she whispered to the nearest technician.

The man shrugged.

She went to Fritz's side. 'Have you heard anything from him?'

Fritz looked up at her, bleary-eyed. 'Not for two hours.'

'Oh.'

'Are those ice flakes actually alive?' Fritz asked.

'I think so,' she said, with the accent on the *I*. 'We'll have to get some samples and do more studies before it's confirmed, though.'

'They're actually eating the new moonlet?'

Wunderly nodded somberly. 'They're swarming all over it. I've got the instruments making measurements, but it'll be some time before we could measure a decrease in the moonlet's diameter.'

'I see. You've made a great discovery, then.'

'I wish I had known about it before Manny went out—'

'Hey Fritz!' the radio speaker crackled. 'Can you hear me?'

'Manny!' Fritz jerked to his feet. 'Manny, you're alive!'

'Yeah, but I don't know for how long.'

Return

Alone in the cockpit of the shuttlecraft, Timoshenko had listened to the chatter between Gaeta and his technicians, then grown morose as Gaeta fell silent. So the scientists have made a great discovery, he thought. They will win prizes and drink champagne while Gaeta is forgotten.

That's the way of the world, he thought. The big shots congratulate one another while the little guys die alone. They'll do some video specials on Gaeta, I suppose: the daring stuntman who died in the rings of Saturn. But in a few weeks he'll be totally forgotten.

Timoshenko had programmed the shuttlecraft to ease through the Cassini division between the A and B rings and take up a loitering orbit at the approximate position where Gaeta was programmed to come out below the ring plane. He knew that the stuntman wasn't going to come out at that precise spot, not with what had happened to him. Probably Gaeta would not come out at all, but still Timoshenko remained where he had promised he would be.

'Hey Fritz! Can you hear me?'

Fritz blurted, 'Manny! You're alive!'

The sound of Gaeta's voice electrified Timoshenko. He stared out the cockpit's port at the gleaming expanse of Saturn's rings, so bright it made him blink his eyes tearfully. Then his good sense got into gear and he checked his radar scans. There was an object about the size of a man hurtling out of the rings like a rifle shot.

'Gaeta!' Timoshenko shouted into his microphone. 'I'm coming after you!'

*   *   *

It took Gaeta a few seconds to recover from the shock of the thruster's sudden ignition. He had no control over it; he banged at the keyboard in desperate frustration, but the rocket simply blasted away until it ran out of fuel and abruptly died. Only then did Gaeta try his comm link. He got Fritz's voice in his earphones; the chief tech sounded stunned with surprise and elation, something that was so rare it made Gaeta laugh. *The old* cabrón *was worried about me!*

'What is your condition?' Fritz asked, getting back to his normal professional cool. 'The diagnostics we're getting are still rather muddled.'

Watching ice particles fly off his faceplate, Gaeta said, 'I'm okay, except I don't know where the hell I'm going. What's my position and vector?'

'We're working on that. Your thruster has burned out, apparently.'

'Right. I've got no way to slow myself down or change course.'

'Not to worry,' came Timoshenko's voice. 'I have you on radar. I'm on a rendezvous trajectory.'

'Great,' said Gaeta. The faceplate was almost entirely clear now. He watched one little ice flake scurry around like an ant on amphetamines and finally disappear.

'So long, *amigito*,' Gaeta said to the particle. 'No hard feelings. I hope you get back home okay, little guy.'

Pain! Holly had never known such white-hot pain. Never even dreamed it could exist. Kananga punched her again in the kidneys and fresh pain exploded inside her, searing, devastating agony that overwhelmed all her senses.

'A simple statement,' Morgenthau was saying, bending over her. 'Just a single sentence. Tell us that you were helping Cardenas to develop killer nanobugs.' She jabbed the palmcomp under Holly's nose.

Holly could barely breathe. Through lips that were puffed and bleeding she managed to grunt, 'No.'

Kananga put a knee into the small of her back and twisted her left arm mercilessly. Holly screamed.

'It only gets worse,' Kananga hissed into her ear. 'It keeps on getting worse until you do what we want you to.'

Holly heard Eberly's voice, miserable, pleading, 'You're going to kill her. For god's sake, leave her alone.'

'You call on God?' Morgenthau said. 'Blasphemer.'

'You'll kill her!'

'She's going to die anyway,' Kananga said.

'Work on the other one,' Eberly pleaded. 'Give her a rest.'

'He's unconscious again. Holly is a lot tougher, aren't you, Holly?' Kananga grabbed a handful of hair and yanked Holly's head back so sharply she thought her neck would snap.

'If we had the neural controllers,' Vyborg said, 'we could make her say anything we wanted.'

'But we don't have the proper equipment,' Morgenthau said. She sighed heavily. 'Break her fingers. One at a time.'

Timoshenko swung the little shuttlecraft into a trajectory that swiftly caught up with the hurtling figure of Gaeta.

'I'm approaching you from four o'clock, in your perspective,' he called. 'Will you able to climb into the cargo bay hatch once I come within a few meters of you?'

Gaeta answered doubtfully, 'I dunno. Got no propulsion fuel left. Nothing but the cold-gas attitude microthrusters; all they can do is turn me around on my long axis.'

'Not so good.' Timoshenko looked through the cockpit port. He could see the tiny figure of a man outlined against the broad, brilliant glow of Saturn's rings.

'Ow!' Gaeta yipped.

'What's the matter?' Fritz's voice.

'I pulled a muscle when I got my legs outta the suit legs,' Gaeta answered. 'Now I'm putting 'em back in and it hurts like hell.'

'If that's your worst problem,' said Fritz, 'you have nothing to complain about.'

Timoshenko couldn't help laughing at the technician's coolness. Like a painless dentist, he thought. The dentist feels no pain.

Gaeta said, 'I'm not gonna be much help getting aboard the shuttlecraft. I'm just barging along like a fuckin' meteor. Got no more propulsion, no maneuvering fuel.'

'Not to worry,' Timoshenko said. 'I'll bring this bucket to you. I'll bring you in like a man on the high trapeze catching his partner in mid-air. Like a ballet dancer catching his ballerina in her leap. Just like that.' He wished he truly felt as confident as he sounded.

Holly lay crumpled on the steel flooring of the airlock chamber, unconscious again.

'She's faking,' Morgenthau said.

'For god's sake, let her be,' Eberly begged. 'Push her out the aitrlock if you want to, but stop this torture. It's inhuman!'

Vyborg said, 'We have enough recordings of her voice to synthesize a statement against Cardenas.'

'I want to make certain,' Morgenthau insisted. 'I want to hear it from her own lips.'

Kananga nudged Tavalera's inert body with a toe. 'I'm afraid some of his ribs are broken. He's probably bleeding pretty heavily internally. Perhaps a lung's been punctured.'

Morgenthau planted her fists on her wide hips, a picture of implacable determination in a ludicrous rainbow-striped caftan.

'Wake her up,' Morgenthau commanded. 'I want to hear her say the words. Then you can get rid of her.'

'One hundred meters and closing.' Timoshenko's voice in Gaeta's helmet earphones sounded calm, completely professional.

He couldn't see the approaching shuttlecraft in his faceplate, so Gaeta spent a squirt of minithruster fuel to turn slightly. There it was, coming on fast, its ungainly form looking as beautiful as a racing yacht to Gaeta's eyes. The cargo hatch was wide open, inviting.

'You look awful damn good, *amigo*,' Gaeta said.

'I'm adjusting my velocity vector to match yours,' Timoshenko replied.

Fritz's voice added, 'Your fuel supply is reaching critical.

Instead of trying to return to the main airlock, it will save fuel if you come in to the central 'lock at the endcap.'

'Is it big enough to let me squeeze through in the suit?' Gaeta asked.

'Yes,' said Fritz. 'Aim for the endcap's central airlock.'

Gaeta said, 'Lemme get aboard the shuttleboat first, man.'

Timoshenko nodded his silent agreement. Get safely aboard the shuttlecraft. Then we can head for the airlock that's easiest to reach.

Deftly he tapped out commands on the control panel, edging the shuttlecraft closer to Gaeta. Timoshenko knew that if he'd had the time he could have set up the rendezvous problem for the craft's computer and have it all done automatically. But there was no time for that. He had to bring Gaeta in manually. He almost smiled at the irony of it. The computer could solve the problem in a microsecond, but it would take too long for him to set up the problem in the computer.

There was no way to match their velocities exactly. He had to close the distance to Gaeta, move the shuttlecraft on a trajectory that would intersect Gaeta's path at the smallest possible difference in velocity. Timoshenko wiped sweat from his eyes as he stared at the radar display. Ten meters separated them. Eight. Six.

Gaeta saw the cargo hatch inching closer and closer. Come on, pal, he encouraged silently. Bring it in. Bring it in. He wished he had some drop of fuel left in the propulsion unit, even the tiniest nudge of thrust would close the gap between him and the cargo hatch.

'Almost there.' Timoshenko's voice sounded tense, brittle.

Gaeta raised both arms and tried to reach the hatch's rim. Less than a meter separated his outstretched fingertips from safety.

'Get ready,' Timoshenko said.

'I'm ready.'

The hatch suddenly lurched toward Gaeta, engulfing him. He slammed into the cargo bay with a thump that banged the back of his head against the inside of his helmet.

'Welcome aboard,' said Timoshenko. Gaeta could sense the huge grin on his face.

'A little rough, but thanks anyway, *amigo*.'

They both heard Fritz breathe an astonishing, 'Thank god.'

Airlock Justice

Fritz and the three other technicians, accompanied by Wunderly and Berkowitz, raced out to the endcap to meet Gaeta and Timoshenko when they docked. Much to Fritz's amazement, pudgy, wheezing Berkowitz kept up with him as they pedaled madly along the length of the endcap. Even Wunderly was not far behind, while his technicians lagged farther along the bike path.

He waited impatiently for them at the hatch to the endcap's central airlock, thinking, I'll have to see that they get considerably more physical exercise. Watching how they panted and sweated, he shook his head. They've turned into putty globs since we've been aboard this habitat.

Flanked by Wunderly and the still-puffing Berkowitz, with the technicians behind him, Fritz marched along the steel-walled tunnel that led to the airlock. They got as far as the chamber that fronted the airlock's inner hatch. A trio of black-clad security people stopped them. A taller black man in tan coveralls was with them.

'This area is restricted,' said the guard leader.

'Restricted?' Fritz spat. 'What do you mean? A shuttlecraft is going to dock at this airlock within minutes.'

The guard drew his baton. 'You can't go in there. I have my orders.'

A woman's scream rang off the steel walls, curdling Fritz's blood. 'What the devil is going on in there?' he demanded.

As Timoshenko guided the shuttlecraft to the endcap airlock, he called to Gaeta in the cargo bay. 'Do you want to get out of your suit? I can come back and help you.'

'No can do,' said Gaeta. 'I've got this *hijo de puta* pulled muscle in my thigh. I'm gonna need a couple guys to help pull me out.'

Timoshenko shrugged. 'Hokay. We'll be at the airlock in less than ten minutes.'

But when they reached the habitat and Timoshenko mated the cargo bay hatch to the airlock's outer hatch, his command screen showed, AIRLOCK ACCESS DENIED.

'Access denied?' Timoshenko grumbled. 'What stupid shit-for-brains has put this airlock off-limits?'

'Try the emergency override,' Gaeta suggested.

Timoshenko's fingers were already dancing across his keyboard. 'Yes, good, it's responding.'

He got out of the cockpit chair and ducked through the hatch into the cargo bay. Looking at Gaeta in the massive suit, he grinned. 'At least I can enter the habitat in shirtsleeves.'

'Tell you the truth, *amigo,* the way my *fregado* leg feels, if I weren't inside this suit I wouldn't be able to walk without somebody propping me up.'

Through a haze of agony, Holly forced her mind to center on only one thought. Don't give them what they want. Don't let them drag Kris down. I'm already dead, I'm not going to let them kill Kris, too.

One of her eyes was swollen shut, the other down to a mere slit. She felt a hot breath on her ear. Morgenthau's voice, heavy and dark, whispered, 'This is nothing, Holly. If you think you've felt pain, it's nothing to what you're going to feel now. So far we've merely given you a beating. If you don't speak, we'll have to start tearing up your insides.'

Holly concentrated on the pain, tried to use it to keep the fear out of her mind. They're going to kill me, whatever she says they're going to kill me. All the pain in the world isn't going to change that.

Someone shouted, 'The airlock's cycling!'

'Impossible. I gave orders—'

'Look at the indicators.' That sounded like Eberly's voice. 'The outer hatch is opening.'

★   ★   ★

Inside the bulky suit Gaeta watched the telltales on the airlock's inner wall flick from red through amber to green. Jezoo, he thought, it'll be good to get out of this suit. I must smell to high heaven by now.

The inner hatch slid open slowly, ponderously. Gaeta expected to see Fritz and the techs waiting for him. Instead, he saw a group of strangers. Eberly, he recognized after a disoriented moment. And those others –

Then he saw two figures on the floor. Bloody. Beaten. Jesus Christ almighty! That's Holly!

'What the fuck's going on here?' he demanded.

Gaeta's voice boomed like a thunderclap in the steel-walled chamber.

Eberly blurted, 'They're trying to kill Holly!'

Morgenthau whirled on Eberly, hissing, 'Traitor!'

Kananga stepped in front of the huge suit, looking almost frail in comparison. 'This doesn't concern you. Get out of here immediately.'

'They're killing Holly!' Eberly repeated, even more desperately.

Kananga called up the tunnel, 'Guards! Take this fool out.'

The three security personnel raced toward him, skidded to a stop at the sight of Gaeta's suit, looming like some monster from a folk tale. A taller man in tan coveralls hovered uncertainly behind them.

'Shoot him!' Kananga bellowed. 'Kill him!'

From inside the suit, Gaeta saw the three guards drawing laser cutting tools from their belts. Behind them, Fritz and the others came up cautiously. His eyes returned to Holly, lying on her back on the floor, her face bloody and swollen, one arm bent at a grotesque angle, the fingers of one hand caked with blood.

The guards fired their lasers at him. They're trying to kill me, Gaeta realized, as if watching the whole scene from a far distance. The sons of bitches!

The red pencil lines of three laser beams splashed against the armor of the suit's chest. With a growl that the suit amplified into an artillery barrage, Gaeta pushed Kananga aside and advanced on the three guards. One of them had the sense to aim at his faceplate, but the heavily tinted visor absorbed most of the laser pulse; Gaeta felt a searing flash on his right cheek, like the burn of an electric shock.

He barged into the guards, smacking one back-handed with his servo-amplified arm, sending the man smashing into the wall. He grabbed the laser out of the hand of the woman and crushed it in the pincers of his right hand. They turned and fled, running past Fritz and his open-mouthed companions. The guard that Gaeta had hit lay crumpled on the floor, unconscious or dead, he didn't care which.

He turned back toward Kananga, who was staring at him with wide, round eyes.

'Trying to kill Holly,' Gaeta boomed. 'Beating her to death.'

'Wait!' Kananga shouted, retreating, holding both hands in front of him. 'I didn't—'

Gaeta picked him up by the throat, lifted him completely off his feet, carried him back through the open hatch of the airlock. With his other arm he banged the airlock controls. The hatch slid shut. Kananga writhed in the merciless grasp of the pincers, choking, pulling uselessly at the cermet claws with both his hands.

'We're gonna play a little game,' Gaeta snarled at him. 'Let's see how long you can breath vacuum.'

The airlock pumped down. Gaeta kept the pincers of his left hand firmly pressed against the controls, so that no one outside could open the hatch. He held Kananga high enough to watch his face as the Rwandan's terrified eyes eventually rolled up and then exploded in a shower of blood.

Epilogue: Saturn Arrival Plus Nine Days

Professor Wilmot sat sternly behind his desk, wishing desperately he had a glass of whisky in his hand. A stiff drink was certainly what he needed. But he had to play the role of an authority figure, and that required absolute sobriety.

Sitting before his desk were Eberly, Morgenthau, Vyborg, Gaeta and Dr. Cardenas.

'They made me do it,' Eberly was whining. 'Kananga murdered the old man and they made me stay quiet about it.'

Morgenthau gave him a haughty, disgusted look. Vyborg seemed stunned into passivity, almost catatonic.

Pointing to Morgenthau, Eberly went on, 'She threatened to send me back to prison if I didn't do as she wanted.'

'Prison would be too good for you,' Morgenthau sneered.

For more than an hour Wilmot had been trying to piece together what had happened at the airlock. Part of the background he already knew. Gaeta had freely admitted to killing Kananga; Cardenas called it an execution. Wilmot had gone to the hospital and was thoroughly shocked when he'd seen Holly Lane, her face battered almost beyond recognition, her shoulder horribly dislocated, her fingers methodically broken. Tavalera was in even worse shape, broken ribs puncturing both his lungs. Dr. Cardenas hadn't waited for permission; as soon as she learned what had happened to them she had rushed to the hospital and began pumping both of them full of therapeutic nanomachines: assemblers, she called them. Drawn from her own body, they were programmed to repair damaged tissue, rebuild bones and blood vessels.

Wilmot agreed with Cardenas. Killing the Rwandan was an execution, nothing less.

'Colonel Kananga deliberately murdered Diego Romero?' Wilmot asked.

Eberly nodded eagerly. 'He put Kananga up to it,' he said, jabbing a thumb toward Vyborg. 'He wanted to be in charge of the communications department.'

Vyborg said nothing; his eyes barely flickered at Eberly's accusation. Wilmot remembered Eberly's insistence that Berkowitz be removed from the department.

'And all this was part of your plan to take control of the habitat's government?' he asked, still hardly able to believe it.

'My plan,' Morgenthau insisted. 'This worm was nothing more than a means to that end.'

With an incredulous shake of his head, Wilmot said, 'But he was elected to the office of chief administrator. You won the power in a free election. Why all the violence?'

Before Eberly could frame a reply, Morgenthau answered, 'We didn't want to have a democratically run government. That was just a tactic, a first step toward acquiring total power.'

'Total power.' Wilmot sank back in his chair. 'Don't you understand how unstable such a government would be? You self-destructed within hours of being installed in office.'

'Because of his weakness,' Morgenthau said, again indicating Eberly.

'And this disgusting torture of Miss Lane? What good did that do you?'

'We had to get rid of all traces of nanotechnology in the habitat,' Morgenthau said, with some heat. 'Nanomachines are the devil's work. We can't have them here!'

Bristling, Cardenas said, 'That's idiotic. If you really believe that, then you must be an idiot.'

'Nanotech is evil,' Morgenthau insisted. '*You* are evil!'

Cardenas glared at the woman. 'How can anybody be so stupid? So self-righteously stupid that they're willing to commit mayhem and murder?'

Morgenthau glared back. 'Nanotechnology is evil,' she repeated. 'You'll pay for your sins, sooner or later.'

Wilmot had his own reservations about nanotechnology, but this Morgenthau woman was a fanatic, he realized.

He turned to Eberly. 'And you just stood there and let them torture the poor girl.'

'I tried to stop them,' Eberly bleated. 'What could I do?'

Wishing more than ever for a whisky, Wilmot took in a deep breath. Tricky waters here. They still have those foolish entertainment vids hanging over my head.

'Very well,' he said. 'My course seems clear enough. Ms. Morgenthau and Dr. Vyborg will return to Earth on the ship that brings the scientists here.'

'We don't want to go back to Earth,' Morgenthau said.

'Nevertheless, that's where you're going. The two of you are banished from the habitat. Permanently.'

'Exiled?' For the first time Morgenthau looked alarmed. 'You can't do that. You haven't the authority to do that.'

'I do,' said Eberly, breaking into a smile. 'I think exile is a perfect solution. Go back to your friends in the Holy Disciples. See how they reward failure.'

Morgenthau's eyes flared. 'You can't do that to me!'

'I'm the duly elected chief administrator of this community,' Eberly said, obviously enjoying the moment. 'It's well within my power to exile the two of you.'

Vyborg finally stirred from his stupor; suddenly he looked startled, frightened. Wilmot was focused on Eberly, however. Can I strike up an alliance with this man? he asked himself. Can I trust him to run the government properly?

'Yes, you are officially the chief of government,' Wilmot agreed reluctantly. 'But we're going to have to find some way to get the entire population involved in the running of your government.'

'Universal draft,' Cardenas said. 'It's been done in Selene and some countries on Earth; seems to work pretty well.'

Wilmot knew the concept. 'Require every citizen to spend at least a year in public service?' he asked, full of skepticism. 'Do you actually think for one instant that such a scheme could be made to work here?'

'It's worth a try,' Cardenas replied.

'The people here will never go for it,' Wilmot said. 'They'll laugh in your face.'

'I'll go for it,' said Gaeta. 'It makes good sense to me, getting everybody involved.'

Wilmot raised an eyebrow. 'What does it matter to you? You'll be leaving on the same ship that brings the scientists in.'

'No I won't,' Gaeta said. He turned toward Cardenas, suddenly shy, almost tongue-tied. 'I mean, I – uh, I don't want to leave. I want to stay here. Become a citizen.'

'And quit being a stuntman?' Cardenas asked, obviously surprised.

He nodded solemnly. 'Time for me to retire. Besides, I can help Wunderly explore the rings. Maybe even get down to Titan's surface one of these days, help Urbain and the other science jocks.'

Cardenas threw her arms around his neck and kissed him soundly. Wilmot wanted to frown, but found himself smiling at them instead.

Sitting in the chief scientist's office, Urbain and Wunderly watched once again a replay of the new moonlet's arrival in the main ring. They saw the ring's bright icy particles swarm around the newcomer, covering its darker irregular form in glittering ice.

'Remarkable,' Urbain murmured. He used the same term each time they had watched the vid. 'They behave like living creatures.'

'They *are* living creatures,' Wunderly said. 'I'm convinced of it.'

Urbain nodded as he smoothed his hair with an automatic gesture. 'Too big a leap, Nadia. The particles are dynamic, yes, that much is obvious. But alive? We have much work to do before we can state unequivocally that they are living entities.'

Wunderly grinned at him. He said *we,* she thought. He's on my side now.

'Already many academics have spoken against your interpretation,' Urbain pointed out. 'They refuse to believe the ring particles are alive.'

'Then we'll have to get the evidence to convince them,' said Wunderly.

'That will be your task,' Urbain said. 'Myself, I will return to Earth on the ship that brings in the other scientists.'

Wunderly was shocked. 'Return to Earth! But—'

'I have thought it all out very carefully,' Urbain said, with a finger upraised for emphasis. 'You need a champion back on Earth, someone who can present your evidence and argue your case against the skeptics.'

'But I thought you'd stay here.'

'And play second fiddle to the newcomers?' Urbain forced a smile, and she could see there was pain behind it. 'No, I return to Earth. I have never been any good at pushing my own career, but I believe I can be ferocious defending yours. For you, and your ring creatures, I will be a tiger!'

Wunderly didn't know what to say. Every young scientist with an unorthodox new idea needs a champion, she knew. Even Darwin needed Huxley.

'Besides,' Urbain went on, 'my wife is on Earth. In Paris, I believe. Perhaps . . . perhaps I can impress her enough to come back to me.'

'I'm sure you could,' Wunderly said gently.

'So the decision is made. I return to Earth. You will be in charge of all work on the rings.'

'In charge . . . ?'

He smiled widely. 'I have given you a promotion. The team coming in from Earth has only three researchers interested in the rings, and they are all junior to you, still graduate students. I have named you as chief of the ring dynamics study. They will work for you.'

It was all Wunderly could do to refrain from hugging the man.

Holly flexed the fingers of her right hand, holding the hand up before her eyes as she sat in the hospital bed.

'Good as new, almost,' she said.

Cardenas smiled satisfiedly. 'Give it a few days. Even nano-machines need some time to put everything right.'

Gaeta was sitting beside Cardenas, the two of them perched on little plastic chairs, close enough to touch each other.

'I'm gonna use nanos the next time I go into the rings,' he said.

'Even Urbain is losing his fear of nanomachines,' Cardenas said. 'He came into my lab this morning and didn't flinch once!'

All three of them laughed.

Then Holly grew more sober. 'Manny, I want to thank you for saving my life. Kananga was going to kill me.'

His face hardened. 'I let him off too easy. Back in the *barrio* we would've done to him just what he did to you and Raoul. And then dropped him on the freeway from an overpass.'

'You guys talkin' about me?'

Tavalera wheeled himself into Holly's room and pulled to a stop on the other side of her bed.

'I was going to come in to look you over,' Cardenas said. 'How are your lungs?'

'Okay, I guess. The medics examined me this morning. They looked kinda surprised I'm healin' so fast.'

'Rebuilding your lung tissue is going to take several days,' Cardenas warned. 'The ribs were easier.'

Tavalera nodded. 'It's funny. I think I can almost feel these little bugs workin' inside me.'

'That's your imagination.'

'I must have a good imagination,' he said.

'Raoul,' said Holly, 'you were really wonderful, trying to protect me.'

His face reddened. 'I didn't do you much good, though.'

'You tried,' said Holly. 'When I needed help the most you were there trying.'

'And I got a body full of nanobugs to show for it.'

Cardenas caught his meaning. 'Don't worry, I'll start flushing them out of your system in a few days. You'll be able to go back home. You won't have any trace of nanomachines in you by the time you get back to Earth.'

'You're gonna hafta to go back by yourself, *amigo*,' said Gaeta. 'I'm staying here permanently.' And he slid an arm around Cardenas' shoulders.

Holly saw the light in Cardenas' eyes. 'But what about your technicians?' she asked. 'Will they stay, too?'

With a shake of his head, Gaeta said, 'Naw. Fritz wants to go back to Earth and find a new *pendejo* to make into a media star. But I'm keepin' the suit. That baby is mine.'

Tavalera looked pensive. 'I been thinkin' about that too.'

'About what?' Holly asked.

'Stayin' here.'

'You have?' Holly asked, her eyes widening.

'Yeah. Sort of. I mean . . . it ain't so bad here. In this habitat, y'know. I was wondering, Dr. C., could I keep on workin' in your lab? As your assistant?'

Cardenas answered immediately, 'I need your help, Raoul. I was wondering what I would do after you left.'

'I wanna stay,' Tavalera said, glancing at Holly.

She held out her hand to him. As he took it in his, she warned, 'Not too tight, Raoul. It's still kind of tender.'

He grinned and let her hand rest atop his.

Cardenas got to her feet. 'I've got work to do. I'll drop in on you two later this afternoon. Come on, Manny.'

Gaeta leaned back in the creaking little chair. 'I've got no place to go. I'm retired, right?'

Cardenas grabbed him by the collar. 'Come *on*, Manny. I'll find something for you to do.'

He let her haul him to his feet. 'Well, if you put it that way . . .'

They left. Holly lay back in the bed. Tavalera still clasped her hand lightly in his.

'You're not staying because of me, are you?' she asked him.

'No, not—' He stopped himself. 'Yeah, I am. I really am staying because of you,' he said, almost belligerently. 'That's the truth.'

Holly smiled at him. 'Good. That's what I wanted to hear.'

He grinned back at her.

Holly called out. 'Phone! Connect me with Pancho Lane, at Astro Corporation Headquarters in Selene.'

Tavalera let go of her hand and started to back his wheelchair away from the bed.

'Don't go away, Raoul,' Holly said. 'I want my sister to meet you.'

Professor Wilmot sat in his favorite chair, gently swirling the whisky in the glass he held in his right hand. Although his eyes were focused on the report he was dictating, he was actually staring far beyond the words hovering in mid-air before him, looking with his mind's eye into the events of the past few days and trying to foresee the shape of the events to come.

For a long while he sat there, alone, slowly swishing the whisky, wondering what he should say to his superiors back on Earth, how he should explain what had gone wrong with the grand experiment.

'Actually,' he said at last, 'nothing has really gone *wrong*. This experiment was intended to test the ability of a self-contained community to survive and develop a viable social system of its own. Unfortunately, the social system they began to develop was definitely not the type that we expected or desired. It was based on violence and deception, and it would have led to a rather harsh, restrictive authoritarian regime. On the other hand, such systems are inherently unstable, as the events of the past few days have proven.'

He sat in silent thought for long moments. Then, taking a sip of his whisky, he continued, 'We are now entering a new phase of the experiment, an attempt to develop a working democratic government. The question is, are the people of this community too lazy, too selfish to work at governing themselves? Are they nothing more than spoiled children who *need* an authoritarian government to run things for them? Only time will tell.'

He thought of Cardenas' suggestion of a universal draft: require each citizen to serve a certain portion of time in public service. It's

432

worked elsewhere, Wilmot said to himself. Perhaps it could work here. But he had his doubts.

He took a longer pull on the whisky, then spoke the final section of his report to the leaders of the New Morality organization in Atlanta.

'You have provided the major funding for this expedition to ascertain if a similar selection of individuals could serve as the population of a mission to another star, a mission that would take many generations to complete. Based on the results of merely the first two years of this experiment, I must conclude that we simply do not know enough about how human societies behave under such stresses to make a meaningful judgment.

'In my personal opinion, we are not ready to begin planning an interstellar mission. In fact, we are nowhere near the under- standing we will require to send a genetically viable human population out on a star flight that will take many generations to complete.

'That is disappointing news, I'm sure, but it should hardly be surprising. This is the first time an artificially generated human society has been sent on its own so far from Earth. We have much to learn.'

He drained the whisky, then continued on a brighter note, 'On the other hand, this group of cantankerous, squabbling, very bright men and women has accomplished some significant successes. We have made it to Saturn. We have avoided falling into the trap of an authoritarian government. We have found a new lifeform in the rings of Saturn, possibly. We are preparing to study the moon Titan with surface probes and, eventually, with a human presence on the surface of that world.

'You of the New Morality may not like everything that we have accomplished, and you may not agree with everything we plan to do – including using nanotechnology wherever it is appropriate. But you can take comfort in the fact that your generous funding has helped to establish a new human outpost, twice as far from Earth as the Jupiter station; an outpost that is prepared to explore Saturn, its rings, and its moons.'

Wilmot smiled at the irony of it. 'In a very real sense, you have shown the rest of the human race how to escape the limits of the Earth. For that, no matter what you think or what you believe, you will gain the eternal thanks of generations to come.'